Making It Up As I Go Along

Making It Up

A NOVEL

As I Go Along

M. T. LENNON

THREE RIVERS PRESS • NEW YORK

Published in the United States by Three Rivers Press, an imprint of the
Crown Publishing Group, a division of Random House, Inc., New York.
www.crownpublishing.com

THREE RIVERS PRESS and the Tugboat design are registered trademarks of
Random House, Inc.

Originally published in slightly different form in hardcover in the United States by
Shaye Areheart Books, an imprint of the Crown Publishing Group, a division of
Random House, Inc., New York, in 2005.

Library of Congress Cataloging-in-Publication Data
Lennon, Maria.
Making it up as I go along : a novel / Maria Lennon.
1. Inheritance and succession—Fiction.   2. Los Angeles (Calif.)—Fiction.
3. War correspondents—Fiction.   4. Women journalists—Fiction.
5. Single mothers—Fiction.   6. Pregnant women—Fiction.
7. Sierra Leone—Fiction.   8. Surgeons—Fiction.   I. Title.
PS3612.E544M355   2005
813'.6—dc22   2004024312

ISBN-13 978-1-4000-8191-2
ISBN-10 1-4000-8191-2

Printed in the United States of America

Design by Lynne Amft

10 9 8 7 6 5 4 3 2 1

First Paperback Edition

TO CHIARA, LUCIA, AND PABLO

I've done a lot of crazy things in my life but you three have to be the craziest. You've changed my life and made me so much better.

TO DAVIDE

for putting up with years and years of crazy. You're a saint, but so am I.

TO MOM AND DAD

You gave it all away—the tools, the belief, the love, the cash—without ever asking for anything back. It's all because of you.

ACKNOWLEDGMENTS

THANKS TO AMINATTA FORNA for her book *The Devil That Danced on the Water*. It's the real thing—the story of an African hero, a would-be philosopher king, her father, who gave his life for a people and a country that betrayed him over and over, but still he would not stop fighting for their survival. It made me fall in love with Sierra Leone and the human spirit with each and every page.

TO THE LADIES IN THE PARK—women who give it all up to pour water into sand and marvel at each and every sand pancake made, day after day, month after month. Raising children fulltime—it's the toughest and most thankless of all jobs, with rewards often only felt late at night when they're asleep, bathed and unharmed. Congratulations. You've survived another day in the trenches. I commend you.

TO MARLY—my favorite part of this whole process, I am blessed to have found you.

Making It Up As I Go Along

CHAPTER ONE

"ONE, TWO, THREE—LATCH."

I glanced around the room, quickly taking in the semicircle of five somewhat traumatized-looking women sitting cross-legged on a carpet that smelled of breast milk and lavender. Had their babies *latched?* It was hard to tell without raising questions as to my prenatal sexuality. If I even mentioned the word "partner" or even worse "no partner" (as was my case), my days at the Pump Station, the holy Mecca for the politically correct, socially conscious, newly nursing moms, would be over.

I looked down at Halla. She was fast asleep, curled under my heavy breast as though still in my womb, totally unaware that she was supposed to be performing on cue. There was nothing in my thirty-eight years that had prepared me for the beauty of a sleeping child in the arms of its mother. It was the face of joy and peace, as though the baby was wrapped in a shroud of faith and its soul was dancing with the angels.

Unfortunately for the church, it was the kind of faith that could not be taught, bought, or guilted into.

"Okay, Saffron—did I get your name right?" The teacher, an ex–Leche League representative who probably pumped milk for her

1

teenagers' lunch boxes, cocked her head to the side as she peered at my sleeping child. "You need to wake her up." Both hands on ample hips. "Now."

"But look at her." I glanced at Halla, a name that a tribeswoman from northeast Sierra Leone had given her when she came up to me, patted my cramping belly, and announced that I was not sick with too much African beer, but with child. She pointed to my stomach and said "Halla" over and over again while she giggled. The irony was not lost on her that she, a woman who could neither add nor subtract, knew about my pregnancy before I did. The name meant unexpected gift. It described my baby perfectly.

The Leche woman stomped over to where I sat quietly mesmerized by my child and squatted next to me. She was earthy, but fortunately still feminine enough. In other words, she was a kinder, gentler version of the in-your-face-breast-feeding dictator of the eighties; the short hair was a little longer, the chin hairs were tweezed, there was even an attempt at wispy bangs and light mascara; the Birkenstocks were trendy now and the soy latte, Starbucks.

"Drag your nipple across her face." She peered down at my breast. "Stop when you get to her mouth and then tease her with it."

I hoped she would go away. I could feel the heat rush to my cheeks as embarrassment pumped through my entire body. I had never liked being the center of attention, I preferred to be behind the camera, taking notes and telling other people's stories. Gretchen—I wasn't entirely sure that was her name, but she looked like a Gretchen—stood behind me impatiently.

"I'll be back." She gave me a nurselike pat of encouragement that was totally utilitarian and devoid of personal feeling. It was the same pat that the ob/gyn nurse had given me throughout my labor and recovery. Because I was doing it alone, she probably rubbed and patted my shoulders far more than she would have patted a woman whose husband was present, but I knew as I pushed and labored that she would forget me as soon as she took off her uniform, found her car keys, and made it to her poorly operating car in the farthest reaches of underground parking reserved for employees.

"That's it." Gretchen walked in a circle behind the nursing mothers, bending down every so often to make certain that their child was indeed "on" properly. "Remember, get the whole areola in his mouth, not just the nipple; that's the only way you're going to keep your nipples from cracking and bleeding."

Nearly all the babies had successfully latched on, their mouths suctioned tightly around the entire circumference of the breast, sucking away as their mothers looked on in raw amazement.

"Excellent." Gretchen stopped in the center of the circle, nodding at everyone. "I don't see an areola in the room and that's saying something." She squeezed out a laugh, most likely the same one she emitted each and every time she delivered the line, and everyone but me managed a responsive laugh. The almost unnatural enlargement of our nipples accompanied by the dark spreading miasma that was the areola—and who even knew what that was before childbirth—was old news by now.

I went back to gazing at my daughter and felt a soft tapping on my shoulder. "You need to wake her up."

"But she's so happy," I said. "Can't I wait a few more minutes?"

"She needs to eat." Gretchen took Halla's two-week-old head in her palm and moved her toward my swollen breast. "Take your breast and tickle her mouth with it."

I looked up from our little powwow and was relieved to see that the other women in the room were not tuning in. They did not care to see my breast, nor were they interested in my humiliation at having to grab it like a sausage. In the ten years that I had covered Africa, Asia, and the Middle East for London's *Sunday Times* and the *Economist,* I had seen my fair share of women breast-feeding their children. Did someone have to teach them how to get their babies to latch on, or did it just come naturally to everyone who lived outside of West L.A.?

Then without so much as moving an arm or a leg Halla opened her pink mouth expectantly. A large part of me wished that she had not done exactly as Gretchen had predicted, at the very moment of prediction.

"Now hold your nipple with your left hand and her head with your right, tilt her head back and when you see her mouth open as wide as it can, push your nipple into her mouth and clamp her head onto your breast."

And then before my very eyes my areola—or that black thing that had suddenly appeared around my nipple like a stain—disappeared into her mouth.

"Like that." Gretchen folded her arms across her chest like a Serbian training officer and moved on to the next soldier.

Yes. For the first time since being birthed, Halla had latched on properly. There was no pain, no frustrated cries, just free-flowing milk for her and physical and emotional relief for me. As I sat on the floor, partially undressed, surrounded by strangers also partially undressed, I finally felt like I was a part of something since leaving the ravaged city of Freetown, capital of Sierra Leone, an African country no one cared about except for greedy diamond traffickers and a few selfless—or selfish, depending on how you looked at it—war correspondents.

I had been there with my pen and paper when the city was overrun in the late nineties with rebels, when the "liberating" army hacked away civilian limbs with the mindless ease of a butcher chopping meat for his counter display. I was among the few who remained when Reuters and the Associated Press pulled their people out, when it became blatantly unsafe for anything that had blood in its veins. I had remained because the man, the surgeon, who had made me fall in love with Africa had remained; I stayed because I had fallen so deeply in love with both the man and place that I could no longer define myself without doing so in their context.

But I was stupid. Neither Africa nor the doctor had ever really claimed me as one of their own. Once the revolutionary fighters started swinging their painfully dull machetes in the streets of Freetown, previously open doors were shut, warm beds and hidden safe houses were suddenly occupied, and the eyes of the West were unwanted. People were no longer acting like people. There was no vocabulary left to describe the evil I saw on a daily basis. Nothing could express the horror—not words, not sound, not even the camera could capture the totality of it.

But it was not the butchery of the people that made me leave Africa; it was the discovery of dozens of handmade tape cassettes in the good doctor's bedroom, like the ones people in new love make for each other. They were addressed to Oscar with curly pink cursive writing and it was this handwriting that made me board a series of planes out of Africa. It was almost the end of 1999 and the war had literally destroyed the entire country. And although I didn't know it yet, I was pregnant.

As I followed Gretchen's commands and switched Halla from one breast to the other, I looked up and accidentally caught the eye of the woman sitting directly in front of me. Her blue eyes did not flinch when we connected, nor did they drop quickly to my wrist to evaluate my watch or my ring finger to ascertain marital status and husband's bank account. Her face was wide open, her eyes deep and warm as though she had enough room to take me in. In them I could see *Good Housekeeping* recipes, Tupperware parties, and prized secrets to successful stain removal.

I yearned to be absorbed.

CHAPTER TWO

WHO WOULD HAVE GUESSED THAT LACTATION COUNSELING was such a lucrative business? From the moment you stepped through the double cream doors into the Pump Station on Wilshire Boulevard in Santa Monica and pushed your stroller across the plush wall-to-wall carpeting, you were initiated into a lifestyle and all the gadgets that went along with it: rooms filled with soft cushions to rest your child upon while nursing, bras, pads, books, embroidered pillows, as though advising all who could read that Mommy was busy doing something so fragile and precarious that there must be a sentinel, or at the very least a sign, at the door. Only in L.A.

It was psychological warfare in the worst way. On the one hand these consultants bombard women with soft sounds and comforting voices that told them that they were doing just fine, that it took time to adjust to motherhood and there was no *wrong* way. And yet under all that mock-Zen smooth talk, they were actually making those choices, the right choices, for them by telling them that they did need help, that they couldn't do it on their own, that they needed the assistance of a lactation consultant as well as an assortment of products to make the whole breast-feeding-mommy-bonding thing go according to plan. And it's like taking the stray cat you found under your car to the vet and being told that it needs a thousand-dollar procedure to live—you simply can't say no unless you're prepared for the consequences, all of which could lead to poor SAT scores, community college, and a job in retail.

You have to have the infant bath soap, the only one Catherine Zeta-Jones and Jodie Foster use on their children's bodies. Otherwise there could be *exzema*. The new Olga nursing bra at $60 a pop and that new elastin belly/breast cream for nursing moms that Jada Pinkett Smith swears by at $75 an ounce—a definite yes—otherwise your boobs could bear a frightening resemblance to Tetley tea bags by the end of the year. The place was a bloody factory and underneath the piped-in soft sounds of llamas mating in the high Peruvian plains in one room and dolphins courting in and around Polynesian motus in the next, there were two large blue-haired ladies perched like birds in front of their computers building customer databases that rivaled Neiman Marcus's and filling their coffer with cold hard cash.

But even more important, by giving the subliminal message that while you could probably figure out motherhood on your own, you could never do it as well and as quickly as you could after a month-long series at the Pump Station, they tapped in on what every new mother knew that she needed but didn't have—a completely neutral mother who never overstepped the line and a group of women who were going through the same things, both physically and emotionally, at the exact same time.

You were being beckoned to join a club, to become a member of a group. And while I was never a fan of groups or clubs, there was something about this that drew me. Perhaps it was the same thing that drew all of us—the need to belong somewhere, sometime.

"You were great in there. Sometimes those lactation people need to back off." She put out her one free hand. "I'm Anika, by the way, and this"—she pointed at her sleeping baby already strapped in his perfectly starched blue-and-white Graco car seat—"is Jeremiah."

"Saffron Roch." I stuck out my hand and, judging by the look of pain on her face, shook hers more like a war correspondent than a stay-at-home mom.

"A few of us from class are going next door for lunch." She lifted an index finger toward the door. "Would you like to come along?"

A few of us? I'd missed two classes and there was already a clique inside my lactation class. "Thanks, but today is not such a good day." I came up with three or four excuses that would get me out of it without closing the door completely. I wanted to make friends— hell, I had been hanging out in the nursing moms' areas of Nordstrom's, Macy's, and Bloomingdales chatting with other first-time moms (and complete strangers) while feeding and changing Halla. I had even called my ob/gyn's office—in London, for God's sake—to chat with one of the nurses who had taken it upon herself to lie to me during my last trimester of weigh-ins. I missed them. I was in new-mom limbo and needed to latch on to something myself.

"Next week then," she said and disappeared out the door. I wondered who the others were. I tried to remember the women in the class, what they wore, how they dressed their children, whether they used pacifiers or not, were pro- or antibottles, and had a pretty good idea of the ladies who would be joining Anika.

There was Sophia Gilot and her daughter, Rain, who stood out in any crowd and not simply because of the name. They were celluloid beauties, both of them. Sophia was the kind of woman who would cause civil unrest in the streets of Freetown. She would never be hired as a correspondent because she would become the story wherever she went. I could say that she was perfect in an L.A. kind of way but that would be unfair. She was beautiful in a universal kind of way, the way young girls and old women in France, Italy, and the Ukraine defined beauty. Blonde hair to her hips, straight but not blown-dry; tight skin, tight everywhere as though she were a Fuji apple wrapped in a sheet of translucent Saran Wrap. Blue almond-shaped eyes and black eyelashes that had to have been dyed were set high in a face that was structurally without fault. Sophia was young, midtwenties I guessed, so I was fairly certain that her face was the result of good DNA and not a skilled plastic surgeon. As for her profession, I would take the easy way out and say she was a model.

I had seen a woman named Alice chatting with Anika before class, and judging by their matching car seats and dark-haired boys, I was certain that she, too, was part of the Pump Station clique. Alice looked like an Alice, very plain with brown hair to her shoulders, bangs, and small round glasses. Her trousers were perfectly pleated down the middle of the leg and she wore an oversized men's white oxford shirt. It, too, was heavily starched and I immediately envied her the housekeeper.

Two things that caught my eye about Alice: the size of her ass (it was huge in contrast to her strangely thin upper body and chest area) and the fact that her hair color, a dark red, began halfway down the crown of her head, giving her the appearance of a pear-shaped multilayered candle. She must have been one of those who believed that any hair color dye should be avoided throughout pregnancy and lactation.

I now believe that many of the restrictions placed upon new mothers—no alcohol, smoking, caffeine, hair color, going out after dark, having fun—were orchestrated by men. Most men seemed to believe that their mothers were perfect, breast-fed them for years, handmade all of their baby food, and lovingly washed their cloth diapers with their own toothbrush until they were old enough to stop wetting themselves or to finally move out, whichever came first. Fortunately, I was one of the few women out there who didn't have a husband telling me what and what not to do.

My shoulder-length dark shag was fully highlighted with streaks of blond that screamed L'Oreal. Highlighting chemicals were probably percolating their way through my system and into my milk ducts, but I preferred to focus on the positive role model I was cultivating for my daughter. A free thinker, a rebel, a single mother, whatever.

I had not done prenatal yoga or postnatal anything, but I did eat. I had not yet lost twenty-five of the fifty pounds I put on and was forced to wear the same military pants and surgical scrubs that I had nicked from Oscar in Africa and worn throughout my pregnancy. If he could see me now, I don't know whether he would be more shocked by my weight or the knowledge that the baby in the carrier was his. Knowing Oscar, it would be the weight.

After purchasing the belly cream, a box of breast pads that were hailed as "revolutionary" by the teenager who helped me, and the line of bath products that Catherine Zeta-Jones used on her baby's ass and on her own face and neck, I left the Pump Station feeling like a member. I loved the place—couldn't get enough of it. I maneuvered the stroller, car seat attached, down the walkway until I spotted the ramp at the end. Ramps were now more exciting to me than lingering eye contact with Brad Pitt.

"Saffron, Saff." I heard tapping on a window to my right and looked up and caught everyone's eyes, all eight of them staring at me from a table laden with food. It looked like Thanksgiving in there with drumsticks, breasts, mashed potatoes, and pureed sweet potatoes. The amount of food was worthy of a photograph accompanied by an article on the excesses of the first world.

I glanced at my watch in feigned conflict—I had nowhere to go, nowhere to be. No one was waiting for me, I didn't even need to check my machine, but I didn't want them to know that. I wanted to come in, get out of the July heat that reminded me of Sierra Leone. I wanted to park my Snap N Go next to theirs and gossip about what the other women, the women who weren't invited to lunch, were doing wrong. I wanted to belong. The door seemed to open of its own volition and suddenly there I was, among them.

"Everyone, if you don't know her name already, this is Saffron Roch." Anika stood. "And Saffy, this is Sophia Gilot, her daughter Rain, Alice Fleming, and her son Michael, who you know from class."

"And I'm the nonconformist," said a woman I had not seen before, "the only one who doesn't want to sacrifice a great set of boobs for a few months of bonding."

"Meet Nancy Schneidermann, bottle-feeder and proud." Anika pulled out a chair next to her and I took it, part of a group.

"I can bond perfectly well over a bottle." Nancy's voice grated like Fran Drescher's before she was humbled by cancer. "Welcome aboard." She saluted.

"And"—Anika shook her head—"they gave her hell for it."

"And," Nancy shook her head back, "you know where they can go."

"Nancy scheduled her C-section so as not to interrupt her husband Stan's big screening," added Alice.

"And party," Nancy jumped in. "Let's not forget the party for two hundred people I pulled together."

"Single-handedly?" Anika teased. "That must have been awfully stressful."

"Ah, give me a break, the caterers sucked, forgot all about the kosher stuff, and I had to deal with the wrath of Stan and the rest of the Jewish mafia."

"A vaginal birth left way too much up to chance," Sophia added carefully as though not fully comfortable with her place among these self-assured women. She was the antidote to Nancy, soft and gentle as though she had never had to fight for her space or protect her boundaries.

"And what's your son's name?" I looked at the enormous English pram, so popular with the Windsor family when Queen Elizabeth had Charles, parked right next to the drink and salsa station.

"Winnie—well, Winston, really," Nancy said with obvious pride, "named after the man who saved the Jews from Hitler."

"A nice English name with a great deal of history," Alice stated as though defending Nancy's decision to name her Jewish son after one of England's heroes.

"Was he Jewish?" Sophia asked, starry eyed. "He must have been."

"Stan and I are convinced of it." Nancy nodded as though privy to some secret information.

"Here we go again." Anika grinned.

Amidst the plates of uneaten roasted chicken limbs and discarded cartilage that I was still unable to look at, much less eat, and untouched eighteen-ounce soft drink containers bubbling with refreshment, I realized that if I wanted to become friends with these people, I needed to ignore the truth and start kissing some serious ass.

After all, I had just landed in kiss-ass central.

CHAPTER THREE

BUT WHAT IS THE TRUTH, RIGHT? I MEAN THAT'S THE PROB-lem, isn't it? That's what it all boils down to. Is there ever any one truth? Or are all truths created equal? Are truths and realities inter-changeable? If I were hungry and tired after having eaten a Balance Bar and shopped all day on Montana Avenue in Santa Monica and you took a girl who had walked all the way from eastern Sierra Leone to Freetown without eating or resting, wouldn't her reality of being hungry and tired be more or less the same as my reality of being hungry and tired—because after all we are both simply hun-gry and tired no matter the location or the activity?

Having a child made me want to believe in the existence of a universal truth, to really go Buddhist and believe that everything was relative, that all pain and suffering or joy and fulfillment were equal, but as of yet I was unable to stop the split screen in my head. The ex-cesses of Los Angeles—the sight of full plates of warm food carefully divided into sections of meat, vegetable, and potato being thrown into bulging trash cans without a second of hesitation, stacks of perfectly white paper napkins tossed as though trees had no life cycle—made me see the thousands upon thousands of people who would kill each other just to jump inside the trash bin of the restaurant where we sat.

Even in Africa I could not see the universal truth, especially when African heads of state and nongovernmental agencies, whose raison d'être was to assist the people, were unflinching in their theft from those very same people. The hypocrisy of it was in Technicolor—it was in the juxtaposition of the djellaba they wore, made from local cloth and dyed with flowers from Africa's earth and Africa's hands, and the gold and diamond Rolex or Cartier watches that dangled from their matte and hairless arms the color of depleted coal. It got me every time.

Their wives were even worse—they, too, would dress in the traditional African dress, a long skirt, a tight blouse, and a hat—wearing African colors like a flag. But from their distended earlobes were diamonds mined from the very same mines that caused the civil war; noses were punctured with diamonds that fell into their craterlike pores; fat wrists were strangled with bracelets made from the same stone that caused young girls too young to read to be raped and sodomized in broad daylight as though their souls could be stolen, depleted just as easily as diamonds from mines.

So I could not see that these women suffered as much as the poorest woman suffered when their children were sick or that they were just as vulnerable to the hardships of life as villagers who were displaced, dispossessed, and disheartened. It was equally difficult for me to see that Nancy Schneidermann *knew* anything on a visceral level about the suffering of the Jews or had ever experienced what it must have been like to be a Jew during and immediately after the war. She could not claim that pain, or the sympathy and respect that went along with it. She did not have the authority to do so.

Or had I just become so inept at the rules of regular social interaction that I had to completely relearn how to act around normal people who weren't in the throes of a civil war, who weren't starving for food or medical attention, but who were craving social interaction and approval?

It was a phenomenon to watch L.A. ladies at work. They talked with such earnestness about feeding the world, compassion for all, the We Are the World mentality, and yet they crossed the street when the faint whisper of homelessness threatened to invade their nostrils. They dumped food as though it was their birthright and didn't seem to see the connection between their actions and the rest of the world.

"Same time next week then?"

"Excuse me?" I looked up from the small cup of coffee that I had been stirring in a daze, completely unaware of what had been said.

"You are coming back?" Sophia stared. "Oh, please say you're coming."

"Face it, kid"—Nancy grinned—"you're fresh meat."

"A breath of fresh air." Alice smiled.

"Thanks." I put my hand over my mouth to catch a yawn. "You don't know how nice it is to hear."

"Is she keeping you up?" Anika asked. "Every two hours, right?"

"It's a source of constant amazement to me." I rubbed my temples.

"That they eat that often?" Sophia asked.

"No"—I shook my head—"that they shit as often as they eat. It's just amazing to me—every time I feed her, there's a huge explosion, like a bloody land mine has detonated, and before I can get her to the changing table it has seeped up her diapers, down her thighs, and through her nightdress. The stuff stains like mustard, so I try to get her clothes soaked right away, then by the time I get her changed and dressed, she's hungry again."

"And then the whole process begins again," Sophia chimed in as though we were harmonizing a duet rather than bitching about diaper changing.

"You could ask your husband—"

"There is no husband."

"You could ask your partner—"

I hated that politically correct euphemism even more. "There is no partner."

Anika lowered her chin and looked up at me like Hester Prynne. "Did you pull a Jodie Foster?"

"Excuse me?"

"You know," Nancy butted in, "a Melissa Etheridge."

"Sorry." I tapped nervously at the table. "But I've been in Africa for a few years and then before that Chechnya, so I'm a little behind in my *People* magazine reading."

Alice lowered her glasses and whispered. "They're trying to ask in the most polite way they know how whether you don't have a partner because you were artificially inseminated."

I truly enjoyed watching Alice, a woman who could be the spokesperson for Talbot's, so prim and proper, ask such a loaded question.

Sophia touched my shoulder. "It's very trendy, nothing to be ashamed of at all, almost the opposite really. Gay is in."

"Sorry to disappoint you ladies, nothing quite as glamorous as all that. Halla's father was a bone surgeon who went off to work with Médecins Sans Frontières—" I was met with a chorus of blank stares.

"Doctors Without Borders?" More blank stares. "It's a nonprofit organization that gives free medical attention to victims of war. I met him in Sierra Leone in a bar one night. It was love at first sight."

They were transfixed, not a single eye twitched, no mouth moved, except for mine. It was like I had turned on a soap opera and they were instantly fully engaged.

"We traveled everywhere, visiting refugee camps, warring villages, wherever he was needed. He'd fix them and I'd write about it." I was slightly aware that I, too, was falling into dream mode. "After it was all over, we planned on buying a farm, somewhere high in the mountains overlooking the coastline, where we could raise our children and he could start a small medical practice, something local, something for the people."

Sophia's eyes filled with expectation. "So what happened?"

"If you'd rather not say . . ." Alice mumbled halfheartedly before Nancy threw her a jab.

"He and I . . ." I hesitated. "We couldn't—" I wanted to tell them the truth but after taking another look at them, knew that I could not. They were too good, too present, too willing to accept whatever I told them. They wanted a good old-fashioned tragic ending to this story. And so did I. "A land mine killed him."

There was a communal intake of breath and three sets of sympathetic hands upon me.

"So you left?" Anika asked softly. "Why?"

Sophia had been silently putting two and two together. "Because you were pregnant?"

Nancy patted my arm and winced. "And he never knew."

"He never knew." I exhaled.

"We're so sorry," Alice offered. "We never should have asked."

I was momentarily struck by guilt, but I could not tell them what really happened to Oscar. When they heard the real story, they would not understand; they would ask me to remove my stroller from the line-up. They would think I was all wrong. I would, once again, be the outcast. But this time it would be worse, this time I would be an outcast at home. They say the true outcast is the one who comes home and, of course, they're right. Outcast: Driven out; rejected. That one line, that one definition, was my diagnosis, my label to pull out whenever I needed an explanation for the events of my life. But being an outcast had always helped me in the past—it worked to shield me from commitment, to console me when I felt excluded, and to put an end to the difficult questions any healthy individual in my situation should be asking themselves.

But it was all just bullshit, all of it. When the British Airways flight hovered over Los Angeles and I saw the twinkling lights, my stomach turned over with a fear that was far greater than anything I had experienced in Africa. I had not lived in California since I had turned eighteen; twenty years had passed. I hadn't saved or planned; I had no home, no job, no husband, no money.

"Will you be staying here for a while"—Alice turned her grieving soulful eyes on me—"or heading back home as soon as Halla has her shots?"

Americans, and particularly Californians, were funny creatures. On the one hand they tried their best to put on their politically correct cloak every time they walked out their tree-lined front doors and hopped into their gas-guzzling SUV rhino-hunting vehicles, and yet underneath it all they were wary of anything foreign.

"This is my home," I said.

"Los Angeles?" Alice grimaced. "But you sound so European."

"Malibu, to be precise."

"You were born here?" She kept at it, trying to understand someone like me, someone who looked like a European but was American and spoke with an English accent that had been softened by the Pidgen English of Africa.

"No, I was born in Corsica but came here with my mother when I was seven or thereabouts." She looked dazed as though there was just too much information coming at her. "It's a long story."

"Don't stop," Sophia protested. "It all sounds so interesting."

"So you're living in Malibu then?" Anika jumped in. "That's quite a drive."

"Well, not if you live in the Colony," Nancy said. "That's an easy one, in town in less than a half an hour, and more importantly, Starbucks in under two minutes."

There was silence. I knew they were waiting for me to give them the location because that one address would allow them to know more about me than a year of long lunches and classes at the Pump Station ever would.

"It's a little further out than that," I said.

"So you won't be going back to Europe at all?" Sophia frowned.

"No, I don't think so." My eyes shot down to her perfectly pedicured toes, where small flowers were painted in pink on the first two, a rhinestone twinkling from underneath the tightly curled petals. I had not seen my own toes since my sixth month of pregnancy and wondered whether toe hair now completely obscured them from view. "Not for a while, not if everything goes according to plan."

Anika looked up from her eighteen-ounce decaf iced tea. "Sounds mysterious."

"Death and taxes are anything but." I shook my head thinking about the legal battle I was about to embark upon. I never thought Heaven would leave it all to me, and what was worse, I'd never wanted her to. Up until ten months ago, all I wanted was a duffel bag, two pairs of clean underwear, and an assignment that promised front-page headlines.

But then Halla changed my world. Now I wanted nothing more than to claim Point Elsewhere, the cove in Malibu where I was raised by a woman upon whose doorstep I was dropped by my mother at age seven. Now Halla would have a home, a home that wasn't dependent upon any man or marriage. It would be hers, free and clear.

There was one roadblock, however, to this sisterhood of freedom, and that was Francis, Heaven's only blood relative, the only person—I think, I hope—who wanted me dead. Well, maybe not the only person, but certainly one of the first in line. And why shouldn't he? He was sitting on a ten-million-dollar piece of property that the law, and Heaven, said was mine.

CHAPTER FOUR

AL SMITH, HEAVEN'S ATTORNEY, SWALLOWED HARD. "IT'S become complicated."

He made me feel thirteen. "I know it's complicated, Al, that's why I'm here."

"Yes." He looked up from his lap. "But now she's been dead for almost two months and while you've been traipsing around the world, Junior and his harem or whatever you call them these days have made the situation more and more difficult."

My stomach tightened at the mention of my so-called older brother. "But the will is legally binding, right?"

Al exhaled loudly as he grabbed a stray nose hair and pulled at it before swiveling his Eames leather office chair toward the window that took up three-quarters of the wall. The offices of Smith and Barney were in a penthouse suite at the intersection of Sunset Boulevard and Doheny Drive. The views from Al's office made L.A. look like the land of Oz, with azure blue swimming pools and emerald green grass spread out like a magic quilt below and above it was only sky.

"Not coming to her funeral was a big mistake, Saffron. A very big mistake, indeed."

"And it broke my heart." Al was a dear friend of my adopted mother, Heaven, from way back when she had taken over her cheating husband's failed real estate business in the forties and turned it into a multimillion-dollar company. He was also the executor of her estate, and had assisted her in drafting the final will, which disinherited her only child, her son, and gave me everything.

"Then why on earth didn't you come?" His voice rose with anger and sadness. "She loved you like the daughter she wished she'd had, and she did everything she could to raise you just as she had wanted to be raised herself. And then for you not to come, Saffron, I just can't understand it."

I had arrived at the small beach house in the hinterland of Malibu in the fall of 1970. It was owned by a self-proclaimed hippie-hater, someone who had worked all of her life and relied upon no man, woman, or government to help her. She ate ham and eggs every morning, paid her Mexican workers less than minimum wage, served them a "weenie" for lunch, and drank Scotch as soon as the sun appeared heavy in the afternoon sky.

Her name was Helen but I called her Heaven, because after hitchhiking with my mother along the path of self-realization where herpes and crabs were the currency, that's where I thought I had landed. A house on the beach, chickens and a vegetable garden in the back, and the smell of hot pies in the oven—domestic bliss peppered with the nonconformist—drew me in and held me there.

I wasn't alone in my adulation of Heaven; she had her very own nonprofessional cult following, partly because she owned all of the land in the cove but mainly because she drew people to her, people who were searching for a mother figure, for a chance to rewrite the past or simply to escape from it.

Her only gripe with the world—and it was a huge one for such a rabid Republican—was that her son thought he was the reincarnation of Jesus Christ. His reddish brown beard was to his sternum, which protruded so far out of his skin it looked like a buried tribal necklace, his silky sun-streaked hair fell over his shoulders. He preferred white kaftans unless there was the option of nudity. His name was Francis but he asked that no one address him by his Christian name. He said we didn't need to call him anything, he would hear our call; he was at one with us all. Okay, whatever.

So Heaven placed all her hopes on me. When I turned eighteen, she sent me to England, a country of manners and a female prime minister. She chose the London School of Economics because it was a man's school, a school of politics and economics, two areas of thought she believed women had to understand if they wanted to succeed in, or at least understand, the world today.

"Under normal circumstances, Al"—I folded my palms against my stomach—"I would have been there, I would have risked my life to be there."

When I received the news that Heaven had passed away via one of her groupies—and by that time she was ninety-one, with more groupies than Mick Jagger—I was in London, flat on my back for my final trimester while magnesium sulfate coursed through my veins in an attempt to prevent the premature birth of Halla.

The funeral was attended by just about everyone who had ever worked for her, and in her advanced years that included mostly doctors, nurses, masseurs, and house help. There was Francis, who according to rumor trotted out in his most opulent of robes and beads, with his hippie friends following in his wake like hairy flower girls.

Francis and his followers came for something but got nothing. While they eulogized Heaven to the Indian sitar—an instrument that, in and of itself, would have caused her to hemorrhage—and threw flower petals and Xeroxed photographs of her into the water where her ashes were strewn, they drank cheap champagne and wept.

"But you didn't come, did you?" He tossed his pencil onto his desk. "She gave you this enormous gift, her legacy, and you didn't even have the courtesy to show up on the day she bequeathed it to you. I'll tell you one thing, Francis sure as hell did."

His undiluted judgment of me made me even more convinced I didn't owe Al an explanation. Heaven knew why I was stuck in London, I knew why I was stuck in London, and that was all that mattered.

"Let's get on with it." He removed a paper-thin light blue file from the top drawer of his desk as if it were something he kept near for easy access. His eyes scrolled halfway down the page, then he cleared his throat.

> *And to Saffron Roch, the woman with whom I share not a single gene, but all of my heart and soul, I give Point Elsewhere in its entirety. You, Saffron, are now the rightful owner of my five acres of beachfront property, including my three homes, my chickens, my vegetables—or whatever is left of them after I've died and you're out getting your bottom shot off and your heart broken in Africa.*

Al glanced up from the page, but I did not reciprocate. That one statement told me exactly when she had drafted her will and I wondered whether she had changed it because of our conversation, because of Halla.

> *All of my belongings are now yours to do with as best suits your needs. This is a hefty responsibility for someone who abhors possessions as purely as you, but it is partly why I*

chose you. The other reason I have made you my sole heir, dear, is because my son is an absolute idiot who has spent a lifetime preaching his freedom from material needs while sitting on his ass on the beach I paid for in Malibu.

But here's the thing: If you should decide to liquidate your inheritance, you must provide him with a similar living arrangement and an allowance for as long as he lives.

I shook my head, unable to process what all of this would mean for me. She had made me a millionaire and made me hopelessly dependent in a single paragraph. "I would rather have nothing but the clothes on my back than have to take care of that hypocrite for the rest of his life. And Al"—I could barely contain my anger—"what is he now, fifty? Why am I the one who has to make sure that he has a roof over his head?"

My mother had left me with Heaven at Point Elsewhere two days after we arrived and never came back for me. I was homeschooled by Heaven, living on the fringes of Malibu on a beach with chickens that laid blue eggs, sucking ice cubes drenched in Scotch, and playing cards while hippies painted dots on their foreheads and practiced the Kamasutra with dedicated repetition.

Under her tutelage, I grew into a very tall woman who knew how to fish, garden, change a tire, build a house, and catch grunions with her bare hands in the middle of the night. Life at the end of Malibu was devoid of roles, pure as a farm. We cut coupons for the market, drove an ancient burgundy Honda that was so gutless it felt like it ran on electricity, and got neighbors to pitch in every time we needed to fix something in the house. I did not know that Heaven was a wealthy woman.

"May I continue?" Al glared at me.

"Go ahead." I glared back.

If left to his own defense, that nincompoop could never support himself and even though it pains me to do it, he is still my son, and I, now you, must provide for him. To say I know you'll do the right thing is foolish, I can't say that. I can only say that I know you'll try. The land—and the community that has arisen because it is my legacy—please treat it with the respect that you have always shown me. It was here that your mother left you some thirty years ago. It is here you must return. Or you must sell. But you can't have it both ways.

Furthermore, if you reunite with your lover, Oscar De Vries (I always told you to steer clear of surgeons, but you did not listen, perhaps you will do so now), and attempt to bring him to the beach, the terms and conditions will reverse irrevocably and you will find yourself the tenant and Francis will be the rightful heir to the estate. If you should choose to sell, I no longer care what you do. If this sounds harsh, then you know it's me and I'm sober.

My eyes met Al's. Having read the will, he was waiting for me. "She's forcing me to choose?"

"That's right, Saffron." He put the paper back in the Tiffany-blue folder and slipped it into his desk drawer. "According to the will, you have the right to either live at Point Elsewhere or sell it, but essentially what she's saying is you can't put it in your pocket and save it for later; if you do, the property will go to Francis, her only remaining heir."

"Don't forget the part about Oscar." I seethed not because I wanted to see him—he was out of my life—but because her control was more complete from the grave than it had ever been from the beach. "I cannot believe she'd be so—"

Al's forehead folded into disapproval. "Speaking ill of the dead brings you nothing and shows me nothing but disrespect."

"Oh, give me a break, you know how Heaven—" I said when suddenly I felt my left breast swell with milk and was overcome by a tingling sensation before milk spurted. That must have been the "let-down reflex" that Gretchen was going on about the last time I went to the Pump Station. Al stared at me as I tried to remember if I put in new breast pads. I suddenly threw both arms across my chest.

"Are you alright?" He leaned over his desk. "You've suddenly gone quite red."

"Fine, just fine." The breast-pad question was now a moot one. I could feel the milk seep through the breast pads, my bra, my blouse—there were even drops of white milk on the hairs of my arms. I stood up and walked to the one spot in the office where I could turn my back to him. "It's just a lot to take in."

"You're cold?" he asked as I took off the gray sweatshirt that had been tied around my waist as a strategic—but useless—ass cover and quickly put it on. I suddenly remembered just how dark rings of sweat appear on gray shirts and threw my shoulders forward so as to avoid any contact with leaking breasts.

The buzzer on his desk sounded.

"Yes?" Al responded, listening carefully. "Thank you, June."

I watched as he got up from his desk and walked to the front door. My time was up, Al was a busy man. "Thank you, Al." I followed him to the door. "I don't mean to sound like an ingrate; it's just a lot to take in."

He stopped in front of the massive mahogany doors and looked me in the face. He was the very image of the father whose picture I would have loved to carry in my wallet and claim as my own. "When were you going to tell me?" he asked.

"Tell you what?"

He opened the door and I was suddenly assaulted by Halla's screams. Her feeding time must have been the same as the letdown, and she was angry at the missed opportunity.

"I'm sorry, Saff, but she just wouldn't quiet down no matter how much I rocked her." June, Al's secretary, handed her to me like a smelly sock.

Al looked at me holding a child, a child who was no longer screaming but "rooting" for my breast. I could see the answers flood through his brain. "Did Heaven know?"

I nodded. "Can't you tell?" The last time we spoke, just a few days before she died, I was still in bed in London alone. I wondered again whether the changes in her will had to do with her telling me that my life needed to be tethered to something, that I couldn't have a child with a man like Oscar. Heaven wanted me home, away from Oscar, away from Africa, away from harm in all of its seductive forms.

"I'm sorry if I was harsh on you earlier." Al nodded and smiled. "I misunderstood."

"It's understandable." I looked down at my baby and couldn't help but smile. "I wasn't exactly forthcoming with an explanation." I artfully unbuttoned my shirt and unsnapped my nursing bra. There was a momentary look of sheer panic in Al's eyes but then he found an imaginary dot somewhere above my head and locked onto it with every ounce of his being.

"Al?" I interrupted his trance. "Where's Francis now?"

"There," he said, still fixated on the spot.

Al's eyes were beginning to freak me out. "In both houses?"

"In all three, I've been told. Apparently, he's of the school that possession is proof of ownership."

"How am I going to do this?" Francis had no concept of boundaries, he knocked them all down so that he could walk unimpeded through life, throughout Point Elsewhere. Heaven erected her lines of defense and fought to protect them until the day she died. I looked down at Halla. She had changed me, I was no longer quite as mean or as dogged as I once was and I didn't know if I was up to the fight. "He's been there for nearly forty years, Al."

"Do whatever you have to. It was her dying wish."
"It might kill me as well."

It had been ten years since I had been back and I was afraid to see what the passing of time had brought to Point Elsewhere, a place where Heaven used to say "time danced but never stuck around long enough to ruin the party." Over the years, no matter where I was, when I closed my eyes I yearned to drive down Pacific Coast Highway, past Broad Beach, where the women looked like Goldie Hawn and their husbands like Danny DeVito, all the way down until the fruit and vegetable stands made from driftwood and funded by the sale of cannabis came into view and the vibe went from Porsche to VW van. I would re-create the drive in my head, taking a left into the broken driveway, where the first house—shack, really—would come into view and then the others. I would see through them to the ocean and the sun that chose to set at the same height as our living room windows each and every evening of my youth.

I would wind my way down the driveway, taking time to notice the height of each Monterey cyprus planted—they marked every Christmas I spent there—and then I would come to a stop at the side of the smaller house, Francis's house. It was built directly on the sand with its blue-framed diamond-shaped windows pointing out toward the ocean like the bow of a ship. There was only one rather large room, a small kitchen, and a smaller bathroom, but I had seen more than twenty people sleep in the living room at one time.

Today I passed the soft cove of Leo Carrillo with its mass of black-skinned, blond-headed surfers and pulled into the center divider at the top of the hill. There, on my left, were the two leaning brick columns and a gray mailbox, with a rising sun painted in crude yellow and orange paint, marking the entrance to the property. I pulled into the driveway and veered to my right, where Heaven's house was. It was hard to believe ten years had passed, and yet the time was in the details. The house was in the Craftsman style and it looked distressed—the gray paint was flaking, the wood cracking, and the glass windows irrevocably stained by the salt air.

"Heaven always joked that the only thing sea air didn't destroy was her roses."

I stepped out of the car, turning to the voice I had known since childhood, the voice of conservatism, family values, and meat and potatoes, and threw my arms around her wrinkled but pearl-encrusted neck. "Sally."

"Hello, dear," she said as though I'd been gone for the afternoon. Her shoulder-length dark hair was styled the same way she had worn it since I'd known her, curled under at the bottom and pinned back along the side. She wore her white leather pumps, blue polyester pants with pleats in the front, and a narrow belt with a small gold buckle. Her blouse was polyester as well and her sleeves were rolled up to the elbows as though she had been pitching in for the war effort. Her long fingers were capped with pointy nails that were painted an awful Sally Hanson pink. On her ring finger she wore the five-carat diamond her husband, Dean, had given her sixty years before when they were married.

"It's so good to see you, Sally." I had gone to their house, a pre-fab plastic-wrapped mobile home on the other side of Heaven's every Friday night between five and seven o'clock for years while they inhaled cocktails and olives like air. It would start out with memories of the old days, then as the gin poured over the vermouth, the talk turned to the dead, and then the arguments would start. Most of the time Heaven and Sally wouldn't get back on speaking terms until Thursday of the following week, just in time for another round of Friday-night cocktails.

"We missed you at the memorial." I watched her forehead wrinkle and her eyes fill with the compassion that comes from attending too many funerals.

It saddened me. "I wanted to come more than you know, but it was complicated."

"Well, we're glad you're back now." She paused. "You are staying, aren't you?"

"Of course!" I threw out a little more cheer than I felt. "Where's Francis?" I took a step back to make sure that Halla was still asleep. I had lowered all the windows in the car and parked in the shade and prayed that she wouldn't wake up until after I met with him. Having to breast-feed in the middle of our meeting would not go a long way toward establishing my cutthroat stance.

"He got back late last night," she whispered. "They've all been up at a festival in Humboldt for the last week"—she smiled demurely—"doing things that young people do."

Humboldt was marijuana and group sex spelled backward. "How's it been since Heaven died?"

"Not the same." She took my arm and we walked toward her house. "Lonely, sad, and strange, you know, like we never know what's going to happen next."

"How's he been treating you?" I glanced toward the shack.

Sally shook her head quietly. "He's always been very good to us, dear. He helps Dean carry his fishing poles to the tide and whenever one of Dean's papaya trees gets too large for the greenhouse, Francis is the first to help."

Occupation is his game, Al had told me, his one and only trick; he'll wear you down like a trickle of water wears a stone. "I'm glad that he's being helpful to you, his mother loved you both so much."

Sally produced the key to Heaven's house from her purse and opened the door. "And evidently she loved you as well."

She knew about the inheritance then.

"The cherished daughter has returned." A huge voice filled the living room. I turned and stared at the man who'd just come through the front door as though pushed from behind by a gust of wind.

Francis had grown into even more of a spectacle than I remembered. His beard was now down to his belly button and his reddish brown hair kept going until his lower back. He was skinnier than I remembered and tanner than some of the Indians I had met while covering Sri Lanka in the early nineties. He wore a long white robe that was similar to what Brahmins wore and a pair of turquoise blue Quiksilver thongs.

"Hello, Francis," I said.

"Hello, Saffron, we've missed you." Underneath all that hair I could see his smile was razor thin; his green eyes locked in on me.

"I've missed all of you." I walked toward him and let him give me one of those touchy-feely, I-am-holier-than-you'll-ever-be hugs.

"Let's have tea and talk." He walked straight into Heaven's kitchen and began to boil water and get the tea bags as though Heaven had never lived there. I felt rage curl my fingertips until my fists were two balls hanging at my sides.

"Sally, will you join—" I asked, but she declined before I was able to finish my question.

Everything was still in its place, but the house smelled of dirt and dogs. I wondered how many of Francis's friends had slept on Heaven's dark blue velvet couches since she had passed away, how many of his pets had peed on her pastel eighteenth-century Oriental rugs and bitten through her handmade needlepoint throw cushions. Francis put the tea bags into two small cups and poured the hot water. "Raw sugar?"

"No, this is good, thanks." I pulled my chair up to the bar that separated the living room from the kitchen and gazed out the window. The view promised such tranquility, such nothingness, and blocking it was Francis—the greedy marijuana-smoking, mushroom-drinking "healer" who used only raw sugar and soy milk in his herbal tea.

"It's been a beautiful summer, Saffron." He combed his fingers through his beard. "You weren't around when she was first diagnosed with emphysema a few years ago and it's been a long road. Doctors, nurses, lung treatments, late-night trips to the emergency room when there wasn't enough oxygen; massages, herbal teas, we did everything. It was draining for everyone involved."

I wanted to slap him.

"But we've done a lot of healing since the spring when Mom finally had the heart attack and passed away."

Who was "we"? Was it a royal "we" or a spiritual "we," as in "I and my followers"? I had no idea who he was referring to.

I was having a hard time forming a sentence. "I'm glad to hear it."

"We wish that you could have been a part of it all." His eyes locked onto mine and rode them.

I could no longer stand it. "Who is 'we'?"

"The community." His hands reminded me so much of Heaven, it hurt. They were square and long with ridges of veins running down them like streams into nail beds that were baby pink and short. He had beautiful hands.

"You mean everyone who lives in the area, or are you referring to your friends who stay here?"

His eyes never left mine. "It's all one."

If I stayed any longer, I was going to puke the refined-sugar, bleached-flour Starbucks blueberry muffin I had picked up that morning, all over the kitchen floor. "Excuse me for a second," I said and walked out to check on Halla, who was sleeping soundly. Anika had told me that babies slept better outside in the breeze, and she was right.

When I returned, I found Francis slicing a papaya in the palm of his hand, juice running down his fingers and wrists onto the floor.

"So you'll be joining us?" he asked without looking up from his fruit. "For good?"

I was certain he knew the effect his words had on me. I was never good with finality, with bird cages. "I'm only a foot soldier, Francis, here to do what Heaven wanted," I said, trying not to show my discomfort at having to share my space with him. "And apparently that was to have her happy"—he looked up—"family," I continued with a smile, "back together again."

"I think Mom would love you to have her house," he said, not hiding the undertones and suggestions that swirled around the issue of the lower beach house and the property that surrounded it. Francis had always considered them his.

"Yes, I think that's where we'll stay." I went along with it for now.

"We?" Francis smiled. "Have you succumbed to the bourgeoisie and married your doctor?"

Suddenly there was a new energy to him.

"No, quite the opposite," I said.

He jumped a little. "What's that?"

"A child out of wedlock—" I stopped myself. I would not belittle my daughter's existence with the sarcasm I felt. "I had a little girl."

Under that mask of hair, I could see his chin twitch and a flash of understanding seep into his eyes. He exited the house through the kitchen door and walked down the railway ties that curled along the side of the mountain and dropped to the lower houses without so much as a wave.

When I went to lock the front door and say good-bye to Sally, I saw Francis sitting by himself, cross-legged, just beneath the sand dune that protected the houses from getting blasted away during those rare but potent California storms. His hair was blowing in the early-afternoon breeze and from behind he looked like a hot California chick. But I knew Francis; he was steeling himself for battle.

I had inadvertently left one war for another, only this time I was fighting it alone.

CHAPTER FIVE

WHETHER IT'S A BEACHFRONT PARADISE OR AN INNER-CITY basement flat, there's nothing quite like moving into your childhood home at age thirty-eight with nothing but a suitcase and a baby carrier in hand, without even the glimmer of a man or a job. Forget outcast, I was a loser.

My furniture was being sent from London by way of the Falklands, which was fine by me because I was dreading its arrival. Even though it was relatively unused, the designs were old and had a musty English air to them, making them totally unsuitable for beachfront windows. My books, and there were far too many of them, would represent all that I was before I had gotten myself knocked up by the wrong man: student of politics, master of politics, voyeur into the lives of the disadvantaged and the taken advantage of, healer, war correspondent. I had considered an all-out breakdown the day I got the call that my container had arrived. It would be like looking in a mirror and seeing the reflection of youth staring back, disappointed and wasted.

Now as a woman with a child, I was invisible. When a woman has a baby, and has said baby attached to her by way of Snugli, she could be Bo Derek in *"10"* wearing a see-through tan bathing suit, cornrows flapping against ridiculously pert breasts, and no one would even glance at her except in that "Oh, look how cute that baby is. What a good mom for taking her daughter out for a run!" way.

Guys might take a passing look and think to themselves that they want their wife to look like that when they're finally ready to stop dating the Pam Andersons of L.A. and settle down with a good girl. A woman who doesn't care about going out, a woman who doesn't want to shop, work out, or drop the kid off with a nanny. A woman who doesn't want a life of her own. Their mother.

During the off-moments when I wasn't thinking about Halla or the Malibu tug-of-war, I thought about Africa and Oscar, remembering the fantasies I had of us that were something out of a twisted Hemingway novella. I was the writer/nurse/invaluable irrigation specialist and he was the doctor who saved lives, who replaced twisted smiles with straight ones, amputated limbs with functioning ones. We would work together all day in our picturesque village that no longer existed in the Africa of today and at night we would retire to our *Out of Africa*–type layout where our young blonde (but so tan they'd pass for natives) children would come running out followed by their loving nanny (dressed in perfectly pressed tribal garb) and their pet chimpanzee, Coco. What an idiot.

Isolation and the hypnotic pulling of the waves were clearly getting to me. I needed to move on to something more real, more grounded. And there was someone I knew who fit the bill perfectly. Retrieving the crumpled piece of paper from my bag, I dialed her number.

"Hello?" she said quickly as though she were waiting for my call.

"Anika?" I cleared my throat. "This is Saffron Roch. Did I catch you at a bad time?"

"Not at all, I just put Jeremiah down for a nap. How are you?"

Her voice was so present, so there, as if she had never been anywhere but here.

"I'm good, I'm good," I said too quickly, not finding that comfortable rhythm that people who are used to casual friendships have. Not only did I not know how to reach out, I didn't have anything to offer. I couldn't invite Anika over to my house, as it would beg too many questions, and despite serious yearnings, I couldn't invite myself over to hers.

"Would you like to meet at the park tomorrow?" Park, park, I can't believe I even said that. I never went to parks, not even in the days when getting drunk in the park was the thing English students did. What in the hell were we supposed to do at a park with a couple of invertebrates anyway? There were no swings for them, no sand toys they could dig with, for Christ sakes—what must Anika think of me? My cheeks burned as I attempted to fill the huge silent void that was about to engulf me. "Or we could—"

"I would love to," she cut in, "but, Saff, tomorrow is Sunday."

I loved the way she said my name, like we were old friends or something. It must have been the lactation class—nothing quite like showing your breasts to a room full of strangers to break the ice. "So?"

"We try to spend Sundays as a family—you know, long walk, big Sunday dinner, that kind of thing."

But the kid can't even keep his eyes open, let alone eat a pot roast. "Oh, I totally understand, I just wasn't thinking." Heat filled my face.

"How about Monday?" she cheered. "Monday would be great for us."

Us. A family at just a few weeks old. Her answering machine message probably included his name in the "we're not here to take your call" or the "we've stepped out" part. She sounded so mature when she spoke, as though all her ducks were in a row, her home was in order, her life made complete sense. She was younger than me, I was sure of it. Did she know that I was older? Was it then condescension I heard in her voice rather than maturity? Was she taking pity on me, the branded elderly woman, unwed, unhitched, and completely unconnected to the community at large?

"Sounds perfect," I said eagerly and then thought better of it. "But it will have to be the morning, we have an appointment in the afternoon." I used the royal "we," the regal "we," the family "we."

Dogs barked in the background. She had dogs, sounded like yellow labs. God, I wanted to go over there.

"Douglas Park at ten-thirty?" she fired off.

I was having a hard time remembering what or where that was. Up until now I thought the primary purpose of a park was to give the homeless a place to sleep, the obese a place to sunbathe, and a city the chance to breathe.

"Right next to the Pump Station, where we meet for class."

I heard it again. Condescension or maturity? Whatever it was, it was fine. I was fully prepared to let someone else in the driver's seat just as long as they didn't drop me off at the curb. "Sounds great," I said, already thinking of lunch afterward but not wanting to appear as though I knew no one else in town. "I'll see you there."

In the short time that I'd had Halla around, I had already found that children, or babies, were the best date a person could ask for— they provided the topic of discussion, the perfect distraction, and the built-in excuse to leave. Even if the person sitting across from you is wearing *Flashdance* leggings and baby pink Capezio dance shoes, you'd think you'd met your soul sister after having discussed babies for an hour. And whenever there is a lull in the conversation, you can simply stare at your child and smile or exhale thoughtfully, and nine times out of ten the person you were talking to would follow. There would be none of those uncomfortable pauses in which you wondered what the hell you were doing there.

And, of course, the excuse. Who could get angry with you for leaving early because you suspect too much stimulation for your little one? How perfect was this setup?

I got in my car at nine-thirty on the dot, thinking it would take me forty-five minutes tops to get from County Line to Santa Monica. I made a mental checklist before pulling out of the garage.

"Front carrier, bassinet, Snap N Go, ten diapers, powder, wipes, a change of clothes—"

I had packed only one change; would that be enough? How long were play dates anyway? I turned off the car, looked back at Halla, who was already sleeping, and made a dash back to the house. Halfway through packing another outfit that would keep her warm in case there was morning fog, I had a horrible visual picture of the car rolling out of the garage and being struck smack in the side by one of those Starving Students moving trucks. I ran out and brought her back in the house. Having perhaps the most acute heat/sound/temporal sensors man has ever known, she immediately woke up and began to wail.

"Shit!" I screamed. "It's already nine-forty, shit, shit, shit." I pulled her out of the car seat and allowed her groping little mouth to find what she hungered for most: my breast. While she nursed, I went through the things I had packed and was fairly certain that we would be covered for the few hours away from the mother ship. I used to feel nothing but apathy when I heard leaders under house arrest complain. Now I felt untainted sympathy.

"All finished?" I was just about to switch her over to the other side, but was thrilled to find that she was already asleep. Thrilled and a bit worried—she seemed to prefer the left side, which meant that my right breast looked and felt like something the Russians built under Khrushchev, while the left nipple was cracked and raw and unable to heal because those vise-grip lips of hers were constantly sucking on it. And to think I used to think of them as part of foreplay. I quietly transferred her back to the car seat and tucked her in.

Less than ten minutes into my drive down Pacific Coast Highway, I heard a sound similar to *pasta e fagioli* being shot out of a turkey baster. I looked in the rearview mirror and saw the stuff seeping through her pink-and-white–striped terry-cloth onesie by none other than Petit Bateau.

"Shit." I turned off Pearl Jam and kept driving. It was now ten past ten. I drove like a madwoman with all the windows down, smelling nothing but shit and thinking of my poor daughter's ass, thighs, and most of her upper rib cage bathing in a pool of it. Then I wondered what was worse in the book of baby etiquette: showing up half an hour late or showing up with a sleeping baby covered in dried shit up to her ears? I pulled over.

"Did you have a tough time getting out the door?" Anika greeted me with her customary warm hug, but her smile faded almost instantly. There she was sitting in the middle of a Ralph Lauren ad, on a light-blue-and-white–check blanket next to a wicker basket with Jeremiah asleep in his spotless boy outfit in his spotless boy car seat. It looked like they'd been there for some time. Ice cubes had melted.

"I am so sorry." I put down Halla's car seat and threw off the bags that were wrapped around my every appendage. "You have no idea what happened." Her eyes were unmoving, on me, waiting for a good excuse. "I left the house at ten but"— her tennis shoes were so white and her navy blue shorts so starched, they were seriously freaking me out—"I forgot a change of clothes, then she shat all over herself—oh, it was awful. The whole car smelled like a rotten compost pile, I had to pull over." I was beginning to feel like I needed a note from the principal. "I seriously need a drink."

"A drink?" Her eyes widened, then she forced a smile.

Did she have a headband on? An actual blue velvet headband? Oh, for the love of God.

"Will lemonade do?" She bent down and picked up a pitcher—made of actual plastic with a friendly pattern of light blue and yellow checks—and poured pink lemonade into matching plastic cups.

I felt like a cow, a flustered moose, with nothing to offer but apologies and rambling. I was grateful, however, that I had made the decision to pull over. Ten minutes earlier would not have been a big deal, but an infant covered in her own shit would have definitely contrasted with the scene that Anika had worked so hard to create. There was the basket, the lemonade, and an assortment of toys for children who could barely move their necks. And her son looked as though he were off to Ascot—pale blue knit booties, gray cotton pants with cuffs, a white cotton undershirt covered with a knitted pale blue cable-knit sweater the color of the booties. He was the picture of masculine dignity, reflecting his parents' wealth and taste better than they could themselves.

"It's beautiful. I had no idea you were going to put all of this together." I thought about my backpack and the cheese-and-mustard sandwich on whole wheat I had shoved into it just in case she didn't mention lunch. "I'm so sorry we're late."

"Please, I understand. I know how hard it can be getting ready with a little one."

"But look at you and look at us." Anika looked like she was about to step aboard her yacht. I glanced at my dirty sweatpants and at my tennis shoes, which were a permanent gray with matching gray laces. My hair was so unruly that I had it tied back in a bandana.

"You look great, what are you talking about! You look as though you're off on an adventure." Anika began to unpack her basket. "Now, I didn't know if you ate meat and dairy—"

"What else is there?"

"Well, there's tofu, soy dogs—" She stopped smack in the middle of the sentence with a look of resignation and comfort, realizing she didn't have to play the hostess with me. "You're absolutely right, there is nothing else." Anika unpacked thinly sliced cold cuts, a bag of country potato bread, and two or three different kinds of sliced cheese. She'd even brought small Tupperware containers of mustard and mayonnaise.

"Do you have someone helping you at home?" I had to ask.

"Three days a week, four hours a day," she said casually, as though it were totally unimportant. "And don't forget these." She handed me two bags of potato chips and a pickle.

But as I nibbled on my sandwich and watched older children squabble over their toys, I thought about all that I would do if I had twelve hours a week to think about my needs rather than anticipate Halla's.

"Joyce comes but sometimes I don't want to let him go, so she'll clean the house, do the laundry, and I'll stay upstairs with him and lie in bed. My husband has been pretty insistent that I use her, though, because he says he wants to have his wife back." She slathered mayonnaise on her bread with the enclosed plastic utensils. When she was done, her knife was absolutely clean, positively monastic. Mine, of course, was dripping with condiments.

"Well, that's pretty common, isn't it? After nine months of pregnancy, just when they think they're going to have you back again, there's the whole nursing thing." I had no idea what I was talking about, having gone through the entire thing, including the birth, solo. I did develop a pretty unhealthy bond with my nurse, though, pleading with her not to leave me, thanking her for being with me while biting the hell out of her hand when a bad contraction came along. She disappeared immediately after I fired off two rolls of photos of the three of us, the proud parents holding baby, and despite my best efforts, remained unfound.

Anika nodded. Her dark hair was pulled off her face and braided down her back like a thick rope. Her skin was olive in tone, suggesting Latin roots, but her square jaw and pale blue eyes threw me off completely. She was average height, five seven or eight, and she had good legs, but she was heavy from her thighs up. At first I thought she was overweight and then I realized that the woman *just had a baby.* I had been in L.A. only a few weeks and was already beginning to think like a native. Frightening.

"It's his second marriage, second family."

My eyes shot to her wedding ring and her necklace and I saw the signs of the "second marriage." There were jewels, gifts that someone our age would have a hard time affording, and the taste was all wrong, seriously dated, verging on retro. "So what you're telling me is that you hide out with your son when your nanny comes over."

"And I organize. I love my boxes, shelves, folders, anything that helps me put our things in order."

"Don't leave much work for the nanny then, do you?" I stood to check on Halla but she was sleeping, for once, like a baby. While her skin remained dark, her eyes grew lighter with each day, and the few strands of hair that she had were completely without pigment. Me and Oscar.

"What did you do before you were married?"

"I was a secretary." Her voice was flat. "I was my husband's secretary."

"Well, you must have been a damn good one." I gave her that cheerleader grin. "He married you, didn't he?"

"He couldn't afford me any other way," she said, but I could tell that she was not yet comfortable with the scenario. Women were not, in general, supportive of secretaries who married their bosses. It was like befriending cancer.

"How long have you been married?" My journalistic curiosities were getting the better of me; I could feel it and yet I couldn't stop.

"A little less than a year." She put both of her hands behind her and leaned back. "We got married when we found out about Jeremiah."

"Great. A perfect reason to get married," I chirped, trying to push away the judgment I felt.

"I was so happy. I had wanted a child since I turned sixteen, and before that I baby-sat just to be around babies."

I loved her candor, which was unusual in a place like Los Angeles, where admitting that all you ever wanted was to have babies—at sixteen, no less—was like admitting you carried the gene for stupidity.

"It's all I ever wanted and my first husband—"

I was getting pulled in faster than a fish on a worm. But then the inevitable happened. Jeremiah woke up and cried. They always woke up crying right when you were getting to the good part.

"What?" I said casually. "He wasn't wild about kids?"

"Here you go." She put him to her breast, unsnapped her nursing bra, and unleashed the monster.

"No, it wasn't that, it was . . . " She paused. "Isn't that Halla?"

"What?" I glanced back to the carrier. "Oh, she's just fidgeting, she's fine." She was actually wailing, but I wanted to get some kind of closure on this story. Halla launched into a full-scale scream that I could no longer ignore, so I picked her up and unleashed my own monster. She quickly refused the right breast, the one that could now serve as a model for a Scud missile, and went for the left one, which fortunately had had time to refill.

Anika adjusted her breast-feeding pillow (which retailed for $40 at the Pump Station) and gave me a thoughtful glance. "What do *you* do in your free time?"

"What free time?" I glanced over at her. "I'm her twenty-four-hour-a-day slave. She's either attached to my breasts or I'm attached to her bottom, wiping it, washing it, and putting diaper rash ointment on it. Her bum has become my life's focus."

"Okay, what did you used to do in your free time?"

We were sitting by a pond of flat lily pads and giant Koi fish the color of ripe persimmon, but it was the ducks and their ducklings that drew crowds from the playground. Children dressed in blues and whites came running ahead of their Mexican nannies and tottered over to the pond's edge just to catch a glimpse of something that they instinctively knew was just as defenseless as they were.

"Follow blood."

"Didn't you say you worked for a newspaper in London?"

"I do, I did." As Halla suckled at my breast, it was hard thinking about my life back then, less than nine months ago.

"So you wrote stories, right?" Anika stuck her finger into her son's diaper to check for you know what. "You traveled the world, wrote stories, and probably had a hell of a good time. I would have loved to travel, to see the world like you did."

Laypeople never got it. Becoming a war correspondent wasn't like becoming a dental technician. You didn't just take a summer course and think, What the hell, sounds like a perfect way to travel the world on someone else's dime. I held two master's degrees in international affairs and journalism, I spoke French and Italian fluently, and was able to make myself understood in Spanish.

And I worked hard for it. After leaving the London School of Economics I did not return to the beach in Malibu and smoke pot with the others. Instead, I worked at the London bureau of the *New York Times* and covered the embassy bombing in Nairobi. Then the London *Sunday Times* had me as a stringer in Chechnya, Afghanistan, Somalia, and Rwanda, before making me the West African bureau chief.

But it didn't stop there. I did relief work for the International Rescue Committee and the Women's Commission for refugees in my spare time. It wasn't that I was a bleeding heart who absorbed pain like a sponge, it was that once you came to a country that was already unlivable for humankind and then added civil war, all there was *was* tragedy. Instead of playing tennis, you worked for the Red Cross; rather than getting a drink or taking a drive, you pitched in at the refugee camps. My résumé made me sound like a Mother Teresa wannabe, but really I was just doing what anyone else would have done if they walked down the street and saw a car crash. These places *were* car crashes.

But these were dark places full of dark emotions that were so far from this pretty little park and this all-American picnic. I don't think Anika could even fathom the darkness that existed in the world, and even more significantly, I was sure she didn't want to. "I did, yes. For the last few years I worked for the *Sunday Times* cover-ing"—I paused, as I always did, before saying the word—"Africa."

Her eyes looked dreamy. "Africa. You must tell me all about it."

I felt like telling her that it was not her Africa, the Africa of elegant safaris with tour leaders who looked like Fabio with rough South African accents; that my Africa was of a beauty you had to wipe the blood off to see. But I didn't want to tell her about my past, I wanted to be in her present, to slip into it like a new coat. "So tell me, is that Hellmann's or Miracle Whip?"

She beamed.

Chapter Six

INTELLIGENCE IS A RELATIVE THING. EVERYONE HAS THEIR own brand of it. While I had always been told I was intelligent, and even more frightening, intellectual, since I had returned to Los Angeles, I felt stupid all the time. I realized that I was lacking in the type of intelligence I needed in order to be happy in a modern society. More specifically, I didn't have the smarts to fill the role of wife and mother, with all the sucking up that it entailed. It was like being politically correct 24/7:

"I believe in you to make the best decision for us." She bats her tired eyes.

"No, that's fine if you want to drive." She bites her lip.

"Oh, you think Tommy should be circumcised?" She holds her breath.

"You're right, I'm sure the name Doris will be back in favor when she's in high school." She quickly thinks of a nickname.

"Sex, sure. I think the stitches should be healed." She winces.

The wife, the nurturer, the liar. But, oh, look at the payback: the house, the car, the life, the Miracle Whip. Marrying a successful man was a sign of adaptive intelligence in modern society. Studying like a dog and getting your ass nearly shot off in Africa for less than the cost of a Ford Focus was not. Nor was falling in love with a penniless doctor with a stump for a penis.

It was all Heaven's fault. She had instilled in me the belief that I must be the master of my own ship, just as she had been after she had caught her husband cheating. Her husband—of whom there were no photos available—had owned the other half of Orange County, the half that the Irvines didn't want. He bought land in Laguna Beach and financed hotels like the Surf and Sand and the Capri. He drank with Cagney and Bogart at the Balboa Bay Club and he cheated on his wife like it was a full-time job. Then in the prime of his life, right after the birth of Francis, he developed tuberculosis and Heaven took care of him.

"For three never-ending years"—she would wag a crooked index finger complete with grained nail in my face—"I cooked, cleaned, and looked after that man. Every time he needed something, he would ring that damn glass bell and expect me to drop everything and come to his bedside begging to help him. And what did he give me?"

"I don't know, what?" I would ask every time, usually during our afternoon card game when the sun was setting in the ocean and the chickens were clamoring to get into their coop.

"Nothing." She would put down her cards and stick that same long nail into her Scotch and shuffle the ice cubes around. "Nothing but bankruptcy and disillusion. Men, dear, are snakes," she would tell me time and time again.

"But you know what I did when I found out about the money and the women?" She would suck the Scotch off her fingertip and point it back at me. "I didn't yell or become hysterical, no, not me. I got even."

Heaven was one of the first women in the state of California to successfully take her husband to court and ask not for spousal support but for the defunct company itself. "I stood there and stared right in that judge's face—"

"He liked you, didn't he? He thought you were cute." I would always cut in because I knew that she loved it. She loved any kind of discreet sexual innuendo.

"Of course not, dear," she would protest, "don't be silly. He knew that Paul was completely incompetent when it came to business and gave me a chance to correct the problem."

And she did. Within five years this petite, dark-haired, and not altogether attractive woman, who had never worked a day in her life outside the home, took her husband's bankrupt real estate company and brought it back to life. Banks lent money to her, unable to deny her moxie, and her husband's friends did the unthinkable—they befriended her and dropped him. "I became one of them, dear. I drank with them, I played golf with them, and I even flew a private plane to Acapulco with them just to get my business off the ground. They treated me as though I was one of them."

"Gin," I would call out and she would sneer.

Her lower lip, now nearly indistinct from the rest of her tanned, shiny face, would stick out in a mock pout. "You're cheating your old feeble mother as she takes a lonely trip down memory lane, you no-good little rotten kid."

"So you never slept with any of them?" I'd nudge her. "Oh, come on, Heaven."

Her mouth would open in a large oval and her milky brown eyes would widen. Her hair was white, pure whipped white, and was always pulled back in a tortoiseshell clip. "Never, dear, never. That would have changed everything. I would have lost their respect, I would have lost everything. Remember," she'd always say at this point, "you must be the master of your own ship. Plot your course, bring those on board you need to make it happen, but drive the damn boat yourself."

"But what about all those people who get married, have children, bake cookies, and plot carpools?" I reorganized my hand so that she knew *I* knew she was peeking.

"Those women are never captains, dear, they're not in control. Their husbands are. When he's tired of them, he can kick them off his ship. Gin." She fanned her cards in front of me like a peacock displaying his colors. "It might sound nice, carpools and baking, but believe me, it's not, not when it's his car and his sugar. I've been there."

She was right. In my thirty-eight years I had seen nothing to prove her wrong, but this knowledge, this keen observation into the dynamic between a man and a woman in a marriage in a mall-and-minivan—encrusted universe, did not help me. In fact, it had made it worse for me and probably made it a lot worse for Heaven as well. All one had to do was look at her son. While he preached togetherness and forgiveness, fury and rage flowed through his veins. He was a boy castrated by his mother's hatred of his father and rendered useless by her successful entrance into the world of men. And he hated her. He hated her until the day she died and then he hated me.

"I can't get no *satisfaction,* I can't get no *satisfaction . . .*" I pointed my finger at every tinted window lined up next to me at the stoplight and screamed the words to one of the all-time morale-boosting songs written and sung by a fellow London School of Economics graduate.

I was on fire, driving back from the park. Play dates were awesome, a grown-up version of the pep rally. Anika had listened as though everything I said was in subtitles and every word provided a clue to the entire picture. I told her about the beach house and she concurred—it was my damn property.

"Why are you even hesitating?" Anika cocked her head to the side. "It's legally binding, right?"

"The will?" I nodded, wondering if she even had a moment's hesitation when she'd moved into her new husband's home.

"Does he have the right to live there?" she continued doggedly.

"He has the right to his home," I said, thinking about the complicated terms and conditions of the will as well as the muddy property lines along the cove itself. Altogether the property was about five acres, including the beachfront property, the cliff, and the promontory overhead. There were no fences, no boundaries, just sand disappearing into water. "Which now seems to include the entire property."

"I don't know you that well," Anika continued, "but you're crazy—we're in California, I can say that, it's a compliment almost. You're talking about a property that's worth somewhere in the range of ten to fifteen million. It's your inheritance, so claim it or he'll do it for you."

"It's not the money," I said. "It's never been about the money. It's about building a life, my life, and there doesn't seem to be any room there for me to do that." Heaven was gone and Francis was everywhere. From the fridge crammed with food that only a born-again vegan would buy, organic this and that, tofu cheese brimming with penicillin-producing mold, to the mailbox crammed with bills addressed unanimously to Francis. Francis now called the shots. Finally his own fiefdom, his nirvana.

"But you have Halla now." Anika jockeyed for eye contact. "You have to make a home for you both." Her voice rose. "You have to lay down the rules with Francis, Saffron, you have to get him to respect you, and the rest will follow."

I had never thought in these terms before. While I was traipsing around the world, I never thought about where the next meal was coming from. It was all about the story. Heaven and home were a universe away awaiting my return if and when I was ever ready.

"It wasn't supposed to turn out this way." I took off my bandana and rubbed my fingers through my hair. "I never wanted to come back alone and settle down here. I never imagined leaving Africa. I never imagined leaving Oscar."

"Oscar?" Anika touched my hand. "Was that Halla's father?"

"Yeah."

"He was the love of your life, wasn't he?"

The tone of her voice told me that she was opening up like a flower. She wanted to hear the story of true love, the kind that can only live in death, the kind that she probably never felt for her husband because what she had been taught to search for was true comfort.

"He was, yes." I wiped my nose and surveyed again the perfect picnic she had prepared. Her life was so orderly, it hurt. Why wasn't I eligible for some of that? Hadn't I given most of my life to good causes and been faithful to myself and honest with others? "Until he put the final nail in the coffin that buried once and for all my hope that men could be trusted."

Anika was visibly taken aback by the venom that shot through my eyes and out of my mouth. "So he's alive?"

"Not to me, he's not."

"Does he know about Halla?"

I maintained eye contact with the dirt. "No."

She bent her head lower. "Do you still love him?"

The trouble with Oscar was that I could envision him wherever I moved. In Africa, he was my point of reference. In London, I could see us taking in foreign films, discussing Rohmer and Fellini over chilled wine and endive salads. No matter where I was, he fit into my life as though the void had been left by him and him alone.

"You do, don't you?" she pressed.

"It's complicated, Anika." I glanced over at Halla. I could already see traces of his biology on her face, like street signs leading her back to him. I had chosen to ignore my own road map and never looked for my own father. "I don't want her first male role model to be someone who's never home, who's more passionate about his work than his family, and who thinks more about his—" I stopped.

"What you want is to build a home for her here." Anika was back on the beach-house theme. "So you set the ground rules for that Hare Krishna and make your mother proud."

"You don't think I'm awful for not telling him that he has a daughter?" Suddenly Anika was my Dear Abby, she was the Moral Majority, the cover girl of *Good Housekeeping,* and I needed reassurance from her. I needed to know that I could still park my Snap N Go next to hers.

"As far as I'm concerned, he lost that right when he did whatever it was that he did to you." She smiled. "And judging from your tone of voice, it wasn't good. So he deserves it."

Now it was my turn to beam.

God, I loved play dates. It had been the single most empowering thing I had done for myself since insisting on the epidural upon admission into London's bleak Cromwell Hospital and getting it. "I can't get no *satisfaction!*" As I turned left off of PCH, I drummed on the steering wheel of the bright red Jeep I had bought for next to nothing less than a week before. Motor vehicles—nothing could induce the high of independence quite like owning your own car.

Recharged and reinvigorated—I even think I lost a few pounds during my four-hour chat with Anika—I now had a plan. First thing in the morning I would walk down to his house, knock on his door, and have a word with Francis. He'd probably tell me that it would have to wait until after his high-colonic evacuation, herbal tea, and meditation, but I would not be deterred. I would come back later that afternoon, that evening if I had to, and with full resolve. As I pulled into Heaven's—no, my—driveway, I was confronted by a man in uniform, standing in front of a collection of sagging boxes with my angry handwriting scribbled across them.

As Halla slept, I directed the movers—two boys who together weighed less than me—where to place my belongings in this house that I feared would never be mine. "The bed in the back bedroom, please; the sofa right here in the living room in front of the windows and the coffee table, well"—I glanced at the paltry display of my worldly belongings—"you can put that in front of the sofa, I guess."

"Ma'am, we've pretty much got it." One of them picked up the coffee table and carried it over his head like a matchbox. "Not exactly what we'd call a big job."

"Table and chairs in the kitchen," I continued as though directing the staff in *The Remains of the Day.* "Desk against the wall at the back facing the French windows. Computer and files on the desk."

After they left, I stood outside in the driveway and surveyed my house. All the things that were once so important to me a continent away were shuffled into all that Heaven held close to her heart. The bedside tables she'd had forever, the wallpaper she'd struggled with and finally hung herself, and, of course, the bed she'd slept in since 1930. And there were my things, the things that had once made my four walls in London feel like home, the things I always took with me and opened immediately whenever I moved. The Harrods bed linens I had carted all the way to Freetown were so thin, they looked like surgical gauze, and the faded duvet cover, once the color of aquamarine, had a cigarette burn on the top left corner. Oscar. The combination of the two worlds felt like a loss deep in my gut. It was like someone got chocolate in my peanut butter, and it tasted like shit.

I sat outside under the magnolia tree with Halla facing the open door. I wasn't sure there was room for us in there.

The phone rang. The phone never rang. I took Halla inside to answer it.

"So did you call him?" It was Anika.

"Who?" I glanced at a photograph lying on its side, a black-and-white of Oscar and me sitting by a campfire in the north of Sierra Leone. It was taken on one of our trips to the refugee camps along the border with Guinea. I stood next to him, hovering over him, while he treated some poor forgotten boy. The boy could have been airbrushed out altogether and it wouldn't have changed the dynamics in the photo one bit. At that point in our relationship, I could see only Oscar.

" 'Who'? What do you mean 'who'? Your tenant is 'who.' "

"I just got home. Anika, give me some time."

"You have to take action, Saff. If you don't, who will?" Her voice rose and fell in waves. "Think about Halla and getting that creep Oscar back."

I grabbed two rolls across my abdomen, pinched hard, and wondered whether I would ever have my old stomach back. "What does Oscar have to do with it?"

"The better you're doing, the more they suffer. And a beach house on the sand in Malibu is about as good as it can get."

"Do you ever give up?" It was as though she was speaking a foreign language to me, but precisely the type of intelligence I needed.

"No." She paused and then spoke to someone in the background. "Wait, hold on, no, it goes over here." "No!" I heard a chastising snap before she came back to me. "Sorry, Joyce is driving me nuts."

"That's alright," I said cautiously. "I've got about a dozen boxes to go through, stuff from London that came in this afternoon." I noticed another frame poking out from one of them and felt my stomach tighten. "More memories than I have room for."

"You're thinking about Oscar, aren't you?" She blew into the phone. "You're moping around, looking at pictures of the two of you smiling into each other's eyes and wondering what went wrong."

I picked up the frame. It was a picture of the two of us outside Connaught Hospital in Freetown. "Something like that."

"Well, I suggest that you think about the look on his face when you caught him with his ass moving up and down into something else in your bed. That's the vision you need to have every time you see a photograph of his pearly whites and healing hands."

I winced. "It wasn't exactly like that."

"You did catch him, right?" Her voice was becoming less enthusiastic. "I mean, that's how you knew that he was cheating, right?"

"I didn't exactly catch him, no. It was worse, if you can believe it." I let my slight, albeit acquired, English accent tighten the words, employing it like snob repellent.

"So if you didn't catch him with his pants down, what happened?"

I was beginning to feel judgment and I feared it. "Can we do this another time, please? I've got a million things to do."

"How about I come down and help?" she offered.

"It's too far, but thanks—"

"Anyway," she continued, as though I had said nothing, "it's almost five. Warren should be coming through the door any second now and he likes to have me home and his dinner ready. You know how it is."

"Uh, no, not really."

"I'm totally insensitive. I'm sorry." Anika took a deep breath. "Put it here, right here." Her voice was becoming faster and faster by the minute and I wondered what was going on in her household. Were there people coming in and out watering her garden, cleaning the pool? Would Jeremiah go to Harvard and make them proud while Halla dropped out of high school after becoming the school slut?

I felt an anxiety attack coming on as my phone beeped. "I have another call coming in—"

"I'll let you go then," she chirped. "I'll see you at the Pump Station on Thursday for sure but let's try and hook up before that."

"Sure, fine." I clicked over. It was my first attempt at call waiting. "Hello?"

CHAPTER SEVEN

"SAFFRON?" THE VOICE WAS LIKE HONEY, SWEET AND STICKY. "Did I get your number right?"

"Who's this?" I had given my phone number out to three people since moving in, and while I wanted friends, whoever this was was seriously ruining my attempt at introspection, analysis, and a good cry.

"It's Sophia. I hope I'm not bothering you." She sounded like a teenager. "But I thought we could meet up."

"Another play date?"

"I didn't know about the first one." Suspicion crept into her voice. "Did you all get together and play without me?"

Damn. I squeezed my eyes shut. Rule number one about play dates: don't exclude other members of the group, but if it should happen, whatever you do, *do not* bring it up. *Do not* mention funny anecdotes of what the children produced, as in poopy diapers, or how much they consumed, as in milk. *Never ever* refer to time spent when not spent as a group; otherwise risk discord, as postnatal lactating women are as close to raw as a human can ever get and are thus frighteningly unpredictable and possibly violent.

"No, no, Anika was just showing me where to take Halla if and when I want to go to the park."

"Oh, that's nice"—she paused slightly—"seeing as how you're new to Los Angeles."

I could hear the return of innocence. "I'm not so much new to L.A. as I am to this whole baby thing. You should have seen me." I laughed at the memory. "It was truly ridiculous, but we survived."

"I think it's great that you even made it out the door."

I had a momentary flashback of the hole I called home in Chechnya, the dank sorrowful cave I shared with a few hundred handkerchief-wearing grandmothers, and I laughed again—this woman had no idea how tough it could be to get out the door. "Is Rain with you now?"

"Yeah, we just came out for a bite. The house is so quiet without Max"—I could actually hear the pout on her face—"sometimes I can't stand it."

"You miss him a lot, don't you?" Max was the husband from France, some sort of fashion photographer, which was how they met.

"He's my life"—she paused—"and Rain."

Yikes. "How about tomorrow then?"

"Brunch at Barney Greengrass restaurant at the top at eleven?"

"Barney's with two babies?" My mouth dropped. "Are you sure?"

"Yeah, they're great," she said. "They used to let me bring my dog and never said a word, not even when he barked."

But you could put the Chihuahua back in the cage. "And then what?"

"We'll walk around, silly."

"Oh, okay then," I said, my head exploding with visions of screaming children, leaking breasts, and seeping diapers, not to mention baby carriers, strollers, car seats, changes of clothes.

"I can't wait!" she chirped, and for a fleeting moment I wanted to punch the front door until I could no longer feel my hand.

I had never been much into ownership. I dreaded furniture, preferring to own nothing more than what could fit in a big duffel bag. My flat in London was a testament to Heaven's love and affection for me, but it did not feel like home. There was just too much stuff like kitchen mittens, valences, and other items I didn't want to know how to use. They felt like the trappings of home, but they weren't home—home was always waiting for me abroad, anywhere there was a story unfolding. Hotel rooms made me smile.

Then came Oscar, and my concept of "home" shifted from a place to a person. Suddenly "home" was wherever he was, whatever he was doing, and that was the beginning of my demise. Now there were pictures in my house of this man, the man who called me his fat beauty, who made me question my ability as a reporter, who made me want to be married for the first time in my life. He was everywhere. In the boxes of clothes that I had not seen since Africa, in the books that he would criticize me for finding truth in, and the cups and mugs we drank coffee out of. Everywhere.

But this was before everything went to hell, before Sierra Leone fell apart, before I discovered Oscar was without honor.

That night after placing all the photos back in a box marked "THE PAST" and storing it out of eyesight, I tossed all of the linens and most of the clothes into trash bags and nearly lost both legs while heaving them out onto the highway for trash pickup. In between feeding, changing, and rocking Halla, I covered my well-traveled sofa with a taupe cotton throw that I had nicked off a British Airways flight. Inspired, I pulled out a red-and-white-checked tablecloth and threw it over the small dining table that had served me so well during my exams. I put my laptop on the desk next to Heaven's velvet chaise longue in the spare bedroom and turned off the light.

I went back in and turned it on. I had forgotten about the small rectangular box that had arrived with the forwarded mail from London, and suddenly my fingers were burning. I wanted to open the box, light a cigarette, pour a glass of wine, and check my correspondence. It was that familiar feeling of my first night home after a particularly long and intense assignment.

"Waaaa! Wa, wa, wa, WAAA!" Halla screamed with a start, as though she had been sitting in a bath of hot salsa.

"I'll be right there," I called, but of course that only made her cry more. "Shit," I said, and stubbed out the imaginary cigarette and pulled out the boob.

I was better prepared at ambushing a pocket of Chechen rebels than I was at having brunch at Barney's with a baby in tow. Parking? Valet was five dollars, the weekly salary of some of the people back in Freetown. The valet was shooting me so many damn hand signals, I felt like a fighter pilot on an aircraft carrier. Self-parking was so far down into the bowels of the building that I would have to stop and nurse before making it up to the restaurant.

In order to successfully complete my mission, I brought the following: the Snap N Go; my Bjorn pack, if we decided to walk and I couldn't face navigating the stroller through doors; and the baby bag, a bright red Kate Spade number filled with ten diapers, an entire box of wipes, two outfit changes, nursing pads for leaks, diaper cream, and powder. The bag weighed more than the baby.

The elevator dropped me directly in the restaurant. A manager walked toward me as I crashed my stroller into the frame of the elevator over and over again.

"Can I help you?"

I was waiting for him to tell me that there were no babies and most definitely no nursing allowed.

"I'm stuck," I said, feeling the heat of eyes on me.

"Here," the manager said as he picked up the stroller and tried to pry it from the spot. "You have to let go first."

"I'm sorry." I let go and it suddenly sprang free. "I can't believe you could get that out so quickly. It must happen all the time."

"No"—he paused—"not at all."

I wondered why he didn't just lie and say that yes, it happened all the time. I thought the whole point of eating in Beverly Hills was to have your ass kissed.

I glanced around the rooftop restaurant at the flurry of activity—everyone who worked there was in motion, constant, frenetic. They swished past me and then swished past me again without ever asking me what I needed. They dodged the stroller as though it were a land mine and might go off at the slightest touch. I scanned the tables—most of which were empty at ten-fifty—looking for Sophia and wondering where we were going to sit so as to offend the least number of people.

"May I help you?"

I looked up into the face of someone who had served one too many breakfast specials, her eyes about as glassy and expressionless as a pair of sunny-side-up eggs. "I'm looking for a friend, but I can't see her."

"Does she have a name, a reservation?"

"Sophia, Sophia Gilot, I think, and I don't know whether—"

"Ah, Sophia. Of course, yes, she's right outside, around the corner waiting for you. Come."

Judging from the way the waitress's attitude changed, Sophia must have been here more than once.

"Come this way, through the double doors, it'll be much easier for you and the stroller." She held the doors wide open and I drove straight through. Sophia was sitting at a large table for four, where there was ample parking for the strollers as well as a view of the city.

"Good morning, Saffron, it's so great to see you." Sophia stood up from the table to give me a hug and suddenly the terrace was quiet. She wore a white gauze peasant skirt with one of those little Mexican blouses in a brick red. The blouse hung open in the front with two laces on either side, blowing in the breeze, begging to be undone. Her hair was loose to her waist; there was no makeup to speak of except for a liberal slathering of baby pink lip gloss.

"You look so beautiful." She smiled. "I can't believe you clean up so well."

"Thanks, I think." I had dressed in a pair of black yoga stretch pants and a long white Indian tunic that I had bought at the Hare Krishna center for ten bucks the week before. I wore flip-flops and my hair was down. My breasts were bigger than ever and my olive skin had a pink translucence to it from the nursing and all the fat I was consuming. Lip gloss and some black mascara that I'd discovered at the bottom of one of my camera bags were all I could manage. It was the most trouble I'd gone to since Halla's birth.

"Is she sleeping?" Sophia leaned over Halla and smiled. "Oh, good, that means we can talk."

"How long has Rain been asleep?" I peeked over at her pink bundle, flat on her back with her small hands placed carefully across her stomach as though she were a still life. "She's lovely," I said and meant it. Seeing a truly handsome baby was about as rare as seeing a really good-looking adult—most of them were pretty darn ugly, which meant you had to lie a lot.

"Well, so is Halla," Sophia replied as though on command, and I let myself think it was true. "I love that little outfit she has on. Baby Gap?"

I nodded. "Third one today. They've unlocked the genetic code—wouldn't you think they could come up with diapers that didn't leak?"

"You're so funny." She flipped her hair over her shoulder. "Are you always like this?"

"I don't know." I tensed. "What exactly do you mean?"

She nibbled the sesame seeds off a particularly phallic-looking breadstick and even the pigeons seemed to swoon. "I don't know, you're just different, you seem so cool. I guess it's because you're European."

"I don't think of myself as European, really."

"Where were your parents from?"

"My mother was from Holland and my father was Corsican."

"Corsican?" Her blue eyes bulged. "Where's that?"

"Corsica?" I waited. "It's an island between France and Italy." Still no clicking. "Where Napoleon was from."

"Wow! That's so exotic. Did you live there?"

"Until I was six. Then I came here to California with my mother."

Sophia lifted her light blue Gucci glasses from her face. "Divorce, huh? Mine, too."

I didn't want to tell her that my parents were never married, that my mother took off in the middle of the afternoon without so much as a hint that she wasn't coming back. Ever.

"Can I get you ladies some coffee—a capp, latte, blended?" The waitress looked at the sleeping babies and sighed as though briefly taken by the memory of her own now grown children. "Decaf, right?"

I scanned the menu. "Do you think they'd call Child Services on me if I had a fully caffeinated cup of black coffee?"

Sophia covered her mouth and giggled. "See, that's what I mean, you're funny."

"Not really, I'm just caffeine deprived and slightly angry in general."

"Don't be angry." Her teeth sparkled and her eyes squealed with blind delight. "Halla is sleeping and it's a beautiful day up here on the top of the world."

"Have you spent a lot of time over there?" She looked as though she'd lost the plot. I went on to clarify. "Europe, I mean."

"I lived in Paris for a few years with Max when we worked together and I absolutely loved it. We lived on the Left Bank right near the Eiffel Tour on a houseboat on the Seine Max had rented. We took moonlit walks along the river, drank cheap wine, and watched life unfold under the bridges."

I had yet to meet a woman who hadn't fallen in love with the city. "Why did you leave?"

"It was the midnineties and the economy was falling apart over there—bus and railway strikes, shops that didn't open because there was no one to run them—it was awful. Max was having a hard time finding work, so he came here."

"But why did *you* come back if you loved it so much over there?" She looked startled. "Max, of course."

The waitress swooped down on us armed with two pots of decaf. "Have you had a chance to look at your menus?"

"What are you going to have?" I asked Sophia. I had already scanned the menu and found nothing that appealed to me. I wanted eggs, bacon, and home-style potatoes but was afraid to inquire.

"The goat cheese salad with frisée is great here," Sophia said with the seriousness of an English professor. "It's what I always have."

After living in Africa, the moment I heard the word *goat* followed by the word *cheese* I felt urpy. Every day I was surrounded by goats, nibbling away at discarded wrappers, rotten lettuce, rotten meats, and soft leather. They were four-legged pigeons, and when we ate anything that came from them, we became the pigeons of the pigeons.

"I'll have the omelet, thanks."

"With or without the yolks?"

"Ah, with." I couldn't help but look at the waitress as though she were crazy.

"Good for you!" Sophia exclaimed. "The yolks are great for your skin even though they may be a tiny bit fatty."

"Two coffees, decaf?" She poured.

"Great." I wanted caffeine. I wanted caffeine.

"What made you come back, Saffron?" Sophia crossed her legs and then uncrossed them again. "By the way, I love that name. So exotic."

At this point I realized Sophia wasn't so much naïve or pure; rather, she seemed like someone from small-town America who had gotten a free ride because of the way she looked.

"Oscar," I said, chastising myself for thinking that way. "It was because of Oscar."

"I know it's a difficult subject for you," Sophia said as she put up her hands, "and if you don't want to talk about him, I'll understand."

"More decaf?" I glanced over my shoulder and was relieved to see that our lunch had arrived. Halla had already been asleep for forty-five minutes and I wanted to eat before I had to go through the entire ritual of whipping the boob out, using the burp cloth, and then changing her diaper, possibly her outfit.

"Please," I said. "And if you have caffeinated, that would be fine, too."

"Are you saying that you'd *prefer* caffeinated?" The waitress looked over at Halla. "Because if you're nursing, it might keep her up."

I wanted to slap the carafe out of her hands and give her a quick elbow to the chin. "Decaf is fine, and by the way, I wasn't saying that I *preferred* caffeinated, just that if that was all you had with you, it wouldn't hurt to mix the two together."

Her lips were pursed together like a marine. "I have decaffeinated, ma'am." She filled my cup and marched off.

"That was sweet of her," Sophia said as she nibbled at her curly lettuce. "People are so caring here."

Sophia handed me a bagel and the pot of creamed butter. "Just tell me how you met, please. Just that."

"How we met?"

"Is it as romantic as I think it is?" She leaned forward. "I bet it has all the makings of a movie, an epic."

"What do you mean?" I wondered whether Anika had told her, whether she was the secret-keeping or the secret-leaking type. I had met so few of the former.

"Oh, come on. Journalist, no"—her eyes flashed—"war correspondent meets Red Cross surgeon devoted to treating ghetto kids in Africa."

You had to laugh at the picture of Sophia sitting on the rooftop terrace of Barney's in Beverly Hills curling her frisée lettuce drenched in crumbled goat cheese around her fork like it was a delicacy and talking about "ghetto" kids in Freetown.

"We met at a bar. I saw him across the room and—"

Her mouth opened wide, exposing a set of perfectly white teeth. "Oh, my God, it was love at first sight, wasn't it? You can honestly tell your daughter that you fell in love with her father from across a crowded room."

"Yes, I did." I sat back in my chair and thought about what the sight of him would do to me at that moment. Probably thrill me just as it had then. "But I fell out of love with him shortly afterwards."

Her mouth opened again, exposing a flawless set of pearl nuggets. "You mean the next day?"

I had to stop myself from counting them. "No, I mean the next hour."

CHAPTER EIGHT

THE FIRST TIME I LAID EYES ON OSCAR WAS IN JANUARY 1999 at a Reuters party at a bar in Freetown called Sonny Markes. It was *the* place to go in town for an after-work drink, and for anyone in the media, it was the same thing as going to the office—it was the place you got your tips, conducted interviews, shot the shit, and soaked your soul after a particularly tragic day, which was pretty much every day in Freetown, where the Revolutionary United Front (RUF) rebels went around amputating anyone who tried to vote for anyone but them.

Sophia interrupted. "Was there an actual war going on while you were sitting there?"

How could I explain to this woman, whose idea of a massacre was a badly gouged ingrown hair, that war was a state of mind over there, that war had been raging twenty-four hours a day for ten years, while people worked, married, and gave birth?

"Yes."

"Sorry." She demurred. "Go on."

That night I had been drinking with my camera guy from the *London Times* and checking out the scene from the bar. The place was packed with Westerners, men and women of all nationalities, everyone lean, tan, and intelligent. And then I saw him and knew—knew what, I didn't know, but I just knew. It was that angular jaw, those chiseled cheekbones that formed question marks under his slate blue eyes, and his soft, soft skin, which I could see from where I was sitting.

I leaned over to my friends and asked, "Am I totally pissed or are the guys better-looking here than they were in London?"

"Take a look at the birds." Rodger whistled and gulped his ice-cold pint. "Nothing like 'em in West Hampstead, different breed altogether."

"Yeah, point taken, but the men. Take a look at that one." I pushed Rodger forward so that I could get a better look. "He has to be as thick as a plank or a complete asshole to be that good-looking. God simply could not be that cruel to the rest of you."

"Well, fuck you then"—Rodger played hurt—"why don't you have a drink with him then, and I'll run along to the pound with all m' other ugly mates."

"Ah, come on, stop acting like a girl," I called after him. "Look, Johnny." I pointed to Rodger, who was walking across the floor with his head down, shoulders slumped. "Rodger's acting like a girl again."

"You've gone off and hurt his feelings again, 'ave you, Saff?" teased Paul, an AP cameraman.

When I came back to take a sip of the truly awful Scotch and tonic in front of me, Oscar had slipped into Rodger's seat.

Suddenly I was sober.

"Was he wearing scrubs?" Sophia interjected. "I love scrubs, especially when they're really worn in. God, I almost fell in love with my OB because of them."

Oscar would never be as obvious as that. He wore a seriously weathered brown leather jacket, its top layer flaking off like molting snakeskin, black jeans, and black cowboy boots. His hair was dark but streaked with gray. His face was lean and dewy.

"What's with the cowboy boots?" I asked.

"I like America," he answered.

"Where are you from?" I stared straight ahead.

"Germany," he said.

"Are you a reporter?"

"More of a butcher, really." There was the hint of a smile at the corner of his lips.

"Whatever." I was not in the mood for the bullshit. It had been three weeks since I'd landed at Lungi International Airport and I had seen enough blood and meat to make any reference to butchers offensive.

"Kidding, alright, levity." He turned to look at me. "I'm a surgeon with the International Red Cross or some other international nongovernmental Doctors Without Borders, smiley-face bullshit organization."

What struck me more than the harshness of his words was the softness of his voice. His accent was German—blunt and crisp as though there was nothing but black and white in his world—but with a soft, almost Roman, lilt to it.

"If you don't believe in what you're doing, why are you here?"

"You bloody Americans are all the same," he laughed. "You're so predictable. So naïve. It's a wonder you're not getting your asses shot off everywhere you decide to take up the cause."

"So that's why you're here?" I asked. "To fix all the shot-off asses of naïve Americans?"

He never took his eyes off the room. "That's far too big a job for a lowly mechanic like me."

Condescending asshole. I had been watching him watch others from the moment he sat down. It was Sunday night, which meant that there were new arrivals from CNN, FOX, and RAI, Italian television, here to cover a week of news. You could spot the greenies right away; they huddled together protectively, as if their safety depended on it.

"See anything you like?"

"I do," he said without moving, "I do."

"Don't let me stop you." I waved at the bartender for the check. We had been sitting side by side for over an hour; it was after midnight.

Oscar took me by the hand. "Shall we then?" He stood and led me out of Sonny Markes and into the Connaught Hotel, which happened to be the closest Western hotel on Rowdon Street.

"But how did he know you'd go?" Sophia asked.

"I don't know." I pushed away my plate and out of the corner of my eye I saw Halla flinch, then twitch. "Damn, she's waking up."

Sophia looked panicked. "Quick. Start pushing the stroller back and forth."

Halla's eyes fluttered like a bird, and as I rocked, I watched her body harden, then go limp.

"So how did he know?"

"I guess I look easy." I shrugged. "I don't know."

"Okay, whatever." She waved her hand dismissively. "Keep going."

It didn't go as planned. Despite our strong attraction and our verbal sparring, Oscar and I were absolutely awful together in bed in nearly every way. When he kissed me, his tongue felt limp and lifeless like a sponge bloated with water. His touch felt awkward, as though he wasn't really touching me but was just doing what he needed to in order to get me lubricated.

But the pièce de résistance was when he slipped off his jeans and I looked for his penis. Sure, I was buzzed, but I could not find it by sight or by touch. Here was this extraordinary Olympian body lying next to me, over six feet tall, so chiseled throughout the abdomen it looked like he had metal under his skin, strong in the legs, massive across the back, and yet the man didn't have a penis to speak of.

"You've got to be kidding me!" Sophia blanched. "Are you sure he just wasn't turned on enough?"

Not one to give up, I went down to look for it. I was, after all, an investigative journalist.

"Ah, yes," he murmured as though in the throes of passion, but there was something about his tone that suggested he would be fully able to perform a complicated surgery while I went down on him, kissing his near-perfect abdomen. I kept going down until I reached it—a furry patch of perfectly Aryan pubic hair, blond and wavy, but not at all curly. I tiptoed my fingers through the hair until I reached the center and found a penis that was worthy of a collect call to Ripley's Believe It or Not.

"Oh, my God." Sophia twisted in her chair.

It was the length of my pinky, and I wasn't sure if he was not excited at all or if this was the best he could do. Either way, it was not good.

"Yuck." She cringed.

I took the little guy in my palm and tried to move it up and down, but it disappeared in the girth of my hand. So I used my thumb and index finger to hold it while I took a closer look.

This man's Achilles' heel *was* his penis. It was God's trick on this man, an otherwise clothed Adonis, and not to mention a pretty awful one on me.

"Come here, beauty," Oscar whispered, and I shimmied my way back up again. I wondered if he knew I was gawking at him, though he certainly didn't seem embarrassed about it. He made no attempt to apologize for it, explain it away, or divert my attention from it. In fact, he was confident, as though he was sporting a flagpole between his legs.

He got on top of me and kind of folded it in and began to move erratically, as though jerking through spasms, while licking my face and rolling his eyes. I looked away, wondering if I had forgotten the art of lovemaking or if he was just about the worst lover I had ever had.

"Ooh, baby, my beauty," he said over and over as his perfectly sculpted ass bobbed up and down. I couldn't imagine he could feel anything at all, because I couldn't. "I'm coming, I'm . . . aah."

For once in my life I was glad that a man announced it, otherwise I would have had to guess. He stopped moving and wiped the sweat off his brow. Then he licked his wet hand.

"How weird," Sophia said.

"Slightly." I nodded and resumed the story.

"Did you enjoy it?" He looked over at me and I wasn't sure how to answer.

"A little strange, but okay, I guess." I pulled the covers up over my breasts and lit a cigarette. "Is there a minibar in this place?"

"You drink a lot." Oscar laid his head against my stomach and licked my belly button.

His eyes were on me, scanning my arms, legs, and face with the cold precision and concentration only a doctor could muster. "You have eyes like a deer, baby blue deer eyes with flecks of viola. But you have the body of an Amazon."

"What's that supposed to mean?" Sophia interrupted. "What an asshole."

I knew exactly what he meant, but wanted to see him make his way through the minefield he had set for himself. Either he was an idiot or he didn't want to sleep with me ever again.

He walked to the bathroom and laid his tiny excuse for manhood in the sink. "If you lost ten to twenty pounds"—he spoke as he washed himself—"you would be magnificent."

"Ten to twenty pounds?" Sophia gasped. "I hope you told him what he could do with his sorry excuse for a penis then and there."

I was seething, lying there on painfully dry sheets while he dressed, but no matter how much I wanted to, I could not reciprocate his hurt. I could not point out his penis.

"I have to go." I took my cheap plastic Nike watch from the nightstand, put my arms and head through my gray knit-jersey dress, strapped on my Puma tennis shoes, and tossed my black backpack over one shoulder. There was one thing I absolutely had to do and that was to leave before he did.

"Don't leave me like a dirty, used-up lover," his voice rose, and I turned to see him there naked, his alarming good looks sadly illuminated by the peeling mirror and neon lights. "Come here and give me a kiss. Please."

I was certain it would be the last time I would see him. We had absolutely no chemistry in bed and he was way too cocky out of it. "Bye." I leaned into his cheek and was surprised when he took my face in both hands and kissed me with a delicate passion that had been missing until now.

"Please say we'll meet again," he said with tears in his eyes and I caved. I no longer saw the penis or the German god—I only heard the abandoned voice.

"We'll meet again." And just like that I fell in love with a man who, if asked at that precise moment, would probably not be able to repeat my name.

"You fell in love with him then and there?" Sophia's cheeks were infused with streaks of color. "After you saw that pathetic excuse for a penis and he had the nerve to tell you to lose weight?"

"It got better," I said.

"Did his dick grow?"

"No." I tapped my breadstick, wishing it was a Marlboro Red. "But his personality did."

She kept glancing over to Rain and then back at her watch. "Let's get the bill before the kids wake up."

The restaurant was now full; every seat in the house had been taken by self-obsessed victims of fashion checking their reflections in the glass doors. The sight of a baby breast-feeding right there in the middle of the patio would look like an accident on the otherwise free-flowing road.

Halla's mouth was opening and closing like a fish. The clock was ticking. "Where will we feed them?" I was starting to get antsy.

"Neiman's," Sophia announced quickly. "It has the best bathroom for babies on Wilshire."

"Why?" Shopping was new to me. Heaven and I would buy our clothes through catalogs, and when we felt like braving the world, we would hit the outlet stores.

"Bigger stalls with actual baby-changing stations built into the walls, clean surfaces, and a comfortable sofa to nurse." Sophia released the brake to her Snap N Go and half the tables turned to look. She was, without question, the kind of woman other women dreamed of being, while men dreamed of slapping a ring on her finger, impregnating her, and calling her theirs.

I followed her out the door as she expertly weaved the stroller in between tables and through the small crowd waiting directly in front of the elevator.

"Thank you," she said with her usual demure tone to the man who held the elevator doors open.

We walked through Barney's and then exited left to go to Neiman's. Neither Rain nor Halla were awake but they had been sleeping for over two hours, which meant that when they woke up, they would be starving. We made our way through the makeup section on Neiman's ground floor, where some of the employees looked like they made up their faces according to their tribal colors, representing their particular region—San Fernando Valley, Torrance, Culver City, or Los Angeles.

"Do you want to try going up the escalator?"

"The escalator?" I winced. I was just getting used to driving the thing on flat ground. "Can't it get stuck?"

"I don't think so." Sophia shook her head. "How would it get stuck?"

Visions of a stroller getting its wheels lodged on takeoff or landing filled my head, but I did not want to appear as concerned as I felt. I was, after all, a war correspondent. "I think we should take the elevator before they start screaming."

"Uh-oh, Halla's waking up." Sophia covered her mouth. "Her face is getting redder. Her eyelids are twitching—, is she still in REM or is she—"

"WAAAAAA—WA—WA—WA." Halla's mouth curled in an angry purple scowl while her eyes remained pursed shut. Blue blood flooded her face as she screamed.

"Wa—wa—wa—waaaa." Rain, also now up, chimed in her more civilized version.

Our two fellow passengers in the elevator moved closer to the door, as though standing up against the cold metal would somehow get them out sooner.

"Here we are," Sophia said, grateful it was a short trip. "It's through the shoe section in the back; follow me."

As we raced to get into the sanctuary for new moms, Halla had nearly everyone on the second floor looking to see what was wrong with her. Her shrieks sounded as though I had just finished some pagan ritual involving hot candle wax. Once inside the room, I picked up her rigid, angry form and lifted up my shirt. The moment she smelled the milk that had already sprung from my breasts, she stopped crying. Sophia and I sat down on the chaise longue, our children latching on in near-perfect unison.

"Does it still hurt?" she asked.

"Like hell," I said as my toes curled.

"By the way, I didn't mean to sound like such a witch back there." Sophia stared at me through the mirror in front of us. "I've had my fair share of bad relationships. I've had guys tell me I was too fat—"

"Oh, shut up," I protested. "You could never have been fat. The fat gene would never be allowed to coexist in that perfect gene pool you swim in."

"Oh, yeah. I've been told I was too blonde, too stupid, too tall, too short, too everything, and I put up with it for years until I met Max. He made me feel unique and taught me to value myself both inside and out."

"So it was the fat thing that got to you," I said, smiling, "not the penis thing."

"No, it was definitely the penis thing." Sophia switched Rain from one breast to the other and I caught a glimpse of her torso. Her body was without fault and I could tell she was as comfortable being naked as I was in my pajamas with a cigarette in one hand and a Scotch in the other. "I can understand falling in love with an asshole, but I could never understand falling in love with a guy who has a deflated balloon between his legs."

"I don't know." My mind filled with thoughts of our first dates, our first weekends together, and I remember being conflicted.

"You like sex, right?"

"I did, yes, until I met him."

"And then you hated it while you were with him?"

"I hated it at the beginning." I glanced down at Halla, who was asleep. I shook her gently and placed her on the other breast. "And then I couldn't wait to sleep with him. No matter where I was, at the office writing a story, out working in one of the refugee camps up north, if I thought about him at all, I felt more aroused than I had ever been before."

"Why?"

"Because I fell in love with *him*."

She stared. "Why?"

Less than two hours earlier, Sophia had thought my life with Oscar was the stuff of romance novels, but after hearing about his small penis, her eyes narrowed as though he was plagued with a disfiguring disease.

"Because he was untouchable."

"With a dick like that, I'll bet."

CHAPTER NINE

"WHY DO YOU THINK EVERY WOMAN—DUMB, SMART, RICH, poor—wants to marry a doctor?" Heaven asked me when I told her I had fallen in love with one.

"I'm sure you're going to tell me."

"Because they're untouchable," she said with textbook authority.

"What's that supposed to mean?" I kicked the fax machine while it ripped and tore at an outline I was trying to send to our London office. Since the truce had been signed between RUF and the Nigerian-led coalition known as ECOMOG a month earlier, in July 1999, the equipment had stopped coming. So had the journalists. Once the bloody battles had come to an end, no more limbs being chopped off, no more enemies left to disfigure, no more baby girls to rape, Sierra Leone was no longer front-page news.

But there was plenty of hell left after nearly ten years of civil war—7,000 dead, thousands maimed, and 150,000 homeless were enough to keep me and two other journalists from the *Sunday Times* there until something else broke.

Heaven's voice sounded like a cocktail of gravel and oil. "It means you can't second-guess them."

I imagined her sitting under the enclosed glass verandah of her beach house with her cards on the table and a drink at her side. I wondered where Francis was lurking.

"That didn't stop you, did it?"

"My point exactly, Saff. Francis's father wasn't a doctor or a lawyer—another good one to marry—and I second-guessed the hell out of him until he eventually went broke and I took over his company. Now, a doctor is like God, totally above the petty things in life, like jealousy or insecurity, that drive us mortals and they love it. They're in control."

"I don't need to second-guess him, Heav, I'm in love." I ripped the illegible page out of the ancient fax and threw it in the trash. "Which is where I plan on staying."

It had been two weeks since I had met Oscar at Sonny's and my heart still pounded when I said his name.

"Where did you meet him?" she probed.

"Why?" I asked. "He's a doctor, a surgeon no less, he's single, German, and he's a bleeding humanitarian." I took a long drag on my cigarette and put my feet up on my desk. "What more could any mother ask for?"

"A surgeon? Even worse. They treat people like cars and look at limbs like parts that either need fixing or replacement. Zero emotion in surgeons. Where'd you say you met him?"

"At a bar."

"I'm sorry, what'd you say?"

"A *bar*," I screamed down the line.

"And he picked *you* up, right?"

"That's how it's usually done, Heaven." I scrolled the screen on my laptop, researching a story I was writing on Francis Stevens, the last man to hold the job of president of Sierra Leone before all hell broke loose. According to everything that I had found, the man was a dictator extraordinaire, the old-fashioned type that ruled for thirty years, had the Swiss chalet in Gstaad and the apartment in Belgravia, and underwent annual prostate exams at the Four Seasons in New York.

"If a man picks up women in bars, he will do it again." She sounded like Franklin Roosevelt. No, Eleanor Roosevelt. "Mark my words."

"Are you saying that it's predetermined he'll be unfaithful to me because we met in a bar?"

"Yes," she said unflinchingly, "that and the fact that he's a surgeon lead me to conclude he will most definitely cheat on you."

"And what would you say if I told you I was the one who picked him up?" There was silence. "That he was just sitting there drinking a glass of *milk* and I went up to him and seduced him?"

Sarcastic laugh. "I'm sure that was exactly how you two met."

I was left with a sinking feeling that Heaven had Oscar's number without ever laying eyes on him.

Change of subject. "How's it going down there? Clouds burn off yet?"

"All but that damn son of mine." Her voice rose. "He's like the cloud that hangs over my every day. Do you know that just the other day I found a bong in my closet? A bong! The man is nearly fifty. It boggles the mind."

"At the lower house?" I shook my head. "How'd he do it this time?"

"I just don't know. I've had the locks changed twice this year and he still finds a way in."

With all that he had, with all that had been handed to him, including a beach house of his own in Malibu, an income courtesy of his aging mother, Francis found a way to take more.

"Whatever you find, don't smoke it." I had a vision of Heaven's small frame crumbled over an outside deck chair. No one down there would be sober enough to call an ambulance.

"When are you coming home?" she asked in a quick, off-handed manner. It was a question that went entirely against her nature to ask.

"Whenever you want me," I said quickly, knowing that I couldn't leave Freetown now, not with the shaky political climate, the refugee situation in Guinea, and, of course, Oscar.

"Hasn't the war ended by now? It feels like you've been over on that God-forsaken continent forever."

"Technically the war is over, but in reality it's just beginning." In some ways the scenes were more terrifying post-truce than during the RUF's last stand against ECOMOG. The battles hid the total devastation of the country and its people. Now the streets looked like Mars—wide open but entirely inhospitable to humans. "I'm one of the few journalists who's been allowed to stay and cover it all."

"Christmas then?"

"Possibly." I exhaled a long thread of smoke. "Hopefully."

"It better be because with all that goes on around here, I might not be around for much longer."

"You're not going anywhere," I said lightly. "Anyway, where can you go besides Point Elsewhere?"

"If Francis keeps this up, Point Dume." I heard the draining of the glass, the muted clinking of melting ice cubes, and the click of the receiver.

War, struggle, rebellion, and death is in all of us, it follows us wherever we go. I fully realized this truth when I spent time at Fando-Yema refugee camp on the border of Sierra Leone and Guinea.

Refugee camps are supposed to treat everyone equally, but everyone was too used to seeing class lines and identifying with political persuasions—the RUF or the Sierra Leoneon government. They brought to the camps their traditions, their struggles, and their hate. They butchered themselves and their children because being displaced from their homes and families made them want to hang on to their war all the more.

Because Oscar was a surgeon with Doctors Without Borders he had access to the entire country—a flash of his identification as well as a little bribe was all he needed to travel from Freetown through the war-torn diamond-rich east to the refugee camps that bordered Guinea and Liberia. The trip was hell on the body: potholes larger than exploded mines, roads that ended in blockades, and impromptu checkpoints manned by teens wearing ragged Guns N' Roses T-shirts and boasting AK-47 assault weapons like giant lollipops.

On my first trip to Fando-Yema with Oscar after the peace accord had been signed in the spring, I realized that war occurred throughout the country like reverberations in a pond. Freetown was just one facet of the mess. The rebels had taken over the countryside close to the diamond town of Koidu, decimating the farming community along the way by chopping off arms and legs and destroying the crops of anyone who hadn't been branded an RUF supporter. We didn't see many of them in Freetown, since most would die before making it to the capital, but some reached the camps, and if they were lucky they would see a doctor.

"There isn't always a doctor here?" I looked at Oscar in horror. "What happens then?"

"They either bleed to death or their veins cauterize due to prolonged sun exposure. Hopefully we catch them before they get infected."

"How many survive?"

"If it's a leg, beneath the knee, they won't make it. The femoral artery is just too big; they'll bleed to death. But an arm, a wrist"— he moved his neck from side to side and slapped at a mosquito— "there's always a possibility."

I watched his face as he said the words and I was especially disturbed at the way he smiled when making the analogy. But damn, did he look good in the open air, in his guerilla-green jeep with the large white cross painted on the door. His graying brown hair fell to his collarbone in soft curls, and he wore light brown aviator glasses. My very own Jim Morrison, complete with stethoscope and loaded with sarcasm. Oscar was better at sarcasm than he was at Hallmark; it was his only defense.

The camp was, in theory, run by the United Nations, but the rebels were the de facto rulers of the camp. They decided who got food, water, medical attention, and shelter—like a mini-Freetown before the peace accord was signed.

"How often do doctors come up?" The landscape that we inched our way through was lush and overgrown because the farmers, who once made their living from cassava and rice, had either been killed or had fled to Koidu in search of diamonds—the African version of the get-rich-quick American dream. The irony was that rice now had to be imported from America.

"Whenever we can spare a doctor in Freetown." He took a long sip of the warm Coke he had tucked in the glove compartment where the flies couldn't get it.

"God help them." There were more than 300,000 Sierra Leoneon refugees in Guinea, most of them in Parrot's Bay, a blip of land that entered Sierra Leone and was for all intents and purposes part of the country.

"We need full-time medical staff just to cope with the injuries the refugees sustain once they've arrived." Oscar's tone was without emotion; he had been making this trip for weeks and was no longer horrified by the conditions. "They can't stop killing each other, and the money to move the camps farther away from the border won't arrive."

"But I just read an article from Reuters saying that the U.N. has gotten West Africa to pledge—"

"Please, American"—he shot me a look over his gold-rimmed glasses—"come back to earth."

"But they've been discussing it ever since the peace was signed. They know it's the only way to keep them safe."

"It goes like this: we get them, we sew them up; they get them, they hack something off. It's cyclical and never-ending. Get used to it."

"Except they only have four limbs to spare." It had only been a month since our first encounter, and although I was desperately in love with him, his detachment sometimes frightened me.

"Not if you chop in lots of pieces." He down-shifted the car and slammed on the brakes as a truck full of armed soldiers came into view. "Medecins Sans Frontiers, MSF doctor." He waved his badge with one hand while he held the other in the air. "Get your hands up"—Oscar shot me a sideways glance—"now."

I was frightened but did not speak. It was the oddest sight—children in torn American clothes with guns smiling and leering at the same time. Were they capable of cutting off the legs of a ten-year-old girl? Did these boys who barely had facial hair rape women until they begged for mercy and quick death?

"You!" one of them shouted. He wore a bright yellow tank top and matching baseball cap that bore the name of a team I had never heard of. "Who are you? His nurse?"

"Journalist." I held up my credentials. *"Sunday Times."*

"English." A younger boy who sat behind the two older boys flashed a perfect smile, a smile without decay. "We kick the English ass."

"So did we," I said, and they must have thought it rip-roaringly funny because they fell backward and held their tight abdomens until the fits had subsided. When they recovered, they waved us through.

It was August, smack in the middle of the rainy season, and the camps were like indoor mud baths with corrugated roofs that amplified the rain to a maddening decibel level. With more than fifty people to a toilet, cholera, typhoid, and malaria ran with the overflow, infecting anyone and everyone who hadn't been infected already. While Oscar worked day and night stitching open wounds, making flaps out of skin and sewing up amputated limbs, and treating the real camp killer, diarrhea, I went in search of young girls for a story I had pitched. But I could find no women under the age of twenty in any of the camps I visited.

"Where in the hell did they all go?" I eyed Oscar across the table we were using to eat our rice and chicken stew, which smelled like the bottom of the zoo. "Is there fish in this stuff?" I winced.

"Isn't there in everything?" Oscar was tired. He could barely feed himself after the two fifteen-hour days he had put in. "Eat, it's more than anyone here's seen in months."

Feeling guilty, I plugged my nose and swallowed. "So where are they? According to the UNHCR records, there were over thirty girls under the age of fifteen here just two days before we got here. Where'd they go?"

"Maybe they went home." He slurped. The man could eat anything.

I pushed the tin bowl away, peeled my blood-red bandana from my head, and wiped my mouth. "Or maybe the rebels took them."

Oscar shook his head. "No, if that were the case, every man in here would go after them, and every mother would be crying about it to every white face she saw. No, they went somewhere voluntarily."

"So why won't anyone tell me where they are?" I was so thirsty, and yet the Star beer in front of me remained untouched. It was hard even to drink an ice-cold beer in a place like this.

"I've got three hours before I have to be up wiping asses again." Oscar rolled over on the cot, curled into a ball, and closed his eyes.

"That's it?" I stared at his back and wished that he had asked me to lie with him. I wished that he would see me as a source of comfort, but he didn't need comforting. Oscar was truly self-sufficient. "How am I going to get my story if no one ever tells me a fucking thing?"

"Good night, my beauty." He turned off the light and was gone, leaving me with the sounds and vibes of the camp, which reminded me of an inner-city pound where dogs paced, too fearful to sleep and too nervous to stop.

"What happened to the 'fat' part?" I smiled.

"I only call you my fat beauty in the throes of lovemaking," he replied with a smile in his voice.

"A poet." I shook my head. "Lucky me."

"You have no idea just how lucky." Oscar yawned. "Now good night."

The following morning, the morning we were to leave, Oscar came and woke me.

"Wake up, sleeping beauty." He nudged me, then pulled off the black mask that sealed my tired eyes from light.

"What time is it?" Pain shot through my back as I tried to sit up. One night on a UNHCR cot at thirty-six was enough to cripple an otherwise healthy woman.

"It's ten," he said, "and I have your girls."

"What?" I jumped up from the bed and swished a bottle of water around my mouth and poured it on my face and the back of my neck. I was surprised not to find a sea of lice springing for cover. "They're back?"

"Oh, yeah." He smiled tiredly and dropped his head down. "Come with me, American."

I grabbed my camera and notebook and followed him through the tents until we arrived at one large tent occupied only by dozens of young women. "Where were they?" I saw no physical signs of abuse on anyone; in fact, some even smiled at me when I entered the room.

"Take a peek." Oscar signaled one of the youngest over to where he sat at the end of a cot. She could not have been more than twelve years old.

"Sit down and put your legs up, please," he instructed, and after a brief hesitation the girl did as he asked.

"Come here, Saffron." I walked over and watched from behind his shoulders.

Her skirt came off and her legs went up. "Spread, please."

She giggled and opened her legs.

"Oh, no," I gasped. There was nothing left of the labia, the inner labia, and the clitoris—nothing but a hole with a short, muddy stick stuck inside. A vaginal mastectomy.

"Who did this to her?" I was breathless.

"Who do you think?" Oscar told the girl to put her legs down.

"I know, I know." I looked at the other women in the room. "Did they do this to all of them?" I looked at their faces and could only marvel at the resilience of humankind. How they were able to chat, to smile even, when they had just been brutally and irrevocably butchered was a testament to the strength of these people.

"No, you don't." Oscar paused. "You think it's the RUF, but it's not."

"Then who?" I glanced at them one by one, all of them tall,

thin, and velvety black with sparkling eyes and great pink lips parting in smiles.

"They did it to themselves, Saff, they did it to each other in a ritual circumcision that allows them to become part of the Bondo society."

"But why?" I was horrified. "They're not even in Sierra Leone, they don't have to do it to each other here, there's no pressure to belong here."

Oscar rose to leave. "Quite the opposite. Here they'll do anything to belong, anything, and going off for three or four days, drinking, dancing without men around telling them what to do, is something these girls live for. Returning a woman is also what they live for. It's their culture; it's even endorsed by the prime minister."

"But how many of them will become infected?" I thought of that gash and that dirty stick, I thought of the rapes that occurred about as often as I showered, and I thought of that hole and the pain that they caused themselves.

"Ah, most of them, but they won't take any medication for it. They'll just nurse huge infections until it travels up to the bladder or, worse, the uterus, and they can no longer go to the bathroom. Then they'll accept treatment." Oscar spoke in front of them as though they couldn't understand what he was saying. The truth was that while they understood the language perfectly, they had no real idea of what he was saying.

"Or die," I whispered.

"Now you're getting the hang of it, American."

I walked out of the tent unable to look at any of them in the eyes. They were a breed I did not understand, and I didn't know if I ever wanted to.

CHAPTER TEN

"WHAT! WHAT! CAN'T YOU JUST WAIT UNTIL WE GET HOME? Please, Halla," I pleaded to the rearview mirror, but her cries only intensified. "Starbucks?" I smiled broadly. The one thing that filled a hole no religion could fill was the Mocha Frappuccino. The thick plastic cups with a rim that was both curved and soft, the sturdy straws that didn't crack or melt after two sips, and the sizes, *huge*, *bold,* and yet strangely conformist. It was a club with its own language and membership that practically validated my move back.

"How about Starbucks? Wait until we get there, we'll stop and I'll feed you, okay?" Cars behind me honked and I pulled into the slow lane to let them pass. Summer traffic on PCH was beginning to remind me of the autostrada in Italy or the autobahn in Germany, clogged with angry and impatient people in a hurry to relax.

I pulled off to the side and wrangled Halla's rigid body out of her car seat. Her screams were so loud and close together, I was sure roadside Children's Services would be tapping on my window any minute. "Here, baby, here you go." I quickly put my breast in her mouth and her body suddenly went limp. At three and a half weeks old she was able to put her hand on my breast and hold it like a can of beer.

Zuma Beach was packed; neon towels blanketed the burning sand; coolers and makeshift umbrellas marked sunbathers' spots while they braved the icy and turbulent water. In Freetown, the beaches were rarely crowded. The sand was the color of cream and so fine it felt like velvet on bare feet, the water tropical in appearance and in temperament—no crashing waves, undertow, shore sharks, or jellyfish—and yet few people went in.

The phone rang from the bowels of my purse. I hadn't even realized it was on. "Hello," I yelled. "Can you hear me?"

"I can hear you, stop screaming. Is this your first cell phone?" It was Anika.

"No, why?"

"Because every time I call you on it, you either scream into it or muffle your mouth against the receiver like it's a walkie-talkie."

"Did I miss something? Are we married?" I teased. "Every time I talk to you you're busting my chops."

"Nancy's inviting all of us over to her house for what she called an 'informal' pool party, whatever that's supposed to mean." A big exhale hit my ear.

"I assume it means casual."

"Of course it means casual," Anika snorted, "but aren't pool parties always casual? Do people actually have 'formal' pool parties?"

This is what happens to women who have nothing to do all day. I shot a dirty look at a passing surfer who lingered just a little too long in front of my window.

"Anyway, Nancy's house is supposed to be amazing." She hedged: "Not exactly my taste, but amazing."

"We'd love to come." I switched Halla to the other side and watched her grab, then suck my nipple like a blowfish. She was hungry and tired of being a passenger. So was I.

"It's for September!" Anika paused. "September."

I waited.

"Can you believe she actually sent invitations to a so-called informal pool party that's not until September?"

"She's well organized." I stopped. "I thought you were friends." I looked out to the beach and watched as people dipped their toes into the tide, only to run back to their towels. "Why is this such a big deal to you?"

"It's not." She paused. "I'm just talking, Saffron, it's just funny, that's all."

I decided to change the subject. "Hey, what's the best way to change a baby with dripping diapers in the backseat of a car?"

"Where are you?" Her voice snapped to attention.

"On PCH. I just left Heaven's house and she began to cry, so here I am, performing a little roadside assistance."

"Oh, my God, did you see him?" Anika switched gears. "What was it like? Is he leaving? Did you fight?"

"First the diaper. Shit." I closed Halla's legs. "The stuff is leaking all over my cream faux-leather seats."

"On your lap, lay her lengthwise in between your legs with her bottom toward you. Unsnap her onesie." She paused. "She *is* in a onesie, isn't she?"

For God's sake. I clumsily cradled the phone against my ear. "No, she's in a black leather cat suit."

"With you, who knows. Anyway, lift her up, put a clean diaper under her, take the old one and scrunch it through her legs, like you're wiping her. Seal it with the tabs—you do use Huggies, don't you?"

"Yes, I do, please get on with it."

"Wipe her, use powder if you have it, and close her up."

When it came to babies, Anika had that exacting self-righteousness that could be a little overwhelming at times, but she knew her stuff. I slid Halla back into her car seat. "Couldn't have done it without you."

"Yes, you could have. Now tell me everything. No—" Her voice rose. "Better yet, come over for pizza."

"Where's the husband?"

"In New York, won't be back until Friday. Come, spend the night even, I hate being alone." Her voice rose to a teenager's squeal. "It'll be so fun. Please?"

It was the best offer I'd had all year. It was the only offer I'd had all year.

"Thin or thick?"

"Thick," Anika bragged. "Any good Italian knows that it's got to be thick."

"Thick it is then." I didn't have the heart to tell her that no pizza in Italy was thick. It was consistently thin and crisp, one of the few things you could count on in Italy.

Anika and her husband, Warren, lived in the old section of Beverly Hills, the section near Merv Griffin's Beverly Hilton, home to big hair and tight lifts, award shows and Continental breakfast banquets. Grass lawns shimmered in the late-afternoon breeze, each individual blade catching a ray of light and a touch of wind. The houses that lined Roxbury Drive, the street they lived on, made me think that Karl Marx and Lenin had it right—it was time for the proletariat to rise.

Their entrance was a modern one, complete with a Japanese garden, Koi fish, and chimes, but every few feet, angular sculptures in Mondrian reds and oranges rose from the moss-covered ground while complicated geometric mobiles hung from high branches as if to jar you from the tranquility the Japanese garden and stream were meant to instill. The house rose behind it like a monument to self— a mass of metal the color of guns combined with shards of twenty-inch glass and planks of rose and cherry woods, making the façade a complex but astounding geometric equation.

"There you are!" Anika shouted from the doorway. In her Gap overalls, pink Izod top, and beaming white Keds, she looked two feet tall against the house, and completely out of her element. I would have imagined her in a Connecticut/Martha's Vineyard–style house, never something quite as cutting edge as this.

"No problem finding us?" She rushed up and unlocked Halla's car seat before I could undo my seatbelt. "Oh, great, she's asleep." She glanced at her watch. "The pizza guy should be here in ten minutes."

I followed her in through the enormous glass doors and couldn't help but stare at the bold wood staircase that crisscrossed like railroad ties until it reached the second floor. "The bedrooms are upstairs, but I'll put Halla down here with us, so we can hear her."

"Great." We went left and winded our way around a dining room that was remarkable for its complete lack of style. It was straight out of an antiques market, complete with a table with lion claw feet and upholstered chairs. Ceramic pots, baskets, and figurines of chickens laying eggs were scattered along the shelves that lined the dining room alcoves.

"I collect them," said Anika, pointing at the chickens. "Warren tries his best to break them."

The kitchen was a chef's dream—double Wolf stoves, Sub-Zero refrigerators, brushed-steel cabinets, and a well-worn chopping block that took up half the room. "You like to cook?"

"I do, yes." Anika pulled out a carton from the fridge. "I'm going to cooking school. Punch?"

"No, but I'd love some water," I said, wishing I could have a glass of wine. No one offered women over thirty-five a drink in L.A. anymore.

She filled the glass from the sink and handed it to me. "Let's go sit down." She took me to the family room, which overlooked the exquisite black-bottom pool and geometric gardens that had nothing to do with flowers and everything to do with form, shape, and symmetry. The enormous blue, yellow, and red–striped cotton pillows stuck in rattan bases and matching chaise longues made me feel like I had just time-traveled back to Hawaii circa 1970. The coffee tables were made of cork and bamboo, but the lamps looked like Louis IX knockoffs. Nothing matched, nothing belonged, especially Anika.

"How much is the pizza?" I grabbed my purse when I heard the doorbell.

"Twenty bucks with tip," she said.

I handed her ten and she took it without a moment's hesitation. I knew people in Freetown who didn't have a single pair of shoes without holes and yet they wouldn't think of taking my money in a similar situation. But never mind.

Though the pizza was awful, I pretended to enjoy it. "It's different than I'm used to, but it's"—I paused, trying to choose the right word, one that would not offend Anika's feelings nor my own integrity—"got a lot of dough."

"Did you eat a lot of pizza in Africa?"

"No, not quite. A lot of sweet potatoes, fish and chips, spicy pork, and fish stews, but not a lot of pizza." The food really was the most vile combination of West African and English cuisine, but for most of us there, meals were an afterthought.

Anika fingered the baby monitor. "Sophia told me you two got together at Barney's and talked about old times."

I wondered how much she told her. "She was missing Max."

"And what about you?" Her voice became deeper, like an insider's. "Are you missing Oscar?"

"He's dead, remember?" I glanced up from my pizza. "I don't want the others to know, please, Anika, now more than ever."

She took a long drink of her punch and proceeded to fold her pizza slice in half and shove it into her mouth like she was swallowing knives. "You never did finish telling me how you found out he was cheating."

"I never started." I grinned.

"We've got all night." She looked like a sixteen-year-old girl trying to get her best friend to divulge her deepest, darkest secret. "Come on, I'll open a bottle of wine."

"Now you're talking."

Since the coup of May 1997, Doctors Without Borders ran its surgical program out of the Connaught Hospital in Freetown. For Oscar, head of the German team, it was home base. He was on call twenty-four hours a day, six days a week, or seven during the particularly bloody days, which was almost every day in Freetown.

Anika sipped her wine cautiously. "Did you go there often?"

"All the time." The hospital was a sprawling colonial building that had been used and used until the floors were thin, the walls were falling apart, and the plumbing was shot. Inside it looked like a Victorian orphanage—white wrought-iron single beds lined up against walls strangely devoid of monitors, IV's, or other medical paraphernalia; just boys and girls with stumps wrapped in dirty gauze. The incessant beeping of monitors, high-pitched intercom interruptions, and the shrill ring of telephones was eerily absent here. Still, unlike most of the African buildings, the British-built Connaught was still standing.

"He stood out?"

"He did more than that." My mind flashed to the first night I saw him at Sonny Markes and I had that feeling all over again. "His eyes caught you, held you, and then pushed you away, only to pull you back again. He wore his light blue surgical robe over jeans and cowboy boots and walked through the halls like there was a beat in his head that no one else could hear. He was cool, he was smart, and he was the best surgeon they had."

"How long had he been with the organization?"

"On and off for five years."

"If he was that good"—she narrowed her eyes—"why was he still there?"

I glanced around her living room at her carefully displayed possessions. It would be impossible to explain to someone like Anika, whose idea of roughing it was having only one washer and dryer. "It's like an addiction. You become so caught up with these people, with their war and the injustice of it all, you can't separate yourself from it. You curse the barbarism and yet you dream of it at night. And when you wake up and smell Africa, you hunger for it even more."

"It must be very beautiful." Anika put two pillows beneath her head on the floor, baby monitor in one hand and a barely touched glass of wine in the other. "Every time I've caught *Out of Africa* on cable, I dream of what it must be like to buy a farm in Kenya or Rhodesia, hire a bunch of Masai, and live out there for the rest of our lives."

"It's not *Out of Africa*, Anika," I laughed. "You wouldn't be caught taking a leak in the houses our friends lived in. Think corrugated roofs covering pulp walls swollen with rain, humidity all year round, and twelve-year-old boys the color of polished ebony chewing bright pink gum in their mouths and pointing fully loaded machine guns in your face. Think of three-year-old girls in ragged pink dresses and diapers hopping on one leg and holding a crutch with one arm because their limbs have been severed by rebels for no other reason than to prove they could."

"Okay, okay"—Anika put up her hand—"I get the point."

"None of us knew why we stayed, it was punishing and thankless. But we did. We felt like we had a job to do."

"Cheating, remember?" Anika cut in. "You were going to tell me how you found out he was cheating."

"Fine." I poured myself another glass and prayed that Halla wouldn't be up soon. "Hey, do you have a breast pump?"

"I think so, why?"

"Because I'm finishing the bottle," I announced.

She grinned. "So you're spending the night?"

"If that's okay," I said and felt giddy for the first time in months.

"What, are you kidding, I'd love it." Anika rolled over. "We could go swimming, rent videos, make brownies, crank-call Nancy."

"Or Francis." I nudged her shoulder. She beamed.

"Let's finish this glass—we have about thirty minutes until they'll be up. The alcohol won't get to the milk by then, so we should be fine. We'll have to pump before the next feeding, though." Anika topped off her own glass. "Now finish the damn story before the kids wake up."

I continued. "Oscar's room at the hospital was tiny. It had been a broom closet when there were actual brooms and mops to clean the floors. We had been seeing each other on and off for several weeks by then but we always met at my hotel room at Mammy Yoko's. I had asked a few times if I could come over but he said the last thing he wanted was to sleep there when he didn't have to. I understood, but I persisted."

"Didn't you get enough of all that gore during the day?" Anika lit a candle and put it in front of my nose to smell. "Lemon meringue pie."

"It wasn't about the hospital." I pushed away the sweet candle. "I was so used to seeing it all, it really didn't faze me anymore. I just wanted to see where he worked, slept, brushed his teeth. I wanted to see what was in his refrigerator, his closet, what kind of sheets were on his bed—"

"Whether any of his nurses or fellow doctors were cute enough to pose a threat," Anika cut in.

I smiled. "At the time I thought he was in love with me and there was no real threat. After all, it had only been a few months."

"And I'm sure there weren't too many girls who look like you wandering the halls of African hospitals." Anika shook her head.

But the photograph, that photograph on his wall. The long, curly blonde hair that fell down her nude back, the perfect ass cocked slightly to the side so that the lines of her hip and the muscles of her thigh looked chiseled and voluptuous all at once. Her stomach was ripped, her breasts looked large though soft enough to ensure their veracity. Her bikini was bright yellow. I may have been pretty, but this girl looked like a *Sports Illustrated* cover model.

I stared at him. It all seemed so strange. He was so damn uncomfortable with me in the room and there was nothing to be uncomfortable about except for heaps of dirty laundry, sheets balled up, and this silly picture on his wall that he was doing his best to block.

There was a small boom box in the corner of his room. I asked if I could play some music. He said he didn't have any. "But what's that?" I pointed to a shoe box under the desk that held clearly marked cassettes tapes. I cocked my head to get a better look. The tops were lined with white labels, the writing was in cursive and the ink, pink.

Oscar glanced over nervously. "That's not mine." Then he took my hand in his and led me to the door. "I feel like a drink."

"You never feel like a drink." I stepped back and took him in. I could see nothing different in his eyes, but small dots of perspiration began to appear along his hairline, filling his pores like drops of water. "What's wrong?"

He opened the door and nearly pushed me out. "I just want a drink, and a change of scenery. Is that allowed?"

Anika wrinkled her nose. "That's a little weird. But then again with a penis like—"

My mouth dropped. "I cannot believe that Sophia told you! What's it been, three days?"

"She's got a big mouth, Saff, I wouldn't tell her things if I were you." Anika shook her head as though it had nothing to do with her at all. "Was it really that small?"

"Yeah, but that's beside the point. Sophia was so hooked up on that and it's really just a detail—"

"Detail, right." Anika patted my shoulder, giving me a look of encouragement. "Let's not get lost in the details." She paused. "Let's get back to the cheating." She crossed her legs and put her glass to her lips. "How did you find out?"

"It was more than just cheating, Anika." I drained my glass. "But it's complicated." I poured. "At the time I was not entirely without guilt myself."

Silence. "Please don't tell me he was African."

"He was African." I nodded.

"Bookmark it here, no more of that war, refugee stuff." She hopped to her feet. "Let's feed the kids, then I'll open another bottle."

As she said the words, I felt my breasts and nipples harden and heard the beginning of Halla's hunger cry. If only everything was as clear as motherhood.

Joseph first caught my eye in the lobby of Mammy's. It was early morning, smack in the middle of the hottest rainy season in years—

August '99. He sashayed through the lobby like a confident woman, wearing navy blue pressed linen trousers, a white starched dress shirt with his sleeves carefully cuffed at the tips of his elbows as though ironed that way, and a pair of polished black leather thongs. Under his arm he clutched a copy of my paper.

Although he was as black as coal, he looked like he had taken the wrong plane and gotten off at the wrong city. He belonged on the runway in Paris or London, and he captivated me. I found myself watching for him every morning at breakfast.

Breakfast at the hotel depended entirely upon what was going on in national politics. If there was a breaking story, the tables were empty, bread baskets were left untouched, and waitresses stood against the countertop looking bored in their dull hotel uniforms. If everyone was waiting on a story, then the tables were crammed, ashtrays were overflowing, and coffee mugs were filled with Cool Daddy gin. The truce signed at Lome a few months earlier had done a lot to clear tables and cut back on waitstaff. Reporters and aid workers were, after all, the hotel's only guests.

So on this early Tuesday morning there were only the two of us. He took tea, ate eggs, grilled tomatoes, and bacon like a Brit, and read the paper back to front. I could not tell his nationality or his profession by looking at him, but I knew he had to be in Freetown for work. Recently declared the most backward and most vicious of all third world nations by the United Nations, Sierra Leone was no vacation spot.

"I'm afraid you'll need a lot more than that"—he pointed to my fruit bowl—"to brave the morning rush in Freetown." He smiled the measured smile of a man who knows his effect on women.

I tried to think of a quick one-liner, something witty and cute but not sarcastic or jaded, but nothing came. I reached for my wallet, which bulged with leones.

"Doesn't your company take care of such a small breakfast?" His voice was soft and light. There was a lot of English there, but the African was interwoven tightly into the accent.

"They do, yes, but I just want to get rid of some of these bills." The leone was now virtually useless, it was so inflated. "They're getting heavier than the bag."

"Perhaps this will all come to an end soon." He stood up to pay for his breakfast and I felt a new flutter coming on when he came to stand by me. He must have been six foot five—he towered over my five-eight frame—but it wasn't his height that made my stomach dance; it was his body. Unlike most tall Africans, his shoulders had bulk and his forearms were lined with threads of muscles and veins. I could see the indentation and bulge of his chest under his shirt.

"That's what we're hoping for, right?" I squeezed out from behind my table and sort of backed out of the restaurant.

He stared. "If you don't mind me asking, why are you walking that way?"

I couldn't tell him that I didn't want him to see the size of my ass. "I suppose it comes from all my years trying not to get my backside shot off."

"You Americans"—he shook his head lazily—"are a very strange breed indeed."

"Yes, we are. For years they've been telling me that and now I finally agree."

"But you make up for it by your beauty." He put out his long black hand. "Joseph."

"Saffron." Our eyes held, and in those few seconds he caught me like a spider.

He crossed his legs and leaned against one of the giant columns in the lobby. "Who is it that you work for? NBC, ABC, CNN?"

"*Sunday Times.*"

His eyes grew wide and then he laughed. "An American writing for a British paper? How do they understand you with your rakish *z*'s taking the place of our civilized *s*'s?"

"So you're English?"

"English educated, but African to the bone."

I dodged the possible sexual innuendo. "Are you from here?"

"I am." He massaged the center of his brow with his thumb and forefinger. "I was."

"Let me guess. An upper-class English-educated refugee"—my eyes narrowed—"who has returned to peruse a very timely career in politics and/or economics."

"A jaded American?" His eyes never left mine. "Now, that's something to write about."

"You haven't answered my question." I was vaguely aware that the lobby was filling with people, but it was merely background noise and movement to me. All I saw was Joseph's flawless matte skin, his narrow nose, and lips that made me think of ripe red grapes.

"U.N., baby." He rolled up the paper and tapped me on the head twice. "Here to keep the peace and spread some love."

I was too embarrassed to respond. I was aware that British forces and U.N. troops were scheduled to arrive in December to monitor the Lome Peace Agreement, as well as the particularly messy process of disarming more than fifty thousand rebel fighters, but I did not think they would come in the form of Joseph.

"And by the way"—Joseph backed away from me, smiling— "you have a truly fantastic backside. I had the pleasure of an unhindered and somewhat lengthy view of it yesterday morning."

I could feel a fire under my face and chest. "I didn't catch your last name."

He stopped in the middle of the lobby and cupped his mouth with both hands as though he were shouting at a soccer match, but instead he whispered. "That's because I didn't give it." And then he was gone.

I took a deep breath and waited for my pulse to return to normal. I glanced at my watch. It was only eight-thirty in the morning and all I wanted was for the day to end so that I could wake up and come down for breakfast again.

There was a hard tap on my shoulder. "I've been outside inhaling petrol fumes for the past half hour, what the hell are you waiting for?"

"Nothing, Oscar, nothing." I cleared my throat. There was nothing quite like the sound of an angry German doctor to snap you back to reality. "I just felt dizzy for a second."

"I bet the twenty kids at the Amp Center are feeling pretty dizzy right now, too," he said, referring to the Freetown center for amputees. "Apparently they've got a two-month-old baby they found yesterday thirty kilometers from here."

"Don't tell me, please," I begged. "I don't think I can stand to hear this one."

His voice was like ice. "One arm and acid burns across her chest. I really do have to go."

I covered my eyes.

"If you'd rather stay here, that's fine, Saff."

"I'm exhausted." I looked at him. "I don't know if I can do this anymore."

"Then go home," Oscar said without sympathy or tenderness. "Go back to England."

I looked for it anyway. "I can't just go back to England, Oscar. I'm the bloody bureau chief."

"But you're the only one left at the bureau," he pointed out. Oscar did not think much of my profession, calling it little more than a parasitic hobby.

"Which is why it's so important that I stay." I stood up. "If I don't cover the aftermath of this wretched war, then who will? Why do you think the United Nations came?" I stammered. "Why do you think the Brits came?"

Oscar collapsed onto the sofa. "I'm sure you're about to tell me."

I jabbed myself in the chest dramatically. "Because of us."

"Are you ready then?" He stood up and picked up my pack.

"You think you're so smart, don't you?" But even I had to smile, he had played me like a fiddlin' fool.

He took my hand in his and led me out of the lobby and into the potholed streets of Freetown.

CHAPTER ELEVEN

"YOU'RE OFFICIALLY FREE TO HAVE SEX," HE SAID AS HE emerged from between my legs, giant headlight attached to his forehead as though mining some treacherous cavern he feared getting lost in. There was always something unsettling about your gynecologist talking about sex while his head was between your legs and his finger was in your ass.

"How's the bleeding?" He pulled off his gloves and tossed them in the bin.

"The pills stopped pretty much everything." I glanced down at Halla to be sure that she was quiet and not about to wake and roar. I had gone out of my way to feed her and change her diaper minutes before stepping out of the house because I did not want to have a pelvic exam with her attached to my breast.

Dr. Lazaroff looked up from his chart. "What pills?"

"The pills you prescribed for the hemorrhage." I stared at him, as if to remind him that he was the doctor. "Four weeks ago."

"I'm sorry." Dr. Lazaroff tapped his Mont Blanc against the palm of his hand. "I forgot."

"That's alright." I pulled the wax paper gown over my legs and tucked it under my naked cold bottom.

"No, it's not." Dr. Lazaroff put down his chart and looked me in the eyes. His light gray hair was cropped short. "I saw you and your baby only five weeks ago when you came in from London, I should remember."

"It's okay," I said, my feelings slightly hurt. "I'm fine, Halla's fine."

"She's beautiful, go and enjoy her." He told me to get dressed and call for birth control.

"Is that her?" Judy and Marcy at the front desk stretched over the glass partition.

I nodded. "Her name's Halla."

"Is that African?" Marcy asked. "I got to write that down."

The waiting room was filled with pregnant women who all looked at Halla and me for some indication of just how rough it was. I felt like a pop star, all eyes on me, listening for scraps of my harrowing birth story.

"No more appointments, hon." Judy clicked her desk with her three-inch red nail. "You take care now."

"Okay," I said, lifting Halla in my arms. "Well, I'll miss—"

"Jones, Betty," Marcy shouted from behind the receptionist glass. "Urine sample, room two."

"Bye." I turned and walked out the door, feeling that I was no longer part of this group, this routine. Green light to have sex, though. Yeah, right.

"Did he give you the go-ahead?" Anika's eyes went wide.

Nancy was next. "Did he actually use the words 'free' and 'sex' in the same sentence?

"Yeah." I was enjoying this. As a single parent this was one duty I did not have to perform. "At six weeks, you're good to go, ladies."

"Because if he didn't use those exact words, then I'm telling Warren that he wants me to check back again in four weeks."

"I get eight weeks." Sophia nibbled at her chicken burrito.

"Lucky bitch," Nancy sneered.

"Last-minute C-section," Sophia continued as though used to the envious sneers of older women. "I was too narrow through the hips."

"Just stop right there." Nancy threw her paper napkin. "I can't take any more."

"But I'm really missing it." Sophia's blue eyes sparkled. "And Max is tired of blow jobs."

There was complete silence as we stared at one another. Nancy, Alice, Anika, and I looked like we each had been hit in the face. "Blow jobs?"

"Shh." I glanced around the restaurant knowing that every table within earshot was listening.

Anika still hadn't recovered. "You're giving blow jobs at four weeks postpartum?"

"No," Sophia said, smiling like a newlywed, "five days, more or less."

"Max has to be the luckiest man alive." Nancy glanced at her nails. "Stan hasn't seen any action since I *found out* I was pregnant."

"No wonder you're so—" Sophia stopped.

"Uptight?" Nancy shot back. "You think I need to get laid? Is that what you're saying?"

"I was going to say happy," Sophia recovered. "I was going to say that you're lucky to have a man who listens to your needs, gives you the space you deserve, and still loves you."

Wow, I thought to myself, what a beautiful save. Sophia wanted to be invited back.

"You're awfully quiet, Alice," Nancy said, moving on to her next victim. Alice had been quiet throughout the entire post–Pump Station get-together.

"We're right on track." She turned her wrist to check the time on her sensible steel watch. "Thank you."

Another excellent save, I thought.

Nancy dipped her French fry into a puddle of ketchup and looked directly at me. "I think the Pump Station should stop wasting all this time on breasts and focus more on the penis."

I nodded. "The Penis Station?"

"Yeah, instead of using plastic babies, they use plastic penises." She looked around the table. "They teach us how to stroke them, quiet them down, make them sleep, make them happy. A sort of postnatal course to life with a penis struggling for attention."

"I like it," I said. "But then again, I don't have one at home, so I would attend for entertainment purposes only."

"And who would teach the course?" Sophia asked. "I don't think Gretchen's ever seen one."

"If she has, either it scared her so badly she never went back or she scared it so badly, it never came back." Anika readjusted her breast pad. "Babies are easy compared to men."

"No," Nancy cut in, "men are the simplest creatures on earth. All they need is sex, food, and quality bathroom time."

"And all women require is a valid gold card," Alice whispered and we all turned. It was the first thing she had said since sitting down. I wondered if she had simply come to the conclusion that she did not belong.

"Touché!" Nancy slapped her shoulder as though Alice's bitter words were not a condemnation of her but a celebration of womanhood. "And on that note, ladies, I will be leaving you." Nancy stood and I once again caught a full-length view of her skintight low-rise jeans and black patent-leather go-go boots, which she had informed me upon arrival were Gucci.

"Where are you off to?" Envy was taking over my brain, becoming a veil through which I could no longer see clearly. I, too, wanted to be off to someplace, to have that freedom of handing over my child to a trusted employee while I did what I did best.

"Home to put Winnie down. I have appointments all afternoon." She threw her freshly stamped Louis Vuitton bag over her shoulder and took out a five-dollar bill.

"There's no valet here," I said.

Nancy grinned like an old and sordid man. "There is when you tip the guy five bucks."

Her car, a garish black souped-up Mercedes 500 sedan with its windows tinted black, reminded me of so many third world dictators who darkened their windows so they didn't have to see the starving and diseased population they claimed to represent. The rest of us were quiet as we walked back to our cars parked along Douglas Park.

"This is me." Sophia stopped and pointed to a very late-model Mercedes sedan. "It's old but it does the trick."

"I'm on the other side." Alice eased her stroller off the curb. "See you next week."

Anika and I kept walking up the street. "Feel like taking a walk?" she asked.

I glanced at my watch. Halla would be awake soon, but I didn't feel like being alone. There was something about Nancy that had unsettled me.

"We can feed them here if we need to," she said. "Everyone here has milky boobs, don't worry."

Sometimes it felt like she read my mind. "I'm not so good at the public nursing thing," I admitted. To see some of these veteran mothers nurse, one would never know just how awkward the whole thing was. You had to lift your shirt, unsnap your bra, and get the baby's mouth right on your nipple all at once. Otherwise you'd expose to the world an enormous breast with a nipple the size of Nairobi, not to mention rolls of descending flesh underneath.

Anika opened her perfectly organized straw basket and pulled out a crisp white receiving blanket. "Let's sit over there by the pond."

It was a glorious afternoon, the fog having lifted after cooling off the park. Children of all ages were everywhere, riding bikes and skateboards and narrowly dodging one another. Moms sat close by nibbling healthy snacks while reading politically correct novels or *Variety* magazine.

"Can you imagine just sitting there and reading?" I shook my head. Nearby on the playing field, girls were being pushed off to the corner while older boys called the show. "What brats."

"I'd be up there so fast." Anika stared with her mouth open. "I can't believe no one is doing anything."

Now the boys were telling the younger girls that they couldn't play there. "I hope nothing like that ever happens to her."

"Oh, it will," Anika said. "But you'll deal with it."

We sat down. "So, do you think you and Warren will stay here in LA.?"

"I don't know, it all depends on his firm, which happens to be in New York."

"Which also happens to be where the ex-wife is, right?"

She nodded her head, but didn't let on whether the split was an amicable one. "Yep, she's there and so are her two boys."

"How does she feel about you?"

"Not great." Anika looked mesmerized by the water shimmering beneath our feet. "She trusted me. I worked for him for six years, I took care of her personal stuff as well as her children's. I knew her very well and was considered a part of the family."

"But did you always know that you wanted him?" I probed. "Or did you just wake up one morning and see him differently?

"I never thought he was within my reach, Saff. I didn't think any of this was. Here I was, a girl from the wrong part of New Jersey; my father, an Italian immigrant and laborer, and my mother a house-wife. Santa Barbara was a soap opera to us, not real life. Beverly Hills was a place we read about. I never"—her eyes went wide—"thought I'd be living in a house like the one I'm in. I pinch myself every morning and thank Warren for the life he's given me."

"So it was something you always wanted?" I had to ignore the sound of Heaven's voice shrieking in my ears.

"I didn't really want it, because it was so far off," she explained convincingly. "I admired it, I guess, envied it even."

"But you wanted Warren?" I glanced at her hands, which were not the hands of a lady, but they cleaned up well. Her wedding band had modest but crisp diamonds all the way around and her watch was a simple gold ladies' Rolex.

"I looked up to him." She crossed her arms and I worried that I was getting too personal. "He's twenty years older than I am, he's in-telligent, well traveled, and we got along great. There was always an undercurrent between us, but he was married and I was raised to re-spect that."

"When did you first know he wanted you?"

"He began asking me about my weekends, where I was going, who I was seeing. When he found out that I was single, he asked me to come with him on a trip."

My eyes went wide. "And you went?"

She beamed like a schoolgirl. "And when we made love, it felt like I had been waiting for this man my entire life."

"Where was it?"

"The Four Seasons, of course."

"Of course." I attempted a smile. It was one of the Ten Com-mandments that Heaven had drilled into my brain. Screwing a mar-ried man the age of your father was bad, not just for the obvious reasons. By doing so, you gave your life over to this person. He's the boss and you're just along for the ride as long as he wants you, and they tire easily. Just ask the one whose place you're taking. "When did his wife and family find out?"

"When she caught us in their Connecticut house in the eighteenth-century bed they'd bought on their honeymoon." Anika looked down. "It was awful, truly awful. She had a vase of flowers in her hands and it smashed to the floor. She walked out and zoomed off in her car."

Children played all around us, totally unaware that their parents would cheat on each other; they would lie, steal, and do just about anything in their power to get their needs met, even if that meant breaking up the home that was the foundation of their lives. "Did she actually see you?"

"No, I don't think so, but she knew."

I stared ahead. "How old were the children?"

Anika's voice faded. "At the time, they were eight and ten."

"Not to sound judgmental . . ." I paused as her eyes flinched. "I could never imagine dating a man I knew was married and had a family, I don't care how in love I was, it just wouldn't happen. Ever."

She wagged her finger in my face. "Never say never."

I took it in my hand and held it. "You don't understand, my mother went from one man to the next, turning his life and everyone else's around until she got bored, packed her things, and left. Her favorite thing was to leave in the middle of the night, after she had slept with them so they suspected nothing. Then off she went, leaving nothing but the smell of her hair on the pillow beside him. My father was her first victim."

"How old were you when she left him?"

"I was three and we sailed off in the middle of the night from Corsica and boarded a ferry for Marseilles. From there we came to California and she worked her magic up and down the coastline a few times over before we found Heaven and she left me with her."

"She abandoned you there?" Anika held her son just a little tighter. "What an awful woman."

"It was more like the stork had finally found me a home." I told her about how well Heaven and I got along. "Plus Francis had made it easy. He had already let her down on just about every milestone a parent looks forward to."

"And that's why you went to the best schools and got the best grades. No wonder Francis hates you."

"I suppose." I stood up and glanced at the field below us. The boys were gone and the field was awash with pink backpacks, pink Barbie bikes, and pink helmets. "Looks like the girls won."

"Don't we always?" she said wistfully.

No, I thought, we don't.

"Let's talk about love," said Anika, sensing my souring mood. "Tell me about the beginning." Her voice was so down to earth, so unaffected and solid, as though nothing I could say would change the way she felt about me. "Not the end."

"Beginnings are so much better, aren't they?" I placed Halla back in her car seat. "Everyone wants a happy ending, especially in this town, but when it comes to love, I'm all out."

"But we're only at the beginning." She pulled out a hidden stash of Milano cookies from her bag and offered me one. "Let's stay here for a while."

So while the girls conquered the playing field and young people kissed by the side of the lake, I remembered my first date with a not-so-young doctor by the name of Oscar De Vries, and in the beginning, it was love.

Red kidney beans, grits, fritters, black-eyed peas, collard greens, yams and sweet potatoes—food that we now associate with black Americans—was slave food, and because Freetown was the first home to freed slaves, it was the national food of Sierra Leone. On our first official date Oscar took me to Paddy's Bar on Lumley Beach, the most happening spot in Freetown, a short drive from the Mammy Yoko Hotel, a favorite hangout for foreigners.

"We'd better eat right away," Oscar announced with his usual Germanesque manner. "Curfew begins in two hours." There wasn't a table or a parking spot to be found after nine at Paddy's, with white U.N. jeeps bulging into the narrow spots and makeshift vehicles squeezing into whatever was left.

"What would you like?" He scanned the splotchy, stained menu.

I waved down the waiter. "I'm having the shrimp in ginger, tomatoes, and cayenne pepper, please. And a Star."

"Do you come here a lot?" He ordered steamed vegetables and handed the menus back.

"Yeah, we do." I looked around the room at the tables of reporters and writers who were about to be shipped out, and for a moment I felt like joining them. "It's a press hangout and a local one, too."

Oscar looked out at the beach and watched waves breaking into ripples on the smooth sand. "Unlike you journalists, surgeons here have work to do."

"You should get out more often," I joked. It was hard with him, like this, after what had transpired the weekend before. Oscar was not an easy man to be with, not lighthearted, not easygoing, but worst of all, he had the knack for making just about everything I said sound stupid.

So far, Oscar had not so much as mentioned the way I looked. I had bought a white tank top and wore it with an African sarong the color of poached salmon. My sandals had a heel short enough not to make me taller than Oscar, but just high enough to make my severely atrophied calf muscles stand out. My hair, highlighted by the sun, fell in long waves to my shoulders. I was tan all over and I had applied baby oil—one of the few moisturizers available in the streets of Freetown—liberally.

"How old are you?" He tapped his bottle of beer and picked up a corn muffin from the basket that had just been delivered to our table.

"Why?" I crossed my arms over my chest. "Did you find that last comment to be immature?"

"Are you always this defensive?" he continued. "So why England?" He buttered his muffin and took slow sips from his bottle.

"My mother thought it was a country where women could get a fair shake."

"I would have thought America, land of the free and all that, would be the fairest of them all."

"Not according to Heaven."

"Heaven?" He momentarily stopped the muffin train that had been going straight into his mouth. "Is that your guru? Don't all Californians have some kind of a guru?" He belched.

Disgust spilled from my eyes. "Enjoying yourself?"

"Carbonation and belching are *fantastik* for the stomach." He curled his delicate fingers into a ball and hit his chest twice. "Digestion is key to a healthy organism."

"Good to know." I lit a cigarette and took a long sip from my beer.

"And that is the key to an unhealthy one." Oscar narrowed his green-blue eyes at me.

"Are you always this annoying?" People were laughing everywhere I looked. We were in Africa, a place where you either laughed or cried, but were rarely indifferent. Pleasures here were simple; life was fragile and good times were fleeting.

"I am a doctor, I am German, and I fix the arms and legs of people who are victims of an ignoble war." He leaned back in his chair, exposing his hairless stomach and skin, which looked creamy to the touch. He wore a bright orange T-shirt, faded khakis that were ripped at the bottom, and blue Converse lace-ups. A jean jacket was tied around his waist. Except for his pale skin, he looked like a recalcitrant student, not the lead surgeon of a highly respected organization. "And most of my patients are repeat customers."

"Are you saying that your work depresses you?"

"No," Oscar said as the waiter delivered his entrée of steamed greens with ginger and chili peppers. "A Coke please."

My shrimp, probably caught that afternoon right in front of us, smelled of the spices of Africa and provided the extra bonus of clearing your sinus and pores. An African facial.

"My colleagues thought I was absolutely mad when I told them I was going the nonprofit route," he said with a laugh, and it was the first time I had seen him relax. "It was almost worth it to see their faces when I turned down lucrative offers at pretentious practices."

"Why did you do it?" Oscar was different; that was obvious from his cowboy boots to his Richard Gere looks, but I was amazed by all that he had given up to be here.

He leaned forward on his elbows and I could smell soap. "I could ask you the same."

"I didn't have to turn anything down. This is my job, Oscar." I threw up my hands in the air. "Although it doesn't look like it, we're in a war zone and that's where I'm supposed to be." I leaned back in my chair. "You, on the other hand, could be in Harley Street being paid a fortune looking after old lords and ladies with gout so bad, your amputation skills would make you the most sought-after surgeon in the West End."

He shook his head slowly. "I'd die first." And he looked like he meant it.

"What is it, London? Being stuck in a city, or is it the monotony of daily life that you can't bear?"

"It's the politics of money." Oscar looked around Paddy's. "It's here, too; it's what this bloody war is all about—whoever controls the government controls the diamonds."

"But it's raw here," I interjected.

"Exactly." Oscar nodded as though surprised that I got it. "There the control is more behind the scenes—you feel like a puppet rather than a player."

"Is that what happens to young doctors in Europe?" I moved closer, enjoying his face by candlelight. "Everyone wants you, woos you until you can't say no?"

"And then you spend your life taking care of people who do nothing but sit and eat; then you marry someone who can do nothing but sit and eat." He pushed away his plate.

"And you spend your days paying for it."

He clinked his bottle with mine. "You're smarter than you look."

"Is that a compliment?" I teased. "Or a complaint?"

"Saffron." He paused. "What a silly name."

Our verbal sparring was like foreplay. "Do you always feel the need to criticize me?"

"What I was about to say was that if you were any better looking, I wouldn't sleep at night for fear that you were being unfaithful to me."

"Unfaithful?" My eyes grew wide. "I didn't think we were officially dating."

"Of course, silly girl, what do you think happened last week?" His eyes went dark. "Do you think I do that with everyone?"

I would bet on it. Everywhere I went with Oscar, heads turned. He had the kind of presence that made people talk about him long after he had left the room. I had no idea why the hell he had chosen me.

"To tell you the truth," I started, "I didn't think it went so well."

He took my hands in his and they were soft like a catcher's mitt. "You're the first woman in years that interests me; be patient, falling in love takes time."

That was the most beautiful thing a man had ever said to me. I felt awash in love, but I knew I did not want to go to bed with him again, not yet.

We walked out to his car at ten-forty, with twenty minutes to navigate the mud slides, potholes, and checkpoints that made Freetown such a collision course. The clouds had pulled back long enough to reveal a sapphire blue sky shot with a map of diamonds that took you up over the northern tip of the Sierra Leonean peninsula and out toward the twinkling lights of Aberdeen Village.

Oscar opened the car door for me. "Would you like to be wealthy, Saffron?"

"What's that supposed to mean?" I said. "I barely make enough money to make my rent and keep my flat in London."

"But would you?" He kissed me on both cheeks softly. "If you could get a large amount of money, and be set for the rest of your life, would you take it even if it meant not being true to yourself?"

"You're talking about your decision to come out here, right?"

Engines turned over, horns honked, and headlights flashed as people rushed to make curfew. "I'm talking about you."

I glanced at my watch. "It's ten till, we'd better go." He didn't move.

"Would you sell out?" His eyes twinkled as though he were playing a game with me.

I threw up my hands. "The answer is no. No." I took the keys and inserted them in the ignition. "I would not sell myself or anyone else for the money. Money means nothing to me. Now let's get out of here before we get shot."

As we nursed our children on a green park bench surrounded by freshly mowed grass, I felt guilty. In this place, a church for the naturalist and an escape from the incessant life of L.A., I had judged Anika. I had felt superior to her when she had confessed about falling for Warren. I had smiled insincerely when she told me to "never say never." She was right, and I was wrong.

Never is always just around the corner, coming for you when you least expected it.

And it was knocking at my door hard.

CHAPTER TWELVE

I HAD AN IMMEDIATE AND VISCERAL DISLIKE OF ANIKA'S husband, Warren. As for Max, Sophia's husband, a Frenchman with far too much hair, he looked like he seduced women for a living instead of photographing them. Alice's husband actually wore a pair of tan pedal pushers with socks and strappy sandals. Enough said. And Nancy's husband, Stan, was oblivious to everything around him except for the cell phone he used like an appendage and the bowl of Ruffles he'd latched onto upon his arrival. I knew this meeting-the-husbands thing had been a bad idea.

We were too protective of one another. We knew things that the husbands did not. We understood one another's needs without making demands. We accepted one another's faults because we knew how hard we were trying. It had nothing to do with the outside world. Until now. Until them.

"Sophia tells me you're a journalist." Max appeared out of nowhere. He was a tall and handsome man, in a trendy I-smoke-twenty-fags-before-my-first-shoot kind of way. His hair fell to the bottom of his neck in a pageboy so perfect it had to have been blow-dried. His shirt was open to his navel, exposing a gold and diamond dagger necklace.

"I was." I pointed to Halla, who was asleep in the Bjorn carrier in front of me, her face nestled in my double D's.

"Lucky thing." He winked, but stopped the moment he saw my stony eyes. "Uh"—he changed tactics—"we're in the same field practically."

I cocked my head and stared heavily upon him. "Really?"

"Well, I'm a photographer." Max looked around for his wife. "Didn't she tell you?"

"Yes, she did." I could not make the effort to bullshit, not now and certainly not with him. "But I'm not sure how fashion and war are the same."

"Travel, for starters." He scanned the crowd again for Sophia, then continued the pitch. "Long nights, empty hotel rooms, waking up alone over and over again." Max grinned. "Awful, isn't it?"

"No, not really." I wouldn't give an inch. "Being alone is far better than being surrounded by a room full of wankers."

Sophia walked up behind him and took his hand in hers. "Ah, there you are," Max said with a heavy sigh of relief. "I've been looking for you."

I would bet twenty bucks that Max would tell his wife on the way home that I was a lesbian and to steer clear of me. Sophia probably would believe him, or at least pretend to.

"Really?" Sophia looked so happy. She reminded me of a young Bo Derek gazing into John Derek's blue-tinted Ray-Bans and seeing nothing but perfection.

"So this is Saffron." Warren came toward me with both hands shoved deep into his pockets. "The woman who has stolen my wife."

"Is that right?" I teased. I wanted to like Warren and, more important, I wanted Warren to like me. "How could I possibly steal her from you when she spends her every waking moment devising new ways to use her Crock Pot?"

He grinned and exposed the worst set of teeth since Michael Caine in *Alfie*. "There are other appliances she could use to make me happier."

Our eyes locked for an instant. Was it a themed party? *A find the hidden sexual innuendo* party and no one told me?

"She tells me you were with the *Times*." He patted his gray hair as though making sure it was covering the right spot. "In Africa, was it?"

"That's right." I tried to sound open to what I knew would come next, the transformation of my life into cocktail-hour sound bites.

"And Halla's father was killed over there?" His voice was measured and patient, used to commanding silence when he spoke.

"Yes." I nodded, hoping Anika hadn't told him anything more.

"We don't realize how lucky we are out here, do we?" He took in his wife and her friends drinking by the pool on a flawless summer day while their babies were being looked after by their housekeepers. "Imagine what an African would think of this right now?" He clapped his hands together. "Imagine you took a poor African and dropped him right here, what his reaction would be." He glanced at Max, who nodded as though on cue.

"Sounds like a great idea for a film." Alice's husband, whose name I could not recall, had been eavesdropping.

"It all depends on the African," I said wearily. "And that particular African's point of view."

"And it's been done." Stan's phone must have stopped ringing for the moment. *"The Gods Must Be Crazy*, great movie." He shook his head. "A little on the slow side and definitely short on special effects, but not a bad show."

Warren touched my hand and I flinched. "Anika has no idea how lucky she is."

"Women don't have a friggin' clue how much this"—Stan threw

both his hands up like Atlas, weary with the weight of carrying the world—"all costs."

Alice's husband was silent. He watched behind thick glasses that didn't make him look like an academic, but rather a grown-up version of the dork who sat in the front center seat of your high school algebra class and tried like hell but still only managed a passing grade.

"I don't know how you guys do it," Max said, looking up at the house. "What did this cost, four"—Warren said nothing and Max's eyebrows shot up—"five million?"

"And that doesn't include expenses, I'll bet," Stan huffed, but Warren remained mute.

"I hope you get laid like you're going to war," Stan said, glancing in my direction and apologizing, "because that's what it is out there. War."

"Saffron understands that, though, don't you?" Warren smiled coyly. "You're the only one of them here that does."

"Actually, my wife does as well." Alice's husband finally spoke. "We were just in Afghanistan with the missionaries there."

I turned. "Alice is a missionary?"

"We both are." He wove his hands together. "Our parents were, too. We were both born in Africa." His eyes shone with the luminescence that blind faith gave. "It's in our hearts as well as our blood."

That explained a lot. It explained her shy and sometimes uncomfortable behavior, her reaction to Nancy's extravagance, but most of all, it explained her husband's pedal pushers and sandals.

"Now, *there* was a good movie." Stan downed his Coke. "Back when De Niro had balls."

"Excuse me," I said and walked across the lawn to where my friends sat looking bored on long deck chairs covered with brand-new fluffy white canvas pillows.

"Cheeto?" Anika held one up and I grabbed it greedily. "Were you bored out of your mind over there or what?"

"What were you talking about?" Nancy asked with a little too much interest.

"Films." I filled my mouth with enough Cheetos to keep me from talking. I could not tell them the truth, that their husbands were talking about how spoiled they all were.

Nancy grabbed her Fendi clutch, so small a slim-fit infant Huggies couldn't fit inside. "Work. That's all my husband ever does." She stood to leave.

"I'm going to check on mine." Alice went to rescue her husband, who had been elbowed out of the conversation and stood awkwardly by a rosebush.

"Let's all go." Sophia jumped off her chair, shadow-boxing Nancy.

"You were right." Anika laughed as they left.

"About what?" I whispered. It felt good to be alone with her again and let my guard down.

"Bad idea." She turned to look at the group that had fractured into two and then into three. "Forced, to say the least."

"That's what you get for trying to beat Nancy to it." I elbowed her.

"I was not!" Anika looked hurt. "Alright," she conceded, "I just couldn't let her throw the first party."

"They're missionaries," I said, whispering again.

"Who?" She dipped a carrot into some ranch dip.

"Well, it's definitely not Stan and Nancy," I teased, "and I'd pretty much say that Max and Sophia are out unless we're talking about sexual positions."

"Alice and what's his name?" She covered her mouth with her hand. "Well, that explains everything."

"Yeah." Halla began to squirm and I took her out of the carrier.

"Except for the complete psychosis that goes along with pushing your religion on people who don't want or need it."

Anika turned quiet and looked down at her feet. "So, what's been happening at the beach?"

"I'm in," I said, "and I'm actually beginning to enjoy it." Still, it didn't feel like home without Heaven. No matter how many things I nailed to her walls or piled into her closet, it felt as though I was waiting for the door to click and for her to come in and fill the room.

Even the lower beach house felt off-limits to me now. I had yet to set foot in it since I'd returned. It was Heaven's jewel; she used to tell me that she wished she could wrap it up and take it with her every time she walked up the path back to her house. Not to mention that Francis wouldn't like it.

Anika shook her head. "What happened?"

"He actually—" I stopped. "You're not going to believe this."

"What?"

"He put a vase of cut flowers in every room."

"Oh, shut up," Anika scoffed.

"And a stuffed animal for Halla." I smiled. "It had seen better days, not new by any stretch of the imagination, but there it was waiting for her when we arrived."

"I still don't believe he's kosher with all this." Anika's eyes bulged. "I mean, how do you go from hating someone to being totally okay with the fact that they've inherited all that you've ever wanted your entire life?"

"He sees it as a fresh start, all of us living there as a family again," I summed up and pulled back my shoulders. "He's changed, and believe it or not, I think I like the new him."

"Uh-oh." Anika shook her head. "He's getting to you."

"He's not all that bad." The pool tempted me, but I could not take off my shoes, not in front of this crowd of weekly pedicures. "It looks like Heaven may have been manipulating the situation to get me to come home."

"Oh, please." Anika narrowed her eyes. "The minute you take a toothbrush down there, he'll be all over your ass."

"No, listen." I grabbed her knee. "Yesterday, as I was moving in, Francis and his girlfriend, Blue—"

She turned. "Blue?"

I nodded on cue. "We all got to talking about the time I threatened to quit the paper."

"You quit?"

"No." I shook my head quickly. "Well, eventually, yes. It's a long story." I turned my back to the party and scooted up closer to Anika to fill her in. "Anyway, I was telling them how much it meant to me that Heaven was supportive of my decision to leave the paper."

"And she was," Francis had said while sweeping the floors. "She wanted nothing more than for you to quit that job with the *Sunday Times*."

"I could always count on her to be there no matter what." I was in the midst of unpacking my suitcases and hanging my shirts in Heaven's bedroom closet. It felt awkward. I felt awkward.

Blue emerged from the bathroom. "You don't have to lie for her anymore." She paused dramatically. "She's dead, you know."

They came into the bedroom, looking at me, staring. "What do you mean?" I asked.

"Tell her, Francis," Blue said. "She has the right to know."

"What's the point?" he answered her directly, without glancing my way. "What good will it do her now?"

"Me," I interrupted. "It's me and I like the truth, so please, shed some light on it." I sat on the corner of the bed, and at that moment felt the passing of time. This was once Heaven's stronghold, this house on top of the hill that afforded her a view of everything that transpired below. And here we were—her son and his hippie girl-friend (who Heaven would have loathed), chatting around her bed while I moved in.

"She wanted you home, Saff," Francis said, doing that thing with his eyes, a kind of hooded fluttering like he was blinded by wisdom, which really got on my nerves. "She hoped that by quitting the job you'd come home."

"But I didn't." I looked at both of them, still not getting it.

"She wanted you to fail," Blue said. "Tell her, Francis."

"No, I won't." He left the room.

"I don't understand," I said to Blue. "What's the big deal?"

"She was not a nice person, Saffy, not nice at all." Blue's voice sounded strangely menacing. "She wanted you to fail. She told us every day that you'd be home before the end of the year one way or another."

"Oh, please." I was slightly taken aback by the picture they were painting. "You didn't know her."

"No, *you* didn't know her. She was obsessed."

"With what?"

She shook her head like I was an idiot. "With you."

"Oh, come on." I started loading socks into the drawers. "You and Francis have a unique imagination." I knew Heaven; there was no need to take any of what Blue said seriously.

"Here's the changing table," Francis announced as he struggled to carry in the three-tired wood structure, which already looked out of place.

When Heaven was alive, her bedroom had been sweet, reminiscent of another time with her tiny pink art deco bed, etched jade lamps with bold Tiffany shades, and her dark brown shag carpets.

"Do you think you can enjoy it here?" Francis wiped his forehead and removed his work gloves. "Soon the beauty of the place will take over, Saffron, and you won't miss her as much. It's a process we've all been through."

"I'm still at the beginning, I'm afraid." Looking around the place, I knew it would take time for the sense of loss to dissipate.

Francis squeezed my arm with that lingering, massaging touch that made me want to jump out of my skin. "We're always here to help." And with that he and Blue had left the room arm in arm and gone out the front door and down the stairs until their two frames, both thin and tan, dissolved into one another.

"So you're sleeping there?" Anika interrupted, shaking her head, still unconvinced. "With your doors wide open, no bodyguard?"

"Oh, shut up." I checked to make sure that Nancy and Sophia were still out of earshot. "You have no idea how supportive they're being. It's incredible."

"Fine." Anika's voice dropped to a whisper. "He gets it if you die, remember that."

"Honey?" Warren waved. "Can you—"

Anika stood to attention. "Duty calls." I watched her stride across the lawn and into her husband's embrace. They both wore Tommy Bahama shorts the color of ripe bananas, ironed and pleated, along with those stringy Mexican sandals that seniors on the cruise circuit are so enamored with. But despite the matching clothes and matching smiles, the million-dollar house and the all-American hospitality, it was as clear as the boldface type on his Viagra prescription that she was his secretary and he was her boss. For life.

I took another long look at them when they came, arms intertwined behind their backs, to see us off. They appeared so unified, with a kind of blind faith in each other that comes from knowing your role and playing it well. From where I sat, they looked exclusive and impenetrable. I coveted that image and yet it saddened me deeply. There was no room for me there.

But I was finding space somewhere else. A place that was slowly becoming mine. Sunday at home, my first home and now Halla's first home.

For as long as I could remember, Sundays at Heaven's place were party days, led by Francis, master of ceremonies, and his partner in crime, George, in the pit—the barbecue spot in between Francis's house and Heaven's cottage. Except no burgers or dogs were being grilled here. They were all devoted vegetarians, eschewing food for spiritual awakening, satisfying their yearning to travel via mushrooms, LSD, and pot.

"They're on my property," Heaven would complain, staring out at the party from behind the curtain. "Look at them," she'd say over and over again, sipping from her tumbler of Scotch. "They're using drugs on my property, I could get arrested." Up went the binoculars. "The state could seize my property from me."

"This happens every Sunday," I would point out. "And look, I think there might even be a Ventura County cop down there rolling joints."

"How can he do this to me?" Her face would be covered with angry red bursts. "Does he not know how bad this makes me look in the community?"

But it was bullshit. All of it. All she wanted was an invitation. As soon as she'd hear the gentle opening of her front door, followed by a "Mom, we're waiting," she would protest until Francis took her hand in his and led her down to the party as if she were a reluctant bride. Then she would beam like a prom queen, the angry red blotches diffusing into a warm pink glow as she greeted everyone. I would watch from the kitchen window, just as she had done moments before. She would not look back. She would not call for me.

There was a knock at my door. "I took the chance that you'd both be awake." Sally stood outside, not making a move until I invited her in.

"For three hours"—I checked my Nike watch—"exactly." I stepped aside and let her come in.

"Since five?" Sally stopped in front of the kitchen. "Babies and old people, they keep the same hours. Dean and I've been up since five, too."

I opened the cabinet and pulled out two coffee cups. "Coffee?" Sally stared at the cups, transfixed.

"Coffee?" I said again. I had the same reaction the first time I had used Heaven's favorite mugs. "It's better than keeping them in storage or giving them away, right?"

"It sure is." Sally snapped back to life. Her hair, which I was beginning to think was a wig, was the same, curled under at the ends and swept back in soft layers. Her pants, true to form, were polyester, wrinkle- and stain-resistant or your money back, fitting nicely with her low heels and pearls. Sally was so middle-class, so middle-American, it was like watching an old June Allison film every time she entered the room.

"Must get kind of lonely here on Sunday mornings." I filled her cup halfway. "Still take four teaspoons of sugar and half-and-half?"

"Now it's just two spoons and nonfat milk," Sally replied, glancing at the cup wearily. "Doctor's orders."

I pulled up my stool so that we could face each other while I kept an eye on Halla, who had just fallen in love with her first chew/suck toy. "Don't they all sleep till noon and then drink until they drop?"

"No, dear." She looked at me as though I were a silly child. "Not at all."

"The parties, remember?" I shook my head at the memory. "Francis was famous for them, drove Heaven mad as hell, too."

"Yes, but that ended years ago." Sally smiled gently. "Years ago, dear."

I remembered Francis saying they had quit drugs a while ago. "Like ten years ago?"

"Probably." She tapped at the cup. "I don't know, I can barely keep track of how old I am, let alone beach parties."

I was having a hard time getting a handle on the whole vibe down here.

"Now we cook, barbecue, see family and friends." She spoke slowly and paused often. "If it's warm enough, Francis takes us out on his boat and then the men cook their day's catch on the beach." Her eyes floated up to the ceiling as she recounted the late-night grunion fishing Francis and her husband, Dean, looked forward to all year, the pole fishing, the harvesting of mussels at low tide.

In less than two minutes, Sally had rocked the foundations of my world. "Did Heaven do this as well?"

"Why, yes, dear. Every weekend," Sally caught a glimpse of Halla. "Oh, may I?"

"Of course." I led Sally to where Halla lay on her back, kicking and spitting. Joy beamed from Sally's eyes as Halla's small pink fist opened to grab Sally's frail pinky. "Look at that!" she cried out. She had no children of her own and seemed fascinated with Halla.

When I had told Heaven about the baby, she didn't seem excited at all. In fact, she barely took notice. "Come home," she repeated like a mantra. She warned me to "get away from that bastard before he screws half of Africa, infects you with AIDS, and kills you both." The woman should have been a professor of human nature.

"You were the closest thing to a grandchild she ever got, you know." Sally moved her long finger in arthritic circles above Halla's head. "One of her greatest regrets was that Francis didn't become a father in her lifetime."

I resisted the urge to mention that at night, after everyone went to bed but me, Heaven would stay awake trying to figure out ways to make her son sterile. "No child should have a man like Francis for a father," she would say. "It will be doomed from the start and I won't be around to pick up the pieces the same way I've been picking them up for years."

Halla began to cry, no longer focused intently on Sally's long coral fingernail. I scooped her up and she buried her face in my chest. "Time for her midmorning snack."

I walked Sally to the door and said good-bye. But as she walked away, she said to herself, "Boy, Francis sure was right." She clicked her tongue twice. "She's looking more and more like her daddy every day."

CHAPTER THIRTEEN

A PICTURE. HEAVEN MUST HAVE HAD A PICTURE OF HIM somewhere, a picture I sent of us doing something glamorously humanitarian, like administering hepatitis injections to a village of orphans.

But I had never sent her one. It would have been like sending her ammunition. Heaven would have found his good looks "chilling" and the faint smile at the corners of his mouth "disturbing." She would find proof in any picture that I sent, proof that Oscar cheated, that he didn't give a damn, that I should cut my losses before they cut me, that I was an idiot unable to see the truth that stared me in the face.

I quickly brought Halla into Heaven's bedroom and nursed her on the bed. Halla sucked as if she hadn't eaten for days. She was able to keep her head up now, and the power of her suction was enough to cover me in hickies should she miss her mark. The milk came fast, full and rich. I vowed that this would be my last session at the Pump Station. It was time to move on anyway; anyone who stayed after the first two months was not only lacking a social life, but had serious latch issues of her own.

"Let's switch now," I reminded her, and when she didn't comply,

I stuck my finger in the corner of her mouth, broke the suction, and plopped her wide-open mouth on the other breast, which had already lost a quarter of its milk on the sheets. Good thing I slept alone.

Halla continued to suck, pass wind, and twist my bra around her fingers, totally unaware of my all-encompassing need to look for that damn picture. I crossed and uncrossed my ankles ten times, lifted my torso, exhaled burnt-coffee breath in her face, and rubbed her back as vigorously as I could before she unlatched and looked up at me like, "What the hell's with you?"

"What a good girl! All finished?" I burped her quickly, apparently too quickly, because she vomited her entire intake of milk all over the shoulder of my cardigan and onto the antique Burmese trunk Heaven kept at the base of the bed. Great.

But despite the bobbing up and down, the soft rocking, the silly walk borrowed from Monty Python, and the Barney song that had spread throughout the world like a bad disease, Halla would not sleep. She must have instinctively known that I was desperately in need of some personal time.

Ah, finally asleep. Inside the chest were stacks and stacks of old *Sports Illustrated* calendars, neatly organized bills, and a pile of letters bound with string. They were my letters to Heaven. I grabbed those first, switching on the light. I smiled at the tight handwriting of my twenty-year-old self, scared shitless in a country where they deemed you an idiot for your American accent alone. Heaven used to tell me that this was my advantage. While I might sound like an unpolished and naïve Californian, I was being educated in their schools and would beat them all.

The paper was the light blue tissue kind used for international mail. Because it was so fine, only ball-point pen would do, and even then you could use only one side. In my hand the letters had an old world feeling. How uncomplicated youth seemed from where I now stood—crouched in the bedroom of my dead adopted mother while my fatherless baby slept. The letters stopped the day I took my first job.

I placed the letters back where I had found them, even though the chest would soon be emptied and its contents thrown away. I thought of how people fought so hard to claim the valuable possessions of the dead, not the valued ones. The things that really mattered to the people we loved—letters, books, clothes—were usually tossed into the garbage as soon as the body was out and the FOR SALE sign was up.

I was about to close the trunk when I caught the cover of the *Sports Illustrated* 1999 millennium-issue calendar.

Curious, I flipped through its pages, which Heaven had heavily marked. In August, which featured a sweaty Latina woman wearing a red bikini and dripping lip gloss, she had written across the last row of dates: *Still with that loser. Could this be serious?*

I turned to September: *Oscar this, Oscar that. Will she never come home? How long has it been?*

In October there were a few notes about doctor's appointments, but it looked as though she had canceled most of them. A large black line was drawn through *Call S. regarding X-Mas.* Then written above, *She's too busy. No war. Must be O.*

November. *DO NOT CALL S.* was written in bold letters through every week of the month.

December. *Maybe she'll be back before I'm gone. But won't count on it.*

I read the pages, stunned. This was not the Heaven I knew, not the woman I spoke to every week. Quickly, I picked up the previous year, 1998, then 1997, and so on, scanning them and seeing similar notes about me throughout.

By the time I emerged from the bedroom, I was in serious need of a bath and a transfusion of Demerol. Besides coming to a very clear conclusion that our culture was doomed if grown women continued to starve and wax themselves into girlhood, I learned that Heaven both hated and coveted me.

"She didn't hate you, Saffron, to the contrary." Francis brought out a pot of chai tea from the house and sat down with me outside. "She missed you, yes, she followed your career with interest, absolutely, but more than anything she wanted you home."

It was a little after two o'clock in the afternoon, and people who drove hours to avoid the urban crowds at Zuma or the L.A. surfers at Leo Carrillo found our beach. It was August and the water was as warm as it would ever get, a chilly sixty-eight degrees.

"But she wrote awful things, Francis." My eyes were wet with tears. "It sounded like she wanted nothing more than for me to fail at everything just to come home."

He smiled. "Now, that sounds like the mother I knew and loved."

"No." I took his hand. "She was not like that with me, not ever." I told him about our phone conversations, about her pride and support, and he nodded throughout without ever appearing to understand a word I said. "Francis!" I pulled his chin toward me and saw that he was smiling again. "Why are you smiling like that?!"

"It's just so Mom, Saff." He lowered his mug. "I've heard it all before, and so have you."

"No, I haven't, that's what—"

He put his tanned hand over my mouth. "You have, you just don't see it yet."

At that moment, with his long brown hair flowing in the breeze and the light blue cashmere shawl wrapped around his bare torso, I could see why people listened to him. I felt like a clumsy student as he, the calm, poised teacher, waited for the realization to strike me. "I don't get it."

"The way she spoke about me, it's identical to the way she wrote about you." He cocked his head to the side, his hair falling like a golden curtain. "The way she spoke to you about me, that's how she spoke to me about you."

I shook my head, baffled. "No, it can't be." Phone conversations ran like tapes in my head, going back all the way to my first years abroad. Heaven constantly complained about him, when she wasn't raving about me. "There has to be some truth, Francis."

"It was what she wanted you to believe, and because you were so far from home, she was able to form your view of what life was like here."

It was true. I had never written or received letters from anyone else. "You were on drugs from morning to night, you killed her dog, Francis, you took over her property with your friends, your groupies, your girls. You made her life miserable," I said, dropping the formalities and the fear that had kept me silent for so long.

"I did," Francis agreed. "But I stopped ten years ago." The smile on his mouth was so resolved, as though he had worked long on this issue and was at peace with it. "She never told you, did she?"

"No." I closed my eyes. The sun made everything feel gold inside and out. In the distance I could hear the waves break with force. "Do you swim?"

He looked out at the ocean. "Never."

The phone rang at that moment and Francis lowered himself into a stretch as though there was no phone, no ring, no one waiting on the other end of the line. He came back up and put his hands together like Buddha. "Excuse me," he said, and walked into his house.

Fifteen minutes later, Francis emerged with Blue by his side, both of them wearing long unrefined cotton skirts the color of wheat. They looked like they had just made love, their faces a flushed translucent pink with a thin veil of perspiration on both their foreheads. Blue appeared shy, and could do little more than smile. I was sitting under an umbrella at the top of the dune, with Halla in one arm and a parenting magazine in the other.

"Saffron?" Francis called out before he entered my space—he was always so careful about that, an irony never lost on me.

"Yeah?" I waved them up.

"There is something I'd like to ask you." He kneeled down in front of me and Blue followed.

I put aside my magazine. It felt so strange to see him this way. He was like an entirely different person. "What I wanted to ask"— he paused to look at Blue and then back to me—"tell you, is that we'd love to have you and Halla in Heaven's cottage."

I stared. "The cottage?"

He nodded. "We think she'd want you to stay there. It was her jewel—"

"If only she could wrap it up and take it with her." I smiled.

"Away from me," Francis said. "I don't blame her, though, I was a real asshole back then."

"Yeah, weren't we all." I touched his hand lightly, still uncomfortable with the camaraderie I felt brewing. It was an awkward happy feeling, and I was not sure whether I could allow myself to trust it.

"Think about it." He stood and took Blue by the shoulder. "It's yours, all of it"—he drew up one long finger and pointed—"except for my little house."

"Thanks, Francis." My eyes burned and my body went slack with relief.

"I'm here to help ease the transition." His eyes wandered past me toward Sally and Dean's place to the surfers down at the beach. "That's all it is, too. Not a beginning or an end, just a transition."

"It will be so smooth, it'll feel as though you've never left," Blue added, and they turned and walked away.

I took a couple of minutes to let everything sink in before remembering what I had come down to ask in the first place.

"Francis," I called after them, but they had already gone inside.

I went up and knocked on Francis's door. It was, of course, the same faded door with the peeling azure blue trim. The deck was in its usual disarray, cramped and crowded with pots and pots of plumaria in various stages of life and death.

Francis poked his head out the door. "Hi, come on in." As I entered, I couldn't believe what I saw. The windows were draped with purple velvet curtains and the bed was made and covered with a spanking white cotton eyelet cover. Side tables had coasters, books were neatly organized on the shelf, and the usual film of dust was gone. The kitchen shone, making the outdated stove look almost retro and trendy. The yellow cabinetry and the white walls made it all look so damn quaint.

"This place looks great, Francis," I said, trying not to sound too floored by the transformation.

"Blue's responsible," he said with both pride and resignation, the way men sound when a woman has come into their lives and taken over.

I decided to get right to the point. "Francis, something weird happened with Sally and I wanted to ask you about it."

"Please." Francis took a seat on the sofa under the violet curtains. I immediately recognized it as one of Heaven's nicer tan sofas she had bought at Smith & Hawkin during my last visit out.

"Did Heaven have a picture of Oscar"—I saw a blank look cloud his eyes—"Halla's father, the doctor I was dating in Freetown?"

He paused a moment or two and then nodded. "Oh, yes, the doctor." Then he shook his head. "Mom sure wasn't too crazy about that guy. No, I don't think she kept a picture by her bedside. Why do you ask?"

I explained what had happened that morning. "Don't you think that's odd?"

"Old, more like it." He stood up quickly. "Sally's in her eighties and doesn't remember half the things she says, you'll see."

I felt him corralling me toward the door. "So you've never seen a picture of Oscar lying around?"

"No, never." He walked me out onto the deck and Halla began to cry. "Look," he said, "it must be time for her dinner."

I nodded and backed off the deck, wondering where Blue had disappeared to and why he wanted to get rid of me so badly.

At eight o'clock, after Halla went down for her last feeding of the night—well, until two o'clock in the morning anyway, when she would greet me with wide eyes, a groping mouth, and a diaper full of surprises—I noticed a car I had never seen before, a silver four-door Mercedes, parked in the driveway of Francis's house, which was dark. I continued peering out the kitchen window, into the cloudless night.

The front door to Sally and Dean's place opened and shut several times, causing the floodlights to burst light across their driveway. From my window I saw Francis, Blue, and a man I didn't recognize walk across the small bridge and onto Francis's driveway. The three shook hands, and the man got in his car and drove off.

I was just about to call out when Francis stopped and, like a bat, swiveled his neck to look intently at the house. I quickly pulled my head in and hid behind the same curtains Heaven had relied upon all those years ago. Something was wrong. Francis's eyes were fixated on Heaven's window in a menacing stare.

Blue shook her head, said something, and led him from the spot he was so rooted in. He left grudgingly.

Feeling every bit the thirty-eight-year-old unmarried, unemployed ex-reporter and mother of one, I got down on my hands and knees and crawled along the wall to the bedroom, where I was sure no one could see me.

As I brushed my teeth in Heaven's antiquated bathroom, I tried to shake the strange scene I had just witnessed.

I caught a glimpse of Halla through the cracked bathroom door. She slept on her back with both arms thrown over her head. Her lips formed a perfect *O* and her cheeks were infused with the kind of pink glow belonging only to sleeping children. Her hair was starting to come in pale and fine. Her chin was square and her jaw was growing more and more defined every day. Her warm, round mass was taking shape into the spitting image of her father. Francis was lying; Sally *had* seen a picture of Oscar, and he had shown it to her.

I eased into bed as if I were traversing a cemetery of mines. If Halla woke up, it could mean immediate crying followed by a good solid half hour of nursing, burping, diaper changing, taking out the trash with baby attached at the hip, and then trying to get her back to sleep. Opting to leave the comforter exactly as it was, bunched up around Halla, I curled up at the very end of the bed, the same side Heaven used to sleep on. Halla flinched and threw up her arms.

I twisted my head and watched her carefully out of the corner of my eye. She did it again. The startle reflex, followed by frowns, tongue slapping, fists balling up, and then it was all gone. The tension vanished and her face was as placid as a baby doll. I wondered whether my mother stayed awake at night, marveling at my expressions. Did she, too, ache with vulnerability at having her heart so exposed to the world? Did she fear getting crumbled under the responsibility of that love? No, my mother was too busy getting high and searching for anything that was elusive enough to keep her in motion and away from me.

I closed my eyes tightly and tried to concentrate on the waves outside, but my thoughts kept wandering. Halla was beginning to look exactly like her father. What would happen when she was old enough to ask questions? Would I run away like my own mother had? After all, I had already walked in her footsteps, I had taken Halla away from her father.

I wanted to go back to Africa, to simplicity. I rolled up the pillow, placed it under my neck, and tried to take myself back there. I closed my eyes and pretended the waves were those of the Atlantic lapping at Lumley Beach. In the black sky would be an explosion of stars, and the air would be rich with the smell of salt and sweet mangoes. I curled up my fists into tight balls like Halla and forced my mind to go back.

And it did.

CHAPTER FOURTEEN

THE ARABS HAVE AN EXPRESSION, INCHALLAH. IT TRANS-
lates into "God willing" and is used as an answer to nearly every
question one could ask.

Medical questions:

> PATIENT: "Will I live?"
> DOCTOR: "*Inchallah.*"
> PATIENT: "Will I die?"
> DOCTOR: "*Inchallah.*"

Technical questions:

> PASSENGER: "Will this plane take off on time?"
> PILOT: "*Inchallah.*"

Affairs of the heart:

> "Will he love me?"
> "*Inchallah.*"

On this continent where God and colonists have toyed with people like cats with mice for centuries, there is an innate knowledge that whatever happens happens, and there is little people can do to change it. They are Buddhists without knowing it. Truth means nothing. Seeking truth is nothing more than a vain attempt to assign meaning and create order in a world where the random reigns. In Africa they understood the futility of it all; *Inchalla* is their motto.

But since I was a journalist, it was my job to seek truth and give meaning. In retrospect, I was impatient and egotistical. God was not willing, so I took my truth, stole it, and it exploded in my face.

Things were brewing in December. The wind, known as harmattan, blew in dry red air from the desert. For once the rain eased up and the humidity died down, the homeless rolled up their plastic sheeting and lived al fresco. This was Sierra Leone's best month, a verdant jungle with tropical flowers in bloom and a warm, sweet breeze.

But with the cessation of the rains came a flood of displaced people. They came to Freetown for medical help, for food, for shelter, but they did not come in search of their family. That would be presumptuous. *Inchallah,* they would think; if it was to be, then so be it. It was a philosophy that came to their rescue when they saw a toddler with one leg or a young girl with acid burns on her face and the initials of the RUF etched on her chest. What other explanation could they have but God?

"You look exhausted," I told Oscar one night over dinner at Mammy Yoko's. Green plastic garlands and white twinkling lights had been pulled out from hotel storage and wrapped around the circumference of the bar. The barman wore a dusty Santa Claus hat, and Christmas music from a different time and place piped into the room like ether-infused muzak. It was horribly depressing and hilariously funny all at once.

"I am." He put down his fork. "It's grunt work." At Connaught

Hospital, the largest clinic of all, Oscar's team was doing between two hundred and four hundred consultations per day. It wasn't the more "glamorous" wounds that got most of them; it was the mundane—respiratory infections, exhaustion, and malaria.

"It won't last," I said, pointing to the crowds of U.N. workers who had swooped in and taken over Mammy's. In a small city like Freetown, their presence caused an immediate stir. Everyone knew that something was going down.

Oscar turned to look at the rows of blue-and-tans at the bar. "Another outbreak?"

"As far as we know, they're here to police the so-called peace." Out of the corner of my eye, I could see two skirts and wondered if there was anything to them. Oscar never failed to appreciate a good-looking woman. Sometimes I wondered what he would be like if we lived in London or Paris. Was it only our current situation that kept him faithful?

Oscar drained his Star beer and ordered another. "The rebels still at it?"

"Only where the diamonds are."

Christmas was a difficult time for people in the field. The holiday itself had so little bearing on any of our lives—except for the missionaries—and yet the angst surrounding it remained. I dreaded Christmas; it had become our holiday of guilt.

The truth was that no one wanted to leave. Sierra Leone was glowing, the war sleeping, and the United Nations had arrived. Things were heating up.

"Do you have anything going on at Christmas?" I asked as casually as I knew how.

"Not really." Oscar shook his head slowly, but his mind was clearly not on our conversation. He had huge circles under his eyes like bruises. He had lost weight.

"You need some time off." I leaned forward. "How about taking a trip to South Africa for the holidays?" My pace quickened. "We could head out to the Cape, embarrass ourselves on surfboards."

"My work"—he yawned—"you forgot about the hundreds of thousands of people who continue to descend on me and my clinic, shitting all over the place like a bad flood."

"You're growing bitter." I smiled. "And losing your compassionate edge."

"Compassionate edge?" He drained his beer. "God, you're awful. I hope you don't write crap like that."

"Oh, come on." I laughed. "It'll be fun, let's go off together." Suddenly I wanted nothing more than to be two young(ish) lovers on vacation with nothing more perplexing than a room-service menu to consider. I wanted to be a couple outside of our regular life. I wanted to be a real couple, in public.

"I can't," he said. "I have to go to Germany."

"What?" I leaned back, surprised. "You just told me that you had no plans."

"Other than going to Germany." He looked at me as though it were a given. "I don't."

"You're in your midforties"—I shook my head—"and you're still making going home to Mom your priority?" As soon as I had said these words, I realized that I had no idea whether his mother and father were still alive. We had never spoken about his family.

"Thank you for your concern." Oscar smiled. "I can assure you that I am not oedipal in the least."

"Why have we never talked about your family?"

"Because you're always talking about yours." The grin was authentic, the look in his eyes affectionate.

I could feel the beer opening up my capillaries, swelling my brain. "But you never told me about Christmas."

"I didn't think it was a big deal." He signed the check. At Mammy's everyone signed. "Look around you, here Christmas is just another day."

"Now you're using my own words against me?" I reached for a cigarette.

He snapped it away. "It was one of the few things you've said that made sense."

"Give me back my damn cigarette." I stared into his face, but Oscar was not in the mood for eye contact. "Why is it always the ones who have somewhere to go that tell everyone else that it's no big deal?"

Oscar lit the cigarette, took a long drag, and handed it to me. "You were saying the very same thing just a few moments ago, and you had nowhere to go."

But I did. I had Oscar to go to. He had become my country, my family, and my sofa to rest upon after too much turkey. I didn't care where I was on Christmas Day as long as I was with him. "Can I come?"

"To Germany?" He laughed. "Are you mad?"

"I promise I'll be good." I put my head on his shoulder. "I won't take up too much space."

"You're huge." He swatted me away. "What are you talking about?"

"Please." I didn't tell him that I was dying to see where he grew up, what his parents were like, and how he acted around them. That I deeply admired him and couldn't wait to see what had gone into the formulation of Oscar De Vries.

But he was silent. "Come." He put his arm around my waist and we walked out of the bar. Had I been less concerned with his lack of enthusiasm, I would have noticed Joseph sitting at the bar, watching every move we made.

Oscar did not invite me to Germany, and I would have spent the entire day in my room with my next best friend, the minibar, had it not been for Ollie Turkel-Bowden's Christmas party invitation.

Ollie Turkel-Bowden held a graduate degree in colonial studies from the esteemed London School of Oriental and African Studies. She was related to the queen on her mother's side and was a flamboyant lesbian. Ollie was massive, often wearing floppy hats painted in light pastels and chiffon skirts with her Wellington boots in the rainy season. She and her partner, a doughy Irish woman named Sinead who had tattoos above her overflowing buttocks, ran the International Red Cross office in Freetown as well as a dozen makeshift rescue centers throughout the city.

Their "fortnight parties" held in their corrugated iron garage on the hills overlooking Aberdeen Bay were legendary in the expat community. They were the only aid workers who had stuck it through all ten years of the war. Most thought they were devoted to the people; Oscar and I believed they were scared shitless to go home. The aid community was teeming with social outcasts who would take up any cause in order to get away from what they feared most—real life and their place in it.

I had been drinking steadily since I woke up on my drool-encrusted pillow at five o'clock that afternoon, still dressed in the same clothes I'd passed out in after gallantly waving off Oscar at Hastings Airport. I found that if I let the interval of sobriety go too long, the word *abandoned* began to knock at the door of my consciousness and, if left unquenched, it would howl for acknowledgement. I did not want to listen. I wanted to pretend Oscar didn't exist.

Charity worker that she was, Ollie had been patiently listening to my alcohol-induced emotional outpouring since I'd arrived at her hilltop home at nine that evening. "But he didn't invite me, Ollie; I asked, I threw myself out there, and he laughed." I would whine every time words in Oscar's defense would come out of her minuscule mouth. There were stretches of time I couldn't account for because I could not stop staring at her tiny mouth. It was pink and arched like Betty Boop's.

She probably didn't use toilet paper. There were Western women who lived in third world countries who gave up using sanitary products altogether. Perhaps I'd write about it for *National Geographic,* I thought to myself while Ollie's mouth moved. That was it, I thought, pushing through the sea of island rum that was now my spinal fluid; I'd become a freelance writer for *National Geographic,* and in no time they'd offer me a ridiculous sum to leave the *Times* and I'd show Oscar what I could do with my Christmas vacation. While he was sitting around eating strudel and wieners that were sadly larger than his own, I would change history with pen and paper.

"So you see," she said, patting me on the knee with a look of resolution. "It's just the way Oscar is, so stop worrying, luv."

But I had no idea what she'd said. I was lost in the world of *National Geographic,* deep in the diamond pits of Koidu and the amp centers of Freetown. I could see the picture for the article's cover page: black toddler, arms reaching up as though in supplication to God. Both arms amputated above the wrist, with diamond bracelets hanging loosely at her elbows.

"Am I disturbing you?" A voice interrupted the *National Geographic* scenario. I didn't recognize him at first, given the unfamiliar surroundings and the tremendous amounts of alcohol. But when he took a seat next to me, my heart leapt; it was Joseph.

I shifted my position, uncrossed my legs, and then tucked them under me. Dangling the scuffed hiking boots was not going to improve appearances much. "Did it look like I was talking to someone?"

"As a matter of fact, it did." His teeth were the perfect length, color, and size for his mouth. "Yourself."

"No," I said, running a hand through my hair and flipping it over to one side. "Just untangling a few kinks in a story I'm working on."

He wore the same flip-flops I'd seen him in months earlier, but there was something about the way he sat, his posture, that made him seem more relaxed this time. "What's it about?"

"Koidu." I reached for the drink in front of me, then stopped the moment the rum hit my lips. "Diamonds and the Diamond Corp who controls them."

"Not a very popular subject." He wore a light blue button-down dress shirt and a pair of dark blue jeans, which he filled like a line-backer.

In the background I could hear an attempted sing-along to Lib-erace's Christmas soundtrack. There must have been fifty people in Ollie and Sinead's corrugated iron bungalow drinking rum and Cokes and gin fizzes. And Oscar? Where was Oscar? Wrapped around a perfect blonde, a specimen worthy of Dr. Mengele himself, Aryan and gravity-defying, drinking peppermint schnapps in front of a ridiculously tall Christmas tree, belting out songs to the fatherland?

Joseph leaned into me, his face and those lips just inches from mine. "Where were you just then?" He put his bottle on the coffee table.

"Troubles." I smiled. "In troubleland where the boyfriend isn't who you think he is and the job isn't what you want it to be."

"Ah." He laid his hands on mine. "You were in life." He lifted me up to dance. "We all need to take a break from life once in a while."

He wrapped his arm around my shoulder and took my hand in his, and with enough space in between us for a third person he began a careful box step. I felt shaky in his embrace, unsure, in awe, and more than a little drunk. We danced, always at arm's length, until the music ended.

"Alright, you two, it's time to say good night," Ollie said as she walked past. "The booze is gone, Santa's bushed."

"May I take you home?" Joseph pulled out keys to his U.N. jeep and waved them in front of my face. "I haven't been drinking."

He pulled a cable-knit sweater over his head, and I watched in quiet admiration as the fabric stretched over his wide shoulders and thick back. "Let me drive you," he said, putting his hand on my shoulder. "I know the roads better than most." Oscar would have told me to take a cab, no question. "I could be your tour guide, so to speak."

"So you *are* from here." I felt the thrill of discovery taking hold.

"I am." He took my backpack and we walked out the door like a couple, wishing strangers a happy new year as we left. "Born and raised."

"Are you Creole?" The Creoles in Sierra Leone were the city elite, educated and opinionated and completely separate from the tribal Africans, such as the Temne or the Mende, which made up the rest of the population. They spoke like American Creoles from the south. To quote Stevens, the man behind modern-day Sierra Leone, *"Dem see soak leopard, dem call am puss"*—some people see a wet leopard and mistake it for a pussy cat—their history was self-made. They were self-taught and they were, in many respects, free from the constraints of tribal politics.

"Temne," he said, "from the north, originally."

Ollie's ramshackle of a house was on a mountaintop surrounded by reeds of green elephant grass that stood over six feet tall and moved with the wind. I walked a little faster to the car. "I don't know how they live up here all alone."

"Scares you?" Joseph opened the passenger door to the jeep and I slid in. It was getting chilly and I was starting to sober up. In the all-embracing buzz of my third rum and Coke, the place was charming, mysterious, and even quaint with its homemade curtains and woven African carpets. Now it was seriously freaking me out.

"I prefer Mammy Yoko's." I clutched my jacket closer to me and leaned forward to check the dash. There were no clues as to who he was or what he did for the U.N.; the car was unusually bare. "Everything under lock and key, phones that work, police, all the accoutrements of the civilized world."

"Civilized world?" His long upper body bounced up as we hit a particularly large hole. "Where would I find that?"

"You sound like a journalist." I pulled out a smoke. "Now, why would you sound like a journalist?"

"You mean I sound like a cynic." He declined the cigarette and I put mine away, too. "I'm not."

"Then what are you?"

"I am an African, a Sierra Leoneon, who now works with the United Nations to try to bring peace to this country, this city of my childhood." He opened his arms wide as though to scoop up the lush mountains, the red earth, and the great expanse of ocean. "All of this was my playground."

I kept at him. "So you're with the peacekeeping force, UNAMSIL?"

He drove for a moment without speaking. "Yes."

"And?" I saw the smile at the corners of his eyes. I knew he was too damn refined, too smart to be just a human shield. "Who else?"

"Can't say." He stared straight ahead, his profile graceful against the night sky.

"The Brits." I shook his knee. "You're with the British army."

"So you've answered your own question." His words were meaningful and slow, very African, very eventual. "Have you ever been to Kissy Terminal?"

We had made it down from the hills above Freetown and were now at sea level. "Yes," I said, "and no offense, but it epitomizes African planning."

Joseph pulled the jeep up to the small dock where ferries ran to and from Lungi airport across the bay. When there was bad weather or swells, the ferries would stop altogether, causing delays and overcrowding beyond imagination. Even in good weather the tide had been known to act up, causing ferries to take up to six hours to cross the small bay. But international planes had stopped landing at Lungi airport, and the ferry had sunk. In the vacant bay the blue and gray diesel water pirogues sat still.

Joseph came around to open my door and took my hand. "There was a reason for it, you know, besides dodgy African planning." He pulled me up on the hood of the car and sat next to me. "It was built to keep people out of Freetown, to protect its people."

"Not anymore." I shook out a cigarette and lit one.

"Not for a long time." He leaned back and watched the African sky, a sky that made you feel as close to outer space as you were ever going to get. "We tried to escape through here when I was ten years old, but the ferries had stopped."

I knew who he was running from. Any man of his age and his academic background had to have fallen out of favor with the puppet master of the country, Siaka Stevens. It was the age-old classic post-colonial African story. The black savior coming to rescue his people after decades of white colonization, only to rob and annihilate them even more. "Did you get out?"

"I did." His chest rose and fell, and I was torn between feeling his pain and wondering what those pecs would look like without his sweater. "But my father was not so lucky. He died in jail with the other idealists."

"So now you're back from the West, riding in the U.N. jeep, armed with education and spurned on by revenge."

He looked over and grinned.

"A bit cliché?" I glanced at him and he nodded. In his eyes, I could see it all. He was so present, so accessible, it made me feel that way, too, like we were right there, together.

"What brings you here?" Joseph turned onto his stomach and I wished he hadn't. His ass was like two halves of a melon and his face was warm, open, and inviting, and to make matters even worse, he hadn't made a single pass at me the entire night. All of this was catching me dangerously off guard.

"You mean what am I running from?" It was the question everyone asked us journalists/charity workers. Unless we were frightfully ugly or hopelessly without potential, we all had to be running or hiding from something. "Myself."

"Too easy." He laughed. "What's with the doc?"

"We work together." I arched my back and stretched. It felt late, but I didn't want to look at my watch for confirmation. "You know him?"

Another grin. "I know his reputation." He tossed the remnants of a bagel at a group of meowing cats.

My stomach constricted. "Are we talking professional or personal?"

He didn't even bat an eye. "Professional."

He put his hands under his chin and looked at me. "But you're involved?"

I didn't want him to stop looking at me the way he did and yet I didn't want to lie. "We are."

"When I was growing up we used to hop on a poda-poda." He shot me a glance.

"I know what they are," I said, referring to the small buses that terrorized the roads, bringing people from the surrounding areas to and from Freetown.

"We used to come here, right here," he said, looking out to sea, "and watch the lights at Lungi. And on Christmas and New Year's Eve after a night of drinking and dancing, we'd still come here. You should have seen what it was like before the war."

I touched his hand and felt his long black fingers coil around mine. "I can't imagine this place whole."

For me Sierra Leone was exactly like one of its amputated children—it had once been beautiful and its people pure, but the war, the diamonds, and the politicking had sucked all the goodness out and left nothing but a truncated and dismembered shell. "It would be strange for me to be here and feel peace."

"It's hard to imagine," he admitted, "but I know what it feels like."

"Will you show it to me?" I could feel my heart pound as I asked him. "Will you take me to the places no one has seen before?"

Joseph held my hand tighter. "You are not mine to take, Ms. Roch, and this country is no longer mine to travel as I wish."

I nodded and left my hand where it was, intertwined in his. Did I feel guilty? It all depended upon whose arms Oscar was spending his Christmas in.

CHAPTER FIFTEEN

I WAS IN SEARCH OF TRUTH. THAT WAS MY MOTTO, AND possibly even the lead sentence of my soon-to-be blockbuster *National Geographic* cover piece on the diamond mines of Koidu. I was to embody the essence of *National Geographic,* to be the young intrepid war reporter, the female version of Sebastian Junger. I saw it all clearly as I filled my flask and packed my duffel bag with enough clean underwear and tank tops to last me the week.

I hailed a cab outside the hotel. "Connaught Hospital, please."

The roads were wet from a few errant showers the night before, and the streets, dripping with red sand from the harmattan, were unusually quiet. Freetown was normally chaotic, lawless, and teeming with industry. Sidewalks were turned into markets, roads were closed off to make way for stalls, and cars zoomed in and out any which way they could. Cabdrivers were, as usual, the worst offenders. But today it felt like a ride through the countryside. It scared the shit out of me.

"Stop here." I rolled down the window to take a look at some of the headlines on display at the newsstands. There was nothing that stood out, nothing to explain the quiet. "Carry on." But something was afoot, I could feel it in my bones.

Connaught Hospital was glazed in red like a rusty ship, but the men who sat in front eating cola nuts didn't seem to care. When the British designed Freetown to resemble a tropical paradise with sprawling white buildings and complicated latticework, they must have assumed that there would always be a workforce armed and ready to sweep away the red sand that blew in from the desert and blanketed the city from December through February.

Oscar's car, a white cruiser that resembled the U.N. jeeps enough to keep me out of trouble, was parked in the back under a makeshift garage. I could take it without causing too much suspicion, but the problem was that his keys were in his room, on his bedside table.

The main staircase was crowded with people, young boys mostly, waiting to see a doctor or just passing the time. They stared at me with zero expression, blank and hollow, without hope or fear of what might happen next. Hope, of course, had been taken away from them and there really was nothing left for them to fear. It had all been done.

"Miss!" Footsteps raced up behind me. "You can't go up there, Miss." But I kept going, in the hope that another tragedy would come between us, and her attention would be diverted. But she kept coming. "That's the doctor's quarters, Miss!"

I swung around. "Ms. Katie, right?"

A look of surprise overtook her doggedness. "Yes?" Her eyes grew wide with suspicion.

I walked toward her and put out my hand. "I'm Dr. de Vries's girlfriend."

"Yes." She nodded, totally unimpressed.

"I forgot something in his room." I pointed and smiled. "I need to get it."

"You can't." Her girth would have been imposing had she been over five feet. "Not without doctor."

I exhaled and dropped my bag. "Look, Ms. Katie, I appreciate your doing your job, but I'm leaving, as you can see, and I need to get something I left in his drawer. Call him, call whoever you need to, but I'm going in that room."

"No one here," she said in tropical English.

"Perfect." I sat down on the step and held my head in my hands. Rules, why were rules so staunchly followed in here and not out there?

"Ms. Katie!" A scream interrupted our standoff. "We need you down here in the operating theater STAT."

"You must leave now." She waved her finger at me and I nodded. There was nothing left for her to do.

As soon as her pillbug-shaped body was out of sight, I continued up the stairs, smiling to myself as bystanders clapped.

I took the key out of my pocket, one of those heavy iron castle-keys that conjured up visions of madhouses. The room was pitch black but as soon as I turned on the one lightbulb, I could see Oscar everywhere. He must have been in a hurry when he left. The bed was unmade and the closet was open, his clothes thrown all over the bed, the floor, and the one chair next to the sink. I missed him terribly.

I picked up his jeans and held them up to my waist, tempted to try them on but too scared to find that they wouldn't fit. His torn T-shirts, running shoes, and nylon shorts evoked images of long runs on Lumley Beach when the sun was just about to set. I would sit on the sand and watch as he went up and down the two-mile beach until the muscles in his legs throbbed and his T-shirt was drenched. Every time he ran past me, I looked up from my book, hoping to find that he was glancing at me, too, waiting for me with a smile, a nod, or even a look of fatigue. But he never stopped to acknowledge me, never came out of that place where Oscar was alone, totally alone, complete.

The key was in the top shallow drawer of his bedside table. I took it and was about to shut the drawer when I noticed a stack of photographs. I sat at the edge of the bed, carefully extracting them from the drawer. My stomach fluttered. I looked at the first photo, then the second and third. They were of us, of me and him, taken on our trip to the refugee camps in Guinea. I looked at my watch. It was getting late, but God, I wanted to snoop.

I stuck my hand further inside the drawer and found a watch and a ring, both old and gold. I had never seen him wear either. I got down on my knees, ready to open the lower drawer when I heard voices. I remained still, waiting for them to pass, but they didn't.

"Nurse says cut the sheets, cut the towels, she tells me, and I'm like there no sheets to cut, man," one orderly complained. "We all out of sheets."

"Shit, man," the other concurred. "There's nothing left to soak the blood but our own shirts."

"Docs all on vacation, MSF, shit, man," he snorted. "Sans Frontières because they're always skipping borders to Club Med."

"That's cold, man." He paused. "Doc Oscar, alright, he work day and night fixing for no pay."

"Any man who leave a wife at home that looks like that one there on the wall"—a broom swished—"got something very wrong in the head, my man. He needs to go to Kissy to fix his head." They both laughed and kept talking in Krio, a language I could barely piece together until I heard the word *wife,* then my brain suddenly became a Krio-to-English dictionary.

I jumped over the bed and my boot caught in the sheet. "Shit," I yelled before I hit the ground.

The brooms fell to the floor. "What's that then?" I heard running, but they ran in the opposite direction of the room, probably suspecting a bomb because of the thunderous thud my ass made when it hit the floor.

"Wife? What wife?" I said over and over again as I drove out of Freetown, past the drunkards and amputees perched in the roots of the city's landmark Cotton Tree, past the empty graffiti and bundles of plastic-coated sheeting stained red. Who in the hell were they talking about, anyway? Not that ridiculous *Teen Beat*–looking picture of the Farrah Fawcett wannabe that still hung on Oscar's wall despite our seven months of dating. That picture, as insignificant as I knew it to be, still irked the hell out of me.

I had to get out, away from the city and the dregs of humanity who had taken it hostage. It was their revenge on Freetown, a city once praised for its educated middle class. Now it was nothing more than a human junkyard housing broken lives and dismembered people.

Further into the countryside, green replaced the dingy red; banana leaves were larger than the hood of the car; fruit, flowers, colors, and smells were so vivid you could close your eyes and know, with complete certainty, that you were in Africa. Wife. Why the hell did they call her his wife?

At the checkpoint to Port Loko, a small city twenty miles northeast of Freetown, my car was stopped and the trunk was searched, not by U.N. forces but by what appeared to be members of the Nigerian-led forces. I rolled down my window, feeling a gust of warm wet air, like hot chicken broth, hit my face.

"Papers." Looking as serious as if he were guarding an atomic bomb, the soldier scanned my American passport carefully, flipping back and forth on the pages and then going back to my picture. When the heavily stamped extension insert fell out of the passport, he shook his head and called to one of his friends. "Busy lady," they whistled, but I had long ago stopped flirting with officials, especially in a country where uniforms meant nothing—and everything.

The soldier behind the silver mirror sunglasses curled his long fingers over the top of my window and whispered into my face. "What you have?"

"I don't understand," I said.

"For me." He smiled and tapped his chest with his index finger. "Pretty white lady, have something for me?"

I was scared. "No, I have nothing. I am a journalist."

"Let her pass." A familiar voice called out from behind the car. "Her," he commanded, "let her pass. Now."

The soldier, who could not have been more than eighteen, acted like a petulant child. He tossed the passport into my lap. I drove through, careful not to hit one of the many bodies who came up to my windows brandishing nothing more than their stumps dressed in dirty linens. This was Africa, this is what the Africans had done to Africa.

Joseph came up to the car and tapped on my window. "Have you completely taken leave of your senses?"

"You promised a tour, remember?" I held the door open. "Hop in."

It was hard to imagine, I said as he filled my mind with a virtual tour of all that Koidu in eastern Sierra Leone had before the war. An air-conditioned cinema, an American-style diner complete with a jukebox and red vinyl booths. An epicurean market stocked with all the right ingredients for a French soufflé, a Lebanese *kofte,* or an Indian curry. Liquor stores stocked with high-priced champagne, boutiques with evening gowns, and even a Volkswagen dealership. This was the Koidu he knew, before Siaka Stevens took power in 1967.

"They stole, too, but it was different," Joseph explained from his desk at their makeshift offices at Port Loko. "Then it was organized. De Beers flew in with their private plane once a week, deposited the cash directly into the hands of the Sierra Leone Selection Trust, and collected their diamonds." He laughed. "Funny thing, diamonds are nothing more than carbon, no intrinsic value at all."

"Value is assigned by consumers," I pointed out.

"Yes, how could I forget." He steepled his fingers in front of his face and paused. "The West."

At that moment he looked like a young activist, albeit a fashion-conscious one. Joseph dressed as though he were off on safari in his British green military pants, lace-up boots, and crisp white shirt rolled up to the elbows. His arms were stupendous, their rich color and defined muscles threatening to throw me off balance.

"Clearly Sierra Leone was better off under the British," I said. "You said it yourself, Koidu had cinemas, air-conditioned diners." I shook my head. "There were Mercedes and Beetles, for God's sake. And what is there now?"

He looked at me from beneath his blue beret but there was no sign of disapproval. "Please, continue." His eyes were focused but kind and, unlike Oscar, he seemed genuinely interested in what I had to say.

"Now there are dead bodies bubbling in the streams like over-turned rafts, armed teenagers high on cocaine hiding in bushes along the roads waiting to amputate arms and legs, which are in turn feeding the stray-dog population." My heart raced. "And Koidu, the city that once had a cinema, a diner, and schoolchildren who walked without fear, has been razed to the ground. There's nothing left of it, just holes where people dig for diamonds at gunpoint."

"Many would argue that before independence, Koidu saw little of the profits from the diamonds." He leaned forward. "That the war today is about the rape of the northeast by the Freetown elite. That it is a war of the peasants, the uneducated, the illiterate demanding equality with Freetown, demanding what's due to them."

I wondered how much Joseph was toeing the U.N. party line. "Then why aren't they chopping off the arms and legs of the government bureaucrats who stole from them? Why are the rebels making deals with De Beers in Liberia and pocketing the cash rather than rebuilding Koidu? Please, tell me." I shook my head in exasperation. "Why is this such a cruel place, Joseph?"

He came around to where I stood. "I don't know," he whispered. "I, too, have never understood the cruelty I have witnessed here. It is of an ungodly proportion, it defies imagination or explanation."

"So what are you doing here?" I stared. "Why did you come back?"

"I have a debt to pay." He rubbed his chest. "For me there is no turning back."

"What's that supposed to mean?"

"It means we will end it." He picked up the keys to my car. "And now it's time for you to go home."

"But," I stammered, "I just got here." I grabbed my bag containing my do-it-yourself *National Geographic* story kit containing a camera, tape recorder, two fresh cassettes, and two new notebooks. "I have to get to Koidu." What I really wanted was to get close to Liberia. That was where the story was, the truth to the ten-year war that wouldn't really end until Charles Taylor, Liberia's president and ultimate diamond broker, said so.

"In case you haven't noticed, there's a war going on." There was a tap at the door and Joseph jumped to attention. "Excuse me." He stepped outside and returned within minutes.

"What now?" I half-smiled. "I'm being arrested?"

But Joseph wasn't laughing. "I have to go back to Freetown immediately." He took me by the elbow and ushered me gently into Oscar's car. I could tell by the hard set of his jaw that I had no room for maneuvering.

We drove in silence, doors locked, windows rolled up, but I looked at the passing scenery differently with Joseph in the car. His family had been killed, but he didn't speak of them. His village, just south of Koidu, had been decimated, but he didn't talk of it.

We were stopped at a checkpoint and Joseph told the armed boys that the vehicle belonged to the U.N. He glanced at me and whispered. "This is Oscar's car, isn't it?"

I nodded, feeling embarrassed. "I borrowed it."

"He's out of the country," Joseph reminded me. In Sierra Leone, a country where you could burn out an entire village without repercussion, lifting someone's car was a big deal. "We could go to jail for this."

"Only if you tell." We drove on in silence until we entered the long straight road that marked the entry into Freetown. Cotton Tree stood directly in front of us; its blackened branches appeared brittle and curled against the night sky. It was nearly impossible to distinguish the lepers from the amputees that made their home among the roots.

"I never understood the fuss, either." Joseph looked up at the tree. "As a child it scared me."

"It scares me as an adult," I said under my breath. Freetown looked and felt more ominous now than it had before the New Year. I didn't know whether it was because I was starting to see it through the eyes of one of its own. We arrived at the hospital. Joseph parked the car under the shed, ran through the hospital's lobby, and disappeared up the central staircase and into Oscar's room. In less than a half hour he returned to the front steps where he had left me.

"What now?" I glanced over at him. It was approaching dinnertime.

"I have a meeting at Mammy's first thing in the morning."

I kicked the mud from my heel and swung my pack over my shoulder. It struck me as funny: he was clean, perfectly put together, and I looked as though I'd been sleeping in a tent for a week.

"Can I buy you dinner?" he asked.

"You can." I bit my lower lip hard to hide the smile that threatened to overtake my face.

Joseph raised his hand to hail a cab. "Quite a looker your man Oscar has on his wall." His voice was without the slightest hint of amusement or intrigue. "The janitors said something about it being his wife."

I stared straight ahead, still biting my lip.

When weren't the janitors gossiping outside Oscar's room? I continued looking straight ahead, trying to lose myself in the sunset over the bay of Lumley.

Instead of dinner at the hotel, Joseph took me to a spot called Number Two River, where the river meets the Atlantic Ocean. White U.N. land cruisers and other non–governmental agency cars competed for space in the dirt lot. "This looks like Club U.N."

Joseph paid the cabdriver a stack of leones and we walked through the brush and into the clearing, side by side. On the beach were privately run thatched huts called rondavels, where drinks and dinner were being served. No one seemed to pay much attention to a white reporter and a black U.N. worker eating an early supper together.

We dropped our bags in an empty rondavel and ordered two beers. On the beach, before a sunset that seemed to burn through the sky, we watched U.N. employees of all different races and colors play a game of football/rugby/soccer.

"Talk about a melting pot, eh?" Joseph smiled lazily as he watched the soldiers fumble the ball. Local boys half dressed but laden with lighters, gums, and lukewarm sodas shouted and giggled as they cheered them on.

We both laughed when two men, Indian or Pakistani, or maybe

half-castes—who could tell?—made a touchdown and dropped their pants and mooned the opposing team. "Do you think they know why they're here?"

Joseph jumped at the answer as if it had already been formulated and was waiting to be recited. "They're here because this is where they were dropped off. They're here because they're paid, clothed, and treated with respect, some of them for the first time in their lives." His long black fingers clasped the wet bottle, nearly encircling it with one hand. They were a flawless black, without hair or scars to interrupt their grace. "They're here because they need a point to their lives."

"And what about you?" Joseph seemed as different from them as I did. Where they appeared carefree and easy to read, Joseph was burdened and complex. His eyes, as luscious as I found them, gave away nothing.

"I am Sierra Leoneon, my reasons are different." He rolled over on his stomach and pushed up onto his knees, then his feet. He stood looking down at me, shielding my face from the sun, like an eclipse. "And so is my job."

"Which is what, exactly?" I followed him to the rondavel, where he ordered fish grilled over a wood fire, skewered roasted vegetables, and jollof rice cooked in sun-soaked tomatoes and sweet onions.

"For a reporter, you're not exactly well-briefed." His breath was sweet with beer and at this point just about anything he said turned me on. "I'm a lawyer," he went on. "International law, with a strong focus on human rights law. I am here to help."

"I get it." I nodded but I was beginning not to care whether I broke through his party line. I was too busy fending off the hormones attacking my brain, signaling me to do things I could not do and supplying visuals that I had to brush away. I had to be decent, I was still with Oscar. I pushed away my beer and ordered a bottle of water.

"So do you think he's married?" Joseph's tone was caring but weighted. "Oscar, I mean."

"No, no." I brushed it off and grabbed my beer. "It's just a picture"—my voice trailed—"of a girl, a model, I guess."

"And he keeps a photo of a model, a stranger, on his wall?" Joseph looked as incredulous as I felt. "Seems a bit strange."

I had to laugh. "Tell me about it."

When the sun was gone, the beach took on an eerie feel, one that made me feel incredibly foreign and, given what I had learned about the political climate, more than a little anxious. Joseph looked up from his plate. "So you plan to marry the good doctor, have a family, and settle in Sierra Leone?"

The food inside my mouth felt like it was growing, taking up more and more space as the seconds went by and he waited for a response.

Joseph smiled as I chewed. *"ER* meets *Out of Africa,* is it?"

His words struck me like a slap in the face, but I pretended to be amused. "Sounds like a good episode." Did he see me as nothing more complicated than an American with an *Out of Africa* obsession? Had he been reading my diary?

"In England and America you can plan your life"—I shot him a look, his right hand went up—"but Africa is like a snake that is silent, pliable one minute and then attacking you with everything it's got the next. We don't walk around with images in our heads like you do of the perfect house, the perfect family, the perfect life. Instead we approach each day with one thought."

I knew it was coming. "And that is?"

"Inchallah."

The word hung in the air like a defining line between the worlds we came from. Our countries were polar opposites, his, the poorest and most inhabitable, and mine the superpower, the holder of the American dream that had become everyone's dream. There was no reason for optimism here; it was considered garish and in bad taste, like a woman wearing diamonds at lunch. And we were the newborns, full of hope and living in the future. And we were buying the diamonds.

Neither of us spoke until music filled the air and men and women danced barefoot on the sand.

"Would you like to dance?" Joseph took my hand, his voice smooth and deep.

My face felt flush with chili and cardamon. "If God is willing."

"He is." Joseph led me out of the rondavel and we joined the others, dancing like elephants stuck in the mud, slow and awkward but smiling all the same. I wrapped my arms around him, feeling a steady pulse at the back of his neck.

"What about you?" I asked. "Do you plan on marrying and raising a family here?"

Joseph swayed back and forth to the music. But before he could answer I put my hands to his lips. "Don't say it," I commanded. "Please, I can't hear it again."

He took my hand away and mouthed, *"Inchallah."*

"You! I told you not to say that." I put both my hands against his chest, but the moment my fingertips made contact, I stopped. I could feel something through his shirt, something raised and thick across his chest. I traced my index finger along the mounds until I came to the last letter. "What . . ." I stared up at his face, speechless and scared.

He removed my hands from his wounds. "Please, no more questions." He put his cheek to mine. "For now, just listen to the music and dance with me."

CHAPTER SIXTEEN

"SO THE BASTARD WAS MARRIED?" ANIKA ASKED AS WE attempted the first round of stretching in our grueling postnatal aerobics class called Mommercize, a word that I found terrifying in and of itself.

"Haven't we stretched enough?" I winced right along with the twelve other women who had propped up their Snap N Go's against the wall to undergo more punishment during our twenty waking hours of the day. "And why did you bring Jeremiah when you've got Joyce?"

"To remind myself why my stomach looks like a three-tiered Bundt cake." She rolled back into a sitting position. "I can't believe he was married!"

"And cheating." I bent with her. "Married and cheating."

"Sounds like my first husband." Anika turned, her face the color of red clay.

"At least you were married." Out of the corner of my eye I spotted a woman wearing an actual G-string over a pair of tights so pink she looked like a side of ham. She wore a matching pink T-shirt with the line *I'm with him* written in baby footprints. Across the wall there was her baby, the poor sod, who wore the same T-shirt with the message *I'm with her.*

"He was a lobster fisherman," Anika turned both ways and whispered, "but his full-time job was drinking and screwing every New England barmaid he could find."

As I took in her well-groomed blonde hair, her black yoga pants and new Nikes, I realized that Anika was a complete reinvention of her former self and I silently applauded her. I could never complete such an overhaul. I would leave behind fragments, forget details, and come out the worse for it.

While most of the children slept, some were being rocked by the nannies who usually tagged along to the mommy events. They were the ones dressed in white nurse's outfits carrying more bags than they had arms and struggling to keep up with a Starbucks-toting mom. The Starbucks cup at early-morning classes almost always meant help waited in the back of the car.

"So what'd he say?" We stood up as instructed and begin to twist from the middle only.

"Ladies!" The instructor, who wore silky jazz pants low on the waist and flaring over her three-inch Mary Janes and a microphone attached to her head, clapped twice. "I mean Mommies." Nearly everyone in the room turned to look at their prize. "No hopping or jumping, remember, give those poor uteruses their well-deserved break."

"Only that he had known her. Her name was Pamela Bunchen, and she was his first love. They had been together on and off for ten years, from the time he was fifteen years old. She grew up in Hamburg two streets from him and their parents hated one another. That, of course, had cemented their liaison."

"Sure it did." Anika winked. "The things we have to look forward to."

"He said that she was the love of his life but that she had a terrible heroin problem which he had been unable to cure. They had broken up over it and she was somewhere in the streets of Berlin, Munich, or Amsterdam scoring drugs and singing tunes with a one-eyed dog and a talking bird." Okay, there was no dog, but there might have been a bird. I still wanted to hit myself hard across the face for having believed it at the time.

"A heroin addict?" Anika raised her eyebrows. "And she looked like that?"

"My thoughts exactly. She looked like fucking Christie Brinkley pre–Billy Joel."

"So that wasn't his wife?"

Anika and I walked across the room. "According to Oscar, she was an old girlfriend, one that he hadn't seen in years and feared might be dead."

She stopped. "But it *was* his wife?" Other women slowed next to us, listening. "And he told you it was an old girlfriend?"

"His very real-life wife who lives in Berlin. And get this, she's some sort of dentist/ballet dancer."

"You're shitting me." Anika and I grabbed two sets of five-pound weights and began doing curls. "He was passing the photo off as his long-lost girlfriend when it was really his wife?"

"And by the time I found out," I said, barely able to believe it myself, "we'd been together for eighteen months."

"And you were pregnant."

I had slept with him. I knew he wasn't the one, but still I slept with him. I dropped the weights on the ground and fell back on the floor. It had been the dirty end to a dirty war, and there was no one left. In the end, no amount of selfless acts could reawaken what I had once felt for Oscar. He was dead to me. And there were no arms left for me to run into. "And Joseph was gone."

"Was that where you wanted to go?" Anika shook her head. "Into a life where you could never belong, to a man you didn't even know?"

"Yes." I stepped back. "And by the way, when did you get so philosophical?"

"It must be the yoga stretch pants." She tugged at the waistband. "They're cutting off the circulation as we speak."

"Ladies!" the instructor shouted. "Water and nursing break." We marched up to our babies, whose eyes were beginning to flutter with need.

"I know you fell for him, but Joseph sounds like trouble." Anika drew a blanket over her shoulder and lifted her sports bra. I, of course, did not have a nursing blanket, so I just whipped it out all the same.

She was right, Joseph was trouble. But it was his trouble, he owned it without ever letting it spill onto those around him.

"He must have lied like a dog when you confronted him," Anika said. "I know mine did."

I was quiet.

Anika stopped cold while the others continued their ode to Barney. "You did confront Oscar, didn't you?"

"I left," I said, wiping my forehead with a bandana. "I think he got the message."

"For such a toughie, you sure are scared," Anika joked.

"Alright, ladies, switch sides if you're nursing on both sides," the instructor's voice boomed. "Burp if you're bottle-feeding."

I did as I was told and switched Halla to the other side. "By the way, why in the hell did you drag me here?"

"To improve your attitude." Anika leaned back against the wall as though tanning in the park. And she wasn't alone in her ease. Everywhere I turned, women were gabbing loudly, hungry for advice and contact. There were G-strings, high-thigh leotards, and low-slung jazz pants exposing stomachs and asses that would ordinarily be worthy of shame. But here there was no shame, only freedom from it.

I pulled at my tank top. "It's going to take a lot more than one class."

Later that night, after Halla went to sleep for her four-hour stretch, I opened the box of mail sent to me by the paper. For some twisted reason, I lit candles and put music on before going into the spare bedroom, where I kept the boxes. The pile looked promising, with lots of foreign stamps. There were two postcards from a woman named Robin, a journalist who had been in the Middle East with me. Apparently, she had made bureau chief in Israel for the *Guardian*.

"Great." I tossed the card in the trash. "She'll never get to experience the joys of leaking breasts or the thrill of Mommy and Me groups where middle-age women sit around and talk about the color of discharge."

There were three account notices from Barclay's Bank advising me of what I'd already known—I was broke in London—and an envelope whose contents told me that I could expect none of the security deposit back from my apartment. "Wonderful."

Then I noticed the blue water stains that his pen made and his loopy cursive handwriting. Oscar.

My stomach fluttered. I had wanted it to be there so desperately and yet I would have been happier had there been nothing. I had left him without a forwarding address and he didn't know how to use a computer—the cut was complete, I'd thought.

The date was December 2000. The bastard had waited two months to pick up a pen and write.

Dear Saffron,

You've been gone for two months now and it appears that you won't be coming back. I should have told you about her, them, I should not have lied, that was clearly wrong. But to put it bluntly, you made the situation happen. I was faithful to you until the day I found that hair, that black man's pubic hair, in our bed.

My heart pumped harder and my pulse quickened. His condescension and complete skewing of the facts took my breath away, but I wanted more.

I was never in love with them. I thought of you, Saff, you were always the one I wanted.

It's all over now, let it be forgotten, I've forgiven you because we fit, you and I, and that is a rare and strange thing. Please come home.

Oscar

"What a load of bullshit." I threw the envelope in the trash. Either he still had no idea that I *knew* his not-so-little secret, or he was pretending I didn't in the hope that I wouldn't bring it up and we could go on as though she didn't exist. Not likely. The next envelope I opened also had a stamp from Sierra Leone but the handwriting was different, slanted and slightly curly. Ollie.

Saffy!!

Where are you! We've been dying to get in touch with you. Oscar said you rushed off to England because of something

*he did. Don't be such a stupid cow, come home, have a drink
at Paddy's and a shag and it will all be over, babe.*

Babe was a simply awful thing to call someone. But coming
from a two-hundred-pound gay Englishwoman, it was particularly
disconcerting.

> *Since you've been gone, the press has had amnesia on the sub-
> ject of Sierra Leone. They signed the peace accord, the war's
> over, who cares. But Freetown's never been worse. The ran-
> dom attacks by rebels in the East have got the natives scared
> shitless, so what do they do? They come to FT and we're
> swamped, both in refugees and rain. And we all know what
> that leads to, don't we? A cocktail of malaria, malnutrition,
> and typhoid. We've got shit for supplies, food is at an all-time
> low, and we're in desperate need of help. Other than that,
> things are rosy. Our garden is coming along nicely. I even
> managed to get Sin to plant roses and climbing jasmine on
> either side of the front door. You must come and see it.*

> *Ollie and Sin*

P.S. Still no word on Joseph.

My heart dropped as I checked the date on the envelope. Her
letter was postmarked June 30, one week after I had left London. I
had left Freetown in October, after searching for Joseph for months.
The consensus was that he was hiding out in Liberia, the rebels had
him, or he was dead. Generating sympathy or help for an expat
Sierra Leoneon working for the British was futile. No one cared, the
country was shattered, aid workers were stretched, the Brits were
leaving, and I'd been fighting a fatigue I did not understand. But I

knew it; I knew it when I left Freetown that Joseph was going to get himself killed trying to wrestle his country back from the rebels. He'd vanished and apparently not returned.

"Point Elsewhere, Point Elsewhere," I said to myself as I paced the small living room. I felt like I was already in Point Elsewhere, I felt like my life should be called Point Elsewhere. I could see Freetown, smell the damp fecundity, and feel the vitality of the people. Life oozed out of every inch of soil, every ripe pink banana, every wide, simple smile, and every tear-filled eye. There, life knocked at your door, it woke you up, jostled you until you became a part of it. And Joseph was somewhere in it.

There was one more letter from Africa, another from Oscar. It was dated June 2001. The month Halla was born.

Saffron,

I've tried to find you for the better part of the year but you've left London and the only other place I knew you'd go was Heaven's house. No luck there, either.

I put down the letter. "Shit." Oscar had the number for the beach house—how did he manage that? I thought back to my many attempts at writing down numbers and addresses where he could reach me, but he always left them behind like a dirty Kleenex. I prayed he got the answering machine and not Francis. There was the small matter of the clause in Heaven's will that was never far from my mind, the one that said if Oscar was to come to the house, I would lose the inheritance.

At first I thought Heaven must have been slightly crazed when adding that condition, but then I realized that it was perfectly in character. Heaven hated men and had done her best to raise me to hate them as well. Oscar had been the first real threat to her world-view of the two of us growing old together at Point Elsewhere. And she made sure he would never come between us.

> *I don't know where you've gone, but it is now clear that you are not coming back. I have made you leave the country you love and quit your profession (which may actually be a good thing), but what pains me most of all is that I've lost my soul mate, the woman I wanted to grow old with.*

"What a lying bastard!" I slapped the letter against my knee. It was almost pathological.

> *I am fast approaching fifty; I have given my life to my career and have nothing but loss to show for it. There are no children, no homes, no bank accounts and no future without you. I have put your indiscretion behind me, it is dead and buried. Won't you rise to the occasion and do the same for me?*

I felt like I was going to puke.

> *I don't even know if you'll get this, I don't know if you still care about me and our life together here. You're probably onto the next war, Afghanistan or Pakistan, and maybe even your next love.*

I closed my eyes; they burned.

It was midnight, seven in the morning in Sierra Leone. I picked up the phone and dialed the clinic. The phone crackled and I imagined the electricity fighting to get through the broken, scarred lines and into Ollie's phone.

"Hello?" She sounded puzzled.

"Ollie?" I said loudly, suddenly feeling like an awkward American. "Is that you?"

"Who else would be up at the crack of dawn, eh?" She laughed. "The boss is who, right?"

"The boss." I smiled into the phone, feeling the flood of my past life take hold of me.

"Tell me about your flight, all the numbers and so on," Ollie fired off in typical fashion. "I'll be there with wings on, my dear, you have no idea how sorely missed you are, and not as a bloody journalist, as a friend. These days there are too many twenty-somethings traipsing around pretending to want to help," she ranted. "How can they bloody help in tank tops and bloody cut-off shorts that show their backside every time they bend over to pick up a bag of rice? We have to get police in to remove them before all hell breaks loose—"

"Ollie," I interrupted, smiling all the while.

"I mean it's bloody ridiculous," she continued, "this is no Club Med, what about respecting these people's cultures, what about the taboo of savagery and all that—"

"Ollie!" I screamed. "I have to talk to you."

"Right, your flight number—"

I could see her searching around her cluttered office for a pen, pencil, or paintbrush. "Have they found Joseph?"

There was dead silence on the other line. "No." Her voice dropped to a sad pitch. "Nothing yet, but we mustn't lose hope, you know. He's a very smart man, knows his way around the country, he'll turn up."

"But he's been gone for so long, Ollie." The words sounded foreign to me, as though they had no meaning. The last time I'd seen him he was in bad shape, living a double life, going deep into his cover pretending to be the savage he could never be.

"I know, dear."

"And you know what's on his chest, Ollie." I took a deep breath. "If they see it, he's dead."

"Yes, I know," she said, sounding remarkably and irritatingly English.

"You know everyone, Ollie." I held the phone so hard my hands were red. "Find out what it will take to find him and bring him back."

Ollie cleared her throat. "He could be dead, you know."

"Dead or alive," I said, "see what it'll take." And just like that Halla woke up and the room filled with her cries.

"You know what it'll take just as well as I do." Ollie paused. "What in the hell is that?"

"Long story." The cries grew louder. "And one that will have to wait until we're face-to-face drinking Cool Daddy gin."

"Cheers," Ollie's voice boomed.

"Find him, Ollie, find him for me." I hung up the phone and ran to my daughter, all four limbs outstretched and angry, shrieking as though abandoned.

It was truly the last thing I wanted to do, but when Alice had invited me a few days earlier to visit the new Getty Museum, I could not say no. She was armed with the perfect solution for every excuse I could come up with.

"I'd love to go"—I nodded self-confidently—"but there aren't any car seats in those shuttles." I winced. "And we'd have the strollers, the diaper bags, my God, where would we put all of that?" I had a mental image of the airport shuttle stuffed full of people and their massive Samsonite suitcases. And for what? To see a few chipped paintings?

"I've taken the liberty of booking us a spot," she said comfortably, "two spots to be exact."

"Oh." Damn, I didn't know you could do that. "But what will we do with the children?"

"I've already been there twice since Michael was born." She handed me the reservation time and the Getty booklets. "It's very child friendly."

"Wow," I said, feeling more and more uncomfortable by the second. Alice was a waiter; she stood there and waited it out. Had she pulled the, "Oh, it's alright, I can cancel those reservations anytime," I would have jumped at it. I would have told her how much I wanted to go, but that I'd rather do it when the kids were a little older.

We would have laughed and walked to our cars knowing the truth, which was that she had offered and I had refused. But not with Alice, no, she waited and let me sweat it out. It was an interview skill, a tactic really, one that I'd lacked throughout my professional career. Waiting was a far more effective tool than words any day.

"There's a family room, places to nurse, rest, change diapers." She folded her arms, making no move to put her son into the car. I felt like I was engaging in a game of chicken.

"Sounds perfect, I guess," I said and watched as a small smile took over her face. She had won.

"We'll meet you at eleven o'clock on Tuesday." She unclicked her Snap N Go. "Down below in front of the tram."

"Alright then," I said, feeling defeated. "We'll be there."

And so I was. On time, no less. Little did I know that she was taking me there under slightly false pretenses.

"Religious art is amazing, isn't it?" She mused over a particularly garish example of Christ being nailed to the cross. "Everything you need to know about a culture is there." In this rendition, large nails were being impaled into his skin and the painter, a fifteenth-century

Italian, had gone to great lengths to show the skin curling away from the embedding ten-inch-thick nail.

I stared on, dazed at the imagery on every wall—red paint the color of freshly spilled blood, the cross in brilliant gold. Women cried and men stared, lost and humbled as their leader was being killed and reborn before them. "I see nothing here that doesn't go on every day out there," I said.

"That's a funny thing to say." Alice shot me a questioning look.

"You know what I mean," I said, dropping the act. In the women's lounges with powder blue carpets and rose-flavored water, where nursing was treated like a sacred act, we could not talk of such things, but out here we could. "War is about greed, Alice, it's always been about greed." I glanced up at a picture of the Madonna. "Not about spreading the word of God."

"I see it as love." She waved her hand over the walls. "These paintings are here because of the love of Christ."

"Money, Alice, money." I smiled, but my heart raced. "The Crusades were about money, the war in the Sudan is about oil, the war in Sierra Leone is about diamonds. The death of Christ was about power. No one fights over Tibet, no one cares about Haiti."

"I am a missionary, I have to believe in this." Alice slowly pushed her sleeping white child nestled in a perfectly clean blue-and-white-checked baby seat through the foyer into the next room, a grand room with canvases as large as a living room wall. But the art did not change. Christ was still bleeding, beseeching, with women huddled sadly nearby and men looking on, robbed of action.

I followed behind her. "Doesn't it ever strike you that these characters never change, it's non-evolving? And we evolve every day. This is nothing but a picture out of an old fable." I put both elbows on top of Halla's pram and looked up. "We don't need to feel little anymore, we don't need to think in terms of good and evil—"

"But it simplifies things," she interrupted quietly.

"For who?" I stared. "For the natives you've tried for centuries to indoctrinate?"

"We've done a lot of good, too," she said.

"I know." I hesitated, trying to cool my temperature. While it was true that some missions offered beds and medical supplies to victims of war, over the years they had done far more harm than good. "But tell me, do you really believe that spreading the word of Christ is helping the people of Africa?"

Alice paused, her eyes bouncing off the walls. Clearly, this was not a new question. "My husband does."

I nodded slowly. "I see."

"He's spent his life there," she said wearily, "and wants to return to the Sudan as soon as Michael can have his first round of shots."

"Will you go?" The Sudan was rough, no place at all for a child; any Sudanese would tell you that.

"I have to," Alice said so quietly I had to raise myself up to hear her. "He's my husband, he's Michael's father."

"He won't miss him for the first year," I said, "so why not stay here?"

"Sometimes I don't know what's worse, the unreality of this place or the reality of that place." Alice pushed forward through the massive glass-and-chrome doors that opened out onto a terrace overlooking the Getty gardens and the whole of Los Angeles.

"I'm having a hard time with that, too." I looked over and felt a certain admiration for the unadorned profile of a woman who loved her husband enough to make his passion her own.

"Would you go back?" She turned to face me.

"If I had someone to go back to"—I glanced down at my daughter who slept soundly—"in a New York minute."

Alice's visible surprise settled into an understanding smile. "You must have loved him very much."

Sadness fell over me. "More and more every day."

Chapter Seventeen

WE DANCED ON THE BEACH UNTIL CURFEW. ANITA BAKER played over and over again until most of the others finished and sat down. We didn't say a word; the music was enough. Small bonfires along the beach flickered in the mellow breeze. I was in rapture with this man.

"Come back to the hotel with me," I whispered in his ear, passion overtaking common sense.

Joseph paused, his hot breath tickling my ear. "Are you sure?"

"Absolutely." My lips were nearly inside his ear.

"But we'll walk in separately, take separate elevators"—he kissed me lightly on the cheek—"avoid the cameras."

"Don't want to be seen with one of us, do you?" I whispered back.

He took my hand and pulled me toward the car. "You *are* an amoral bunch."

Mammy Yoko's was busy. Incoming U.N. personnel were being delivered to the city's most popular hotel by the truckload. It was also just past curfew and the lobby was crammed with people who looked like they were inexplicably thrown out of a nightclub and were looking for the next party.

Joseph was waiting in my room, standing with his back to me, looking out the window.

"I didn't see you." I threw my pack down on the coffee table and approached him. "I was worried you got held up."

"I slipped right past you." His voice was quiet. "No one saw me."

The letters on his chest came back to me at that moment, questions popping up in my mind.

"Joseph." My voice was shaky. I needed to be told the truth. "What does it mean?"

His back was broad, his physicality apparent but not intimidating. "Who am I, you mean?"

"Yeah." I lit a cigarette and sat at the edge of the bed. "That, too." Strangely, the sexual cravings that I had felt earlier at the beach were gone and in their place, real questions and concern.

He turned to face me, with his shirt unbuttoned and open. My eyes trailed down and stopped at the *U*. It looked as though it had been carved into the breastplate; the center was deep, the skin splaying out at the sides, like burnt sausage, curling back into the muscles. The scar tissue went from mauve to black.

"Dear God." I stared without moving. I had seen dozens of these markings, but they were fresh, florid pink and still wet with blood and infection. This was old, judging by the tissue, but the look in his eyes told me that the pain was very present.

"Unfortunately, they were rather zealous rebels, new recruits"— he turned back to the window—"and enjoyed making their point seen and felt."

"When?"

"Less than ten years ago." Joseph stopped. "We lived in an important region, as you know, and my parents were important people within the industry."

"Diamonds." I exhaled tiredly. It was tiring, all of it, like seeing the same child shot over and over again for a pack of gum he didn't take. Rebels storming villages and branding men like cattle. If Sierra Leone hadn't been so rich, the people wouldn't have been so poor.

"Did you think I was one of them? One of Foday Sankoh's right-hand men? Or did you think I was a spy?" He turned and walked toward me. "Sent by Sankoh to infiltrate the U.N. and government forces?"

"I like that one." I nodded. "Intriguing, sexy even." Joseph kneeled by my feet and put his chin on my knees.

"How did you get so beautiful?" Comments about my looks had the same effect on me every time, no matter who gave them. They made me deeply uncomfortable, like I was naked and under the microscope. "Plenty of cigarettes, wine before lunch," I joked, "getting your ass shot at ten months of the year."

"Where are you from?" He would not stop looking at me. "Where do you get those blue eyes that scream Hitler Youth and then those dark curls and olive skin that make me think of Sardinia?"

I had to laugh.

"What's so funny?"

"No one has ever guessed," I said, embarrassed. "My father was Corsican, my mother, Dutch."

"You say *was?*" Joseph peered at me. "Are they dead?"

"No, I don't think so." I turned away. "Are you tired?"

"I am." He dropped his line of questioning. "I'm glad we did this."

I pointed to the bed. "And not that?"

He grinned. "And definitely not that."

"I think it's over between Oscar and me." I sat on the bed.

Joseph was quiet. He took my hand in his.

I pulled him down next to me. "May I?"

He nodded and studied my face as I carefully buttoned his shirt all the way to the top. In the wrong hands, the letters spelled a death sentence. "Will you lie down with me for a bit?"

Joseph took my face in his and kissed me good night. I put my head in the curve of his shoulder and closed my eyes.

When I woke the following morning at sunrise, he was gone.

But on the left side of my bed, Oscar's side of my bed, there remained a small sample of his DNA.

"So that's the pubic hair story?" Anika crossed her arms. "That's Oscar's entire explanation for cheating on you? The discovery of what looked like a pubic hair in your bed?" She drained the last of her Frappuccino as we sat in Starbucks waiting for the clock to strike and Nancy's party to begin. "For not telling you he was married?" She shook her head in disapproval. "Weak, very weak.

"And he's a doctor on top of it," Anika mused. "Wouldn't he know the difference?"

"I guess he didn't have his microscope handy."

"Did he ever?" Anika teased.

I glanced at my watch. "We better start packing it up."

"Hold on." She waved me back to the chair. "They'll need to eat again soon, let's wait it out here."

"You just want to be late."

"That, too." She pointed her large green straw at me. "So you didn't do anything with Joseph that night other than spoon?"

"Yeah." I cringed at her choice of words. "That about sums it up."

"Have you ever wondered why you're not having sex with any of these guys?" Anika looked around the room and lowered her voice. "I mean, what is it with you?"

"Don't tell me you and Warren are at it every night?"

"Yeah, I actually don't mind it with him, hated it with the last one, but with him, it's different."

"Must be the age," I jabbed, but she licked her lips as though I had hit the nail on the head, so to speak.

"I never knew it could be so good." Anika looked away.

Under the ceiling of a three-million-dollar house, with nothing to worry about but who's going to clean your carpets next week, I'll bet.

Even though she flitted around dropping recipes like Betty Crocker, Anika was jealous. It was in the way she pretended not to be impressed, the way she chatted with the uniformed staff as though she had been surrounded by waitstaff her entire life and was therefore kinder to them than, say, the average nouveau riche high school dropout. It was in the way she had declined Nancy's invitation to take a tour of the house when the rest of us panted like puppies, the way she glanced dismissively at the impressive Boteros that were spread across the walls like wallpaper.

Nancy's home, bought and paid for in full, was on Mapleton Drive in Holmby Hills, where it would appear that each inhabitant had a Napoleonic complex greater than the next. This was the street of serious money—not Merv Griffin blue-haired money, but serious international-arms-dealing, drug-smuggling money, the kind with bald, dark, fat men wearing gold Cartier glasses and pointy black crocodile slip-on shoes driving mustard yellow Bentleys—money. There were so many rooms in the scaled-down "but genuine *refrabrique* Versailles," as Nancy put it (with a French accent that made my eyes water), that we were taken to only the most important—read ostentatious—ones.

"The projection room, Stan's baby." She wagged her finger at us and we all smiled like schoolgirls. "Other than Winston, of course." The room had twenty red leather seats, with individual art deco side tables for popcorn and soft drinks, or drinks from the fully stocked bar. "This is where it all comes from," she gloated. "Stan's genius blooms here."

Stan made his millions backing films. As his successes became uniquely consistent year after year, he was able to raise money without question and take a cut of the film's profits.

"This is the master bedroom." We all stood by the large French doors and stared into a showroom of white and yellow wealth. There was no dirt here, no stains, no unmade bed. There was no toilet in the bathroom, only a bathtub in Italian marble separated from a shower by a sheet of stained Murano glass.

Then, in the far corner of the suite, I spied a picture of Stan.

I walked across the spongy alabaster carpet with nearly the same trepidation as I would across an alligator-infested river. I picked up the frame and had to stop myself from laughing.

"Stan." Nancy touched the hugely bloated face staring back at me with narrow beady eyes and gave her fingers a kiss. As hard as I looked, I could not see genius blossoming from this man; he would have eaten it.

"Where was this taken?" There was only so much one could say when holding such a terrifying picture. Anika would have loved it. He wore a straw hat, white Izod shirt, and khakis to his knees, and everything clung to him as he held up his drink and posed with a black man in a high-collared, starched white uniform who appeared weary under the weight of his client but eager for a tip.

"Let me see." Sophia reached for the frame and I could see a smile instantly form on her lips. "He looks so handsome here, Nancy. What a great shot."

Not only did the picture prove to every passing stranger without a shadow of a doubt that Nancy had married him for his money, it also reinforced my belief that Sophia was a liar. A big-mouth and a liar.

"Bermuda, my first trimester." Nancy narrowed her eyes and ran her fingers through her short wavy hair, the color of gold-beige foundation. "I was ten pounds lighter there."

"But you only gained twenty pounds altogether," Alice, the voice of absolute objectivity, chimed in. "How could you still have ten pounds to go?"

"Now let me think." Nancy put her fingers to her head and tapped her temples. "Could it be because I've only lost ten?"

Alice didn't respond. She didn't seem as acquainted with caustic humor and sarcasm as some of us were, like the chain mail we put on every day before our morning coffee.

"I think Alice's point was that you look like you've already lost all of the baby weight." As much as it killed me to compliment Nancy, I had to stick up for Alice. She seemed so out of place with her dark roots and red bangs, not to mention moral fiber. The only fiber Nancy had was the kind she bought at the pharmacy for those days when she'd dipped into the potato chips one too many times.

Nancy looked at me and winked. "Boy, you journalists don't miss a beat."

Downstairs Anika was in the kitchen watching three Filipino women pull sheets of puff pastries out of professional-grade steel ovens that lined the wall.

"Hey, Saff, come here, you've got to taste this." She handed me an egg roll. "Saff, this is Maria, she's one of the chefs here. Maria, this is my good friend Saffron."

"Hello," I said as Anika introduced me to everyone in the kitchen, first and last names. "We'd better get outside; Nancy's got something for the kids."

"What can the kids possibly do or see at three months of age?" She wiped a crumb from my face and hit the speed-dial on her sleek phone. "Hold on, I just want to see whether Warren's landed." She put her hand over the mouthpiece. "He's on his way to London," she whispered loudly. "Big project over there, might even meet the queen."

I tapped my foot against the million-dollar marble, most likely flown block by block from Nero's last Roman palace to Stan's. "If the plane crashed, you would have heard about it on CNN." I pointed to the door. "Come on."

"Sweet." She grinned. "Come over later, we'll finish that bottle of wine."

"I thought I did."

"I'm talking about the second one you opened." I stared and Anika nodded. "Oh, yeah, I saw that one, too."

"It's impossible for a middle-aged woman to drink around here." I pulled her through the double doors. "It's time you made an appearance."

"What?" She threw up her hands. "Nancy can't wait?"

It turned out that Stan had purchased two lots, one for the house and one for the garden, and with all the taste of a Brooklyn movie producer, he had turned the latter into something his son would use in the not-too-distant future to get girls to sleep with him. There were underwater caves, waterfalls, and shallow Jacuzzis surrounded by palm trees, bamboo, and wide banana leaves. "Are those birds real?" Sophia asked the question that I had been dying to ask. We were surrounded by the long rolling squeaks and deep intermittent squawks of tropical birds.

"Another thing Stan did." Nancy pointed to a black box. "Computer-generated," she said. "Makes you feel like you're in the tropics."

In the park behind the pool, Nancy had set up red-white-and-blue Adirondack chairs with matching blankets in a semicircle. "You can either put the babies on the blankets or on your lap, whichever is easier for you." Drinks—all nonalcoholic—and organic low-fat party foods were at the front. No wonder Stan reached for the Ruffles.

When we had gotten our plates, claimed our babies, and rooted our large bottoms—Sophia and Nancy not included—in our uncomfortable but oh so patriotic Adirondack chairs, the show began. First there was a clown, who came up and made our children cry, then music and a bubble show that rivaled the water dance at the Bellagio for a finale.

When it was over, we were all speechless. Sophia's eyeballs looked dry from lack of blinking; her face displayed a kind of quiet awe mixed with rapture that people had when they wanted something so badly. Anika had cradled Jeremiah to her chest—face down—the entire time in a sort of quiet protest of Nancy's extravagance. Alice looked slightly traumatized, as though she had entered an entirely different world with values she could not comprehend.

It was my first children's party in Los Angeles, so all I could ask was who was this for? It certainly wasn't for the nearly sightless invertebrates we were all holding and it couldn't be for us. We were of absolutely no importance in Nancy's world, certainly not worthy of such display and expense.

When we left the house, Alice came up behind me but said nothing until I had finished putting Halla in the backseat. "Can I ask you something?" I turned. "You were in Africa for five years, right?"

I closed the door. "On and off for eight."

"How does all of that"—she pointed at the house, which rose behind us like a monument—"make you feel?"

Alice looked at me with such earnestness. This party had answered her query, the question that had kept her up at night, the question she had asked me when we stood on the Getty balcony.

I knew what she wanted from me; she wanted confirmation, she wanted truth. And I could see it, the truly wasteful nature of it all, the superhuman ass-kissing, the meaninglessness. But I wasn't there yet. I wasn't ready to renounce it, to give up on it. This was to be my life. I had nowhere else to go.

"It makes me . . . it makes me. . ." I paused, regretting it before I said it. "It makes me feel grateful to have all of you as friends."

"Me, too," she hedged, "yeah." As Alice walked back to her gray Volvo station wagon, I was painfully aware that with those few words, that simple discounting, I had made her feel that she was an outcast here. And that, I knew too well, was a terrible place to be.

The drive home was unbearable; the laws of Beverly Hills had made driving with any speed or creativity impossible. Brain death was required of all who entered the city limits. I felt like escaping. I wanted to get away, to travel, to live someone else's life. I'd had it with the Pampers vs. Huggies debate; bottle vs. nipple; Beverly Hills vs. Beverlywood. I couldn't take the perfectly manicured front lawns, the complete regard for timely stops at traffic signs. I didn't think I could stomach one more session at the Pump Station.

But more than anything there was a hole in my stomach that reopened each morning and grew every time I checked my in-box for news of Joseph. Somehow, I felt that distance would bring about the end of Joseph.

Take the money and run, a voice leaked through the barrier of my subconscious. *Ten million dollars can buy back his life. Your life.*

Traffic in Beverly Hills was mind numbing, not like in Sierra Leone, where you could have your windows washed, buy a paper, a new set of towels, a gun.

I imagined pulling my jeep off the road and driving straight through the center divider, all the way down Sunset Boulevard. In

Freetown, driving outside the lines was a viable alternative to sitting in traffic and it felt damn liberating.

We were not moving, I was going nowhere. Halla began to cry. "Fuck!" I screamed. "Fuck, fuck, fuck!!!" Halla wailed.

"I can't take this anymore." I lowered my cheek against the steering wheel. "I'm not cut out to be a full-time, I-have-no-other-interests, stay-at-home mom, I'm not like them." Tears ran down my cheeks and I felt numb as Halla continued to shriek. It was all so ridiculous—the house, the party—but what really got me was the lie. The lie women told themselves and others, that they were in love with the person they slept next to each night.

But what really pushed me over the edge was Sophia. No, you can't smile with a schoolgirl crush, bat your eyelashes, and say "He's cute," because clearly he was not. He looked like a man-eating ogre. Her comment was so outlandish, so troubling, it merited a call to Family Services. Did she really believe that by looking at his photograph and kissing ass in absentia, she would secure her place at Spago? And then she actually had the nerve to invite me to juice with her over on Rodeo.

"Juice?" I looked at her like she had completely lost it.

"Yeah." She laughed lightly, totally unaware of the grudge I was holding against her for opening her big mouth. "You know the stuff you mix with alcohol to make cocktails?"

I looked at her as though she'd said Stan was handsome again. "I'd never waste perfectly good alcohol on fruit juice."

She looked at me for the first time. "I'm just kidding, Saff, what's with you?"

She had the nerve to ask. "Nothing." I didn't have the nerve to answer.

"I can't wait to hear more about Africa, Oscar, and how you got on after that first date."

"His penis didn't grow, Sophia," I said and left her in the garden, staring after me, slowly putting the pieces together one by one until she understood.

Sell, sell, sell.

How could I belong here? I didn't, and I didn't want to. And yet when Alice asked me the one question that—despite my best efforts—had been knocking at the doors of my consciousness, I couldn't answer it truly. It was this lie that made my head swell with anger. This place, with all of its complex mind-fucking and masterful manipulation, was eating me up. Africa had kept me true. Alice knew it and so did I.

Heaven will never know the difference.

But I would. I would know that I had broken the will of a woman who'd taken me in when no one wanted me; a woman who sent me off to do great things. The woman who'd waited a lifetime for me to return.

The car was becoming stifling with Halla's hot screams. I turned my head, put one hand over the back of the car seat, and shook it. "For fuck's sake will you please shut up!" When I went to shake the seat again, I caught a woman in the next lane staring at me with a look of horror on her face. I saw the horror of me in her eyes. My heart continued to beat off the rage that I had been in the throes of, and my cheeks burned with heat and shame. Halla continued to scream but there was nowhere we could go, nothing I could do. We were stuck there on Sunset Boulevard between Mapleton Drive and Beverly Glen, she in her car seat and me in my life.

Halla kept crying as we made our way around the accident at the intersection of Beverly Glen and Sunset, which took two hours. By the time we got home, she had cried herself to sleep. Her eyes looked like two red welts and her fists were still clenched. I felt as though I didn't have the right to touch her after the way I had behaved.

Weekends for a new mother were hard. Just imagine everything that you'd enjoy doing on your day off—going to the gym, the movies, the beach, the spa, shopping, eating out, biking, blading, bowling. And then consider doing it with a baby who can't sit or be carried and needs unhindered access to your breasts every two hours or, when the crying is bad, every half an hour. You will also require immediate access to a baby changing table in case there is a leak or, worse, a two-way eruption, as well as a spot to completely change outfits because of said eruption. Then consider the company, because no one wants to go out with you anywhere. The only place for a new mother and baby is home, which can start to feel like house arrest.

If I went below, I'd get all the Hindu-Buddhism shit, which was no good at all while I was feeling selfishly sorry for myself, and if I popped over to Sally and Dean's, they'd load me up with cheap gin and drag me down memory lane *again*. I did not want to live on memory alone.

"I used to be doing that," I said under my breath as I closed the windows, pulled the drapes, and turned on CNN. "I knew her"—I clicked the channel—"and her"—click—"and her." Christiane Amanpour's face filled the screen, her eyes excited with the news she was about to deliver. We're storytellers, I thought to myself as I watched her in front of the Wailing Wall in Jerusalem. I stared at her eyes, watched the way her lips moved, and listened to her use of words; there was absolutely no waste. "How do you do it?" I wanted to pour myself into her. "How can you be a mother and an active war correspondent?"

"So I take it you left the baby at home then, Christiane?" a British interviewer asked. And then I heard it come from her lips, as though in answer to me. "My husband, James, and I share the responsibilities. When I travel he stays in London, and I do the same for him." Her lips moved as though they were frozen. Her lips always looked as though they were frozen. "It's the only way that works for us; that way we each have our careers and family."

"And you do it brilliantly."

"Piss off." I clicked off the television and fell asleep to open windows on crashing waves that roared into a chorus of *sell, sell, sell.*

CHAPTER EIGHTEEN

"LEAVE?" ANIKA ATE THREE MICROWAVE BROWNIES, THE kind that you mix with water and cook in the enclosed microwaveable bowl, one after the next. "You can't leave, not now." She poured a full glass of fruit punch and drank it. "Where else on earth will you get handed a ten-million-dollar beach house, a best friend, and a ready-made husband for Halla?"

I leaned back in one of the many Adirondack chairs she had purchased for her garden the day after Nancy's pool party. The realization that I'd had in my car about leaving all of this and moving back into the depths of hell had been coming on like a bad flu. I was now totally infected.

Anika refilled my glass with the most vile fruit punch ever. "You're seriously considering taking your daughter there? To Sierra Leone?" She glared. "A place no one would take their pet?"

Santa Ana winds had swept through the night before, eliminating any trace of pollution from the sky. It felt like Hawaii in Anika's backyard, soft warm winds sweeping through just in time to dry the water from your skin after a dip in the pool, which was heated to a perfect eighty-four degrees. This was the life, there was no question about it, but it was not my life.

Anika dipped into a bag of contraband Doritos. "It's because of your brother, isn't it?"

"He's not my brother." I filled my mouth with chips. "There's nothing genetic about our relationship at all."

She lowered her voice. "Is it the money?"

"I would be lying if I said it wasn't." I felt horrible guilt just saying the words.

"Money can be an awful thing." Anika closed her eyes and reclined further in her chair while our children slept.

It was a double-edged sword in L.A. If you had money, either through marriage or family, it was okay to discuss it, but if you didn't and talked of selling an inheritance in order to get it, you felt like a gold digger with no respect for family.

"So can poverty."

"Yes, but you're not poor."

"No, I'm not." I didn't want to get into my personal finances. It was one thing breezing into town and introducing yourself as a hotshot war correspondent from Africa who happened to grow up in Malibu, it was another admitting that you lived off an allowance at the age of thirty-eight.

As Oscar had said in his letter, at the age of fifty, he would have nothing but scars. I had a property that I was coming to believe would never feel like mine and I was itching to get out. I could feel it, my time was coming to an end.

Anika took my hands in hers and held them tightly. "So why do you want to sell so quickly?"

The intensity of her emotions touched me. "I have a friend who needs me."

"Well, I need you," she said, resuming her tanning position, "a lot."

"Yeah." I glanced around the garden, the pool, the spotless floor-to-ceiling windows. "Somehow I think you'll survive."

"Well, who is it?" she asked. "Who's taking you away from all this?"

"Joseph," I said quietly, "my friend Joseph."

Suddenly energized, Anika rolled over onto her stomach. "Ouch!"

I winced with her. "The boobs?"

Anika rolled back. "You would think that after nine months of not being able to sleep on your stomach, God would give us a break."

"Don't you know that God doesn't give breaks to women?"

"What did Joseph do now?" she asked.

"He's disappeared." I explained the e-mail from Ollie and the fact that I hadn't heard from him in nearly a year. "No one knows where he is."

"And you want to use the money—" She stopped.

"That about sums it up." Money was the only way to find out what really happened to him. Dead or alive, that kind of money would deliver him to me, since it was the only thing people were interested in over there. Some things are universal.

Anika studied me long and hard as though she had finally figured out the puzzle. "It's *him* that you love; it's always been, hasn't it?"

"I don't know. Oscar dazzled me at first, but Joseph quieted me. He feels like my center."

"Does he know it was him?" She scooted forward. "Oscar, I mean."

"I don't know," I said again. It all seemed so long ago.

"Was he different when he came back from Germany?" Anika asked. "Sweet and guilty?"

I tried to remember that day. Oscar was a complex man, nothing American about him at all. He arrived that afternoon and came immediately to my room. There was a swift knock at my door, which I ran to answer.

"I've missed you," I announced as I fumbled with the handle.

The door opened wide and there stood Oscar, looking as if he'd just come back from the Boer War. "That's quite a homecoming," he said with a grin. "Not entirely sure it was meant for me, but entertaining all the same."

Anika interrupted. "You thought it was Joseph?"

I closed my eyes and nodded.

"You're back." I walked backward, away from him, and tied the sash of my robe even tighter around my waist. His appearance made me feel cold, and I could feel myself pulling back, waiting for the next comment, the next criticism.

"Arrived this morning, went to the clinic to see how things were holding up." He plopped into my chair. "Disaster, of course, with all these local doctors playing doctor. Absolute disaster."

"Let's go for drinks on the beach." I picked up my jeans and pulled a light sweater from the closet.

"How about we go to bed instead?" he said with slightly glassy eyes and a wide grin.

I scanned the room looking for any trace of Joseph, who had left only that morning. The sheets had not been changed, nor the bed made. "I've been in all day, working," I said, "let's go out." He looked unconvinced and unwilling, but rose from his chair.

The Cape Sierra Hotel on the tip of the peninsula had been described as a fiscal blunder, built with nonexistent government funds to impress foreigners and get more foreign aid. But I loved the view there—magical, tropical, otherworldly.

"Did you miss it?" I asked Oscar over a cold beer at the bar. There was a wait for the dining room, with everyone anxious to get their fill before it was time to shove off into rebel territory.

Oscar sat back in his chair, relaxed and slightly complacent. "It's only been fifteen days."

"Felt longer." I touched his pinky with my hand. "Did you have a good time?"

He shrugged. "Germany is not a place I would call 'fun' really, and spending most of the time with my mother, well." He paused to drink.

A table opened up, and after ordering our meals, I launched into my idea for a saleable article on Koidu. Halfway through my pitch, Oscar put down his fork and knife and pushed aside his hamburger. "I've missed you, you know."

I looked at his face and saw the old Oscar, the one I'd gone to Parrot's Bay with, the one I'd watched heal penniless and powerless strangers night after night. "Me, too."

"I want to sleep with you." He took my hand. "Tonight."

"Why?" Anika interjected. "I just don't get it."

It was true, we made terrible love together. For us, it was the pull of making love, the mental and emotional sparring that provided the fire, not the physical act itself.

When we returned to the room, Oscar took a hot bath. Flight filth, he called it. I took the opportunity to scour the place for any signs of Joseph.

Oscar emerged wearing a towel around his tight waist, looking every bit Nietzsche's Superman. He was about to lie down when suddenly his body stiffened.

"What's wrong?" I touched his shoulder. "Did you forget something?"

Oscar didn't move or speak for a full minute. Then he stood up, turned his back to me, and slipped on a clean pair of shorts and a white T-shirt.

"Change your mind?" I said, feeling a guilty surge of relief.

He lay back on the bed, his body curled tightly into a ball, the sheets pulled up over his shoulders to his chin, like a small boy.

I sat up on my knees and looked down at him. There were tears running down his face. "What the hell's wrong?"

"There's a black pubic hair in your bed, Saffron," he said solemnly, "a black man's pubic hair."

"That's impossible." I pulled him toward me, but he wouldn't budge. "Well, a black hair, maybe, we're in Africa for God's sake, but a black pubic hair, no way."

"I'm a doctor." Oscar reached over and turned off his bedside light. "I know what a pubic hair looks like."

"But he never mentioned it again," I told Anika. Except to make a joke about my "black boyfriend" and ask me to give him the courtesy of changing the sheets in between my lovers.

Anika rolled onto her side and curled her body toward me. "Where was Joseph through all of this?"

"Gone," I said. "Like a cloud of smoke." I felt as though I had lost my new best friend. During that time, from February on, the U.N. peacekeepers were being harassed and taunted by every rebel out there, some 45,000 pissed-off palm-drunk kids with weapons. The peacekeepers were easy targets, since UNAMSIL's mandate was to keep the peace and that meant a policy of nonviolent nonintervention.

"When he did show up, Joseph's arrivals were hushed and quick—a dinner at a local seafood hut here, drinks at a nondescript bar there. He followed me home one night, his cab creeping along slowly, one block at a time. It scared me shitless until the door opened and I heard his voice." I closed my eyes and tried to relive it. The look on his face, the intrigue. It was all so incredible. "He took me to a local spot on Aberdeen, a place I would never walk into alone. A place I would not think Joseph would know." His face was drawn; his eyes darted around the room as if he expected someone to slip through the beaded curtain without a sound, aim a gun, and fire.

"What happened?" Anika gulped.

I took his face in my hands and held on for as long as I could. "I've missed you," I said. "Now, where the hell have you been?"

He carefully removed them, as though he didn't want me seen touching him, and placed them on the table. I knew it was for my protection. He said he'd been upcountry trying to talk some sense into the rebels. He put his head on the table and tapped it slightly. "But there is no hope; there will never be any hope. Greed has eaten their brains."

"They won't demobilize?" The sight of Joseph made my body feel like it had been starving for months. He had created a hole in me and no one could fill it but him.

"They want war," he said.

I looked at him and knew. "They're coming?"

"Possibly." Joseph and the rest of the team had been in discussions with rebel leaders in Massaika and Makeni, their two most important strongholds. "We urged them to continue on the road for peace, to enter into elections and rule side by side with Kabbah, and underlined that all war crimes had been commuted, but still that was not enough."

"What is?" But I knew the answer. Nothing.

"Just the diamonds." He told me he had to leave in ten minutes. "We have a rendezvous at Port Loko tonight."

"With who?" I said with a heavy heart. "The West Side Boys?"

He nodded. "And two other bandit groups that are threatening to attack U.N. forces."

His voice was cold, his accent more African than usual. I could not begin to imagine the magnitude and range of his emotions. "How are you?"

"Fine." He didn't look up. "I miss our time together."

I stopped. His face was so vivid, his eyes so full of pain that I could see his demise. I could not get the picture of his chest out of my mind. What would happen if the other U.N. soldiers saw *RUF* etched across his body? What would the Nigerian forces do, or even the rebels themselves? Joseph was everyone's most tantalizing scape-goat and war prize. "Two weeks later, fifty U.N. officers were ab-ducted. It was the beginning of spring, May, to be exact. The rebels were closing in. Freetown was surrounded."

"How awful." Anika's eyes were wide, but she had no idea. Not even I could fathom what Joseph had gone through trying to push back the rebels from the city gates. But he had succeeded, and he had lived.

As the far-away sounds of running sprinklers and buzzing lawn-mowers silenced us, I wondered what genetic stitch had made me totally unable to settle down.

"The truth is, even if Joseph weren't missing," I confessed, "I think I would still sell." Heaven's twisted logic weighed on me every hour of every day. "The way she's structured the will, I have to choose between living my life and living hers."

"So you go back, find Joseph, then what?" Anika asked. "You marry him?"

I shook my head. I was done with fairy tales.

"You go back to work?" The word sounded like a death sentence on her lips. "Why work when you don't have to?"

"There's nothing that I'd want more than to work." I heard a squeal that sounded like Halla. I jumped at the chance to check on her. Strangely enough, in the days since I had decided to move back, I was far more at peace with being her mother.

When I returned, Anika was flipping through a *Modern Garden* magazine. She picked up the pitcher and bowl of chips. "Want any more of these?"

"No, thanks, I can barely fit into my maternity pants." I fol-lowed her into the kitchen.

Anika removed an enormous domed pot and plugged it in. I watched her as she diced an onion, threw in four slabs of bacon, emptied the entire contents of a jumbo plastic bottle of barbecue sauce, and unwrapped white paper that covered the ribcage of a cow.

"Who are you trying to kill?" I teased.

"It's Warren's favorite." She seemed undaunted by the comment. "And it gets me out of my sexual duties for the evening." She pushed the ribs around with a large poker until they were smothered in sauce. "Maybe even two," she winked and added another half cube of butter.

If the women of Africa were as frigid as the ladies I had met at the Pump Station, AIDS would have far fewer victims.

She closed the lid and set the timer. I watched as she moved throughout the kitchen, preparing dinner without ever dirtying a pan. "How long does that thing take?"

"Five hours for ribs"—she sucked the wooden spoon—"so good the meat just falls off the bone."

I had to shake my head to rid myself of the images her words evoked.

She went into the pantry and returned with a roll of Hungry Man biscuits.

I was stunned. The quantity of food was grounds for a medical docudrama. "Are you having company?"

"No, it's just the three of us." She continued to twitter about the kitchen like a fifties housewife.

"But Jeremiah doesn't eat."

"We're a family." Anika defended her position. "We sit down at the table together every night. That's what families do."

"You see?" I picked up my diaper bag. "I'm not the settling kind."

When I had dreamed about having a family with Oscar, in the days before I learned he couldn't keep that tiny excuse for a digit in his pants, I saw a farm in the north of Sierra Leone, not too far from Freetown, but far enough to have some land, cows, and quiet. I dreamed of evening meals under the cloud-speckled sky with our children, our friends, and anyone who needed a meal and a place to sleep. I dreamed of being two people devoted to something so much greater than ourselves, and I dreamed of our children being colorless and nationless, like us.

In my dreams I had never envisioned crock pots or matching cutlery, dinner times or seating assignments. I was not trying to create and sustain my family through ritual; we were free and we were a family no matter how many times we were able to eat together.

But clearly it was a dream. In reality, Oscar was a cheat and a liar, Joseph was missing, and I wasn't making dinner for anyone.

Anika picked up Halla and handed her to me. "But you'd like to be."

"Yeah," I said, as if through a thick fog. "Sometimes I would."

Family. Family is meant to provide the link to the outside world, a bridge built by the parents for the children to succeed as adults.

So what happens when a mother abandons the father, steals the baby, and then abandons the baby? What happens then? Since Halla's birth, my mother's face had been a constant fixture in my subconscious, surfacing in sleep and in those moments when I felt overwhelming love for Halla. How could she have given me up?

I scanned the pictures, the stories on the walls of Heaven's house. Not a single person who shared my blood or Halla's blood was in the polished frames before me. Blood or money? Unwittingly, I was walking in my mother's footsteps and taking the money.

There was a knock at the door. "Yes?" I covered my chest with a burp cloth.

"Saff?" It was Francis.

"Come on in." I pulled a blanket up around Halla and let her continue using my nipple as a pacifier.

Francis stopped when he saw us. "I'm disturbing you." He backed away. "I'll come back."

"Oh, stay," I said. "It might not be too pretty to look at but it's not contagious."

Francis sat down at the edge of the sofa. "Al asked me to leave these with you." He stared at my face with great concentration, not letting his eyes go below the above-the-neck area. "It's just the trust stuff."

Suddenly I was tired. "Can I ask you something?"

"Of course." Francis was quiet.

I looked down at my feet and then up again. "Do you think I'm doing the wrong thing keeping Halla from knowing her father?"

"Yes." He paused thoughtfully. "I do. In theory I believe that every child has a right to know his or her parents and my practice supports that theory." His eyes grew sad as he talked about his brief relationship with his own father, how Heaven had kept them apart with lies. "Your mother did the same to you, Saffy."

"I know." His words brought my own concerns into focus. "The most selfless thing I could ever do—"

"And the most loving," he interrupted, "would be to give your child the chance to meet her father and decide for herself the kind of relationship she wants to have."

"Despite all the enormous shit that would come along with it." I laughed. "Because let me tell you, Oscar really is a shit."

"But you love him, don't you?" Francis's eyes were the color of fine marbleized turquoise.

"I did, yes." I pushed back the cuticles on my fingernails to avoid his stare.

"And now?"

"And now"—I exhaled, not wanting to get into it—"I am thinking not of myself but of Halla."

"Then you'll do the right thing."

"Do you understand that what you're saying has consequences?" I eyed him carefully.

"All decisions have consequences." He stood.

"Some are greater than others," I responded in a very David Carradine meets Grasshopper kind of way.

Francis smiled as though my words were a waste of my breath, as though he had known all along that I would sell. For him it was a forgone conclusion.

"Well?" I waited, hoping he would ease my conscience, but instead he walked to the door. I wanted him to stay, I wanted to talk to him about what I felt was becoming inevitable, but he was already on his way back to the beach.

A moment later there was a soft tap at the door. "Is that you again?" In spite of myself, I rushed to open it. "I thought you—" I stopped when I saw the pink robe and the matching pink slippers. "Sally?"

"Hello, dear." She smiled, her cheeks folding into a dozen folds. "I'm so sorry to bother you . . ."

"You can always bother me." I opened the door wider. "Would you like some tea?"

"Well," she continued the script without entering, "this came for you, by way of me." She held out the familiar tissue-thin blue envelope and my stomach dropped. "Must have gotten stuck between the catalogs and coupons."

I backed away from the paper-thin blue envelope. I wasn't even sure if I wanted to see it, knowing there was a chance it wasn't from him. On the outside, where the return address should have been, there was nothing, just three empty lines.

I grabbed it. "Thank you." I quickly closed the door. Carefully, as though it belonged to someone else, I slit the top of the envelope with a steak knife. The letter felt disappointingly slight. I peeled back the first page and smiled at his script, so recognizable and yet so foreign to me. My African, my love.

Then I saw the stamp in the upper-left corner. Pademba Road Prison, Freetown, Sierra Leone. Prison. They had caught him.

CHAPTER NINETEEN

I HAD FEARED THIS. SINCE OUR DANCE AT THE BEACH WHEN I first felt the letters on his chest.

I looked at the postmark and saw that the letter had been mailed to the West African branch of the *Sunday Times* in December, two months after my departure from Sierra Leone. It was now September, nine months later, and I was terrified of what I would find written inside. I had interviewed people at Pademba Prison, and I could not bear to think of Joseph behind those gates. My eyes quickly drifted down the page.

My dearest Saffron,

How your face brightens my day and holds my thoughts like a dream, a dream that keeps me from facing the realities of life at Pademba. It has not changed here, I don't think, since the great dissenters of Stevens's corrupt regime in the sixties and seventies. Executions occur in the dead of night and bodies are summarily removed and dumped in a place only God can witness. And to think that there are over fifteen thousand United Nations soldiers and British forces right outside these dank walls ensuring that the peace is adhered to. It has been weeks, no, months now and I have not received a sentence and I am a lawyer, of all things. It's almost funny, really, if you think of it.

I am writing to you, not for your sympathy or support, but to tell you that I never lied to you, never betrayed you. I've loved you since the moment I saw you in the cafeteria back when life was so simple. I loved you then and I love you now.

There is little that you or I can do with that information, however, because I am quite sure they'll never let me out of here. The rebels think I'm a traitor, the government forces, the Kamajors, think I am a rebel, and the British seem to think I am a very good spy, which reveals how frighteningly inaccurate their information really is.

I did not abandon you, Saffron, I was taken from you. I only hope that the decisions you made had nothing to do with my disappearance, and that you are happy, whether that means you decided to stay with Oscar or not. It's all water under the bridge, as they say, but at least it's clean water now.

I'll write when I have news, good news. Remember, Inchallah.

Amnesty International had no listing of a Joseph Hanna; neither did Human Rights Watch. I went to the United Nations Web page and searched for news on Sierra Leone, but there was no mention of hostages. I tapped away at CNN until I found a backlog of stories from the time I left; I did the same with BBC and every other reputable news organization. I besieged Ollie's in-box with a bevy of e-mails, all of which asked the same thing: Is there any way to find out whether he's still alive? But Joseph was not to be found, not even between the lines.

I combed my address book, looking for names of people I had known in Sierra Leone—journalists, lawyers, aid workers, doctors, and nongovernmental employees—who might still be there, firing off e-mails asking if there was anything they could do. I knew chances were that I would hear nothing.

It was nearly six o'clock in the morning when Halla's body arched and stretched, indicating that she wanted out of the cold uniformity of the bassinet and into my arms. She gulped as though she hadn't eaten for days. By the time I'd fed, burped, clothed, and attempted to give Halla my full attention, I had a response from Ollie.

Saff,

Received confirmation that Joseph is indeed being held at Pademba. Trial slated for next month. Accused of treason. Not good. Will write more when more comes in. In the meantime, pack and fly.

Ollie

Pack and fly—the good old days when I'd cram two pairs of underwear and a couple of tank tops into my overnight bag, stick a toothbrush in my pocket, and not count the days. The last time I'd done that was when Ollie and I had gone looking for Joseph in August 2000 after the rebels had kidnapped eleven British soldiers in northern Sierra Leone. No one had heard from Joseph in weeks. We were convinced that he was one of them. How we managed to come back alive nearly brought us to the church doors. We thought we were invincible, that our good motivations and our pure hearts were our armor. We were stupid.

But off we went in a tired medical vehicle, cruising through darkened, slippery, washed-out roads to find one man who neither of us knew very well but knew well enough to know that if the tables were turned, he would do the same.

When we arrived at the city's checkpoint, the achingly tall Nigerian U.N. officer stared at us, two unaccompanied white women, with a look of damning judgment. They were tired of white people doing stupid things. "And who might you be? Papers."

"*Sunday Times?*" He shook his head. "We're in the middle of a war, Miss, you can't come in, no reporters allowed." But Ollie's ID got an altogether different response. "Please." He ushered her in with a wave of his pink palm. "We need all the help we can get."

"Not without her." Ollie stared at him straight in the eye. "She's my right hand in this."

"What ID did you show him?" I asked seconds later, impressed to the core.

Ollie fished through her wallet and produced the winning card. "Attending physician, Aberdeen Clinic," it read, accompanied by a murky photograph of her.

"You're not an actual doctor, are you?" I stared at the card.

"Made it halfway through med school. Good enough for these parts, I'd say."

We drove up to a long, narrow cement building that had a line circling around it two or three times. There were hundreds of people in various stages of illness, some standing and carrying infants, some sitting, and others lying down altogether. Some, particularly the ones faced down, looked dead. Above the open door of the building, a small plaque read PORT LOKO MEDICAL CLINIC.

There did not seem to be a central command or any type of organization at all. Inside the clinic there were no beds—"They take them out from under the patients at night," the one and only nurse there told us when we asked.

"Then lock the door," I said, feeling glib.

She pointed. "They took those, too." I felt like an ass.

Every scrap of floor space was being used, kids sandwiched against adults with IV bags lying next to them on the floor. Needles were sterilized and reused until they were too dull to pierce the skin. Small metal buckets of urine and feces dotted the hallways and were often lying on their sides, emptied of all contents. No wonder malaria was rampant.

"Where are the doctors?" Ollie finally got up the courage to ask. There was always that second, that moment when you could not ask, not engage, and just leave. I was tempted.

The African nurse, who must have once been so proud of her starched uniform and the elevated status it brought her, now seemed oblivious to the blood-splattered skirt, the dirt and grime that ringed the outside of her sleeves and collar. "There is one doctor, a local resident, who has remained," she replied.

Ollie looked at her pointedly. "No one else?"

I knew what she was getting at, and so did the nurse. "No, ma'am, there are no Western doctors here. They were evacuated when the rebels came back."

"There must be someone in charge here," Ollie's voice began to rise, her British sensibilities finally shaken. "There are far too many people here for there not to be someone in charge."

The nurse continued. "Most of the patients here have malaria, ma'am, and diarrhea. We give them medicine and tell them they can go home, but they don't have homes." She shook her head. "So they stay here."

"What about the U.N. command?" Ollie continued her search.

"They are not doctors," the nurse said.

"Right," Ollie said as she took my arm. "We're off."

The drive to the command center, an abandoned building two miles into town, was excruciating. Ollie was furious.

"It's one thing to have no supplies," she huffed, "it's quite another to have open jugs of contaminated urine and feces throughout the hospital. I will not have it."

I was proud, so proud to be in her company. "You go, girl." I held up my hand and slapped hers.

"It has little to do with me," she continued, "and everything to do with the unit running the clinic. Never, not in my ten years in this country, have I seen a U.N.-occupied town with a hospital in such poor condition."

Ollie Turkel-Bowden was not a regular woman, she was an Eleanor Roosevelt. Ollie was selfless, classless, and colorless—the only thing she cared about was the improvement of the standard of living for all. The end.

Who else could claim such humanity? Alice? Nancy? Anika? Certainly not me.

But Ollie followed no one. She saw through uniforms, past authority. When we arrived at the U.N. command center, Ollie was beside herself. I could see the disappointment in her eyes, as though she was deeply aware that we were losing the war, that the U.N. and the aid agencies were beginning to reflect the chaos of the country. I knew the lens she looked through, the corrective lens of the British, the lens that said we must be better than this, we must win this.

The command center looked deserted. Makeshift office desks were unoccupied. Fax machines were off. Lightbulbs were missing from the desk lamps. The offices had been raided of supplies and personnel.

"Where is everyone?" Ollie exploded.

"Who are you?" A rather indignant Pakistani officer, who had been peacefully smoking a hand-rolled beetie at his desk, glanced up from his Arabic newspaper.

"Ollie Turkel-Bowden," she announced, throwing her girth as well as her somewhat fraudulent ID card on his desk. "Who's in charge here?"

I stood behind her, leaning against the wall, watching. I did not want to throw in with her, for fear that when it came time for me to inquire about Joseph, they would have already told us to piss off. But the officer did not move from his desk. Ollie walked farther into the offices and peered into the back rooms. For such a large space, it was quiet—no machines humming, no telephones ringing, no rustling of paper.

"Look"—she threw up her arms—"aren't you people working here? Half a dozen people outside the clinic have died waiting for care, and hundreds are rotting on the hospital floor." Ollie kicked the young peacekeeper's boot and he jumped. "Get off your ass and call your supervisor."

The young Pakistani stood, all five feet of him, and raised his chin up to Ollie's massive, heaving breast. His mouth grew wide and he screamed, like a comic book character, *"There is no supervisor, you stupid English cunt!"*

Ollie's face grew redder and redder as she watched him sit back down, flick, straighten, and fold his paper across his legs. "Is there a Joseph Hanna around?" Her voice had a controlled edge to it that frightened the hell out of me.

He did not bother to lower his paper. "Tell me." His Indian-English accent dripped with sarcasm. "Do I look like Joseph Hanna to you?"

Ollie looked back at me and I shrugged. We were going to get nothing from him. I shook my head and cocked it toward the door, and to my total surprise she nodded and walked toward me.

But then Ollie stopped. "There's one last thing."

The peacekeeper grumbled, "Now what?"

Ollie stood straight in front of him, turned to the side, and in a single motion bent her knee and lifted her giant leg to a near-perfect ninety-degree angle, then shot out her foot in a powerful blast to his face.

"Oh, my God!" I covered my mouth and watched as chair and man flipped over and crashed against the wall.

"Don't you *ever*, and I mean *ever*, use the word *cunt* in such a degrading and unappreciative manner." His face was still covered with the newspaper. "It's a thing of beauty, the cunt, every woman's own Mona Lisa." Ollie straightened her long skirt, pulled at her shirttails, and signaled to me that it was now time to leave.

We learned from the Nigerian soldier back at the city checkpoint that there were only five U.N. officers left at Port Loko. The country was, technically, once again at war and it was now the British and the Sierra Leonean army who had to maintain order on the ground. And without U.N. presence, no doctors or aid groups would risk their lives bringing supplies outside Freetown, the one city the rebels had been unable to get to. But there was one last question to ask.

"Do you know a Joseph Hanna?" I asked as sweetly as I knew how. "He's been stationed here on and off since January." The officer shook his head slowly. "He's from here, Sierra Leonean by birth, a Temne from the north, but schooled in England."

Ollie shot me a look of wonder. "You seem to know quite a lot about our man."

"No." The officer stuck out his lower lip and rolled it down. "I've been stationed here since December and there's never been a Sierra Leonean U.N. officer and there would never be."

"And why is that?" I asked with a note of exasperation. "Enlighten us, please."

"Because there are no native peacekeepers with UNAMSIL," he said easily. "It would be a conflict of interest."

I was silent. Ollie spoke up. "Do you have a roster of the officers' names here at Port Loko?"

He shook his head and smiled. "Against the rules." I held out my camera and offered it to him.

He took it. "It'll take a few minutes."

Ollie and I waited without speaking, our minds racing with the possibilities and berating ourselves for having been so incredibly, earth-shakingly stupid.

The officer returned with a clipboard. My index finger scrawled down the sheet but my mind was already gone. There was no *Hanna,* no *Joseph* even.

According to the U.N., Joseph Hanna had never existed. Period.

I stood and looked out at the cloudless morning. I took it all in, the houses, the sand, the water, everything I could, and closed my eyes tightly as though making an imprint, a mental Polaroid. This was the home of my childhood, but it was not my home. It was time to say good-bye.

I dialed quickly, feeling the adrenaline rush of the all-nighter take hold of my stomach. "Hello, Al," I said into the phone. "I'm selling."

There was a long pause followed by a fatherly chuckle. "Bad morning?"

"No," I announced firmly. "Everything's good, Al, I've made up my mind."

"Take more time, Saffron," he said in a stern voice ringing with parental disapproval. "Get used to the place, decorate, plant."

My heart pounded. "Time is something I don't have."

"I can hear that something has upset you," he continued, "but you mustn't act on impulse. This was Heaven's life's work, and her life's gift to you."

"I could never build a life here." A gift should be returnable, yours to do with as you please. "Al, I don't want it."

"Did you not enjoy your time there with Heaven?" I could feel him recoil from the phone, as though I was ungrateful and greedy.

"It's different, and I can't explain." I rubbed my eyes. "I don't have the time to."

"But what could be more important to you than Heaven?"

"My life is more important, Al, my own life that I have failed so miserably at."

"I think you're continuing the trend."

Ouch. I could not respond, I could not tell him that I was cashing it all in to save a man's life, a man who was good to the core, whose courage was boundless. If I told him about Joseph, he'd say I couldn't save the world.

"And what about George?" he asked. "You'll have to advise him as well, Saffron."

My heart beat faster. "Oh, shit." I had forgotten about George, Francis's right-hand hippie and Heaven's right-hand man who had lived there for over four decades and had nothing but the motor home he parked on her property.

"It won't be easy for George, you know." Guilt dripped off Al's words. "He doesn't have the resources Francis will have."

God, I felt like hitting myself, or better yet, Al. "You really don't want me to sleep tonight, do you?"

"No." His voice was annoyingly measured. "I want you to think all day and all night if you have to. Your decision is one that has a lot of consequences and can hurt a lot of people, both alive and dead."

CHAPTER TWENTY

FRANCIS'S CALL WAS UNEXPECTED. WHY BOTHER TO CALL, when he could simply walk up the hill and whisper a silent OM into the keyhole? Al must have gotten to him immediately, the only explanation for the sudden lunch invitation to a restaurant I was floored that he even knew of, much less could pronounce.

"Chinois on Main?" I repeated into the phone. "Wolfgang Puck's restaurant?"

"That's the one," Francis answered. "Is tomorrow at one o'clock good for you?"

"Fine." One o'clock, I thought to myself, couldn't be worse. The restaurant would be hopping with fat, balding moviemakers while stick-thin actresses laughed at every belch and nursed a plate of vegetables.

Call me superficial, a hypocrite even, but the last thing I wanted was to be seen with Francis, with his long red beard and his vests made of recycled yak. He was fine on the beach, good-looking maybe, but not in a four-star restaurant.

And Halla! No one brought a baby to a place like Chinois on Main, where behind those massive art deco doors, women did not "do" babies. Their help did it for them, feeding them, diapering them, taking them to the park, and putting them to bed at night. Mom was there for the big stuff, the stuff that really mattered like the weekend photo op.

I got there at twelve forty-five and the tables were already almost full. "Oh, how sweet." The hostess made a face at Halla as though she had never seen a baby before. "Will she be staying?"

"She will," I said meekly, "if that's okay. Do you have a reservation for Francis?"

"Francis what?" She smiled politely.

"He doesn't use a last name," I said and she nodded quickly as though she was used to first names like Arnold, Sylvester, Tom, and Clint.

She scanned the almighty reservations book in front of her and slowly shook her head. "What time was the reservation?"

"One o'clock." Halla was sound asleep. I had done everything in my power to stretch out her awake time so that I could feed her at twelve sharp and have her fall asleep in the car ride over.

"Sorry, nothing."

"How about Saffron Roch?"

She barely glanced at the book. "I'm afraid not."

The asshole didn't even book the table. How typical. "Do you have anything available now?"

She glanced at her watch and shook her head. "I have something for two."

"I'll take it." The restaurant had filled up in minutes; soon it was standing room only. Every now and again someone would catch a glimpse of Halla's car seat and say, "Is that baby real?" Fortunately Californians ate early and quickly. By two o'clock the place was thinning out.

After sitting for an hour and a half waiting for Francis to show, I felt deflated and fatigued.

"Can I get you something small"—the hostess opened the menu—"like the goat cheese salad?"

What was it with the goats and L.A.? "I try to avoid anything that comes out of goats," I said, standing up. Halla began to fidget and I knew what was coming. "But I will use your bathroom."

The ultramodern, ice-cold restroom had two stalls, no baby changing table, no sofa or plump chair to sit on, just the toilets with aluminum covers. But Halla didn't care. As soon as she latched on, the let-down kicked in, and she was swallowing milk like a beer guzzler.

When we emerged half an hour later, the lunch room was empty except for one table. I stopped dead in my tracks. "You've got to be fucking kidding me."

Francis waved me over, Blue at his side. "Great, we'd thought you'd left." His voice was smooth.

"You were supposed to be here two hours ago, Francis."

"You're ticked, aren't you?" he said, turning his head to get a glimpse of Halla. "Come have a glass of Mersault and share some appetizers."

"Mersault?" I shook my head. "I thought you didn't drink."

"On special occasions." He winked. "Here's to Blue." He clinked his glass to hers and beamed. "My wizard."

"That's great, Francis." I plopped down at the table and let them pour me a glass. "We could all use one of those."

I sipped the wine, which tasted like warm, creamy lemons. "So what's this all about?"

"I've spoken with Al," Francis said, eyes flashing, "and thought we should talk."

"Why here?" In all my years at Point Elsewhere, the farthest Francis had ever gone was Point Dume fifteen miles away.

"Blue and I enjoy coming into town every now and again."

They nodded in unison. "We thought it would be good to do this away from the beach."

"And he loves the duck here." Blue rubbed up against him.

"Duck?" My mouth dropped. "You've been a vegetarian since I've known you."

"Special occasions," he said again. "I've mellowed."

"That's for sure," Blue chimed in. "He's a totally different person now, the anger is gone. His body and mind are not fighting anymore. A lot has happened since she passed on."

"I know it was never easy between you," I conceded, "and living there with her must have been hard at times."

"You have no idea," he said, voice lowered. "Toward the end she was so full of hate and feared that people were only out to rob her. It was almost as if all that bad karma was eating her from the inside out."

Heaven had been born poor and stayed that way until she married. It was an experience that permeated her waking hours, her sleeping hours, and was at the root of every decision she ever made. She questioned people's motives before they even reached her front step, and most of the time she was right. Francis had never known poverty; he could afford words like *karma*.

I caught sight of my fingers and saw that they were trembling. I shoved both hands under my bottom. "I understand, Francis, if you hate me for what I'm going to do with Point Elsewhere." I looked down at my lap. "I know Heaven's hating me now. Al hates me. George, Sally, and Dean will also hate me."

Blue looked at me hard. "Then why are you doing it?"

"Because . . . " I bit my lower lip, not wanting to share the details of my life with these two, but realizing that I owed them an explanation for what I was about to do. "Because a very good friend is about to be executed for something he did not do, because I miss my life and feel like I'm in jail out there." I waited for someone to jump on me for that, but no one did. "I want out. I want to go home."

"And that's home for you?" Francis asked. "Africa, civil war, starvation, and pain?"

It was an awkward moment. Here was the guru sipping a two-hundred-dollar bottle of wine in a restaurant that charged thirty dollars for a plate of spaghetti, a self-proclaimed seeker of truth ready to pounce on a plate of roast duck before returning to his ten-million-dollar pad on the sand.

"It is," I announced calmly.

He wiped the corners of his long mustache with a white napkin and quietly burped. "Then you must."

It was a tough question, but I had to ask it. "Even if it means selling yours to do so?"

"I'll buy a new one."

"But you've lived there most of your life," I said, "all of your friends are there, your lifestyle—"

"If I remember correctly," he interrupted, "my lifestyle will not change."

"That's right," I jumped in. "Oh, absolutely, whatever you want." I eyed Blue. "Whatever both of you like, it's yours."

"You know what I'd really like"—Francis pulled back as the duck was placed in front of him—"is to be free." He picked up his utensils and began to cut. "For most of my life, I've felt like this bird. Point Elsewhere was my cage. I could never leave it as long as she was alive."

"Because I was gone?" I hedged.

He nodded. "Someone had to be there to take care of her, and that was me."

"Now we can go," Blue said.

"Really?" I leaned forward to pour myself some more wine, but

Francis took the bottle from my hands and poured for me. About one third of a glass. He needed to do more work on control issues. "You're not angry?"

"Relieved, more like it." He and Blue fell into each other and kissed. Yikes. "A place of our own."

"Where I can decorate and maybe even have one of those." Blue smiled at Halla, who was still asleep. "She's perfect. What's her name mean?"

"It means unexpected gift."

"Where's her father from?" Blue continued innocently, or so it seemed.

"A long story, I'm afraid." I crossed and recrossed my legs and had to force myself not to grab the bottle of wine in front of me and pour until empty. "And not a very interesting one either."

"Oscar, isn't it?" Francis asked, a bit too casually. Then he suddenly switched gears. "When will the property be placed on the market?"

"As soon as I can find a good agent," I said, unsure about what had just transpired.

"I have just the man for the job. Tom is the name." He fished into his hand-tooled leather wallet and took out a card. "Tom Rourke."

I looked at him, hoping that I appeared willing, but past experience had shown me that Francis was not terribly reliable when it came to referrals. "Tom." I offered a half smile. "Who?"

"A good friend of Mom's," he said. "Someone who's been down here ever since we have and won't steer you wrong. But you don't have to use him; it's only a suggestion."

"No." I took the card and scanned the numbers. He was, after all, a friend of Heaven's. "I'm grateful," I stammered. "I need all the help I can get." It was already September and Joseph's life had a time limit.

"He'll know what to do." Francis pushed away his half-eaten duck. "You'll be amazed."

"Will you be using him to find a new place?" I tiptoed into a territory that I was still not altogether sure was friendly. Where would they go, I wanted to ask, what would they buy? And when would they start packing?

"Oh, most definitely." They nodded. "Tom's the man."

Oddly enough, they appeared less conflicted than I was. "And what about George?"

"We'll take care of him." Francis called for the bill. "He's family."

"I'll contact Tom tomorrow then." I wanted the shortest escrow possible.

"Let us do that for you," Francis offered.

"Do you think he can do it in less than thirty days?" I asked. "I need to be gone by October."

I couldn't read the look on Francis's face. Was it surprise, horror, shock, or amusement? I was just about to take it back, to offer apologies for my lack of compassion, when his blank countenance curled into a smile.

"I'm sure he can," he said, nodding firmly. "I'll see to it."

Thirty days to sell. In thirty days I would be a multimillionaire with absolutely no ties to anyone or anything. It would be gone, all of it, the beach in my pocket, reduced to a card less than a quarter of an inch thick. But Heaven was in the back of my mind and in the forefront of my thoughts. Still I could feel her acute disappointment more than I could feel my impending relief.

It surprised the hell out of me that Tom Rourke was slick, not in the usual L.A. kind of way with the gold watch and the open dress shirt, but slick in a Malibu kind of way. He actually wore Uggs in the dead of summer.

"You must be Saffy," he said when he arrived at the house, sticking out his hand and then covering mine with the other. "Great to finally meet you."

"Saffron, actually." I smiled slowly, trying to free myself from his grip. His teeth took up most of his lower jaw. His tan was that of a local.

"Sorry," he said, lowering his sunglasses. "After the years I've spent listening to Heaven and Francis go on about your travels, your escapades, I feel like I know you."

I had never heard of him in my life. "Well," I tried, "call me Saffy then."

He smiled and replaced his glasses. "You're a lucky lady, Saffy." He took my arm and led me back to the front of Heaven's cottage. "I've had two appraisals and they've come in within a couple hundred thousand dollars of each other."

"And that means what exactly?"

He jumped when Halla let out a cry, as though he had not noticed her before. "She's beautiful." He touched her cheek awkwardly. "It means that their appraisals reflect the current market, which"— Tom smiled so brightly I nearly wanted to duck—"is extremely high and therefore favorable to you."

And you. "How much?"

"Listing price at nine million, nine hundred and fifty thousand." He watched me and waited for a sign, any sign. "What do you think?"

I shifted Halla's position in the hope that she would go back to sleep. "You don't think that's too high?" I unbuttoned one strap and removed her from the pouch. "Sounds high."

But Tom was ready with a prepared litany of why that was the perfect listing price for this product in this market. "Market analysis clearly shows that this kind of beachfront property in Malibu—"

"County Line," I interrupted. "Technically we're considered County Line."

He shook his head. "Even better. Don't you read the papers? No one wants to live in the Colony anymore, it's just like L.A. but with no decent restaurants." He waved his hand out before us. "No, no, everyone wants this, this is the last remaining beachfront property in Malibu." And there it was again, the guilt.

"Have you spoken with Francis about the price?"

"No." Tom looked surprised. "You're the owner, technically, not Francis. He's just the occupant."

"Right," I said absentmindedly. I could feel Halla tense and twist her body against me. In seconds she would let out an angry squeal. "I have to go."

He nodded, half-smiling, half-confused. "So I'll go ahead and list it at that price?"

I kept walking. "Sure, leave the paperwork for me to sign." Halla began to scream. "But if the property doesn't sell within fifteen days, lower it."

Tom looked puzzled, but Halla's cries made it impossible for me to continue. "Talk to Francis, he'll fill you in."

I went inside quickly, trying to beat the clock before milk sprayed through my bra. Halla was angry now; it had been nearly four hours since her last feeding. Not only was she insistent, but she was becoming increasingly particular. She liked to lie across my chest and grab at a soft cloth, preferably my T-shirt, and twist it in her tiny fingers. And she didn't like to be rushed.

I noticed Sally and Dean leaving their house, closing the gate quietly behind them, and walking across their lot toward Francis's house. Parked right next to his car, a dilapidated Toyota truck, was a silver four-door Mercedes. It looked identical to the car I'd seen the other night.

I unbuttoned my bra and Halla did a nosedive. Her eyes rolled back and her fists uncurled, her body going completely slack. She was relaxed and 100 percent in the moment. I was anything but. What the hell was going on down there?

There was a quick knock at the door. "Yes?" I covered my chest with the nearest towel.

"Saff?" It was Francis.

"Come on in." I pulled Halla further onto my chest.

Francis stopped when he saw us. "Bad time again?" He sat down on the sofa. "Tom asked me to leave these papers with you." His stare was fixed to the right side of my head. "Did it all go smoothly?"

"He wants to list it at just under ten million," I said. Francis nodded approvingly. "He seems to feel that anything over that would scare buyers away."

"That sounds about right." He crossed his legs. "The houses are small and most buyers would probably tear them down."

"Yeah." I shook my head at the thought of a bulldozer crashing through the place but Francis didn't reveal any emotion at all. "So you know Tom well?"

"No, not really." Francis was quiet.

"But he was here the other night, wasn't he?" I fished. "For dinner?"

Francis continued to stare at my head but his posture grew straighter. "I don't know what you mean."

"The other night. I saw his car, and later he was standing outside with you, Blue, Sally, and Dean."

Francis was slow to respond, but then nodded as though the evening had completely slipped his mind. "He *was* here. Came by out of the blue to show me some of his other listings. Sally and Dean were over for coffee, so I introduced them." He paused. "I'm sorry I didn't call you. It was late, and . . ." He pointed to Halla, now sleeping soundly on my chest.

Clearly I had rumpled his terminally flat feathers. "That's fine, totally fine."

He apologized again and stood to leave.

"No worries." I refastened my bra and put Halla in the bassinet next to me. "Are you and Blue going to be okay when obnoxious people begin to trudge all over your lives?"

Francis stood at the partially opened door. "People have been doing it all my life," he replied, his voice smooth and calm. "But it will all be over soon."

CHAPTER TWENTY-ONE

"WHO HERE PLANS TO PUMP?" GRETCHEN TOURED THE ROOM like an officer surveying her unit on the final day of her command.

No one spoke, moved, not even a flinch. Anika held back her laughter. The carpet still smelled like lavender and breast milk, a scent of the past.

"Oh, come on," Gretchen continued. "I can't be that good."

"I bought one." Anika raised her hand cautiously. "We have to go on a trip soon. I have to give him a bottle."

"Just as long as you balance that with equal time on the breast"—she looked at all of us—"pumping, the bottle, isn't all that bad as long as it's not a substitute for what's real."

"Did you get the double pump?" I whispered to Anika. "The Medela?"

She nodded. "I actually went to a movie last night."

"I've been using it since day one," Nancy whispered back. Of course, it was the top of the line, could squeeze out a gallon of milk a second.

"Can I borrow it?" Sophia leaned in. "I've been dying to try it."

"All right, ladies"—Gretchen sat cross-legged—"take your

breast and tickle the cheek." She nodded as we complied on cue. "Good, very good."

Alice's eyes were waiting for me, seizing mine the moment I looked up. "Are you going to start pumping, too?"

"I guess," I said. "What about you?"

She nodded half-heartedly, then shook her head. "I don't know what I'm going to do."

That about summed it up. It was our last class at the Pump Station. At three months old, Halla could smile, frown, cry real tears, and hold her head high, which is more than I could say for some of my friends. As Sophia, Nancy, and Anika lost their baby fat and overcame the uncertainties that came with their new station in life, they picked up their prenatal attitudes. We'd hit the three-month mark, and like it or not, life was moving on. Our old lives were slowly taking over.

The last few postpump lunches were a series of long, empty silences, as there was little left to discuss. It had taken twelve weeks, but we'd figured out the basics of babying, and conversation on any other topic besides the finer points of milk storage seemed pointless. Sadly, we had very little left in common.

"You'll keep in touch, right?" Nancy tossed her untouched Cobb salad.

"I'll call you," Sophia replied. "Max has been dying for the four of us to go out to dinner."

I watched as Nancy smiled and brushed her off all in the same instant. She had no intention of ever going out to dinner with Sophia and Max, there was no reason for it, nothing for her to gain.

"Anika, take care," she said as she grabbed her purse, which was the size of an envelope. "Let's do another pool party. No"—she winced—"scratch the pool. Stan broke out in hives the last time."

"I'm sorry," Anika offered. "I wish I'd known, I have cream for that."

"I'm sure you do." She shook her head. "Saffron"—she tapped

her finger against my forehead—"don't waste that brain of yours by hanging out down here too long."

"What brain?" I suddenly felt incredibly sad. The group was breaking up, dissolving, and for some reason I hadn't anticipated this. I thought it would remain intact despite my departure. And why wouldn't it, given the common bond?

"Bye, Alice, watch your back," Nancy said, squeezing a folded ten-dollar bill into the busboy's hand. He relieved her of the carrier and the baby and escorted her outside to her waiting car. She hopped in and sped off. None of us knew whether she glanced back or waved; her windows were impenetrable.

Across the room a table of new mothers caught my eye, their newborns all asleep. I sipped my lemonade and watched them talk excitedly, getting pieces of conversation—poopy diapers, sleepless nights, the six-week checkup, and the dreaded "when we can have sex" topic. Terrain that we'd covered long ago.

Our table, with one chair empty, was strangely quiet. "Where should we meet next time?" I jumped in to fill the void, to prolong the inevitable. "We can go to the beach—"

Sophia interrupted. "But aren't you selling the place?" Her eyes went wide. "Where will you go when it's sold?" Her jaw dropped just a little. "With all that money?"

"Will you go back to Africa?" Alice leaned forward. "And bring some of it there? God knows the missions in Sierra Leone could use your support."

"My house?" Anika took over. "What about my house? We have plenty of room."

But no one was ready to commit. We all got up to clear our plates and pack up our diaper bags.

"Let's talk later in the week," we all promised hollowly as we exited the restaurant. Anika and I hugged Alice and Sophia and watched them walk up a side street.

"So." Anika turned. "When will it be?"

"I hate to say it." I threw my bag over my shoulder and walked toward my car. "But the sooner the house is sold, the better."

Anika followed quickly behind. "Are you heading out to the beach?"

"Yeah." I glanced at my watch. "I've got a thing at four o'clock."

She looked at me questioningly. "With an agent?"

I nodded.

Anika stared at me. "Didn't I mention that Warren's a broker?"

"Oh, shit." I drew a long breath. "I'm sorry, everything's happened so quickly, it didn't even cross my mind." I explained how Francis was taking care of the whole thing, had even contacted the agent, an old friend of Heaven's. "It's one less thing for me to deal with, if you know what I mean."

"Would have been a nice commission," Anika continued, "and Warren's good." She paused. "The best."

"Sorry, Anika," I said again as calculations ran through my mind. "I wish I could give it to you, it's a lot of money."

"It's all right." She hugged my shoulder. "It's not like we're starving."

"Nope." I took the key from my pocket and unlocked the car. The day was cold, overcast; strange for September. I didn't want to reveal to her how sad I felt that this chapter was coming to a close. What had once seemed deep, profound even, was as tenuous as any other relationship.

"Call us if it doesn't work out with him." Jeremiah wiggled in his car seat and yawned. "I'd better get him home." It was their date night, Anika explained like a blushing young girl. "I want to get him fed and bathed early so I can get a dress." She smiled. "Thank God for the pump."

The pump. A new dress, I thought to myself. An intimate dinner out with your best friend, where conversation was unobstructed and the promise of passion hung in the air. My mind flashed to his face and I had to close my eyes tightly. It wouldn't be long, I hoped.

"Sorry!" Anika leaned forward and hugged me. "I'm so sorry! I can't believe I did it again. Warren tells me all the time, 'Keep your mouth shut,' he says."

"I'll call you in a few days." I kissed her on both cheeks. "To find out about your date."

Thank God Heaven was already dead, because she would have had a heart attack if she had seen the hordes of real estate agents climbing all over the place on Monday, doing what they called caravan, peeking into every shower and closet, under every toilet seat and bed.

The questions they asked ranged from the bizarre—"Have there ever been any cult slayings that you know of, ritual sacrifices, suicides, anything that might be off-putting to a buyer?"—to the complicated—"Are you zoned for that barbecue pit? Are you on septic? Where's the property line exactly?" I handed them all over to Tom and Francis, who seemed to enjoy fielding questions, offering information, and deflecting interest in questions he had no answer for.

At the end of the day we were exhausted, unable to stand or talk. Blue had called for Chinese takeout, which cost us twenty bucks in delivery alone. It was worth it. We sat, the seven of us—me, Sally, Dean, George, Blue, Francis, and Tom—with our backs to the dune and the ocean in front of us, dining on mu shu chicken, stir-fry vegetables, and broccoli beef.

I opened the small boxes right and left, unable to find a solid dose of carbohydrates. "Doesn't anyone ever order rice anymore?"

George began to massage his lower abdomen with his fingertips. "Blocks the colon—"

I threw up my hand. "Fine."

"So how'd it go out there today?" Sally asked, sipping vodka and Seven from her plastic cup.

"Haven't seen that many people running around since Pearl Harbor." Dean smacked his knee with his arthritic hands.

"It was pretty amazing," George said so quietly that I was quite sure he was upset. He hadn't left the confines of his motor home the entire day and closed the curtains when the agents came to sniff around his lot.

"And I thought only bad TV anchors wore bright suits and white pumps," I said.

"The Malibu look has changed," said Francis, who was fasting and drank only ginger tea. "We used to know everyone down there in the city." By "city" he was referring to the small town of Malibu that had sprung up on Cross Creek Road, near the Colony and the million-dollar movie-star rentals. "It was Topanga all the way."

"But the prices have nothing to do with Topanga." Tom scanned his green notepad. "We're going for nine point five million."

"Hear! Hear!" I shouted, but immediately wished that I hadn't.

"What will you do with it all?" George asked me point blank. Besides drinking hallucinogenic mushrooms and hearing voices, he had spent the last two decades of his life helping people in any way he could, whether it meant delivering a paper to a bedridden lady down the beach or caring for Heaven's every whim.

I looked down at Halla, hoping she would cry or crap, anything to provide a distraction. I was dishonoring a woman's dying wish, displacing her family and making an enormous amount of money doing so. "Charity."

They nodded and smiled awkwardly, visions of shopping sprees along Rodeo Drive dancing in their heads.

"What about Africa?" Sally added sensibly. "You've always loved that country so."

Continent, I screamed silently.

Francis popped by for a visit later that night as I was getting Halla ready for bed. He looked relieved to find me with both breasts out of sight. "I can see you're doing something new."

I smiled. "The spontaneity of motherhood can never be underestimated."

"Nor it seems the predictability." Francis pointed at my laptop, which was open on the table next to me. "May I?" And without thinking, I slapped the screen shut.

He looked at me, startled. "Just never seen one before."

"How rude of me, I'm sorry," I apologized, flipping it open and turning it toward him, "an occupational response, I guess."

It was obvious from his reaction that this was indeed the first laptop Francis had ever seen. His eyes went wide and he even shot out a high-pitched whistle when I changed the screen. "It's so fast! Is it a new one?"

"It's about a year old." I sat down next to him and put the slim gray machine on his lap. It was an incongruous picture, the hippie and the laptop. "You can even do your house hunting online."

"How?" His fingers danced across the keys as if he were a kid playing secretary. Heaven told me once that Francis had been an excellent student before all the drugs.

"Give me the name of a big real estate agency in Humboldt." I crouched over the keyboard, ready to strike. "The connection's slow, it'll take forever to download a picture, but let's give it a try."

"Um." He glanced up reflectively. "I don't know, I never went to one."

"What do you mean?" I stopped. "How are you going to find a house in less than thirty days without an agent?"

Francis patted my hand. "The same way we found this one, through our network of friends."

"Okay," I said, more than slightly concerned. "What's Tom's company's name?" I tried again, hands ready. "Let's see what's for sale in Malibu."

"Um." He rubbed his hands together and squeezed his eyes shut. "I'm so bad at this." He got up and laughed nervously. "That's why computers aren't for me."

"Coldwell Banker, Prudential . . ." his face was blank. "Sounds like pen and paper haven't worked out so well either." But I had to smile. Francis was a throwback to another time, a part of the counterculture who would not, could not, change.

"Looks like someone could use a change." From the side of her bassinet, Francis caught a whiff of Halla's postnurse expulsion, which was never pretty.

"Bath, more like it." I swept her up in my arms. "I'll be back, grab yourself a tea."

"We're back," I called out when we emerged twenty minutes later, but the room was empty, the door was closed, and the computer sat buzzing along on the coffee table just where I had left it. I closed the windows and shut the computer down before taking my place on the sofa next to my baby. A book, *Runaway Bunny*—the tale of a seriously controlling mother bunny who tracks down her young bunny and thwarts his desire for adventure until he finally gives up and returns home—a pale yellow cashmere blanket, and one small stuffed pink bunny surrounded us. The surf was our lullaby.

I sat on the sofa and looked down at Halla, who was becoming more and more like a person every day. "It's just you and me." But as soon as I said the words, I knew they weren't true. They'd never been true. There was a whole life out there that Halla was a part of. Africa awaited her just as much as it awaited me.

What better place to end my career as an L.A. mom than over lunch at John's Garden, a small deli in the outdoor shopping area on Cross Creek Road, a popular hangout for local celebrities and the photographers and fans who made them want to quit their career and become waitresses.

It was Sophia's idea—well, Max's actually. That morning he had packed up her lunch, dressed her, and sent her off to where he felt her time could be "more productively spent." It was where the Hollywood dads hung out, he told her, where Joel Silver, Grazer, Spielberg, and Bruckheimer went to watch their kids eat sand. It was where she needed to be, daily, he said. Max wasn't all stupid.

"That's Jodie Foster." Anika nudged me. "No, don't turn—" She hit me again. "Oh, now she's looking over here, great."

"No, it's not Jodie," Sophia said as though they were dating. "She's doing a movie and doesn't let her babysitter come all the way out here." Sophia shook her head. "They go to a park in Beverly Hills."

"Don't look, but"—Anika elbowed me again—"Lisa Rinna at two o'clock."

"Oh, my God, you're right." Amazement washed down Sophia's face. "There she is with her daughter—aren't they beautiful?" Sophia's brain ticked away as clearly as Big Ben. "I hear she's got a new show coming out."

In the months I had been frequenting parks and baby classes in Santa Monica and Malibu, I had noticed that babies often looked very different from their mothers—which, I had come to realize, was not because of their fathers' DNA, but due to the fact that the mothers had usually had so much work done that they most probably looked nothing like their own baby pictures, much less their babies.

Women here had a uniform look—bone-thin, bee-stung lips, button noses, Asian eyes, and shiny pink skin stretched tight over hard, jutting cheekbones and square jaws—but their little girls gave them away, no matter how good their surgeon. Their daughters carried their genes, and their faces told the story—large hawk noses, small black eyes like hamsters' with eyelashes to match, thin lips, and porky hands leading to an even porkier frame. I wondered how long it would be before their children were in the chair.

"Will you stop staring!" Anika seethed. Sophia had actually turned Rain in the other direction to get a better look at the ex-*Melrose Place* star.

"I wonder where she goes for Mommy and Me classes." Sophia brushed the sand off her cream-colored yoga pants. "I'll be back."

Anika and I watched her leave. From a distance, she looked like she fit in, reigned even, with her flawless natural beauty and her taut, tanned body, but on closer examination, you could tell instantly that she was a foreigner here. Her eyes were just a little too wide, too in awe, and her words came quickly as though she was trying to impress. Her packaging was flawless, but the goods were flawed.

"But to have that ass." Anika shook her head and smiled. "I wouldn't have to do anything—Warren could just look at it and that would be enough."

"And what about world peace?" I turned. "If Madeleine Albright had an ass like that, well, there might just be peace in the Middle East."

"Want ice cream?" Anika slipped Jeremiah from his swing, and we walked to the end of the square and waited in line for frozen yogurt, fat-free, the only kind they had. "It's a conspiracy," she whispered. "You can't even get fat here; they won't allow it."

We stood in silence, watching the young couple in front of us kiss each other's necks while never losing their practiced look of cool. I wondered what people like these considered a real problem. I wondered what would kill their love for each other. The loss of money? Fame? An affair? In a society that worships appearance more than substance, could any of these relationships endure amputation, rape, financial ruin, or hopelessness?

"I'm scared, Anika." I stared ahead. "What if he's already dead?"

She shook her head, clearly at a loss for words. But it was not words that I wanted from her.

"He's in jail for treason." I bought two cones, swirled with chocolate sprinkles. *"Treason,"* I enunciated. "It basically spells death. Anywhere, even here in the land of Oz."

"Any news on the trial?" she asked, as though they actually consulted a calendar over there under the dripping walls of the prison.

"It's still set for the beginning of October, but who knows." Ollie had e-mailed me after speaking to the courts, the district attorneys, and anyone else who'd listen. But there was little else she could do for him. He needed an outsider, a Brit, to represent him, but no one would even talk about a complicated case like Joseph's without a deposit. "Who knows if he'll make it through the rest of the month?"

"Let me ask you something." She cocked her head to the side. "If you got a call today that he was dead, would you still go back?"

"Yes," I said without hesitation.

"So it's clearly about more than just one man." She licked her cone like a pro while I stood still, allowing mine to drip. "It's about you, not him."

"And him," I said.

"And him." She nodded. "But not *just* him."

I closed my eyes. "No, not just him."

"Then you know what you have to do." Anika took out her lip balm. "You need to go home, feel challenged, alive the way you do when you're sitting in a run-down bullet-pocked hotel writing about tragedy."

"You have a knack"—I grinned—"a real knack for words."

"I'm from Jersey." Anika rubbed her lips together and surveyed the crowd. "This is my Africa." Her eyes sparkled. "I could take notes on these people for years and still not understand what the hell they think they're doing."

Just then Sophia came running toward us waving her phone book. "I got it!" she screamed silently. "I can't believe I got it!"

"Her number?" I asked. "Her assistant's number?"

"No, even better." She exhaled a long stream of breath that smelled of honeydew melon, I swear. "The Mommy and Me class her daughter is going to."

"Let me guess." I shook my head. "It's all the way out here in Malibu and you're going to drive over an hour on the outside chance that she might take pity on you and hire you as a walk-on on a show that has yet to exist?"

"Uh . . ." Sophia looked at me as though I had clearly lost it. "Yeah."

"You see?" Anika swallowed the rest of her cone. "To me this is still fascinating stuff."

"And to me"—I linked my arm in Sophia's and kissed her on her warm, translucent cheek—"it's time to go."

CHAPTER TWENTY-TWO

HOW WAS I TO KNOW THAT THE AIR HAD BEEN SLOWLY leaking from the real estate balloon? As per my usual stroke of luck, the Internet market that had been fueling the crazy American economy had gone bust. Properties like mine, according to Tom, were popping up all over town.

"But you told me there were no properties like mine," I whined to him over a lukewarm chai latte prepared by Blue. "You said ours was one in ten million. You actually used those words."

"The market's fickle." Tom's dark sunglasses hung from a black rubber rope around his neck. Today, fifteen days after he had put the house on the market, he looked a little less slick. "Around here it can change faster than a woman's bust size."

I chose to ignore that one. I handed Halla to Blue, who smelled of patchouli, and watched as she took her for a stroll. "Are you saying we should lower the price?"

"No." He shook his head and crossed one Ugg boot over the other. "Not quite." He lifted an official-looking briefcase and took out a file on comparable properties. "Prices are holding, but the market's gone a little soft. Stocks are dropping, then there's the whole technology market, which has hit a bump, and the Internet business, which can't come up with a way to pay for itself."

If I wanted an analysis of the market, I'd read the *Wall Street Journal.* "My question is, Do you think we'll need to lower the price in order to sell by the end of the month?"

He shook his head. "No, what I was trying to tell you was that—"

Here we go again. "Do you have any solid buyers?" I interrupted.

"Yes." Tom leaned forward. "If you'd let me finish. I was trying to tell you that we have some very interested parties, two couples in fact, both in the entertainment industry, which as we all know is still going strong."

I forced a smile. "I want to make sure that you understand, Tom, the property must be in escrow within the next two weeks." The end of the month. Ollie had been in daily contact with the authorities at Pademba who'd "promised" Joseph's trial would not be until October, that no decision would be made before that. It was too big of a case, they explained, to sweep under the carpets of justice.

"Absolutely," he said, beaming one of those team spirit smiles. "Francis told me all about your time line and I *will* make it happen."

"It's now September fifteenth." I put Blue's hand-crafted yellow tea cup in the old sink in Francis's kitchen. "Reduce the price to nine million and get it into the MLS book by the beginning of the week."

"Let's sit the open house tomorrow and see what kinds of nibbles we're getting." Tom spoke softly, obviously trained to deal with situations such as these. "It'll be Sunday, it's supposed to be beautiful, so we should have a lot of traffic. Let's hold off on the price reduction until Monday."

I agreed. "But if you have anyone serious, tell them we're flexible."

"Definitely." He beamed. "I just want you to be happy, Saffron."

I nodded uncomfortably. I wasn't used to that. I preferred being broke and entirely uncatered to.

I invited Anika, Sophia, and Nancy to the open house. Alice was already booked—God had a way of taking up your Sundays, she'd explained. I told the others to bring their husbands and anyone they knew who might be interested in acquiring a one-of-a-kind original Malibu oceanfront compound. I filled each house with wildflowers, freshly baked (previously frozen) chocolate chip cookies, and freshly brewed organic coffee (I left the bag out so they'd notice). It was to run from two to four in the afternoon.

At five past two, there was a knock at my door. "Hello there." Anika beamed.

"Where's Warren?" I opened the door wide for her stroller.

"At Neptune's Net." She shook her head. "We must have driven past the place three or four times before finding it. He said he needed a beer." Anika swept past me like a recently hired interior decorator and stood in the kitchen. "This is incredible."

"Hold on," I stopped her. "Isn't there an open house sign at the top of the driveway?"

"No," she said, disappearing down the hallway to the bedroom. "Is this only one bedroom?"

"Two." I put Halla in the Baby Björn carrier. "I'd better find Tom. There should be a sign."

"Oh, no," Anika cautioned, "not with ten-million-dollar properties. Who wants every Tom, Dick, and Harry stomping through their homes, fondling their possessions?"

At that moment Warren walked through the door. They kissed on the lips—after they'd been apart all of five minutes.

"Isn't that right, dear," she purred, "high-end properties don't have open house signs with great big blue arrows pointing people to their doorsteps, do they?"

Warren's eyes glowed. "No, dear, they don't."

"Oh," I said, puzzled. "Then who are open houses for?"

"For clients who already have agents and are actively looking and prequalified to buy a ten-million-dollar property," Warren said.

"See?" Anika smiled. "He knows his stuff."

I nodded. "He sure does."

After Sophia and Max arrived, we all walked down the driveway to the two beach houses that sat perched at the last sand dune, ready for another great storm to come and test their resolve. Just that week, Francis had filled flower boxes with Heaven's favorites—Martha Washington geraniums in salmon and fuchsia—and placed them in the front windows of both houses. "This place is insane," Max claimed. "A great place to shoot, fucking great."

Sophia covered Rain's ears, then caressed Max's cheek. "It's absolutely lovely, Saffron. Was that Heaven's house?"

"Her cottage, she called it." I led them over the flower-lined walkway and up onto the porch. The house felt strangely clean, devoid of the smells I had always associated with her house, namely white wine and damp rooster.

"Have you ever slept up there?" Max pointed to the loft above and I nodded. I had lost my virginity there gazing out the sunroof, under the stars, listening to the waves below. How long ago that was.

I continued the tour through the gardens, barbecue pit, and chicken labyrinth. "And this is Francis's place." I opened the door to find Tom deep in a phone conversation. "And our Realtor."

"A throwback to another time." Warren cleared his throat and tiptoed uncomfortably through the small space, his hands folded behind his back as he looked up at the mystical books that lined the shelves.

Tom was nodding and smiling at me at the same time. I glanced at his so-called headquarters, and I looked for flyers with glossy photos of our property.

"Where are the flyers, Tom?" I asked, even though he was still on the phone.

"Flyers?" Anika pulled me aside. "What flyers? You don't use flyers on a property like this. It's all word of mouth, Saff.

"But if no one comes, then your Realtor isn't doing his job"— she continued glancing in his direction—"and the listing should be pulled. Isn't that right, honey?"

"On the button." Warren came over and scooped Jeremiah into his arms. This Ricky and Lucy thing was getting a little old.

"This is one hot property," Nancy said as she arrived, cracking her gum. "A little out there, but worth the drive, right, Stan?"

Stan mumbled something and then took the entire plate of cookies out onto the porch.

It was already three o'clock, halfway through my first open house, and the only people here were my friends from the Pump Station. "There's no one here! How am I ever going to sell this place," I groaned and put my face in my hands. "I have to sell it, you don't understand, I have to get back."

"Get back where?" Sophia seemed exasperated with me. "If I owned even one of these cottages, I'd never leave."

"It would take you over an hour to get anywhere anyway," Nancy added.

"I think what Saff is trying to say is that she needs to get back to Africa." Anika squeezed my shoulder. "And the only way to do that is to sell this place."

"You'll sell it, don't worry." Nancy patted my knee. "Even though I think you're crazy. Who wants to live in Africa? Have you checked out the line at immigration recently? It doesn't take a journalist to see that it's going the other way."

"If you don't have an offer soon"—Anika's voice was calm—"Warren can help get it sold. He's amazing."

"And I can house-sit," Sophia offered with a laugh. I glanced up at them, the three standing around me in a protective semicircle. They were my friends. They came from different places and had different agendas, quirks, and faults, but they were all here now, for me.

And just like that, two people appeared at the top of the drive. Then two more and so on and so on. A steady stream of potential buyers continued until half past four. By five o'clock we had our first offer, and by six o'clock I was asleep on the couch with Halla lying like a kidney bean between my breasts.

"We need to have a party." George's mouth opened wide. "One last party."

"The party to end all parties," Sally declared.

"But we haven't sold it yet," I said, feeling sadness grip my heart. It was a stunning day, and here we all were, smack in the middle of an empty beach, having sun-brewed herbal tea and playing a game of cards.

"I hate to break it to you," Blue offered, "but it looks solid."

I nodded. "So Tom says." There was a full-price offer on the table and Tom was in the midst of putting together a fifteen-day escrow.

"All cash." George leered and I sank back into my chair. "Ten million bucks." The talk of money made me wish I could disappear. I felt like a treacherous mercenary, no matter how certain I was about my decision.

I stood up and went inside the cottage to collect myself.

"It's alright." Francis followed me inside. "They don't understand. They can't." He put his hands on mine, and their resemblance to Heaven's made me catch my breath.

"I feel so awful," I said shakily, "but there's no way out for me."

"You're doing the right thing."

"I'll give you money, Francis," I cried. "I'll give you half, more, I'll give it to—"

"I don't want it." Francis put one hand over my mouth. "I have all I could ever need."

"What about George?" I looked out to the table where he sat drinking a cold beer. "Surely, he'll need something."

"He'll be fine." Francis laughed. "George has always been fine."

"Will he go with you?"

"He doesn't even need to pack," Francis said, "just kick the bricks out from behind the RV, throw the car in reverse, and he'll follow wherever I go. He'll always have a home with me."

"How about a party?" I glanced his way.

"It's not such a bad idea. We'll have a little beer, some wine, and invite anyone who has ever meant something to us down here at Elsewhere." Francis pulled at his beard. "Shall we see what the others think?"

"Let's do it." We walked back out. Sally and Dean looked up from their cards. "So what's it going to be?" Dean croaked. "Are we going to honor this place and the woman who built it?"

"We are." Francis took my hand.

"The offer looks firm, Al." I watched his face, but he gave nothing away.

"I'd like to see the contract," he said, tapping his pencil on his desk. "If you have a copy."

I didn't. I had signed it that morning when the offer came in and left it on the dining table. "It's a full-price offer, all cash, no major contingencies."

Al looked up. "Do you have a deposit?"

I nodded. "According to Tom, the deposit, twenty percent of the list price, has been wired into an escrow account. They've agreed to a ten-day escrow and if all goes well with the inspections, the money should come in by the end of next week, around September twenty-seventh." I was excited. "They're Hollywood people, he's an entertainment lawyer and the other guy's in the music industry. They want to build some sort of compound with a sound room, a screening room, basically lots of room to make as much noise as they want."

Al didn't seem too interested. "And where is your little one today?"

"At the beach with Blue," I said, pulling my purse tighter against my chest, readying myself for a jab that seemed imminent.

"You've become quite friendly with Blue and Francis, haven't you?" He looked me up and down. "You're even dressing like them."

"Just because I'm wearing thongs and a floral skirt, Al, doesn't mean they've successfully recruited me."

His nod was imperceptible. "But you trust them enough to leave your baby with them."

I exhaled. "Yes, I trust them. You were right, they are good people."

"No." He shook his head. "I never said they were good people, Saffron. I could never make such a blanket statement and neither should you—they're dangerous."

"The people or the statement?"

He grinned. "Now you're beginning to sound like a lawyer."

"What an awful thing to say, Al." I took his hands and held them firmly. "Will you come to the party on Sunday?"

Al placed his hand on my lower back and ushered me to the door. "I wouldn't think of missing it. Heaven would have demanded it."

I looked up at him. "Didn't she always."

Early Friday morning Tom tapped eagerly at my door. "Is the house packed?"

"And good morning to you." I stood in my pajamas. Halla was down for her morning nap and I was trying to catch up on correspondence with Sierra Leone.

He stuck his nose around the semiclosed door and took in the clutter. "This is not good, Saffron, this should look like no one lives here, get my drift?" According to Tom, the buyers were as anxious to be in as I was to be out. They were ready to take possession right away. Because they were paying cash, there was practically nothing to impede a smooth changeover. Except, of course, Francis.

"Have you been down to Francis's house yet?" I asked. Judging from his vague answers, Francis still hadn't chosen a place to live. "Has he spoken to you at all about where he's going to move?"

Tom nodded. "He's mentioned Humboldt and he's mentioned Malibu."

"But he's got like fifteen dogs and ten cats, and he's got George and Blue." I went back to my desk and closed the laptop. There were still two unread messages in my in-box, one from Rodger at the *Times* and the other from Ollie. "And he's got nearly a half a century of shit down there.

"I know, I know." Tom came in and pointed to the sofa across from me. "Mind?"

"No, of course not." I pulled on a robe. "Coffee?"

"Not if it's decaf." He winked and followed me to the kitchen. "Francis says money won't be an issue. The sale will give him more than enough time to look."

"But what if he doesn't have the house cleaned out before the first?" I was nervous. "Can that affect the deal in any way?"

"It will all go as planned, Saffron, as promised," Tom assured me. "I'm still showing the property, and fielding offers in the case that something might happen, but I don't see it. It's rock solid—you want to sell and they want to buy." He stopped. "Now I'm going to contradict myself."

"Oh, no." I put up my hands. "Not that, anything but that."

"I was just going to say," he continued, pulling my hands down to the counter and holding them there, "that money, on either side, is not a deal breaker."

But it was. It was a deal breaker, a lifesaver, and the key to my future. It was everything to me, and despite my best efforts at denial, I found myself willing to do anything to get it. In the short months that I had been here, I had seen what it could do. It bought the "we"; it bought family.

"All you need to do is have fun at the party this weekend," he said, "and from what I'm hearing, it's going to be one hell of a going-away party."

I pulled my robe tighter around me as I waited for the coffee to brew. I almost dreaded the party, like an acid flashback to all of the hippies who had flocked to this beach on Heaven's dime. It would be a drunken reverie, a rehashing of memories made interesting only by time and distance, friendships overexaggerated for the sake of self-aggrandizement, and a few more free cocktails.

At ten o'clock on Sunday morning, I tiptoed down to the beach. The party was scheduled to begin at eleven. The number of people coming was a mystery, but Francis had put the word out to his friends in Topanga, so chances were the police would be arriving before midday.

"Good morning," Blue called out from the beach where she was sitting in a still lotus position. "Would you like me to refresh that for you?" She pointed to my coffee cup.

"I'd love some. How long have you been up?"

"Since five." She and Francis had already been to the catering company to pick up the kegs and the food.

As we walked toward Francis's house I noticed that the outside of Heaven's cottage was closed with a small sign asking people not to enter. I smiled. "Thanks."

"This is for her, too," Blue said, sounding strangely mature. "And for them." She pointed to the barbecue pit, where I saw the bare feet of two, four, six, eight, ten people.

"Friends of Francis?"

"And mine." She walked us into the house, which smelled of cinnamon, cloves, and freshly baked carrot bread. Coffee bubbled from a jet black Krups coffeepot. "Black, right?"

I accepted. We sat down on Heaven's beige sofa, which was now covered in purple and pink Indian saris and embroidered pillows.

Their house was a strange mixture of the bohemian no-strings-attached look and of domestic subservience. I wondered the obvious. "Do you want children?"

"To tell you the truth, I wish I could be one, I wish I could latch on to my mother's breasts and drink from her, be caressed by her and reassured all at once," Blue said dreamily. "I wish I could experience what that kind of love would feel like."

"The ironic thing is that you have to be a parent to feel it," I said proudly. I had changed.

"No." She shook her head slowly. "I've found it with Francis. I've latched on to my soul mate."

The New Age stuff was getting too heady for me. I stood up and took a look at the bookcase, which remained as it had been for years, overflowing. In fact, there were no signs of boxes anywhere, the house was just as it had always been. "Have you any idea where you and your soul mate are going next week when the movers come?"

"Francis has a few tricks up his sleeve." Blue stood to refill my cup and led me outside. The sun had burned a hole in the thick marine layer and the clouds were evaporating like smoke. Surfers, who had only moments earlier appeared shivering and huddled against their boards, were suddenly stretched out like seals, soaking up the warmth.

Then I noticed the steady stream of people making their way down the red-brick driveway to our right, looking like a casting call for *Jesus Christ Superstar.* Long hair, dreadlocks, saris, Punjabi pantsuits, white Yogi turbans, skull caps, Op shorts, and thongs abounded. They carried duffel bags, towels, and suitcases on wheels, leading dogs and cats and even a white turkey that gobbled as it walked by. I stood in silence as they streamed back to Point Elsewhere.

"How many people do you think will show up?" I asked Blue as they made their way to the pit, where Francis was already holding court.

"Hundreds," she said, and I nodded back. Like Heaven, I was in the fortunate position of being able to walk upstairs and shut my doors, so I did not care. "Some people have come from as far away as Africa."

"Just as long as they're gone by tomorrow."

Blue looked me straight in the face and laughed.

CHAPTER TWENTY-THREE

CURTAINS CLOSED, BABY DOWN FOR A SCHEDULED ONE-hour nap, a cup of hot English Breakfast tea, and a small but deceptively high-calorie berry scone by the side of my laptop. The silence was better than Vivaldi. I clicked to open my e-mail from Ollie. I took a deep breath.

Saffy:

Red Cross still hasn't been allowed in. The official party line is that they are nationals, prisoners of the state, and are therefore property of the state, not the international community. Rather selfish of them, I said, but their reaction was barely a grunt. One of them actually laid his head down at the window and took a nap while I continued to harp on about the injustice of it all.

Kabbah's government is in control now, but because there remain pockets of RUF resistance, they're taking no chances. Anyone allegedly with the RUF is taken straight to Pademba. I believe that Joseph, caught in the quagmire of

his unusual circumstance and seemingly questionable loyal-
ties, will die there if you don't come now.
     We miss you terribly and wait for your return.
Yours,

                                                           Ollie

That day in Port Loko over a year ago, when Ollie and I had gone looking for him and were told by the officer that there was no Joseph Hanna working for the U.N., we both came to the conclusion that he had to be a British agent. It all added up.

We talked of nothing else on the ride back to Freetown. Had he infiltrated the Makeni rebels or was he working farther north, gaining information to assist the Brits in the cleanup? Neither of us knew the details, but by the time we reached my hotel, there was little that could convince us otherwise.

Also in my in-box was an e-mail from the United Nations, once again claiming that there was no Sierra Leoneon national by the name of Joseph Hanna working for UNAMSIL or any other U.N. body in Sierra Leone from December '99 to the present. The British, of course, had no record of him. The rebels had decimated his entire family and village, leaving Joseph without a past. Perhaps that was why he joined the secret service, to feel as though he belonged to something that was, in and of itself, a secret. A family that didn't exist, a job that couldn't be traced, a life spent in the shadows. A true outcast. The manifestation of my inner self.

There was a knock at the door. I looked up from the screen but remained as quiet as I could. The knocking continued.

It was Blue. "Hey, you," she said, seeming to sway a little. "Why don't you join us? It's really mellow." Blue dangled an outstretched arm to the beach. "I've put out some hummus and pita bread, Francis has the barbecue going, and Dean brought over the fish he caught this morning as an offering."

"Maybe in a bit," I replied. "I just put Halla down for a nap."

"Just don't come too late. There are a lot of people we want you to meet and who want to meet you." She turned to go, skipping as she hurried to rejoin the party, her skirt sailing around her small frame like a parachute taking flight.

The party was in full swing by the time I entered the fray with Halla in the carrier. There was a sitar, a guitar, and a flute going in the pit while on the other side of Francis's house a boom box blasted Cat Stevens.

I poured myself a glass of wine and toured the party like a sightseer at an amusement park. "Hey, Al." I stopped when I saw the only man wearing a suit. He stood in the background like a *National Geographic* anthropologist taking notes, watching the fervor mount. "Having a good time?"

"Fine." He wiped his splotchy brow with a handkerchief. "Lovely, yes." Everyone was dancing now, swaying this way and that. There was a tremendous amount of kissing and hugging going on, and a few had even slipped off their T-shirts, freeing their pendulous breasts.

I was actually beginning to enjoy myself when I saw her heading toward me. I did not recognize her at first, and probably would not have had Blue not introduced us directly.

"Saffron." She took my hand and clasped it to the other woman's. "Meet Monique, your mother."

We stood motionless, staring into each other's eyes. She wore a sheer dress that looked like batik, and it tied around her neck like a halter, exposing her wizened shoulders and jutting collarbones. Her hair was blonde and fell to her hips. Her eyes were a transparent blue. "You look Dutch," I said.

"That's because I am Dutch," she said in a smoothed-out California drawl.

"We look nothing alike." I looked around us nervously. Blue and Al had disappeared.

"You look like your father," Monique replied. "The best part of him, that is."

"I wouldn't know." I pulled my cardigan over Halla, who peeked out of the carrier. I did not want Monique to see my child, to share baby stories, or find any similarities in appearance. Halla was off-limits.

Monique looked directly at her. "Is she yours?"

"Yes." I nodded. "Did you have any others kids?"

Monique shook her head. "No, I spent my life nurturing my spiritual child, so that I could help others find theirs." She took my hand and led me to the top of the dune. "Leaving you here was just the beginning of my sacrifice."

"Your sacrifice?" I turned to her. Her audacity was chilling. "Dumping your seven-year-old because you wanted to take off with a bunch of guys and fuck your way up and down the coast was your sacrifice?"

"Had I kept you," Monique said calmly, pulling her hair back in a knot at the nape of her neck, "you would not be the person you've become." Despite the tie-dyed dress and tan suede Birkenstocks, I could tell in a second that she was European. It was in the way she moved her hands, the way she paused slightly before beginning a sentence, and the way she touched me whenever she wanted to make her point.

"And who is that?" I baited.

"Graduate of the London School of Economics, war correspondent, humanitarian." She glanced up at me. "Heaven and I kept in contact until her death." I must have worn the shock visibly, because Monique laughed. "Yes, she told me everything, she shared her pride."

"You actually thought about me?" I tripped over the words. "I didn't think you gave me a second thought. Why didn't Heaven tell me?"

Monique took my hands in hers. "Because she thought you'd look for me, try to join me if possible, and she didn't want that." She paused. "Neither did I."

"Why?" I stared, feeling hurt and manipulated.

"Because you would have ended up like one of them." She pointed to the pit. "A hanger-on, lost and scrounging." Her eyes grew moist and she took a deep breath. "Like your mother."

"What about my father?" I dug my feet into the sand and watched her hands. They were delicate. "What was he like?"

"Oh, honey." She patted my knee. "He was awful—handsome, but awful. The first great thing I did for you was to get you out of there. He was a misogynist of the first order and a cheat."

My thoughts immediately flashed to Oscar. The tapes, the women, the wife. "Is that why you left him?"

"That and he was an asshole." She tried to touch Halla's head, but I pulled away. "What about you? Will you be raising her by yourself?"

"I'm not sure." I didn't want to say more and I didn't have to.

"Will you go back to Africa soon?"

"Yes." I turned my head to look at her. If she weren't my mother, I probably would have liked her. There was something wise and light about her, an old soul that had been beaten and burned and had come back to stick around anyway.

"Africa's your home," she said. "And California is mine." She worked at the Topanga Wellness Center, she said, providing help to the elderly who could no longer care for themselves. She bathed them, fed them, changed their diapers, and read them stories at night. "That's all they want, you know," she said of her work, "to be treated and loved the same way a mother cares for her baby."

Tears stabbed my eyes at the benign cruelty of her statement. How would I have been had I felt her love and dedication? Would I have been able to form lasting friendships, forge deeper bonds, and ultimately marry?

"We bounce off our pasts, Saffron." She stroked my arm. "I bounced off restrictive parents who were obsessed with maintaining my virginity until they could marry me off to the biggest Edam cheese farmer in Holland."

"Edam cheese farmer?" I laughed.

She nodded, her filigree hoops dangling. "And I gave you up. If you bounce off me, you're bound to be a good mother. Just do as I say, not as I did."

"I'm glad we met." I realized I meant it.

"I'm glad we met, too." Monique stood before me, her tanned, naked toes emerging from a heap of warm sand. Her voice was sweet but disciplined as though she had spent a lifetime in self-analysis. "Just remember, do as I say, not as I did."

I could feel my heart open and ache simultaneously as I watched her walk away. There went my mother, whose body I was created from, whose breasts nourished me, and whose hands held me. And then she was gone, disappearing into the crowd that she had chosen thirty-two years ago over me.

I ran. I ran from the house, the beach, the freaks, the encounter with my mother. I had always thought that motherhood was cellular, that a woman's body did not forget that it had borne a child, even when the heart or the mind had. But it was clear her body had forgotten.

My feet slapped against the wet sand, which had grown hard

and cold with the setting sun, until they stung and finally went numb.

I continued on, making it halfway to Leo Carrillo before Halla woke with a startled cry. I had been holding her tightly against me, cupping her feet in my hands while I walked briskly. Clearly she was wondering what the hell was going on. It was now sundown and she was ready for her bath and milk. Babies are such creatures of habit, I thought to myself as I walked back to the house. But then again, aren't we all.

As I approached the embankment, I could see several bonfires on the sand surrounded by semidressed men and women swaying to the flames. The fire marshal would love to shut this one down, I thought as I made a straight line for the railway ties that would lead to Heaven's house. I didn't want to see Blue or Francis, hear stories about Heaven, or run into Monique again. I was done with it, I was done with it all. By the end of the week, I would be home.

I made it to the third step, halfway up the hill, almost home, when I heard a voice down below call my name. I stopped, my lungs struggled for air. Sweat beaded along my forehead. I waited to hear it again.

"Saffron?" he said it again. "It is you, isn't it?"

I turned. When I saw him, I nearly lost my balance and sat down with a heavy thud on the wood tie. Halla began to scream. "No, no," I whispered, "shh, please be quiet." I bounced her quietly up and down, willing her to stop.

"It is you then." Oscar began to climb the steps, one by one, his perfectly beautiful frame coming closer with every second.

"What are you doing here?" I managed to say. My head felt as though it was wrapped in a cotton swab. This couldn't be. Oscar could not be here.

"I came to see you." His voice had the sweet German lilt he used whenever he tried to make good, when he had just gotten done doing bad. His shirt was characteristically unironed and flapped behind him in the night breeze.

"Your hair's a little longer," I said, "a little grayer."

"All because of you." He sat down next to me and stared up at the moon. "Beautiful spot." Oscar leaned back on his hands and took in a deep breath of night air. "Why didn't we ever come together?"

"All those nurses." The sting felt like yesterday's. "How could you, Oscar?"

His mouth moved, but no words came out. He stood, smoothed his hair back, put both hands on his hips, and looked down at the ground.

"*All* those nurses?" He looked up from his study of dirt. "What do you mean?"

"It was the tapes," I said. "The tapes in your room sparked my curiosity." After our last night together, I could no longer stand it. The tapes with the pink writing had been eating away at me for months. "I found them"—I paused—"or they found me."

"You were drunk that night," he remembered. "We'd been to bed."

I was drunk that night. A month had slipped by since Ollie and I had gone to Port Loko in search of Joseph. All eleven British soldiers had been returned, and still no word on Joseph. He was dead, I told myself. It was over, I convinced myself as I slipped in between the hotel sheets and tried to feel something other than empty.

We joined together one last time in a passionless attempt at lovemaking, his mouth hot and hard on mine, his eyes pursed shut, his hands eager but ineffective. I lay still, arms at my sides, until he began to snore softly. And then I took off.

"I went to your room," I said. I went in search of the tapes, in search of one truth, of one ending.

"You didn't have a key," he struggled.

"I did have a key." I had taken it from his pocket while he slept and entered his room. I listened to one after another, one more revolting than the next. Bad ballads, love songs sung in dozens of drippy languages, from women he never cared for, didn't even know.

Oscar expelled a deep breath, as though to lift a massive weight. "It only started because of the pubic hair I found in your bed."

"Don't." I put my hand up to stop him. "It gets better."

That night I was on fire. I had far too much alcohol in my system to stop. On my way down from his room, I was stopped by the ever-vigilant Ms. Katie.

"What are you doing here?" her voice boomed.

"I have to drop something off for Oscar," I said. Then a light had struck. "He wanted me to send something to his mother, but I can't find her address. Do you have it?"

She took a second to size me up and then, for some unknown reason, took me to her files to look it up. "No, no mother, but I do have his wife on file."

"A wife." I nodded. "Perfect."

"Shit." Oscar tapped his forehead with his curled fist. "Ms. Katie. Never could tell a lie."

"The janitors had tipped me off earlier." I told him what I had overheard, minus the lifting of the car keys part. "They couldn't get over a man leaving a woman who looked like that. I chose to ignore it; denial's a lot more fun."

"But I have"—his eyes poured into mine—"left her."

"It's too late." In his eyes I could see the woman in the poster staring at me, mocking me with that ridiculously muscular midriff.

"For who?" Oscar's voice rose slightly. "For her?" He glanced at Halla, who watched his every move. "Haven't things changed now?"

"Is that why you came?" I turned. "To try and claim her?" I could feel the blood begin to pound again and Halla began to squirm. "Because you'll never get her." I stood. "I'll take her away so fast, you'll never see her again." And just at that moment, I caught a glimpse of my mother walking across the beach alone, head down. Suddenly she stopped and turned to look up at the house or at me. I could see her; could she see me? "Mom?" I called out, but my voice was just a whisper. My mother continued her walk down the coast away from me.

"Saff?" Oscar tried to get my attention. "You don't look right, are you feeling okay?" He put his hand to my forehead and I turned, tears filling my eyes.

"Oscar?" He nodded. "Oscar?" I said again and I wept. That night, our last night, felt like the end of it all. End of Oscar, end of hope for a life with Joseph. But it was also a night of beginnings, the night of Halla.

How can I describe what it was like having my worlds collide all at once—my mother, Oscar. There were so many questions to ask him, so many things to explain. But instead I cried and cried in his lap until Halla's cries rose above my own.

"She's hungry." I wiped my nose on his shirt. I stood to go, but Oscar took my hand. "She eats more than I do, if you can believe that."

"May I walk you?" he asked and I nodded.

He watched quietly as I fed her and gave her a quick sponge bath in the sink. I said a silent prayer that he wouldn't comment on how much she looked like him. We took her to bed and formed a circle around her with our bodies.

"What's her name?"

"Halla." I smiled. "It means unexpected gift in African dialect."

"And it describes her perfectly." He watched as I pulled her to my chest and she latched on. I felt aglow in the light warmth and love of his eyes. "You're a natural," he whispered. "I knew you would be."

"Pump Station," I whispered back and laughed when he shook

his head. "Silly classes where L.A. women go and are taught, for a few hundred dollars, how to get their children to latch on."

He wrinkled his nose. "Sounds very American."

It was, but it was also so much more.

I looked down and saw that she was falling asleep. I tried to move, but she grabbed my nipple and pulled it back into her mouth.

"Can you forgive me?" he whispered. "For all of it?"

"It's done." I let my head fall to the side, I was exhausted. It was water under the bridge, all of it.

"Will you come back?" Oscar leaned his head against his arm, and the fine skin of his face dropped to the side. I could see his age, but it didn't matter. He was still one of the finest-looking men I had ever known.

"Yes." I attempted to ease out from under Halla, but she would not let me go. Her fists took hold of my T-shirt and her legs curled up into my stomach.

A look of relief came over his face and he smiled. "I'm a changed man." He scooted closer to me. "We can get married, I'm free now." His eyes lit up. "And buy that ranch house out in the country now that the war is over."

They were the words I had been wanting to hear. But I had changed and so had the dream.

"I'll be coming back on my own." I paused. "Well, not totally on my own, with Halla." Oscar looked away and I could see that he was on the verge of tears. Seeing us, lying there on the bed, all the ingredients for a family, so tangible. But after a short string of words, all was suddenly lost and he was alone. "But we'd love to have you in our lives, if that's at all possible."

"Is it because of what I did back there in Freetown?" His body tensed. "I thought you were cheating on me, Saffron, I would never have done any of it had I known that you'd been faithful."

"No." I reached out and touched him. "It's not that."

"Pamela and I haven't slept together for years," he stammered. "She wouldn't give me a divorce and she wouldn't come to Africa. I was stuck, don't you see? There was nothing I could do, and it was a nonissue by the time you and I became serious. I totally forgot she even existed."

"Good thing you had the poster to remind you," I said, unable to help myself.

"Is she finished?" He pointed to Halla, who had substituted her index finger for my breast. I nodded and slipped out from underneath her. The living room was bright with light and I quickly turned everything off so that the crowd below could not witness our reunion.

"Can I get you a drink?" I went to the bar and pulled out a bottle of Mersault.

"No, I'm fine," he said, but I uncorked it anyway and found the largest glass in the house. "She told me that she would grant me a divorce if I came home for the holidays. So I went."

I took a long drink and felt the lemon tartness clear my throat while the alcohol softened my mind. I sat next to him on the sofa. "I'm sorry then, Oscar."

"Reconsider." He took the glass from my hands and drank. "I've changed, I'll be more attentive. The fighting is over, we'll take more trips, spend more time with each other."

I reclaimed my glass. "Did you know that Heaven died?"

"No"—he shook his head—"I didn't. I'm sorry."

"I wasn't even here, you know." Outside the party raged on, boom boxes blaring over the sitar, drunken laughter taking over the earlier meditation. "Those people down there are having a good-bye party because this place will no longer be theirs by the end of the month. Did you know that?"

"No, I didn't," he said again, growing slightly impatient. "But what does all of this have to do with us?"

"I'm the one selling, Oscar." I stood at the window. "I'm the one taking this place away."

A small smile curled his lips. "And the money?"

"Ten million dollars—"

"It's all yours?" he interrupted.

"No, less actually, after taxes and after I find Francis and Blue a place of their own."

Oscar cleared his throat. "Why are you doing this?" His eyes narrowed. "Why are you selling this place, her legacy, you used to call it, and moving back to Sierra Leone?"

"It doesn't make sense, does it?" I smiled. I didn't have a job, a man, or a home to keep me there and yet it was the last place that popped into my mind every time I went to sleep at night and the first place I wanted to see when I opened my eyes. "It's where I want to die, if that makes any sense at all."

"I understand. Oddly enough"—he shot me a glance—"and without nearly the sentimentality, it's where I want to die as well. Perhaps when we're old and gray, we'll be together again." He nodded pensively. "The last remaining colonials."

"I want us to be friends," I said with a heavy tone. "I want Halla to know her father."

Oscar walked to the door. "It really is a pity, you know."

"What?"

"Giving it all up, giving me up, for something that doesn't exist," he said. "There's nothing left, Saffron. What you think is there is gone, all of it. You'll see."

"Maybe there is something left," I said, wondering how much he knew.

"Americans." Oscar shook his head. "You'll never change."

"I hope not," I mumbled and watched him walk out of the house, out of my life.

Chapter Twenty-four

THE WAR WAS OVER, AND SO WAS THE STRUGGLE. YOU could see it in their faces, the lack of fear, the flashes of hope. King Jimmi's market in central Freetown had always been as good as any political indicator, and I had never seen it as resplendent as on that October day. In an alley that led into the soft blue ocean, women carried massive woven baskets on their heads while others propped multicolored umbrellas around their bowls of grains and spices, in case they were hit with the last remaining rains of the season.

"But it's not over," I said to Ollie as she walked from stall to stall, filling the basket that she had expertly duct-taped to a luggage trolley. "What about all of those people in the refugee camps?" I stopped and bought an orange that had been peeled and licked the dripping juice from its bottom.

"Can you believe all this?" Ollie pointed to the greens, the clear yellow tomatoes, the red bananas, and the fat mangoes. "Started coming in when you left."

"Don't you mean when the rebels left?" It was hard to take it all in. People lounged on chairs, women nursed their children, men held portable stereos, listening to an inter-African soccer match. The place was bustling and people looked happy.

"One and the same." Ollie continued her search for Irish oatmeal, stopping to chat at nearly every stall in between. She had reached the status that few aid workers ever achieved, that of an honorary Sierra Leoneon, and clearly people loved her. "It's been a year since you've been gone and the war was declared over last January."

"So why are there still eighteen thousand U.N. peacekeepers?" I said, trying to keep up with her.

"Liberia, dearie." Ollie stopped to admire a bright yellow sarong that was hanging by clothespins. A young girl wearing a tank top in a pink so blinding I had to look away pulled down the skirt and handed it to her. When Ollie took out a wad of cash, the young girl shook her head slowly and pushed the skirt into her hands.

"Don't you ever pay for anything?" We bumped and pushed our way through the market.

"No one lets me." Ollie rifled through her makeshift shopping cart for a final check and decided it was time to go back to her place and sample the Daddy Cool Gin that had been slipped into her cart moments before.

In my absence, Ollie and Sinead had moved into a two-story home on Tower Hill overlooking the bay and the entire city of Freetown. Though the décor was distinctly that of *corrupt African politician* circa 1980s, with chipping ornate gold work and deep red carpets with threads of gold feathered into corner tassels, the appliances were newer than anything we'd ever seen in Sierra Leone.

"Watch out," Sinead cautioned as Ollie unloaded her groceries into the massive Frigidaire refrigerator, "she's gone and turned into Julia Child."

"We moved in the day after Kabbah's reelection." Ollie took my hand and led me through the kitchen and into the dining room, continuing the tour through the living room with its acres of wall-to-wall red carpeting and floor-to-ceiling mirrors until we reached the back of the house. "You're sleeping down here."

"No, Ollie," I stopped her. "As soon as Halla wakes up, we're moving in to Mammy's." The flight had been arduous—Los Angeles to Brussels, and after a seven-hour layover we caught the twice-weekly flight out of Brussels to Lungi International Airport, where Ollie met us with a U.N. helicopter, still the only safe way to cross the bay. By the time we had arrived, I felt as though I had crossed the world and left an entire life behind me.

"At a hundred and fifteen a night?" Ollie stepped back. "My, oh, my, we've certainly gone up in the world, haven't we, Miss Malibu."

I winced. "Is that how much it costs these days for a single in a bombed-out third world country?"

Sinead cut in. "If you want ocean views, it's a bit more."

"So will you stay?" Ollie pleaded. "We have four massive bedrooms and I feel horribly guilty, I do."

"Then I'll stay," I said, feeling relieved.

"Let's drink." We filled tall crystal glasses to the brim with ice from the refrigerator and Ollie poured the gin of Sierra Leone into our glasses. We sat out on the veranda overlooking the mountains, listening to the splash and whoosh of streams below.

Sitting there, up on the hill that had always been the property of the enemy, it felt wrong.

"You look awfully serious." Ollie squeezed my thigh. "Far too serious for such a happy occasion."

"But it's not happy." I stood and put my drink down. "I don't know how you two can drink from those glasses and pretend that there still aren't people in jail being beaten with their own feces, or hundreds of thousands of refugees too scared to come home. Up here I feel like one of them, and not one of us."

Ollie's smile was tight. "Look, moving back into the shack we used to live in won't get them out of jail."

"It won't get Joseph out either," Sinead said quietly. "It looks a lot worse than it is, Saff. We haven't changed, we just got a great deal on the rent up here."

"And we deserve it," Ollie threw in. "You got your Malibu, and we got our Tower Hill."

Sinead walked over and rubbed the back of my neck. "All that stands in front of you now is Pademba." The appointment they had made for me to meet with Joseph and his lawyer was for the following day.

Suddenly I was scared. I had nothing left in my life but this one moment to look forward to. "Can you keep Halla?"

Ollie grinned. "Are you kidding? Sinead's gone positively maternal on me already."

I trusted these two women. In my heart I knew they were good people. But hadn't I trusted Francis? And Blue and Tom? Hadn't I felt in my heart that they wanted the best for me and my daughter?

"Enough already." Ollie put my drink to my lips. "You look like you're going to cry. I can't have any of that, not up here, not next to Sinead, who will soon follow suit."

I ran my fingers through my hair and wiped my eyes. "I don't know if I can do this." I turned my back to the view and stared at the last two friends I had in the world. "What if they've moved him? What if he doesn't want to see me? What if when I see him, I don't recognize him anymore?"

Ollie didn't pause. "Then you go home, build yourself a bright new life in Malibu with the millions you now have at your disposal."

"Or you stay here and build the farm you've always dreamed of for Halla and yourself," Sinead added.

"Have you seen Oscar?" I eyed both of them. "Recently, I mean."

"He's off to Europe, he said," Ollie's tone was brusque, "an extended vacation." Like Heaven, she had little time for dramatic scenes of wallowing self-pity.

"With his new lady friend," Sinead added, but immediately stopped when Ollie shot her a look.

"You were broken up," Ollie cut in. "It had been a year and he moved on."

"To a Swedish aid worker, I believe," Sinead popped in. "White hair down to her ass and the body of a fifteen-year-old girl. Lucky bastard."

"I see." And there it was.

The appointment was for ten o'clock the next morning. It was a clear, sunny day, a beach day, I thought as I paid the cabdriver and walked up to the gates of Pademba Road Prison. Joseph had been in there for at least a year, maybe more. It looked positively Gothic from the outside, imposing and crumbling all at the same time.

After taking my name and passport number with a kind of polite swiftness that took me by surprise, the guards asked me to wait for my turn. There was only one meeting room and we would be next, they said.

I had not slept an hour the night before due to Halla's jet lag and the fact that I had forgotten to pack an adapter for the new breast pump I'd picked up. By the time I saw the first shadows of light dance across the window, I had been hand-pumping for three hours, and I didn't know what hurt more, my hands or my nipples.

"She wasn't planned now, was she?" Ollie poked her head in with a hot cup of coffee as I dressed for Joseph. I wanted to look the same as he remembered me, a journalist; together.

I was struggling with wardrobe, with hair, with the extra five pounds that would not budge. "That question would fall in the irrelevant category." I shot her an angry look. "Should I go for the jeans and blouse or the linen skirt and short-sleeve top?"

Ollie pointed to the jeans. "You'll be in there all day, darling; the less attention you call to yourself, the better."

I slipped on the jeans and struggled with the blouse until I felt her hands at my neck fastening the buttons. "Are you angry with me?" I whispered.

"I'm not angry, Saff, just a bit confused by all of this." Ollie sat on the side of the deep tub. "Since when has your life depended upon a man?"

I turned away from the mirror. "What do you mean?"

"Isn't it obvious? You used to be about so much more, the people, the work, the country even. And now, since you've come back, it seems as though you've hinged your life upon Joseph."

"I've always been his friend, Ollie." I stepped back. "And I've always made it my goal to see him free."

"Yes, but this seems altogether different." She looked me up and down. "You're not approaching this as a friend, a professional journalist going to bat for a colleague. You're primping and sweating like a wife going to have a conjugal day with her husband."

"I want to look right," I said defensively.

"You're latching on, Saff." She shook her head slowly. "But it's all smoke and water, all of it."

Tears stung my eyes. "Maybe," I said. "But it's all I've got left."

"There you go again!" She slapped her knee. "Talking like some suburban housewife. What in God's name happened to you out there in America?"

"Life," I said to the mirror and watched as she walked out of the bathroom, no doubt disgusted by what she thought I had become.

I woke to a soft nudge at the bottom of my rib cage and found myself sitting in a fully occupied room. There were not enough seats to hold the many women and men who stood, sat, and squatted while they waited their turn to see someone inside. I clutched at my hair and pulled it away from my neck. I had been sleeping for three hours—it was now one o'clock.

I stood to stretch, but the person next to me shook his head.

"I wouldn't do that if I were you," he cautioned. "You'll lose your spot and have to join them against the wall, or better yet, the floor."

I turned my head and took a good look. He was African, spoke with a slight Krio accent, wore round spectacles, and had his Afro gelled down and parted on the side. He wore a tan waistcoat and a light blue summer suit, along with the smartest white canvas wingtips I'd seen outside of London.

"You must be Henry George." I stuck my hand out. "I'm—"

"Yes, I know who you are," he said, "you've been sleeping on my shoulder for the past few hours."

His slightly indignant and strangely British attitude was already grating on my nerves. "How much longer do we have to wait?" And who the hell hired you?

He brushed at the sleeve where I had been sleeping. "Until they say it's our turn."

The pleasantries were now over. "How many times have you visited Joseph?"

"Twice," he said.

"When?" Despite the stares and resulting giggles around us, I continued our conversation looking straight ahead, just as he was doing.

"Upon his arrest and once in preparation for a hearing, which was later postponed."

"When was he arrested?" So far I did not have a clear idea of the events.

"November of last year."

"What was the charge upon his arrest?" If he had been arrested for something other than treason, we might have room to wiggle.

He looked at me as if I should have known the answer. "Treason, of course."

"Treason, how?" I turned to face him. "He was working for the United Nations and the British who were working with the incumbent government. How could Joseph be tried for treason?"

Henry George wagged a long black finger in my face. "No, Ms. Roch, you've got it quite wrong."

I leaned forward, my breath quickening. "Then clarify, please."

"Dr. Henry George and guest, please report to the front window." A small speaker at the front of the room crackled like a walkie-talkie.

"Come." He picked up his new leather briefcase and waited for me to walk in front of him, gentleman that he pretended to be.

"Wait," I said, "treason against who?"

"Shh," he cautioned. "It's our turn now." He signed a dozen copies of some form before we were buzzed in to the main hall, where our bags were taken and searched, as were we. I had been to Pademba on more than one occasion covering a story, almost always that of a good man wrongly accused by a corrupt government bent on seeking absolute power. I had the grim feeling that I was about to witness more of the same.

The walls were cracked and leaked liquid, like a dam waiting to split. The dirt floors absorbed the sounds of our shoes. We were escorted into a room with a white Formica table, long and narrow with six metal chairs around it. Young guards stood against the walls, looking like children dressed for Halloween. Their pants were ill-fitting and their shirts hung loosely at their slim necks. They smiled as if this whole thing was fun.

Joseph sat at the middle of the table, head down, palms face up, with two guards flanking him on either side.

"Joseph?" I whispered. "Joseph?"

"Good morning, my good client." Suddenly Henry's voice was full of rhyme and song, as though they were on the same team. But Joseph did not look up. His head was shaved almost to the skin and looked as though it might fall to the table at any second.

"Joseph." I walked forward and pulled out a chair across from him. "It's me, Saffron."

I reached out and took his hand, but the moment I made contact, one of the guards slapped a stick down in between us, just missing our forearms. I yanked mine away, but Joseph's arm remained where it had been, he hadn't even flinched. "Jesus, Joseph." I covered my mouth. "What in God's name have they done to you?"

"I've come to tell you for the last time, Mr. Hanna"—Henry opened his legal case and removed a large manila envelope—"that I can't help you if you don't help me. You will rot in here, I tell you, unless you sign these papers and be done with it."

"What papers?" I looked at Joseph and then at Henry. "What are you talking about?"

"The court has made it their ruling that if Mr. Hanna signs this declaration, a confession that he was working with Sankoh and his Revolutionary Front, they will give him no more than two years." Henry glanced up at me. "They've even stipulated that his partisanship could be viewed as coercion of a sort, due to the involvement they had in the death of Mr. Hanna's family, et cetera." He put one hand on his hip. "It's really very generous, given the circumstances."

"Which are what?" I did not like this man.

"That while pretending to be a member of the U.N. peacekeeping force, my client here plotted to take down the government of this country, an act punishable by death."

I knew that was not true, I would have staked my life on it. "Joseph?" I called him again, but he would not look at me. "Will you please say something?"

His lawyer laughed. "He won't talk to you."

"Why?" I stared at him. "What did they do to him?"

"How would I know." He snapped his briefcase shut. "I've not yet had the pleasure of Mr. Hanna's conversation." He turned toward the door and signaled to the guards to open it up, the interview was over.

"Joseph," I whispered again. The door clicked.

"It's time to go," the guard called out to me, and as I backed away I watched Joseph lift his head. His eyes stared through me, through it all. "I'll get you out of here," I said. I watched his eyes come into focus until both were on me, momentarily locked on to mine. "I promise." There was a look, an imperceptible nod of his head, then it was over, his head dropped and his eyes deadened. He was gone.

Henry George walked stridently through the checkpoints and held the doors open for me until we exited the building and stood in the harsh light of day. "A waste of your time, sorry." He explained that he had told Ollie as much but she had been insistent. He neglected to mention that she had also applied pressure to his seniors. "The judge has given him a deadline and it is fast approaching."

I shielded my eyes from the sun. "He won't be found innocent, will he?"

My question took him off guard. "Well, no, probably not."

"And why would he be?" I said, amazed that he had lasted this long in Pademba. When the legitimacy and stability of the nation was at risk, they couldn't free Joseph no matter how innocent they proved him to be.

"Well said, Ms. Roch." He took his car keys from his pocket. "If there is anything else you'd like to discuss, please call, you have the number." Henry George walked to his car. "And now I must leave you."

But I followed. "Oh, but there is one more thing I would like to mention." I stopped at the shining door of his sports utility vehicle. "You're fired."

His neck twitched. "But you can't fire me." He held his keys to my face and shook them like a talisman. "I'm appointed by the court."

"You will be replaced by a lawyer of his choosing," I said. "And that will supplant your authority."

"With what money?" His tiny nose narrowed. "That man, that mute, is penniless and without family or friends. There is no one who will pay the considerable cost of the legal battle he faces, a battle that he will lose as sure as I am standing here."

I wanted to form an intelligent response, one that would make him feel stupid and burned and small. But instead, and despite my best efforts, I lifted my middle finger high in his face and said, "Fuck off."

I should have seen it coming—Joseph's demeanor changed with each visit, his nerves were shot, his story no longer made sense. But I had been too in love, too caught up in the war to see that it had already claimed him, and would claim me, too.

The last time I saw him was in late July, two months since that night at the bar in Aberdeen. He looked like a different man.

"I had to see you"—he exploded, breathless and excited, into my hotel room—"before something happens."

He was in tatters, hardly recognizable to me. He wore striped bathing shorts and a tank top emblazoned with bright colors. His thongs were dirty and small chunks were missing from the foam where his heel had been resting for some time. But it was Joseph, and Joseph always made me happy.

"You look awful." I smiled at him. "What have you been up to now?" Although he never confirmed or denied his whereabouts, Ollie and I were certain that he was embedded with the RUF somewhere up north working undercover for the Brits.

"More of the same." He closed the curtains and switched on the bedside light. "I'm sorry for coming so late."

"You took a big risk," I said.

He shook his head. "You know I can't speak about—"

"I meant Oscar." I crossed my legs and pulled the blankets over them. Joseph looked away shyly. "I'm kidding, Joseph, I haven't seen him in weeks."

"I didn't think of that"—he shook his head—"too many other things to worry about."

He did seem more worried than the last time we'd talked weeks earlier, after a group of British paratroopers had been kidnapped by the West Side Boys. "Can I get you a beer?"

"I can't drink anymore, too many stories to keep straight"—he rubbed his hands across his eyes—"too many lies to tell."

"You smell." I saw a small smile. "Do you know you smell?"

Joseph raised his arm. "Part of the disguise."

"Get in the shower, use some of my girlie products." I stood and took him to the bathroom and he followed silently. "Do whatever you need to do to wipe away the smell of foxholes and charcoal."

"I only have an hour," he said. "I have to get back before they start to miss me."

"I miss you already." I opened the shower door and watched as he disrobed.

"Be a lady"—he gave me a look that melted my heart—"and turn around."

"It's tough." I wanted to peek, and I had planned on peeking, but I held my ground. He emerged smelling of soap and damp skin, a stark white towel wrapped around his taut stomach.

"Stop it." He backed away. "You're making me nervous."

"What?" I fluffed up the pillows and leaned my head against them. "What am I doing?"

"Staring at me like I was a steak." He pulled on his shorts.

"No, no." I put my hand up. "Not yet, please. You look like some godawful rebel in those."

He stopped still. "That's what I am."

"No, that's what you're pretending to be." I went toward him and put my arms around his neck. "When will this be over?" I touched the sides of his cheeks and took in as much as I could. "I need to talk to you."

"About what?" His cheek turned to mine.

I kissed it. "About us." And kissed it again. "I want there to be an 'us,' Joseph."

"And Oscar?"

I turned his face to mine and looked into his eyes, which could not settle down. "I want there to be an 'us.' "

He turned quickly. "When the war is over, Saffron, that is when we can talk about things like this, not before. It would be tempting fate."

"And when will that be?" I took his hand in mine and pulled him back. "Another ten years?"

"Think diamonds." He pulled away, tossed aside his towel, and slipped on his clothes. "As soon as the mines are in safe hands, the country will be in balance." He came closer. "And we will be free."

"Screw freedom." I wrapped my arms around his neck. "All I care about is you, us."

But Joseph was already gone. "I have to leave." He peeled my arms from around his neck.

"Are you heading to Koidu tonight?" I followed him to the door. "Can I come?"

"The more you know"—he took my face in his long fingers—
"the more you'll be tempted to talk, and talking assures only one
outcome in this game."

I felt my heart swell with pain. "What's that?" I whispered.

He kissed me long and sweet on the lips. "Death." Then he was
gone.

It all seemed like a game back then, in the heat of it all—it always did in war zones. As reporters and aid workers we somehow
felt apart from it all, as though the violence we stood in front of
would never, could never, permeate the lens, never spill over onto
us. But it did.

It was well past four in the afternoon when I returned to Tower Hill.
I could hear Halla's cries from outside the house and felt my heart
race.

"Thank God!" Sinead cried as soon as she saw me coming
through the door. "Ollie left an hour ago, said she couldn't stand it
anymore."

Halla was bright red, verging on purple by the time I got hold of
her, and when I did, her entire body went rigid in search of my
breasts, which were hard as rocks until she got her mouth on one of
them and the milk flowed.

"Ah." Sinead threw down the burp cloth and collapsed on the
chair next to me. "For the love of Christ!"

"Tough day?" I smiled. In seconds Halla was as quiet as an
angel, curled up on my stomach, nursing. She was all that was right
with my world.

"Tough day?" Sinead leaned forward. "She's been crying since
the moment you left. We gave her the bottles, but she wanted no
part of them. I've been rocking her, singing to her—"

"That must have been it."

"Stop joking. We tried everything to make her happy, but nothing would do."

Ollie came through the door looking more disheveled than usual. "I thought you were tough, Ollie, could stand it all," I teased.

"Not that, anything but that." They sat on either side of me and watched as Halla nursed quietly. "And now look at her, an angel."

"I saw him."

"And how was he?" Ollie glanced over at us. "Did he look alright?"

"Did you know he hasn't spoken a word since his incarceration?" They shook their heads. "Did you know that his lawyer is essentially an employee of the state trying to get him to sign a confession of treason?"

"No, we didn't know," Ollie said, shooting Sinead a sharp glance. "Should have perhaps, but didn't."

"And what will he get if he signs?" Sinead assembled the tea—toast, jam, and butter on a massive sterling silver tray. England at your fingertips.

"Henry George, the asshole lawyer, said he'll get two years or less, but I don't believe a word of it."

"Why not?" Ollie stared at me, glued to every word.

"They're setting him up, Ollie. They're saying he was a rebel, posing as a U.N. official, plotting to kill Kabbah and bring down the government. He's got the bloody initials carved in his chest and chances are he was discovered with the rebel forces in Koidu, bartering with Taylor in Liberia."

"Diamonds for guns." She nodded.

"Exactly."

"Then why can't we get the Brits in on this one?" Sinead called from the kitchen. "How can they let one of their own sit in jail and face execution?"

"I fired the lawyer." I switched Halla to the other side and relaxed into the sofa.

Ollie nodded. "Should have been done long ago. We must hire the best."

I looked at her and felt excitement as visions of Ollie's trust fund connections danced in my head. "And it has to be someone from Britain, someone completely without ties to West Africa in general and Sierra Leone in particular."

"And we must do this immediately." Ollie stood. "Saffron, I'll contact friends in London, international lawyers who've experience in third world politics and criminal law."

"And I'll set up another meeting with Joseph, if at all possible." I patted Halla on the back lightly until she belched and thick yellow liquid dripped down my shoulder. "Ah, she was hungry."

"Lovely." Ollie picked up her purse and keys. "You'll have the money wired in the morning then?"

"What money?" They both stopped what they were doing and stared at me.

Now it was my turn to explain.

Chapter Twenty-five

HEAVEN: "You are too quick to believe."
ME: "Because I want to believe."
HEAVEN: "You are too quick to trust."
ME: "Because I want to trust."
HEAVEN: "No, what you want is to latch."
ME: "I was abandoned by my mother. I had no friends."
HEAVEN: "And it's abundantly clear to all who stand before
you."

This was the song that played over and over in my head. It was Heaven's favorite tune, one that she sang when I asked to go to high school and every time I attempted to interact with kids my own age. She was protecting me from my own self, she would say with a tired smile and a tight hug. She said I wanted it so badly that they—everyone outside of Point Elsewhere—would be able to smell the desperation on me and I would be left standing alone, used and hurt.

And she had been right. On the last day of September, I had been left utterly alone, used and hurt. I had not felt that much shame in being me since my mother had left me all those years earlier.

"The whole thing was a lie?" Sinead rubbed my back. "The house was never really for sale?"

I felt like such an idiot it was hard for me to go on. "No." I stared ahead numb. "The real estate company was fictitious, so was the escrow account. The Realtor, Tom, was, of course, an actor."

"But didn't you look into it, Saffy?" Ollie stared at me. "It was ten million dollars, after all."

I couldn't look at her. "I trusted them, Ollie." Heaven's words came back to me again, but I shook them off. "I'd never bought or sold a home before," I said lamely. "It made sense. There were open houses, potential buyers. I trusted him, all of them, they were singing the same tune. I mean Sally and Dean, a couple of eighty-year-olds, for God's sake, were in on it."

"But didn't you get that he might be a little angry?" Ollie's eyes widened. "You were selling the place, his world, out from under him, Saffron."

"I wanted to believe that they weren't angry, and Francis had done his best to convince me of it. But deep down I guess I knew that they had to be."

"Well, of course they'd be!" Ollie went to the kitchen and poured herself a glass of gin.

Sinead gave her a backward glance. "I thought you were heading back to the clinic."

"It was ten million dollars, luv." Ollie took a deep swallow. "Of course they'd be angry. I'd be downright homicidal."

"But Oscar." I closed my eyes. I never thought that he'd play a part in my financial overthrow, when he'd never shown the slightest interest in money. "Why would he come all that way, go through all of that, for money?"

Sinead came over to where I sat. "Men are assholes. Didn't Heaven ever tell you that?"

I thought back to my conversation with Heaven about Oscar,

about the nature of doctors, of surgeons, and knew that Heaven would have no pity for me if she were alive today.

"He must have been paid handsomely for his role in their little drama." Ollie's face grew red. "How long do you think he'd been there before you saw him?"

"Couldn't have been more than a few days." At first, I had wondered long and hard about the details, but they had since lost their importance.

"And that was enough to get you disinherited?" Sinead spoke softly. "Couldn't you explain to Heaven's lawyer that you didn't know, that you didn't invite Oscar, had nothing to do with him being there and all the rest of it?"

Francis had been far more computer-friendly than he let on. He had accessed my computer and sent e-mails to Oscar while I breast-fed and bathed Halla in the bedroom. "Apparently, they had quite a correspondence going from my e-mail account, and it was used as proof that I invited him, that I wanted to be with him."

"So your word stood for nothing?" Sinead asked.

"Al's opinion was that Heaven's word had stood for nothing, so why should mine."

"Well, the man's got a point there." Ollie poured gin into our tea cups. "Might as well drink, we haven't a prayer in hell now."

I jerked so fast, Halla began to cry. "I thought your family was loaded."

She put both legs up on the coffee table. "We've been broke for centuries. There's some real estate, of course, but how much do you think a rotting castle in the Scottish Highlands goes for these days?"

I took a long sip of gin and blew out fumes. "I'm thinking a lot less than beachfront Malibu."

Ollie tipped her hat. "And to think you, shining star of the *Sunday Times,* were duped out of ten million by an out-of-work actor and a bunch of hippies."

"And a surgeon." I smiled in spite of myself. "Let's not forget the seriously fucked-up surgeon."

There had been moments over the past few weeks when I believed that my mother had been a part of the whole thing, that somehow her presence was a ruse. The night before I was kicked out of Heaven's house, with nothing but my suitcases and my daughter, I had written her a letter. Strangely enough, her guilt—or innocence—mattered to me. Since having Halla and losing Heaven, my mother mattered to me.

I had sent the letter to her at the hospice in Topanga where she said she worked. That may have been a lie, too, but I sent it anyway from the last mail slot I could find before I boarded my plane for Belgium.

She had written back, care of the *Sunday Times,* and as I stood on the African sand, listening to the high squeals of children playing touch tag on the beach in front of me, I opened the letter. Her writing was unfamiliar to me, but her tone and words could belong to no one but my mother. My heart dropped little by little as my eyes flew down the page.

Saffron,

It has taken me thirty years to find the good in people who are essentially bad, but you seem to find it at first sight. But with this love in your heart comes a price, and you have paid the heaviest of all. Anyone who knows Francis knows that he would never let the beach go without dying or killing, whatever was necessary, whichever came first.

At least you and your daughter are still alive and you are back in Africa, your chosen home. Let the money go, it will only cause you anguish, but learn from your mistake. It might well be the costliest mistake ever, but it is not the worst mistake you could make. That honor I hold as my own and hold it against my heart day and night like a shield, until I find a way of making it up to you, not erasing it, but easing it.

    Until then,

                             Monique
                        (your mother)

I returned to Pademba Prison ten days later, which according to the secretary was the first date available. When I arrived, however, Joseph was no longer available. He had been moved to solitary confinement.

"Why?" I stared at the kind-looking man with tight gray curls and a skullcap. At least he had God, and with this job, he would need him.

He looked up at me, but didn't see me. His attention was caught and held by Halla's face cradled in the Baby Björn carrier. "She's a pretty little thing."

"Thank you." I smiled. "But why have they moved my friend?"

"Can't tell you." He looked at Halla again, then scanned the file in front of him. He scanned the pages up and down, one by one. I felt hope. But the deepening crease between his eyes and the deep intake of breath told me that there was nothing to hope for. "Seems he's been tried"—he picked at a spot on his head—"and found guilty."

"What!" I leaned over the partition and nearly grabbed the file off his desk. "When?" I shook my head. "How? He hasn't even got a lawyer."

"Five days ago," he read slowly, trying to make out the thick black cursive. "He was tried and found guilty of treason."

Perspiration rushed through my pores and dripped down the inside of my arms. I hadn't even noticed the line that had formed behind me. "But he had no lawyer, we were getting him new counsel."

"Seems he was represented by one Henry George, court-assigned counsel from day one."

I could barely retain my composure. "What's the sentence?" I tapped my fingers while he continued reading slowly. No doubt George had him set up for the maximum sentence and Joseph would be in jail for life.

"Death." He closed the file.

The blood drained from my face, my fingertips felt numb. "Death?" I managed.

"Death is the only sentence for treason, Mum." He smiled at Halla, then picked up a fuzzy stuffed lion that had been perched on top of his computer screen and proceeded to enact a one-man puppet show.

Halla giggled. I fainted.

According to Henry George, Joseph had sent for him just hours after our visit. He was ready to talk, he said. In the brief meeting, he explained that he had been working with Sankoh to overthrow the government and had signed the confession. Immediately after leaving Pademba, Henry George took the signed confession to the courts and spoke in closed chambers with the judge. Trial was set for the following day.

"How could he be tried in a closed court?" I stared at Ollie from under the covers of her guest bed, where I had been forced to stay since fainting that morning. "No jury, no notice?"

"There is no opposition, Saffy. No one will stand up for someone accused of treason, not here, not at a time like this."

Sinead folded her arms and looked down. "And the signed confession probably didn't help much either."

"When's the execution set for?" I couldn't believe I was saying those words.

"One week from tomorrow, Friday the twenty-fifth of October." Sinead picked Halla up in her arms and kissed her lightly on the forehead. "I can't bear it."

"What did your friends in London say?" I looked at Ollie.

"Since it's now an execution, higher stakes and whatnot, there might well be some interest." She ran her fingers through her cropped gray hair. "But the money is a central problem. No one is going to fly out here to West Africa and work for free, darling."

Sinead rocked Halla gently while she stared out the tall window. "We did."

"Fuck." I threw back the light comforter and pulled jeans on over my pajamas.

Ollie watched me as I collected my things. "Where do you think you're going?"

"Somewhere I can be effective." I looked over at Sinead. "Can you keep her for a few hours?"

"Ah, no." Sinead looked up, a film of terror over her wide blue eyes. "I, I'm not sure—"

"I just fed her and there's formula in the nightstand." I ran over and kissed Halla on the head. "If that doesn't work, give her a banana, or a crust of bread to gnaw on until I get back."

"Has she ever eaten anything before?" Sinead stared.

"No." I ran to the bathroom. "So it should keep you busy for a while."

I hitched a ride on the first poda-poda that came by. It was close to sundown, and the poda-poda was only half filled since it had already dropped off most of its passengers and was on its way back to the city for the next round. The air was dusty and hot, the people on board were full of life. Men smiled, girls flirted, and rival radios blared eighties hits into the evening sky. This was Africa, vibrant and chaotic, lulling and terrifying. It made you feel alive; it made you feel a kind of terror that could never be duplicated in an organized society, where right is applauded and wrong is punished. Joseph had done nothing but fight for the people of Sierra Leone and he was going to die for it. This, too, was Africa.

With the war over, the British gone, and the president sworn in, the *Sunday Times* had all but boarded up their office. Sierra Leone was no longer a hot spot, but because the U.N. peacekeepers were staying on to monitor the Liberia problem, the overflowing refugee issue, and the nasty ongoing diamond trade, the London office had recruited one person to run the show, an ex-colonel in the British army who happened to live in Freetown. I let myself in with my key and startled the hell out of him.

"What in God's—" Hugh Lawson-Smith looked up from the paper he'd been reading and adjusted his glasses higher on his nose.

"I'm so sorry." I looked away as he lifted his pants from around his ankles and yanked them up. "Usually people shut the door when they're on the loo."

"I was unaware that the key was in circulation." Hugh flushed the toilet. "Won't be a moment." The tap was turned on to full blast as he worked the soap into a frothy lather.

I went to my old desk and picked up the phone. "Rodger?" I waited, hoping he would be civil. "It's me, Saffron."

And he was. "Saffron," he called out in a thick American accent, "as in American baby Saffron?"

"That's me." I smiled.

"What the hell are you doing back in Sierra Leone?" Rodger had been less than kind when he found out about my pregnancy and my immediate withdrawal from the job, so much so that he made it impossible for me to continue working for the paper in London. "Not trying to resume your position, I hope."

But old dogs could change, right?

"Because there's nothing to resume." He went on, "War's over, story's over, honey. Go back to knitting booties, luv."

Maybe not. "I need a favor." I ignored the snide clichés. "A friend, Joseph Hanna, is in jail and has been sentenced to death."

"Happens every day," Rodger said blandly.

"Yes"—asshole—"but not to someone who was working for the British government as a source or possibly a spy."

"Possibly?" Rodger's voice piqued.

"Well . . ." I looked over at Hugh, who really was the epitome of the middle-aged Oxford-educated British civil servant. He stood at the entrance of his office, my old office, looking as though he was waiting for permission to enter. "That's where it's a bit muddy."

Rodger's voice and attitude changed altogether. "What do you want me to do?"

"I want you to splash this story across the front page of every edition of the paper, all over the world. I want the British and the Africans to take notice of how they're treating one of the heroes of the war and to get him the hell out of Pademba before they kill him."

"Saff." He paused. "If he's an African national and still in jail, the British aren't going to do anything to stop the execution." Rodger explained that if he was Special Forces acting as a spy, there was little they could do. "It is, after all, a domestic issue and the last thing the British want to do is to tell them how to run their affairs." He chuckled. "Particularly after spending billions of pounds on them."

"They're going to kill him, Rodger," I said, feeling tears pool in both eyes.

"And don't tell me"—sarcasm dripped—"you love him, right?"

"That's beside the point." The thought of Joseph's life coming to an end in seven days was more than I could bear. "If I can get his story splashed across the front page, Rodger, I can get the spotlight on this execution and maybe the Africans will bow to the pressure. They've done it before."

Hugh took a seat and continued to read his paper. "But not for treason," he mumbled without looking up.

"It could backfire, Saff; no one likes to be told what they can and can't do." I could hear the clicking of his keyboard. "Let me fire off a few e-mails and see what I can find out about your friend and his involvement with the Special Forces."

"Apply pressure, don't let up, Rodger." I felt like collapsing into the phone. "I've got seven days, maybe less."

"Yeah, yeah." And he hung up before I could thank him.

"Tough spot you're in." Hugh folded his paper back and then down until it was the size of a sheet of paper. "I do agree, however, with what Rodger appears to have said."

"And what's that?" I asked.

"Diplomacy," he said. "Behind closed doors, that is."

"He was on a mission." I reached for a cigarette and then tossed it back when I remembered that I was not the same person I was before, I was someone's mother. "For fuck's sake, helping the government, Kabbah's government, and now they're killing him for it."

"A small price to pay for the legitimacy of a new government," Hugh said evenly, his words chilling me to the bone. It was exactly what one of my political science professors would have said, and I knew it was right. The execution of RUF rebels for treason was a perfect way to bolster the new government and appease the millions of refugees and amputees who clamored for revenge.

I glanced down at my watch and jumped. I had been gone nearly three hours. Halla would be ready for her bath and night feeding and Sinead would be ready for a bottle of gin. "I have to go."

"I'll keep you informed, if I may," Hugh offered. I jotted down my numbers in case there was a call.

But there were no calls. For two endless days and nights, no one called or e-mailed. "What the bloody hell?" Ollie stared at me on Monday morning. "A man's life is on the line, and no one can pick up the phone?"

I could only think of Joseph. Did he know that he was going to die on Friday? What did he think of us, out here doing nothing? What did he think of me?

"I still can't believe that the British haven't lifted a finger to help him," Sinead said disgustedly. "They're British, for God's sake, they're supposed to do the right thing. It's what our country is based on, it's practically sewn into the Union Jack."

"That's if he really was working for the Brits. No one really knows what Joseph was up to." Ollie drained her tea cup. "It's all a mystery, isn't it, Saff? The Brits certainly would be loathe to admit to the use of local spies in foreign affairs."

"Shit." I scanned the faxes from one human rights group after another, but they were all the same, all useless. Sorry, but sorry was all they could say. "And more shit." I took my cup to the kitchen.

Ollie followed. "What about the Malibu money? Are you planning on fighting the decision?"

"No." I poured and turned to face her hard eyes. "It would be too late anyway, Ollie. The money would never get here by Friday even if I were able to reverse the decision, which I won't."

"Why?" She stared at me.

"Because they hate me there." I took my cup and started toward the living room.

Ollie put out a leg to bar me from leaving. "Are we talking Malibu or across the entire state?"

I didn't want to talk about it. I wanted to forget the whole thing ever happened; I was disinherited as suddenly as I was inherited and I wanted to leave it at that.

"Why do you fight for everyone but yourself?" Her massive leg remained in the air, although it didn't need to. I wasn't going anywhere.

"Fighting for Joseph is like fighting for me. I love him, Ollie."

"That's all well and good, Saff, but Joseph is a separate person from you. He comes from a different world, and most likely has plans for himself that aren't centered on you and your little girl."

She was right, of course. At night when I closed my eyes, I could see, like a splash page on a Web site, the farm in the countryside just north of Freetown, high in the mountains but still close enough to an ocean view. I could see a free legal clinic and the two of us working tirelessly to reclaim property for the refugees. I could see him with Halla, warm and kind and accepting of her nightly tantrums and boundless energy. Joseph had been swapped for Oscar and the fairy tale was complete.

"What are you saying?" I looked up at her and saw that she was deadly serious.

"Listen to me." Her stare was piercing. "According to all the information I've been able to gather, Joseph Hanna doesn't exist."

"It was a name given to him then." I shrugged my shoulders. "Part of the mission, who cares? We know, I know that Joseph is who and what he says he is, Ollie, no matter how much crap you spout at me."

"Would you stake your life on it if you weren't in love with him?" she asked.

"Yes," I said without hesitation.

"Okay then," she said brightly. "Let's hope Rodger has been able to apply the right pressure in London."

"Incoming fax," Sinead shouted. "Looks like an e-mail for Saffron sent to the *Times* office in Freetown and faxed to us here." She held it up and I grabbed it.

After reading the first two lines—*Saffron, I was so angry with you for leaving like that, without even saying good-bye. But then I took it upon myself to look into it*—I tossed it in the trash. It was from Anika and I could not bear to read about her sleepless nights over the right preschool for Jeremiah or her thoughts on Cheerios as finger food.

"Who's it from?" Ollie went to the trash bin.

"Leave it. It's from another world, from someone whose biggest problem is organizing her sock drawer and devising creative meal choices for her geriatric husband." And for a short time, it was someone I wanted to be.

By Tuesday afternoon there was still no word. Rodger's contact in the foreign office hadn't confirmed or denied that a man known as Joseph Hanna worked for the British government while it was involved in the conflict in Sierra Leone. Henry George had called me at the *Times* office to ask whether I knew of anyone who would want Joseph's personal belongings.

"There's not much," he sniffed, "nothing to hold onto, really, but it's my job to ask."

"Just like it was your job to defend?" I countered.

"Look." He paused. "You're the only one left who seems to care, so why don't you take them."

"It would be my honor." I grabbed a cigarette and before I could stop myself it was lit. I was inhaling and feeling better than I had in months. There was little evidence, I thought to myself, that nicotine actually passed through the breast milk anyway, and I puffed away.

"Friday afternoon at the prison then. It will be waiting for you."

I forced myself to ask the next question, the one that I was coming to accept as an eventuality, something I could not change. "And where will he be buried?"

"It is the government's policy to bury rebels in unmarked graves so that they may not be honored or vilified."

"How decent of them." I dropped the phone in its cradle.

"Saffron, someone's here to see you," Hugh called out when he saw that I was off the phone. From the moment I caught him with his pants down he had been nothing but a perfect gentleman and had lent me his office for the duration of the campaign.

I swiveled my chair around and was just in time to catch his entrance. He was as beautiful as ever, and I felt my throat go dry.

"Hello, Saffron." He stood leaning against the doorway, wearing cowboy boots and a leather jacket. His hair was sticking straight up.

"Cut your hair?" I didn't know what to say to him. I couldn't look into his eyes.

"Yeah." He sat down. "That bad, eh?"

"Yeah, I guess." It looked fucking great, he looked fucking great. "Why are you here, Oscar?"

"To tell you how sorry I am." He shook his head slowly. "I wish there was something I could do."

"I think you've done enough." I stood to escort him from the office but collapsed into the chair when I noticed I was still wearing my pajamas. Shit.

"I know we parted badly in California," he continued, seemingly unaware of my overall sloth, "but I thought you wanted to be friends. I thought you wanted me in our daughter's life."

That was it. "How dare you even bring her up? You have single-handedly ripped her inheritance from her. You've destroyed everything, Oscar—you have no idea what you've done by playing your little part in Francis's game."

"I have no idea what you're talking about." He stood back.

"Oh, shut up." I lit another cigarette. "You were there." I took a long drag. "You're the one who put the nail in the coffin, so to speak."

"Look." He stood and put both fists on the table. "I know I've been a shit, the whole marriage thing, the girls even, it was stupid, all of it. I realized that in Malibu when I saw Halla. I knew that I couldn't be what you needed, what you deserved."

"But that wasn't enough for you." I looked at him long and hard. "You had to take away everything I owned."

"I don't know what you're talking about."

"Why are you here?" My temples were pounding.

"Because I heard about Joseph and the execution." He moved back. "I wanted to see if I could help in any way."

I felt something strange take hold of my stomach. "Why did you come to Malibu?"

"Because you asked me." He pointed to the computer. "You e-mailed me, said you had a baby, our baby."

At least I wasn't the only sucker in the room. "It was Francis who e-mailed you."

He looked confused. "Francis, why?"

"Who picked you up at the airport?" I shook my head. "Was it Francis? Didn't you think it was all a bit strange that I didn't come to pick you up myself?"

"You had a newborn and didn't want to sit in the car that long," he said.

I was dumbfounded. "Is that what he told you?"

"No," he said, his tone growing more irritated by the second. "It was what you said in the last e-mail you sent before I took off."

"And when did you meet Al?"

"The day before I saw you." Oscar closed his eyes as though trying to recall the sequence of events. "We drove to his office in L.A. after they picked me up at the airport. They said he wanted to meet me. Had heard all about me, all the rest. We met again at the party."

"Didn't you wonder where I was?" I cried. "Didn't you think it was all a bit strange?"

"They said you had to go up to Santa Barbara to pick up your mother for the party," Oscar said, looking confused. "Why shouldn't I have believed them?"

"No reason." I felt like laughing. "Except that your little visit cost me my entire inheritance. Everything."

The enormity of it all must have hit just then because his knees buckled and he fell back into the chair. "Ten million dollars?"

I nodded. "Heaven made it part of the will that if you set foot on the property, I would lose it."

He cradled his head in his hands. "Thought highly of me, did she?"

"No," I said softly.

"I've done a lot of stupid things, but never have I done them for money." Oscar walked to the door and turned.

"Good-bye, Oscar," I said, and I meant it. The ties were gone, and I felt free.

He didn't budge. "What will you do now?"

"Go home." I gathered my things from Hugh's desk. "We go back to our lives."

"What life?" Oscar came over and took my hand in his. "You don't work here anymore, you don't have a place to live."

"No," I said, suddenly feeling strong. "But I have me and I have Halla and as long as I feel what I feel and listen to my heart, good things will come." I opened the door and he followed me out into the streets of Freetown.

"You'll always have me." Oscar took me in his arms and he felt like a friend. "Whether you like it or not."

"Thank you." I walked away. I was going home to Halla.

"Saffron!" Hugh shouted after me, but I kept walking into the traffic. "Wait! There's a call on line one, a Mr. Henry George."

"Not now." I waved my briefcase behind me and kept walking. "You take it."

"Says it's urgent, imperative he speaks with you!" Hugh yelled out the front of the door.

I looked down at my tennis shoes covered with red dirt. I had never wanted to hear that prick's voice again. I turned. Hugh was still standing in the doorway, bright red and waving the phone. I walked back quickly and took the phone from his hand.

My voice was tight with rage. I had chosen this man to be the sponge of all my hatred. "What could you possibly have left to say to me?"

"It's done." His voice was almost a whisper. "You'll find everything at the front gate of Pademba, Ms. Roch."

"Now?" My heart stopped. They'd already killed him. I shut my eyes tight.

"When was it 'done'?" I asked slowly. I wondered whether his last view of the world had been when the sun was high in the sky and sounds of morning traffic and schoolchildren filled his ears as the noose tightened, or was it at night, when owls and bats made ominous chatter, breaking the silence of his fall?

"Now," he said hurriedly. "It was all very quick, done quietly."

"I'm coming." I hung up before I could hear one more word.

The road to Pademba prison was packed with late-afternoon commuters, screeching poda-podas, and weaving mopeds. Clouds of dust obscured the view and pollution stung my eyes, and for a moment I seriously wondered whether this was the best place to raise Halla. In the distance, I saw a square cardboard box sitting against the prison gates and I felt my knees buckle. That was all there was left of Joseph. I ran to it, dropped to my knees, and cried.

Cars raced by, but I no longer saw them; the weightlessness of the box engulfed me—that and the realization that this man, a man whose family thought him capable of greatness, had no remaining relatives; that this man worked for an organization that would not claim him and died for a country that would not remember him; that this man was reduced to several ounces in a broken-down, abandoned cardboard box.

"Saffron!" I heard a scream but did not turn.

"Saffron!" Ollie's voice shot through the traffic. Something was wrong.

"Stop!" She threw up one hand while she ran through the red dust. Someone was with her, trailing behind.

"This is all that's left." I held out the unmarked box with nothing but a piece of tape holding it closed.

"It's not what you think, Saff." Her eyes were watery from fine red dirt and exhaust fumes. "Just drop it and come with us."

I stared. "It's over, he's gone." I looked up to find that Sinead and Oscar were suddenly standing in front of me. "What are all of you doing here?"

Panic tore through me. "Where's Halla?" My pulse quickened. "What's happened?"

"She's fine, fine." Sinead turned, and there was my daughter tucked into an African back sling. "Happy as can be."

"Drop the box," Ollie repeated, "and come with us."

I stared at them, all of them. "Are you crazy?" I screamed. "How can you ask me to do that?" I cradled it in my arms. "It's all I have left of him."

Oscar took the box from my hands. "Open it."

"No." I shook my head and felt new tears. "I don't want to."

"Look." Oscar flipped open the folding top. "It's just papers, stacks of old newspapers."

"Assholes," I cried, "heartless assholes." But what had I expected? Joseph had been arrested most likely wearing nothing more than a torn T-shirt and shorts. He would have no possessions.

"Come on, luv." Ollie took my hand in hers and pulled me down the length of the prison walls. "We have to be quick." We turned into the first side street past the end of Pademba prison, stopping in front of a tall mildewed door with an imposing curled-brass door handle.

I wiped my nose with my sleeve. "What's this place?"

She put a white sheet of paper in my hand. "Read it."

I tried to focus my eyes on the fax. I squinted until the words began to bounce off the page and my heart pounded through my chest. "Is this true?" I stared at all of them. It couldn't be.

"Seems as though you sold them short." Ollie folded her arms across her chest. "Not that I blame you, Californians and all."

"Anika did all of this?" My mind raced. "She called Al?"

"And brought it to his attention that the real estate agent was a fraud, and that Oscar's arrival was a setup," Ollie explained. "She told him Francis had orchestrated the entire thing to disinherit you."

"How'd she know?" There were no lines to read between. It was all so terribly simple, and I felt the quick bite of self-recrimination. Why hadn't I fought for myself, for what was rightfully mine?

"She mentioned that a woman named Monique found her number by the phone at the house and took a chance."

"A chance?" I said.

"A chance that she was a friend, a true friend," Ollie said, "and she was."

Sinead picked up. "It was really this Monique woman who was suspicious when she'd discovered that the house hadn't been sold and Francis and his girlfriend were moving into Heaven's cottage."

"Who's Monique?" Oscar asked.

"My mother," I said, with a surge of feeling.

"She called Anika, who then tried to contact the real estate agent, who didn't exist," Ollie said quickly.

"And when Anika couldn't find Tom's name, she went nuts." I smiled. Anika was not one to let something like this go, especially when it involved real estate.

Ollie produced another fax. "Lucky for you she found Al."

I took a deep breath and coughed. The poda-podas were in a queue lined up outside the prison, waiting for the light to change. Children's arms stretched out of the bus and waved.

"He must have loved that one." I could just see Al being presented with this information at cocktail hour.

"Enough to believe it." Ollie shoved the paper under my eyes.

I began to read it, but lost interest after the second legal paragraph. "I thank you, I really do, but why do I have to do this now?" Anika and Monique had saved the day, the truth had been discovered, and for that I was both indebted and grateful. But the fact that I was a millionaire had very little importance to me at that moment. "I just want to go home."

"Read!" Ollie's jowls shook.

"I can't." I shook my head and held Halla tightly. "I want to go home, Ollie, please let's go home."

"Don't you want to know what happened?" Oscar put his arm around me.

"I got it back, right?" I nodded. "All of it back?"

"No." They shook their heads. "Not all of it."

"Fine," I said. For a moment I wondered how they'd managed to do it all so quickly, to deal with Francis, liquidate the property, and so on, but I stopped. I would have to think about it later.

"A few million short," Ollie continued.

I stared. "Million?"

She rapped at the old door twice. "Million."

The door opened from the inside but there was no one there, only darkness and a vacuum of cold air. Ollie moved away from the door, Sinead and Oscar following suit.

"Why are we here?" I wrapped my arms around my stomach. I felt tired and ill. "I want to get the hell out of here. I never want to see this place again, is that too much to ask?"

Footsteps pounded the hallway and I turned. A man the color of ash was suddenly shoved to the edge of the door.

"Take him," a guard said with a laugh. "He's bought and paid for."

It got quiet, so quiet. My mouth went dry. "Joseph?"

He did not look up. His head, shaved and covered in scabs, was down, his hands still covering his eyes as though cuffed. He was so very thin, his pants barely fit. The T-shirt he wore was in tatters.

"Let's get him to the clinic." Oscar put both arms underneath him and lifted him easily.

But I could not move. "Joseph?" I asked. "Is it really you?"

"Yes, luv, it's really him." Ollie yanked me from my stupor. "Now let's get on with it."

We ran through the streets until we reached Oscar's parked Land Cruiser.

"Get in the back"—Oscar pointed to me after placing Joseph in the padded corner of the vehicle—"and talk to him."

"I'll take Halla." Sinead reached out but I shook my head. I wanted her as close as possible as I crawled in next to his crumpled form. He looked like a rumpled package in the corner of the jeep, propped up but discarded.

"Joseph?" I reached out to touch his knee. It shook. Did he think he was being taken somewhere terrible? Did he not register that he was free, that we were his friends? Did he know it was me sitting next to him? "Why is he still not talking?"

"Shock," Ollie said.

"Not to mention dehydration, malnutrition, torture, and infection, to name a few," Oscar jumped in. "Give him time, Saff."

"Joseph?" I pulled myself into the spot next to him. I still couldn't believe that it was him; I hungered to see his eyes, to hear the warmth when he spoke, to see his lips curl into a smile. "It's me, Saffron."

"And Ollie, Sinead, and Oscar," Ollie called out from the front. "Don't leave us out now, babe."

"See, she's calling me babe again." I tried to take his hand from his face but it would not pull away. "Did I ever tell you how much I hate it when she calls me that?"

"Don't get too close," Oscar said, "he may lash out, Saff, it's not uncommon."

"Babe," I continued, "simply awful." I held his wrist but no longer pulled. "I will never call my daughter that." I looked down at her. Halla was wide awake on my lap and quiet.

"He should be alright after we get him to Connaught." Oscar looked in the rearview mirror. "If this bloody traffic ever lets up."

"This is Halla." I looked at his head and could see the marks of his incarceration. The holes, nicks, and scars flashed images of night beatings. "She's heard a lot about you."

"Haven't we all," Ollie interrupted.

"I didn't get a chance to tell you about her because you were too busy getting yourself in deep shit up north." I felt his hand drop down, his fingers going limp.

"Shit!" Oscar honked the horn but still we didn't move. "This is impossible!"

I leaned forward to touch him. His skin was warm and dusty and reminded me of a boy after a long day's play. I loved him so much. I didn't know why, but I did. I used to look away when prison inmates kissed their wives, unable to understand how any woman could still want to be kissed by someone who occupied that kind of filth, a man who'd been exposed to nothing but the hell of mankind.

Now I knew. Love. I would have taken him in my arms and held him until he became whole again, if given half a chance.

"How's our boy doing?" Ollie called out.

I pressed against the slight bump in his neck and felt the beat, the same one I'd felt when we first danced. Slowly, his face turned toward mine. He opened his eyes and took my face in, and in his eyes I saw relief.

"Hello," I said.

"Would it be alright to sleep now?" his voice croaked.

"Yes, you can sleep now." I took his head and rested it against my pounding chest.

"God damn it!" Oscar shouted. "Why do they give these people driving licenses?"

"Easy, luv," Ollie said. "You have to let go if you want to survive out here in the jungle. It's bloody unpredictable, isn't it?"

At that moment my eyes took in the view, the entire scene: the chaos of the African streets, vendors weaving in and out of stalled traffic selling peanuts and peeled oranges; hands flying, gesticulating from car windows while pedestrians looked on with eyes that asked, *Where are you all going in such a rush?*

Oscar continued to swear in German, honking and shouting

with the ease of a local; Ollie chastised Oscar, and Sinead told them both to be quiet, Joseph was trying to sleep. Halla stared at all of us, much in the same way as I stared at all of them, with a look of astonishment and wonder that this eccentric and damaged collection of people was our family.

I was in no rush. I was home.

About the Author

An honors graduate of the London School of Economics, Maria T. Lennon now lives under a heap of Disney paraphernalia in a slightly disheveled tree house in Laurel Canyon, Los Angeles, with her husband and three children. Visit her at www.mariatlennon.com.

AUTHOR'S NOTE

There are three major stages in a person's life that no one can prepare you for: birth, death, and becoming a mother.

When I had my first child, it felt like the world stopped. No, that's not right. It felt like I'd stopped and the world just kept on going in blatant disregard for the extremely awkward situation I found myself in. Breasts exploding, stomach deflating, baby crying, husband leaving. Days spent indoors, apart and separate from the functioning world; nights little more than two-hour sleep intervals interspersed with feeding and diaper changes.

On the off chance that you do make it out, strangers randomly pop into your face, peek at your baby, and tell you just how lucky you are. You're not sure you agree.

Your relationship with the world is broken. It's hard to relate. It's hard for your friends to relate to you. Your perception of yourself changes. You are no longer who you once were. And you're not quite sure how to be. The only people in the entire world who understand you are other new mothers, mothers going through the same thing at precisely the same time as you. But where to find them? You find yourself looking forward to your OB checkup, you loiter in department store restrooms, settling into sofas the color of milk, hoping that the door will open and a new stroller will struggle through.

When you do finally find a group of new mothers whose babies and nipples are on target with your own, they become your support group. It must be like alcoholics, I think, because during those first six months, there is no one who understands you better. And nine times out of ten these are women you would never, ever hang out with in your prebaby years. But none of it matters, nothing else matters, nothing except the baby and this new world that you are navigating through with an equal sense of fear and wonder.

It is a magical period, and as with most magical periods, it is finite. It usually seems to happen at about six months, when the newness has worn off, when the answers come more easily and philosophies begin to reflect the individual rather than the group. Breast is replaced by bottle. Attachment parenting is replaced by nannies, and mornings in the park become morning runs through the park. Past lives creep in for attention and beckon you to return. Husbands resume their role as friend and confidant, careers fight for attention, and the group disperses.

Life resumes. But until then you're just making it up as you go along.

—ML

READER'S GROUP GUIDE

ABOUT THE BOOK

When her adoptive mother, Heaven, dies, bequeathing her a $10-million beachfront property, new mother Saffron Roch returns to California to claim her legacy—and to protect it from Heaven's bitter son, Francis. Saffron brings with her her baby girl, Halla, leaving behind Halla's cheating father, Oscar; a dream job as a correspondent in war-torn Sierra Leone; and the chance at true love with a virtual stranger. The full story of Oscar, Saffron, and the intriguing Joseph comes out as Saffron confides in her friends from the Pump Station, a breastfeeding education center in Los Angeles. Saffron is glad for company—especially as her interactions with Francis take an unexpected turn—but she can't help thinking that the lives of almost all the Pump Station ladies are both extravagant and shallow, and completely unlike the world she valued so highly in Africa. Nonetheless, Saffron forges a tight bond with Anika, whose frank gossip and optimism are both silly and soothing, and whose friendship will help Saffron in ways she never imagined.

QUESTIONS FOR DISCUSSION

1. Saffron alternately refers to California and to Africa as "going home." Discuss the concept of home as presented in the book. How does Saffron's idea of home differ from that of her friends in L.A.?

2. Why do you think Saffron joined the class at the Pump Station? Is her membership there out of character?

3. Saffron makes costly and painful errors of judgment throughout the story. Given her track record, do you feel confident in her decision to trust Joseph? Why or why not?

4. Saffron feels that she has sold out by not talking honestly with Alice in criticizing the extravagance of their Pump Station friends. Why can't she relate to Alice, whose experience most closely resembles her own? Do you think this is dishonest or unkind?

5. What does Saffron learn from Anika's friendship? Do you think Anika learns anything from Saffron?

6. Monique tells Saffron that she will be a good mother because "we bounce off our pasts." Where do you see this concept at work in the book? How does it apply to Francis, for instance?

7. Why do you think Saffron is unable to see some of the obvious signs that Francis and Blue are leading her astray? Were you fooled by Francis? Why or why not?

8. What do you think of Oscar? Does he love Saffron? Was Saffron in love with him?

9. When Saffron sees a picture of Nancy's husband, Stan, for the first time, she is struck by his unattractiveness and marvels at how Nancy can moon over him as she does. What do you think of her response to the picture—and to her friends' relationships in general? Do you think she judges them fairly? Why or why not?

10. Do you feel that Saffron is a reliable narrator? Considering that her first version of the story she told her friends included the false detail of Oscar's death, are there other details you think she may still be withholding or editing for her audience?

11. What do you consider to be Saffron's biggest mistake?

12. What do you think of Heaven? Was she a good mother to Saffron? Is there anything she should have done differently to protect her adopted daughter?

13. Would Saffron be a more compelling heroine if she made smarter choices? Do you like her? Why or why not?